CinnamonPress

0135668346

Published by Cinnamon Press
Meirion House, Tanygrisiau, Blaenau Ffestiniog, Gwynedd LL41 3SU
www.cinnamonpress.com
The right of Marg Roberts to be identified as author of this work has been
asserted by her in accordance with the Copyright, Designs and Patent Act,
1988. © 2016 Marg Roberts
ISBN 978-1-910836-37-8
British Library Cataloguing in Publication Data. A CIP record for this book
can be obtained from the British Library.
Designed and typeset in Garamond by Cinnamon Press. Cover design by
Adam Craig © Adam Craig.
Cinnamon Press is represented by Inpress and by the Welsh Books Council
in Wales. Printed in Poland.

Acknowledgements

During the many years it has taken me to write this novel I have had:
the love and support of my husband, Pete;
the advice and encouragement of Novelink, a women's writers'
group (Penny Harper, Katrina Osborne, Jeanette Sheppard and Judy
Tweddle) which meets at the Oken Tea Rooms, Warwick, and my
writing buddy, Angela Lett;
Rachel Duckhouse who drew the explanatory map.
Thanks to you all and other supportive writers and tutors.
The turning point in this project was the Cinnamon Press
mentorship scheme. Thank you Jan and Rowan for your belief and
help.
The quotation from *Ecclesiastes 3 v.1, 3 and 8* is taken from the *New
Revised Standard Version Bible*, copyright 1989, Division of Christian
Education of the National Council of the Churches of Christ in the
United States of America. Used by permission.
The publisher gratefully acknowledges the support of the Welsh
Books Council.

Historical Background

On 28th June 1914, Gavrilo Princip, a Bosnian student revolutionary, shot and killed Archduke Franz Ferdinand, heir to the Austro-Hungarian thrones. The Austro-Hungarian government declared war on Serbia who was seen (rightly or wrongly) as the source of the agitation leading to the assassination. Other nations took sides and on 4th August 1914, Great Britain declared war on Germany because it invaded Belgium en route to France. Great Britain and Serbia thus became allies. A number of British doctors, nurses and VADs volunteered for service in Serbia, including women's medical units.

In October 1915 four armies invaded Serbia. Its army was driven into a small corner of the country. The Serbian government therefore ordered its army, its cadets and its government to evacuate to Corfu through neutral Albania.

Author's Note

A Time for Peace is a work of fiction. I have undertaken research into the events of the First World War in Serbia, prior, during and after 1914-15. References to the Sixth Army, the Jevo regiment and named battles in the novel are imagined, as are the atrocities committed on civilians in the Balkans, although similar ones are documented. My descriptions do not refer to real events or attempt to apportion blame but rather to imagine the effects on decent men and women on both sides.

Serb cadets were part of the exodus from that country, as a government response to invasion and occupation by enemy forces. It is difficult to be certain as to their ages—some may have been as young as twelve. As far as I know, there is no record of women leading such a group. However, women certainly played a significant role in medical units in Serbia and elsewhere. I have made brief mention of the Scottish Women's Hospital but the Women's Medical Corps attached to the Jevo regiment is fictional.

Marg Roberts, 2016

Serbia and its neighbours: 1913-1915

A TIME FOR PEACE

For everything there is a season, and a time for every matter under heaven: ... a time to kill, and a time to heal; ... a time to love, and a time to hate; a time for war, and a time for peace.

Ecclesiastes 3 v.1, 3 and 8.

In memory of my parents and grandparents

Chapter One

Belgrade, Serbia, August 1914

Stefan Petrovic should have been enjoying himself, for he was dining at the Karakjodj, the most expensive restaurant in Belgrade. He picked up his wine glass so a waiter could reach across and remove the unused cutlery and side plate. The food had been excellent. He had sampled hors d'oeuvres whose names he had never heard of, whose flavours, even after tasting, remained a mystery to him. He had chosen *jagnjetina* for his main course and appreciated the lamb's sweetness, enhanced by rosemary and thyme.

Another waiter lit the three-branched candelabra in the centre of his table, and as Stefan leaned back into the comfortably upholstered dining chair, he tried not to think of his wife waiting at home. His friend Tomislav was celebrating his promotion to General of the Sixth Army. Stefan himself, newly appointed as colonel of the Jevo regiment, was dining among generals and divisional commanders. He should have been honoured to eat in such company, but he felt uneasy.

The dining room in the Karakjodj was carpeted and adorned with glass chandeliers. On a warm evening at the beginning of August, the sun having almost set, Stefan considered it the most splendid place. He sat with two of his men and their orderlies at one of the round tables at the opposite end of the room to Tomislav's, whose top table was decorated with ivy and stephanotis and fragrant, cream-coloured roses. Stefan rested the palm of his hand along the scar on his thigh, which had healed well though it itched from time to time. To try and relax, he moved his fingers to the beat of the traditional music being played on a dais in the conservatory. In the mirror on the wall to the left, the grey-green dress uniforms were framed within the candlelight, decorated with the gold and silver braid shoulder straps, gold and silver buttons, the many coloured campaign ribbons and the occasional gold Obilich medal.

When Tomislav had said, 'Bring two friends from the regiment, for it is friendship that binds Serbs together,' Stefan had chosen Rajko and Mikaiho. Mikaiho, a widower, was part of his extended family. His feelings towards his cousin were those of duty rather than affection. Rajko was a good friend; Stefan loved him as only men who fought alongside each other could.

He leaned across the table to speak to Rajko, who gripped his glass as though an enemy might wrench it from him. About to say that a beer would be most welcome, Stefan decided it might be interpreted as reflecting badly on their host. Though his jaw ached from courteous talk, he asked cheerfully, 'Enjoying yourself, brother?'

Rajko's eyes were bloodshot. 'Yezthankyou, zir.'

During their twenties, they had both liked carousing. Ten years later, Rajko still did, but Stefan cut back after he was wounded in the last campaign. Mikaiho, sipping water from a champagne glass, muttered under his breath.

Stefan examined his wristlet. He'd an appointment at home at ten-thirty with an American journalist and would be glad to leave. Another potential embarrassment. No, he would not dwell on it; nothing might come of it.

After the main course, Stefan was surprised to see Tomislav get to his feet. At first he presumed he was to make an announcement, but he edged his way behind the seated officers. They'd met at Military Academy when Stefan was considering an academic career and Tomislav was politically out of favour. He'd aged in the last few days; his moustache was more white than grey. Despite the jaunty shrug of gold braid shoulder boards, he stooped. He strode through waiters in black suits and bow ties who were serving desserts of intricate sugar confections piled high on cut-glass dishes, rose and lemon flavoured Turkish delight, *baklava* and *kadayif* pastries.

Stefan's discomfort increased. His friend was making his way to their table, singling him out. He jumped to his feet, ready to make the introductions but Tomislav, after greeting them, motioned a waiter to bring him a chair, which he positioned to Stefan's right. The orderlies moved back to allow Tomislav more space at the table.

'I hope you're enjoying yourselves.' Tomislav leaned forward as he used to when lecturing, never from notes, but standing in front of the lectern, flicking a white silk scarf, enthusing about strategy, encouraging debate.

'Thank you, sir,' Stefan said, 'The evening does you credit. You were introduced to Major Rajko Kostic and Lieutenant Mikaiho Nis as we came in, weren't you?'

Tomislav appeared to be examining Rajko intently. 'I'm glad you could come, Major.'

Stefan hoped his friend could hide the extent of his drunkenness.

Rajko removed his elbows from the table, rubbed his fingers on the linen serviette on his lap. He picked up and replaced his wine glass as though, like Mikaiho, he'd been drinking water. Then he said, 'I am proud to be here, sir.'

'We are a select gathering and I am glad you could come. I believe you and Stefan are old friends?'

'Commissioned together, sir.' Rajko cleared his throat.

Stefan clarified, '1902.'

'Longer than us, eh?' Tomislav glanced at Stefan, who thought he was going to say more; however, he continued to observe Rajko before adding, 'You have an excellent reputation, Major, not only against the Turks but you did well for us at Bregalnica.'

Rajko's face flushed. He mutely opened his mouth; he could be reticent on a first meeting.

Stefan boasted, 'He was the only one in the regiment to win the gold Obilich.'

Tomislav turned to Mikaiho. 'And we have your cousin. Allow me to welcome you, also. Your action at Bregalnica earned you promotion and, if you prove as brave and intelligent a soldier as either of these men, you will do well.'

'It is an honour to fight for our glorious Serbia.'

'Are you from the same village?'

Stefan wasn't sure to whom the question was directed or even if, aware of the answer, Tomislav was being polite. He said, 'The Major is from the borders with Montenegro and the Lieutenant from Orasac.'

Tomislav said to Mikaiho, 'Both these gentlemen are loyal soldiers of Serbia.'

Mikaiho sprang to his feet. 'I am willing to die for my country, sir.' He saluted, his face pale against black hair and moustache. 'The whole regiment is proud of your promotion, sir. It is an honour for us all.'

Stefan shuffled his feet. Mikaiho was slightly too keen.

Tomislav said, 'Please sit down, Lieutenant. We have a hard battle ahead, but tonight we celebrate that a peasant from the village of Struganica can reach the height of public service. We, too, can enjoy the best that Belgrade provides. Now is the time for dancing and drinking. Tomorrow we will defend our country from its enemies.'

Stefan was relieved Tomislav couldn't read his unease. Though it was true Austria had taken the initiative and declared hostilities, Stefan wished his government had complied with their old enemy's demands. Victory was unlikely after their army and hospitals had been decimated during last year's fighting, civilians and soldiers killed by the countrywide typhus outbreak which followed.

He pointed to the wall behind the top table where portraits of Serbia's heroes hung. 'I confess I never expected to dine here…at the Karakjodj…' His hands dropped. '…where King Petar himself entertains.'

Smiling, Tomislav nodded. 'Like you, I was born a peasant, and would not presume, but when good fortune occurs we celebrate in the manner of princes. One day, Colonel, when you take my place, I hope you will invite your commanders here to celebrate.'

'Thank you, sir.' With an effort, he kept his voice level, trying to mask his depression at such a prospect.

After a brief chat, Tomislav returned to his table.

A waiter reaching to remove unused glasses, asked, 'More wine, sir?' Stefan put a hand across his. Half past nine. He would slip out and go home in half an hour.

Smoke drifted over the tables. His jaw ached from smiling politely and he looked across to the top table where Tomislav was holding forth. He feared the government was exploiting his friend. With Serbia only days into its war with Austria, the politicians needed him, so they had promoted him to general of the Sixth Army. When Tomislav caught him looking, he turned away.

Stefan paid scant attention to Rajko and Mikaiho's struggle to converse. Instead he prepared for the arrival of the journalist, picturing him in a Western-styled suit, ringing the bell outside the gates of his enclosure, waiting a moment for the porter to admit him, walking across the cobble-stoned courtyard, climbing the stone steps to his house. He imagined this man who'd access to train seats, hotel rooms, berths on a liner all the way to Southampton, England, sitting at the bench in front of the fire, accepting a glass of *shlatko* from the welcome tray his wife, Stamenka presented. He swirled the wine, savouring its warmth.

Stefan forced himself into the present. The dessert dishes had been removed. The clock in the foyer was striking the hour as waiters served coffee and liqueurs. Stefan chose *sljivovica*, which reminded him of the plum orchards of boyhood. Throughout the room men were pushing back chairs, stretching legs, discreetly loosening waistbands. To his right in the conservatory, the floor was being cleared for dancing. Two violinists were leaning against a pillar while the *guslar* strummed. Stefan began to listen to the conversation.

'Mules are best through mountains.' Rajko spoke in certainties.

His cousin leaned across the table, his face close to the candles. Stefan sighed as Mikaiho waggled an admonishing finger at Rajko. 'No.'

Mikaiho had yet to learn caution in unfamiliar company, Stefan thought. He didn't appear a worldly young man.

'Donkeys are best,' Mikaiho asserted. Two orderlies exchanged smiles.

'What do you know?' Though he appeared more sober now, Stefan recognised the anger in Rajko's voice.

'We have donkeys at home. They do what we say and carry more than mules.'

11

'Donkeys are for fools. What do you say, sir?'

Stefan replied after a moment, 'They both have their place.'

'Our young lieutenant here, he too has his place. Isn't that right, sir?'

Rajko was perhaps insinuating that at twenty-five, Mikaiho was a novice.

Stefan sipped his coffee. Rajko was the senior of the two and ought to be conciliatory, but Stefan's sympathy lay with him.

Mikaiho pushed forward so far across the table that his brows risked being singed by a candle. 'Our mule was frightened by a shot and tore down the track so our turnips and cabbages spilled out and were trampled on...'

'That's a matter for little boys. I'm talking of the mountains of Albania and Macedonia.'

'We don't live in the mountains.' For a moment, Stefan felt sorry for his cousin.

'So don't talk of things you know nothing of.'

At the top table, a waiter refilling glasses blocked the figure of Tomislav. The generals and their adjutants were obscured by smoke. During the short silence, Stefan picked out the love song, a song of long evenings dining on boulevard pavements with Tomislav and their respective wives. The *guslar* was singing, '*Ruza! Ruza!*' in accompaniment to his own strumming.

'In the Turkish campaign...' Mikaiho began.

'Yellow belly!' Rajko jumped to his feet, a glass of wine in his hand. His chair and newly acquired walking stick crashed to the floor.

Stefan's orderly, Dragan, stirred by his side. Stefan didn't need to look at him. He was forty-five, old for the army and served Stefan well, but tiredness and drink caused him to nap on long evenings. He would be resting, chin on his chest, like a bird dozing on a branch. Should Stefan choose to rouse him however, he'd do whatever he ordered. For the moment he was best asleep.

'Major! Sit down now.' Stefan raised his voice just as the *guslar* stopped playing. It didn't help that Mikaiho was in the right. Whatever happened, Stefan mustn't let the tiff go any further.

The two men turned towards him. Stefan was aware that the divisional commanders at the next table had stopped talking though the officers on the top table were far enough away not to have noticed or were pretending they were not distracted. The violins and *gusle* began a mournful ballad.

Rajko began to speak, but Stefan interrupted. 'We are the general's guests. For God's sake, do not spoil our regiment's good name.'

He could have added that Rajko's accusation was unjust. Mikaiho had led his unit with the cry, 'Prince Marko will aid us,' and they'd held their position. True, he'd not remained at the head of his unit, but that was inexperience.

Sitting down, Rajko gulped the contents of his glass. An officer on the next table resumed the conversation. At the top table the generals were laughing; Tomislav was preening his moustache.

Stefan reached for the box of cigars and handed it to Rajko. 'Pass them round, brother.'

Rajko glowered round the table, his eyes as black as raisins, but after a moment, he took a cigar and passed the box to Mikaiho.

Rajko's arm was shaking as he picked up the three-pronged candelabra and held it towards Stefan, who steadied the central stem with a hand. Amid the guffaws of men on the other tables, Stefan lit a taper from one of the candles and started to light his cigar. Not long till he could leave. Perhaps he would feel more settled when arrangements for Stamenka and their son, Mitar, were finalised.

It was a quarter past ten before Stefan felt able to leave. If he skirted the edge of the restaurant, he could walk through the conservatory, on through the gardens, without drawing attention to himself. He suspected Tomislav wouldn't think well of his choosing a family appointment in preference to this all-male celebration. Reaching for his cigarettes from inside his tunic pocket, he smelled sweat. The silver case slipped in his hands and he removed a glove so he could open it more easily.

He'd not accepted the offer of the journalist the first evening they'd met in the Gornji Café, but asked, 'What do you get out of it?'

'You pay me of course.' The journalist went on to say he'd family in Chicago and understood Stefan's concerns, but Stefan felt uncomfortable at the mention of money. He could afford to ensure his wife, son and mother were removed from the arena of fighting; his men were not so privileged.

Later, on telling Stamenka, he'd been surprised by her reaction. She'd missed her parents when she moved to Belgrade to marry. Now she would travel to England with thirteen-year-old Mitar as long as Stefan promised to join them after the war.

He struck a match, watched it fizzle into flame before lighting his cigarette. He'd been angry when the Austrians declared war. It wasn't unexpected. They'd wanted revenge for the murder of the Austrian Archduke by a Serb, wanted to demonstrate they remained a mighty empire. The British, French and Germans were crazy for war, and the Russians would do anything to keep a foothold in Europe, but Serb politicians were equally foolish. He spat strands of tobacco into his hand. He'd bitten straight through the cigarette.

He stood up and stepped back from the table, wondering how Rajko would react. He was dancing, swaying with the violins, his stick, shoulder height horizontal. His friend was unquestioning in his support for the war. When Stamenka took the train to Salonika, would Rajko condemn Stefan for lacking faith in the army?

There was a roll of thunder, but too distant to bring the threatened rain. Stefan caught a whiff of *sljivovica* and he glanced up at Tomislav sitting with his guests. He felt a wave of affection. The politicians had known what they were doing when they promoted him; they needed a leader who was popular with the people at a time when some of the military warned of a long struggle. Nonetheless, he hoped Tomislav remembered people and politicians could be fickle.

In the distance, another reverberation. Not a storm then. Probably a bomb that hadn't exploded. There was nothing he could do. Engineers would deal with it.

Just as he took a drag on his cigarette and Dragan was rousing himself, Tomislav looked across. Damn. He couldn't slip out. He would have to walk over and make his excuses; he extinguished his cigarette.

'Wait here,' he instructed. As he approached the top table, Tomislav bounced to his feet. 'Stefan! I was just saying we must not let the enemy spoil our evening.'

'Indeed, no.' Stefan drew closer, ready to shake Tomislav's hand. He would explain he'd business and pray Tomislav didn't ask questions.

'And yet… a bomb in the wrong place can kill innocent men and women. I'm looking for a volunteer to find out what's going on. We can hardly sit drinking and making merry while our people are suffering.' His friend was exaggerating. Civilians didn't expect a General to concern himself with a bomb when the enemy was gathering on the other side of the river in preparation for invasion. Tomislav's arm was around his shoulders, his breath warm on his cheek.

They shook hands. 'Stefan. I knew I could depend on you. Send word if there are deaths and tell the people their army will take revenge.'

As Stefan hurried along the gravel path through the restaurant gardens and towards the main street, he caught a whiff of roses and lavender, favourites of Stamenka's. All he would do was assess the damage, ensure any survivors were being rescued and send a message to Tomislav. Then he could go. The journalist would wait half an hour.

The torches on either side of the path flickered. Behind him, Stefan heard his orderly's footsteps, the tap tap of Rajko's stick. Already irritated with Tomislav, for sending him on a useless errand, his ill humour was increased by Rajko's presence. At times like this, he wished his friend's bravery extended to risking an operation to remove the bullet lodged in his knee.

Rajko panted by his side. 'No-one heeds the warnings.'

'Take your time, brother.' Stefan tried to sound reassuring.

Rajko went on, 'They think because we've had one victory, bombs won't explode.'

'It seems to be on Ulica Morava.'

Rajko paused, leaning on his stick. 'The Bulgars will attack next.' Rajko spoke in short bursts and Stefan waited, tapping his foot.

Rajko went on, 'Then the Turks. The whole world hates us.'

Stefan snapped, 'You should take the offer to retire and return home to your wife.' His wife was reputed to be a dark haired beauty. Stefan couldn't remember him going home on leave; no doubt she'd found someone else.

'Who knows, even the Greeks could turn against us. All before our damned allies set foot in Serbia.'

Stefan grunted. The sensible response was, Why the hell are we fighting, if we can't win without the help of allies? Serbs, a passionate people, were rarely sensible.

As Rajko began to walk again, Stefan increased his pace through the gates of the Pavilion gardens. Dragan stepped closer. The avenue of trees on Bulevar Foccicia was poorly lit and the side streets dark. The smell of barbecued meat from restaurants drifted towards them, along with the sound of women's voices.

At King Petar's statue, a train of ox-drawn wagons clattered along the cobblestones. The cavalcade had no beginning and no end. If he waited for it to pass, minutes would be wasted. He stepped into the road, his shoes slipping on shit and urine, as he moved towards the steaming mouths of bullocks, the stinking hindquarters of oxen. He didn't want to witness the wounds of the men lying in the wagons, but couldn't ignore their groans when one wagon obstructed his path.

Fighting nausea, he peered over the wooden side panels, able only to distinguish a blur of shapes. Humps, which moved. Grey blankets. Grey hair. Bodies heaped like logs outside his house. He recoiled, as an arm dangling from the wagon, snaked towards him, touched his sleeve. Not able to stop himself, Stefan's eyes followed the fingers, the trembling

16

hand, the ragged sleeve. Shadows flickered across the wagon, before retreating. It was too dark to distinguish a person, but in his mind he saw a man lying on heaving bodies, and in the instant the wagon moved on, from within it, a voice called out, 'Serbia is great.' He pictured an ashen face under a crust of black blood, a bandage in tatters. Through a mist of tears, he saw, or imagined, faces drained with pain, eyes pleading for mercy, calling out to their country.

The rich food from Tomislav's celebration rose from his belly, sprang from his throat, before he'd time to control it. He grappled for the handkerchief inside his trouser pocket, wiped his mouth and chin, and flung the handkerchief and vomit to the ground. He gulped night air as though it were water, and stumbled behind the backs of wagons to the other side. Dragan wasn't far away, but he'd lost a sense of Rajko's whereabouts. In the distance, a woman screamed.

On the pavement he waited. Ancient stone buildings loomed through the murky darkness, and a boy of about six darted from a shadowy doorway. Stefan stretched out his arms to catch the child, for it was dangerous for youngsters in the city, but he swung towards the traffic, and though Stefan ran after him for a yard or so, he was too slow. The experience added to the unreality of the evening.

A moment later, he was joined by Dragan, who used his handkerchief to remove the vomit. Stefan hated the smell, but Dragan spat, wiped, spat again, wiped and wiped until the front of the tunic was clean. When Rajko joined them, limping, Stefan's impatience returned. The three men moved on.

From a side street, there was the sound of heavy, rapid footsteps. Stefan hurried ahead, relieved when he recognised one of his own men.

They saluted.

'What news?'

'A bomb by Gornji café.'

Stefan grimaced.

'Yes, sir. Students and soldiers. Over there.' The voice was pained. 'We're checking the site.'

'Well done, brother. Do you need reinforcements?'

'There's not a lot we can do, sir.'

Stefan ordered Rajko to return to the Karakjodj and report to Tomislav. The Gornji was where he and Rajko had drunk as students, young officers, and where Stefan had first met the journalist. If it had been any other public building, he could have left the job to the engineers.

It was as Stefan expected. Where the café had stood, smoking rubble shuddered like men in shock. While he looked down the street, Stefan wiped his arm across his mouth, which tasted of masonry grit. A few women huddled on the pavement. A cordon stretched the width of the side street, while soldiers evacuated families from houses. A woman in a night dress carried a baby in a black shawl, followed by a dog. Now and again, a figure ran up or down the street.

Stefan peered at the remains of the café. There was no sign that an hour ago students and soldiers crammed into its bars, drinking, smoking and laughing. This was where he'd celebrated his promotion a few days ago.

The engineer in charge, his uniform drenched with ash dust, said, 'Terrible business, sir.'

'Many survivors?'

'Not yet.'

If the Austrians had been able to choose the site on which their bomb fell, they couldn't have done better. It felt a bad omen. It was the hub of patriotic fervour. The men stood in silence.

'See to it, and show me where to dig.' It would be at least an hour before he got home, and it would be difficult for Stamenka to occupy the journalist. She wouldn't think it decent to sit with a foreigner for long.

It was first light by the time Stefan staggered past the shop where his father used to work, its doors shut to the street. The bench his father built, had disappeared many years ago. Stefan used to watch him planing, sawing, whittling, but that wasn't the picture that stayed in his mind this morning. He saw him, eyes shut, black hair under a red fez, sprawled along the bench

18

in the evening, when his work was over, a glass of *rakija* in his hand.

Already birds were singing, and someone was drawing water from the well near to his mother and older brother's dwelling. There was no foreign vehicle in the courtyard, but if the journalist had come by horse, that would have been stabled.

He dragged himself up the steps to his house. The shutters to the living room were closed, so he couldn't see if the room was lit.

He pushed open the door. A low candle flame trembled in the centre of the long table. He tripped over the rug, stumbled almost to his knees, before he regained his balance. The room smelled of wood ash, candles, and polish. It was a woman's room. What had the American thought? Were they too poor? He'd heard all the houses in America had electric light, though that could be propaganda. He staggered across to the bench in front of the dying fire. There was no sleeping figure. Head in hands, he sat down, relieved.

Only when Stamenka, fully clothed, emerged from their sleeping quarters, did he stir.

'Do you want to inspect Mitar?' she asked.

'Did the journalist come?'

The door snapped shut. She stepped towards him. She smelled of wood smoke and lavender oil. 'I thought you'd returned to barracks.'

In her black gown, she reminded him of his mother when he was a boy. Nothing about her dress reflected modern city life. He resented her refusal to dress like an officer's wife. A flash of anger followed by an urge to run away.

He pursued his question. 'The journalist?'

'I must light a candle to celebrate your return.'

He reached for his cigarette case. He mustn't blame her for his disappointment. His throat was too dry to smoke. He let his hand fall.

'We were expecting the American journalist,' he said wearily.

She strode across to the fire, as though shooing chickens, lit a taper from the embers and held a protective hand around

19

it, as she carried it to the table. The candles in front of him flared into primrose flames, and when he turned to look at her, noticed red blotches on her cheeks where she'd lain against the blanket. Perhaps she thought he'd cancelled the appointment.

'Do you like the new tapestry?' She held the candle above the bookcase his father had built for them, when they married. He gazed at the tapestry. A patchwork of mud, wooden stakes, mountain trenches, burned out buildings among wheat or maize stubble.

'He was to take you and the boy to freedom,' he said glumly.

She poked the fire, added a few logs, lit the candles in the recesses, and pushed the books on the shelves so they stood like men in line. At the table, with her sleeve, she rubbed the photograph of him in dress uniform.

'You are a brave soldier for Serbia.' She lowered her eyes. He knew she boasted of him to other women and the priest. He squirmed on the bench, embarrassed, his body yearning for rest.

She tucked the bunch of dried thistles back into the wooden feet of the photograph frame. 'A bomb destroyed the gymnasium.'

'Mitar?'

'It was a Saturday.'

'We were to finalise the arrangements for your leaving.'

The burning candles tickled his nostrils and he sneezed. After he'd wiped his nose, he said, 'There are things about war that are too shocking for me to tell you.' Women weren't resilient. It wasn't just deaths on the battlefield, and they were bad, but the men in wagons, officer cadets buried alive. He couldn't admit to her, to anyone, how much every death mattered.

She said, 'They're running out of space in the cemetery.' She sat down on the chair nearest him and frowned. Her fists were clenched. 'Turks have left us their curse…'

His voice rose to quell her words. 'Superstitious nonsense.' In his memory his father shouted at his mother, and he turned his back on her, and stared at the logs catching alight.

There was a click, and the door to the sleeping quarters opened a crack. He couldn't see the boy, didn't want to talk to him. Stefan believed, though others didn't, that Belgrade would soon be occupied and he, the boy's father, would be unable to offer protection. He turned to look at Stamenka. She'd shrivelled into the chair. The door closed.

'Have you been afraid?' He tried to soften his tone, but though quieter, his voice was still harsh. He pushed himself to his feet. Whatever had possessed him to think he could get them away? He would go back to the barracks, catch some sleep.

'I'll fetch Mitar,' she offered tentatively.

'No.' On an impulse he stepped over to her chair, knelt and touched her hand. 'We have been apart too long.' He stroked her fingers. 'We need peace.'

Her palm was warm, as she placed it over the back of his hand. 'The journalist who was to take us to safety did not come.'

He sighed. Straightening, he looked across at the tapestry she wanted him to admire. He remembered her as his sixteen-year-old bride. What had happened to the yellow, blue and red tapestries she'd brought, the ones she'd displayed on the day of their betrothal? Why was she sewing tapestries as dark and desperate as the trenches? He looked down. Her eyes were full of tears, and he didn't know how to comfort her.

'Maybe he will come tomorrow,' she said.

'An unexploded bomb went off near the Gornji café. Many were killed.'

'You think he's dead?'

'I don't believe he will come tomorrow, or the next day.'

It occurred to him, he was relieved his wife and child wouldn't be travelling on a train out of Belgrade. He didn't want them to leave. He trembled with shame, and pushed the thought away.

'Then you must take us, Stefan.'

He gasped, jumped to his feet. 'I am Colonel of the Jevo regiment. It is not possible.'

'We're not safe in Belgrade.'

She was asking too much. Desertion? The candles on the table flickered, illuminating her face. What if all three of them left? Blinds pulled down, the train would steam through the night. They'd sit opposite, Mitar holding his hand.

'The army will protect its people,' he lied.

Slowly she stood up, her fingers round his. She led him to the table, leaned to blow out the candles. 'I fear you love Tomislav more than us.'

Numb with what she'd asked him to do, he gazed at the reddening wick.

'Lie with me,' she said.

Chapter Two

Regimental hospital, Jevo,
South of Belgrade, October 1914

In the late afternoon, the ward had fallen into darkness. An oil lamp fizzled on the wooden desk on a dais, candles burned in the alcoves of deep, narrow windows. Men were crammed two, sometimes three, to a palister. Many wore the ripped and bloodied clothes they fought in, hadn't been bathed, weren't dressed in the royal blue pyjamas of the Women's Medical Corps.

Closing the door, Ellen Frankland looked round for the nurse-in-charge.

She hated these first moments on the ward. Rotting flesh. Suppurating wounds. Stale blood. At her feet a man clutched at the air above his blanket. Hair stuck to an ashen face. In the same bed, another patient, on his side, groaned in his sleep. Drops of rain dribbled onto the floorboards, as Ellen removed her sou'wester, and shook it.

When the women's unit had arrived at Dobro Majka, the regimental hospital, a week ago, Matron determined to establish order and prove to Colonel Petrovic their unit could save lives. Ellen had responded, by distempering walls and ceilings with other orderlies, by day and candlelight. The next morning, they'd filled the palisters with straw and covered them with sheets and grey blankets. And now, that transformation was smothered in smells, as strong as those in the courtyard, where patients queued for beds among tethered oxen and mules.

Unbuttoning her mackintosh, Ellen strode along the central aisle until she reached the foot of the bed where Rose squatted. Her fingers slipped on the oilskin, finding it hard to concentrate, distracted by so many wounded men, so much pain. Rose didn't look up from where her patient slurped from a glass, eyes closed. Three shared the palister. A small man in the middle stared at the ceiling, a blue knitted hat on his head.

Ellen squeezed the folded sou'wester into a mackintosh pocket. 'May I register one of Dr. Eyre's patients?' she asked.

'From the casualty station?' Rose twisted, seemed to take stock of Ellen.

Embarrassed, Ellen blushed. To hide her discomfort she said, 'Dr. Eyres wants to operate straight away.' She'd been helping another orderly lift the wounded man from the mule ambulance chair when her surgeon friend had hurried to examine him.

'You're new to field hospitals?'

Ellen nodded, ready to apologise for her inexperience.

Rose continued, 'It's always the same. Either they arrive days before they're expected, or not at all. It's a good sign, this activity.'

Conscious of mud falling off her boots, Ellen didn't move. She volunteered, 'I thought … I thought it would be tidier than this.' Some confusion was expected among tent wards, hastily erected by men from the Jevo regiment in the recently cleared orchard, but not here in the main building.

"Fraid not. Every Matron I've come across says the same, "No-one to be admitted to the wards until they've been bathed, shaved, their wounds dressed," but straight after a battle it's damned impossible.'

Rose stood up. Ellen liked her. In her apron pocket she carried a white handkerchief dabbed with lavender water, which she held in front of her nose every time she thought a man a bit 'whiffy'.

'Can you cover while I take my break?'

'Is it allowed?'

'I'll only be ten minutes.'

Ellen made way for the nurse. She couldn't anticipate a problem, and if there was, she'd only to run to the corridor and shout for another orderly.

'If you think it's all right.'

Rose was bustling towards the trolley. Before she put the beaker down, she asked, 'What's wrong with your patient?'

'He's blind.' When he'd arrived, he'd been unable to raise his head or support his body. 'Dr. Eyres said it might be exacerbated by shock.'

'Write, "head shrapnel".' Rose dropped the beaker on the bottom shelf, moved to leave. 'There's another one you can add while you're at it.' She pointed to a bed close to the door. 'Ivan Velec. Left leg, gangrene. I'll check you've done it properly when I get back, so don't worry.'

Rose's straight forwardness reassured a little, but in charge of patients who didn't speak much English, Ellen felt uncertain. At home, where she managed her father's household, and was spoiled by her fiancé, self-doubt never occurred.

She tucked her mackintosh under the desk, stepped on to the dais, and sat on the high stool. Rose must think she was doing all right or she wouldn't have left her.

She decided to fetch Ivan's nametag, so she could enter both names at the same time. Gangrene meant amputation. She shivered despite the muggy warmth. It seemed cruel, but Audrey had told her that where gangrene took hold, there was no choice.

Her boots clipped, as she strode down the aisle. Some men watched, others shouted, cried in their sleep, chatted, one called a greeting.

She recognised an Austrian prisoner of war she'd met yesterday. Gustav. He was gazing at a jar of holly, she'd placed in one of the tiny alcoves. She'd write in today's letter to her fiancé, how her German enabled her to exchange pleasantries. Gustav had become a person, with a life outside the hospital, and the experience encouraged her to continue her off-duty classes in Serbian.

Ivan, lying very still on his back, wore a homespun jacket, his legs covered by a blanket, through which blood trickled onto the floor. She wondered if it mattered, if she ought to call a nurse. No, Rose had looked at him, she wouldn't have left if his life were in danger.

While she stretched to reach into his jacket pocket, she spoke calmly in English, 'I'm going to take your identity tag,' thinking as she did that she must learn more vocabulary for when she was on ward duty. A sharp kick jolted her shin. She wobbled under the blow, surprised by Ivan's strength. At first, she took it as a rebuke. She peered at him, but his eyes were

25

closed, his skin ice pale under several days' growth. She chided herself. The movement was involuntary, not personal. She extracted the tag and returned to the dais.

The register was open at page 4. Now she was becoming accustomed to the sounds, she could better identify who made them. The man next to Ivan snored fitfully.

The man in the blue woollen hat, in the middle of the palister where Rose had kneeled, was whimpering, calling out for his mother, *Majko, majko.* The cries were distressing, and Ellen wondered if he thought he was on the battlefield. The third occupant of the bed was sitting up. He'd been shaved and the stump, where his hand had been amputated, was bandaged. He was talking to the patient to whom Rose had given the drink.

She smoothed the name-tag with the edge of her hand. *Ivan Velec.* In the language class during the journey to Serbia, she'd learned the rudiments of pronunciation. The 'v' like an English 'v'. The 'c' like the 'ch' of 'church'.

The nib spluttered as she scratched the capital 'I'. After his name, she wrote 'J' for Jevo under the column headed 'regiment', and 4th October for the date of admission.

'Please, miss!' The man, who'd been chatting, waved. He shouted, 'Water. The boy wants water.'

Balancing her pen on the register, Ellen jumped down. As she hurried along the aisle, to the earthenware jug on the trolley, she adjusted a loose strand of hair with a comb. If Matron saw her, she would be in trouble for not wearing a cap.

Water splashed the back of her hand. How hot the ward was. After a morning and afternoon heaving the wounded out of wagons and mule chairs, and then lowering them on stretchers, she felt grubby and sweaty. Still, it was good to be useful. Maybe when she'd learned how to wash and dress a wound, make conversation, she would feel more confident.

As she approached the threesome, she asked, 'Who wants the water?'

'He's gone, miss.'

She positioned herself at the foot of the palister. 'Who wants water?' She spoke more slowly, thinking he'd misunderstood. In the next bed, a patient with jaundiced skin fingered rosary beads.

'He's dead.'

Her hand shook, water spilt on the blanket.

'He wanted a drink,' she stammered. She thought the patient accused her. Men on neighbouring beds listened. 'He asked for his mother,' she pleaded.

Still holding the beaker, she shuffled between the palisters, not quite believing. Her feet became entangled in the loose blankets and sheets. Mud crumbled on the floor.

'I'll have that water, miss.'

She continued to edge towards the man who'd died. What was she supposed to do? What if he was asleep or in a coma? When she got close, she handed over the drink.

Colour had drained from the dead man's face. The eyes stared. Strands of black hair lay across his forehead, below his knitted hat. He'd been too young to shave. His body seemed smaller close up. She couldn't stop trembling. She was aware of the beaker being returned, but she was obsessed with this man, this boy soldier.

'He looks young,' she whispered.

'He was fourteen.'

'A child.'

'A soldier, miss.'

She placed her hand on the boy's cheek. It was warm. Black eyebrows, long lashes. She tried to interpret his expression, to search for reassurance his death had been peaceful. Wouldn't it have been better to die on the battlefield? She closed his eyelids. She'd read that's what you were supposed to do. Unable to cover his face with a sheet, without disturbing the others, she removed his hat and laid it over his face. Blood stuck to her fingers and she wiped them on her skirt.

Just as she'd returned the beaker to the trolley, the door opened with a flourish and Matron, in white gown and head-dress, entered the ward. Ellen rubbed her bloodied hand on her skirt once more, jabbed loose hair in a comb and hurried to the dais. As she scrambled onto the stool, she noticed that behind Matron, the dark hair under Serb military cap, the silver pips of Colonel Petrovic.

'Who has obstructed this doorway?' Matron said.

'There's not enough room, Ma'am.'

Matron strode down the aisle, surveying each row of beds. Last night Ellen had taken her cocoa as she'd held the hand of a patient with a high temperature. Ellen hadn't seen her initially. Unassuming, insignificant. But not this afternoon.

Turning to the colonel, Matron announced, 'You can see the problem. We need another admissions' tent.'

'You're doing good work, Ma'am.' The colonel spoke English with a slight German accent.

'We could save more lives.'

Ellen wondered how to tell Matron of the death. The body needed to be removed, she was sure that was the procedure.

'Excuse me, Ma'am,' Ellen began.

'Miss Frankland, please get on with your work.'

The oil lamp spluttered. Ellen sat down, picked up her pen. In the column 'Reason for admission' she wrote, '1. leg gangrene.' As she blotted the entry she glanced over to the colonel. He was crouched over Ivan.

When he straightened, he addressed Ellen. 'Ivan Velec from Orasac, my birth village.'

'He came in today, sir.'

'They lost a son last year. I hope you can save him. They'll need him to work on the land, when they get old.'

She ran her hand over the blotting paper, thinking that if Ivan had gangrene, he wouldn't be able to walk.

'Where's the nurse-on-duty?' Matron said sharply.

'She slipped out.'

'When?'

'No more than a minute ago.'

'A minute?'

'No more than two, Ma'am.' She hoped Rose wouldn't be in trouble. Soon, Matron would notice that she wasn't wearing a cap.

'I want to report, Ma'am…'

'Three in a bed, Colonel. Look.'

28

Ellen jumped from her chair, off the dais landing with a thud. 'That's what I wanted to explain...You see, just a... second ago, while I was fetching him some water, that boy... the one in the middle...I put his hat over his face... because...' Out of the depths of her stomach, a sob began to surface. She pushed it down. '...because, Ma'am...sadly he's died.'

The colonel joined Matron. He was younger than Ellen expected for a colonel. Perhaps, forty. Weather-beaten face, thick eyebrows. In his grey-green uniform, gold shoulder boards and buttons, a dark red collar, campaign medals and polished, black riding boots, he was as impressive as a British officer.

Matron said, 'Have you checked his pulse?'

She shook her head, saying sorrowfully, 'He was fourteen.'

Matron slid between the beds, knelt on the edge of the palister, holding the boy's wrist. As she got up, she said gently to Ellen, 'I expect he was dead, Miss Frankland, but that's why we always have a nurse on duty. If there is nothing that can be done, she can at least record the time of death.'

Wanting to ask the colonel if he knew the boy, if he was from his birth village, Ellen turned to him. He was holding his gloves in his hand, his nails were trimmed, the cuticles pushed back to the half-moons. He seemed to be examining her face.

'Why did you come to Serbia, Miss Frankland?'

'To save lives, sir.' It wasn't entirely true; she was repeating what Matron said. She could hardly say she wanted to see a bit of life before she got married, and even that wasn't quite accurate.

Matron was nodding approval. 'We could do more, Colonel Petrovic.'

'Priority has to be given to the movement of troops, Ma'am, or Serbia cannot survive.'

Matron began to walk towards the door. She spoke briskly. 'We're on our last bandage bale. We can do nothing without bandages. They're at the railway station in Jevo. In a few weeks, we'll have our own motor transport, but in the meantime, your men die.'

He rubbed his hands together. 'I will arrange vehicles.'

'And gauze. And Dr. Eyres must have her anaesthetic.'

'Of course.'

Ellen returned to the dais, so she could add blind Vukasin's name to the register. At the door to the ward, the colonel turned back, and said to Ellen, 'It is not always possible to save lives, but we're grateful for what you're doing.'

Later that evening, stretched on the bed, Ellen looked up from her writing pad at Audrey, who was reading a medical book at the table by the window, a tiny frown between her eyebrows. She wore a dressing gown over her pale blue nightdress, having just had a bath. Two grips pushed curly, shoulder length hair, out of her face.

Ellen had Audrey to thank for this room in the old nunnery because the other British volunteers were bedded in dormitory tents. And though she was grateful, she also felt intimidated. Audrey, one of the first women surgeons, was clever, never stopped thinking, talked mostly about her work.

The wall was cold on her back and Ellen adjusted the pillow. It was the first time she'd not known what to write to Edward; she'd written every day during off-duty.

'It's difficult to describe death, isn't it?' she commented.

'Don't.'

'We promised to tell each other everything.'

'That's ridiculous.' Audrey looked at her watch. 'Are you going to the mess for cocoa?'

'I'll finish my letter, if that's all right. I'm worried I haven't had one from Edward.'

'Nor me from Douglas. They're busy.'

'I suppose so.' Ellen leaned down to dip her nib in the inkwell on the floor. It felt a long time since she'd seen Edward.

He'd been extraordinarily kind, when she'd told him she wanted to join the Women's Medical Corps as an orderly. Papa had refused permission and Edward had looked into the situation. That involved touring the largest military hospital in England, and discussing Ellen's plans with the matron. He'd spoken to Audrey, appointed as orthopaedic surgeon at Dobro Majka, and at length on the telephone to Lady Alice, the founder of the Women's Medical Corps. Satisfied, that his future wife would be acting patriotically, without coming to any harm, he'd tried to persuade her father. That he'd not done so, was his only doubt about her venture.

With a sigh, she began,

My Dear Edward,
I have been thinking of Lady Alice at St. Thomas' hall. Those peacock feathers, that emerald dress, the tilt of her hips. Yet it's difficult to imagine her in Serbia, particularly at Dobro Majka. She was elegant and I was impressed, but my recollection of her description of the Women's Medical Corps does not match my present experience.

Resting the nib on the page, she remembered that afternoon at St. Thomas' hall. The mingling of women's perfume in the rows around her, the swelling of her feet in satin shoes, too small for walking on London pavements in August, the buzz in her stomach. Straight after the meeting, she'd telephoned Edward at his club, had enthused that Lady Alice believed women could play an active role during the war. Obviously it included witnessing death, but she (and perhaps Edward) had glossed over that.

'If you're not going to write your letter, you may as well fetch our drinks now.' Audrey spoke sharply.

'It's harder than I thought.'

'Death?'

'Writing. I was different at home, I wonder if Edward will recognise me.'

'After a single death?'

'It's something you're used to I expect...'

'Any death is tragic, especially of one so young, in a needless war, but being here will help you decide what to do with your life.'

It was hard to explain to her pacifist friend, that though she grieved, she accepted death. Her uncle Victor had died fighting in the Boer war.

However, there was no point in trying to finish the letter with Audrey in the room. She would get up early tomorrow, take pen and ink to the chapel, and write by candle light as she'd done before. She picked up the sheet of blotting paper from the coverlet and laid it across the half page she'd managed to get down.

'You know I don't want to be a doctor or a nurse.'

'You can't be a soldier!'

'That was a misunderstanding.'

'Only you could possibly imagine that a respected woman like Lady Alice would suggest women fight.'

'It was silly, I know.' She wished she'd never blurted out, in an unguarded moment, she wanted to be a soldier.

'I'll make us hot water bottles and bring over cocoa, shall I?'

Ellen tucked the letter inside the writing pad. As she put it in the drawer of the bedside locker along with the letter she'd already written to her sister, she took a deep breath.

'I want what's best for you,' Audrey went on, 'that's all. Maybe we could see something of the country while we're here. Colonel Petrovic suggested to Matron that we take a ride into the villages. I'm sure she'd let you come with me.'

Ellen bent down and picked up the inkwell. 'If you like.' She doubted anything would come of it; Audrey sometimes worked through her off-duty though Matron didn't allow nurses and orderlies to.

As she carried the ink well across the room to the stand she kept inside the wardrobe she said, 'Your fiancé is a surgeon so he won't be shocked by these things.'

'There's a lot here that would surprise him.'

'In some respects, Edward is leading a more sheltered life than I am.'

'Ellen, Edward is twenty-eight. He's running a factory making motor ambulances, negotiating with the Ministry of Defence. If he doesn't know men die in war, he's living in a different world from the rest of us.'

Ellen nudged the drawer shut. Why did Audrey have to lecture her?

Audrey went on, 'Life is not a melodrama with you the tragic hero. You wanted to find out what war's about, and you are.'

As she crossed the room for last night's hot water bottles, Ellen was silent. When she'd started at St. Catherine's as a weekly boarder after her mother's death, Audrey, a Sixth Former, was asked to help her settle in. Ellen, aloof in her desolation, hadn't been dramatising though Audrey had presumed so.

At the door, with the hot water bottles in her hand, she clarified. 'All I'm saying is, that I think I know more about the human cost of war, than Edward.'

She didn't admit to Audrey that it disturbed her, the unfamiliar feeling of wanting to protect him.

Chapter Three

Dobro Majka, outside Jevo. October 1914

The crisp, evening air burned Ellen's throat, as she made her way through the winding paths to the operating tent. Apple trees had been chopped down to make way for the Unit's tents, and she followed the lighted lanterns on the stumps to the far end of the hospital grounds. As she turned into the final alley, she straightened her shoulders, tried to ignore the stirrings in her tummy. Ahead, the tent loomed like a prehistoric bird, the corner flags, wings preparing for flight. The electric generator Audrey had paid for and collected from Belgrade last week *thrump, thrump, thrumped*, by its side. Gladys, the theatre nurse, was waiting under a lantern hanging from a wrought iron post.

While they shook hands, Ellen was conscious of the basket to the left of the entrance. In the flickering light, she glimpsed legs, shins and feet, hands, finger knuckles, arms. It was a place she avoided, her imagination stirred by stories of amputations, the smell of blood and decomposition.

Gladys nudged the basket with her foot. 'Don't take this as normal. You'd lose your job at St. Bart's if you left limbs lying about.' She sidled close, 'It's primitive here.'

Ellen twisted from her, hands clasped, stared into the starry sky.

'Have you got a parcel from home?' Gladys went on. Wisps of grey hair shone in the lamplight. Gladys was another of the older nurses. She'd left two children with her sister, her husband having enlisted. 'My mother's sent biscuits and chocolate if you want to join us after supper. That scrambled egg and beans was awful, wasn't it?'

Ellen disliked communal eating at Dobro Majka, hated the dried egg mix and had managed only a slice of bread and jam. The prospect of chocolate sickened her. 'We've had worse,' she said politely.

She'd herself to blame for being here. Audrey meant well. Last night as they'd chatted drinking cocoa, Audrey had suggested she observe the operation on Vukasin, so she would have a fuller picture of what happened in the women's medical unit. Upset by the boy soldier's death, tired at the close of a day, Ellen had succumbed. Matron had given permission for Ellen to be present during one operation in the early evening, emphasising to Audrey that Ellen needed ward experience before specializing.

Gladys, tall, with broad shoulders and a broad Cockney accent instructed, 'Now, you must take off your boots, nice leather, and put on those overshoes.'

She pointed to a three feet long rack, on which were balanced several pairs of wellington boots. Ellen removed her gloves, ready to unfasten her laces. Her heart fluttered.

'Do you think it will snow?' Gladys asked cheerfully.

Seeing nothing but the ordeal ahead, Ellen was slow to reply. She hoped the operation wouldn't last long. Audrey couldn't estimate, but sometimes she came to bed long after Ellen was asleep. Gladys pushed on, 'This head. Even at St. Bart's he mightn't make it.'

Impulsively, Ellen confided, 'I don't like it when they die.'

'I used to cry and cry, after a patient passed on. You learn to be tough.'

The laces knotted. Ellen's fingers trembled, she fumbled.

'Audrey thought your patient might feel better if I spoke to him in Serbian, though I'm not very good.'

'Is she your friend?' Gladys stood hands on hips as Ellen slipped one foot into the boot.

'Sorry. I should call her Dr. Eyres. We met at school.'

'Must be older than you, surely?'

'Six years.'

While Ellen slid on the second boot, Gladys gabbled. 'The Serbs are useless. Their doctors and nurses died from typhus last year with their patients. Their army isn't that good either.'

'They won their last war.'

Gladys went on, 'Every time you come in or go out, you must douse your shoes. Like so.' Raising her skirts, she swished first her left, then her right foot. Ellen suspected the demonstration was exaggerated. When she'd told Rose where she was going, she'd advised not to be taken in. 'They like their bit of drama,' she said.

'You do it,' Gladys ordered.

Ellen wriggled her toes. Her foot felt tiny and cold as she swished it in the trough of disinfectant. In the distance, men sang to the mournful strings of the *gusle*. Gladys kicked at a flurry of leaves.

'Be careful, mind you don't slip.' She watched Ellen for a moment before marching over the duckboards into the tent.

The heat inside hit Ellen. The bulbs hanging from cross beams and rickety stands, were brighter than those elsewhere in the hospital. She stuffed her gloves in her pockets, pulled off her scarf and unbuttoned her greatcoat. Among the distinctive smell of disinfectant, others intruded. She quashed her queasiness.

Used to the wards, where there was barely space to walk between each palister, the high table where Vukasin was lying under a white sheet, appeared isolated. Furniture was crowded in the area close to the entrance. Washstand. Trolley. Coat stand. Tin bath. Cupboard. Small sterilising unit. Stacks of buckets, bowls and jugs. A canister of water.

Audrey, in a white coat, pulled instruments from the pockets of an apron, which ran round the sides of the table. Behind her, on a bed tucked into the corner, another patient lay asleep.

Audrey hurried over and shook Ellen's hand. 'Good of you to help out,' she said briskly, 'We've dressed the patient. All you're required to do, is talk, reassure him. Nurse Gladys will give the rules of theatre.'

Gladys hung up her coat and slipped on a green gown. As she tied the belt at the back, she said to Ellen, 'Wash your hands before you do anything. At Bart's we learned how easily bacteria can be introduced into a clinical environment.'

She turned quickly to Audrey. 'Shall I gown you, Doctor?' Holding a green cape, she walked over to Audrey who'd removed her white coat.

As she unhooked her tunic cuffs, Ellen wondered what Edward would make of the fourteen year old's death. Maybe he would discuss it with the matron of the military hospital. He liked to understand why things happened.

Gladys, having fastened Audrey's gown, shook a green hair net.

She explained, 'To lessen the chance of infection when we're near the patient, we wear a face mask. White. It covers the nose and mouth. Dr. Eyres uses this to keep the hair from her face, but it's physically demanding work, so she likes to keep as cool as she can.'

'Preventing infection is our greatest challenge,' Audrey agreed. 'Everything and everyone has to keep clean.' She turned to Gladys. 'Make sure you keep your eyes on Miss Frankland. She won't appreciate the risk having come from the wards.'

Ellen resented the tone.

'How is he?' she asked.

'We won't know till we get in. Most head wounds die. He's done well to survive the journey and the night.'

Ellen prayed she wasn't about to witness another death.

Audrey breezed on, 'I'll be looking for the size of the entry hole and the brain matter protruding through the exit hole. From that I can make certain deductions. For example: bullet. Chances of recovery? Poor.'

'You wouldn't operate in that case?'

'Trauma is a strange beast. All we do, is provide the best clinical conditions for his survival.' She turned to Gladys, 'Get yourselves ready and we can make a start.'

Ellen looked over at Audrey, who leaned over the patient. Ellen thought how remote the theatre felt. In the mess, even when it was cold, tent flaps were partially open. They smelled grass, observed apple and plum trees while they ate. In the wards, she glimpsed passing shapes and shadows, but here within the double walls and double roof, she felt entombed.

Gladys threw Ellen a green gown. 'The Serbs have no clue about the need for cleanliness. Matron telephones Colonel Petrovic every day to tell him to cover the cesspool, but he doesn't.'

Matron would tell them it had something to do with poverty and the resulting lack of education, Ellen thought.

'You'll need to roll up your tunic sleeves to your elbows,' Gladys said.

'I can take it off if you like. It's boiling.'

'No need for that. I remember my first operation. It was Matron who recommended me for theatre, thought I'd an aptitude and she was right. I was ten years a nurse by then.'

Audrey said to Gladys, 'When Ellen has washed her hands, help her gown up. Then she can give the patient a cigarette.'

Ellen was relieved when she stood by Vukasin, that he had more colour than yesterday. Like most of the soldiers, his skin was weathered. Fresh blood trickled down the side of his face, by-passing a scar, strands of red hair escaped his bandage. She wondered if his sight had returned.

Using one of the first questions she'd learned, she asked. *'Kako vi ste?'* She'd understand a 'very well, thank you,' but nothing more involved.

When he didn't answer, she fumbled through the back slit of her gown for cigarette case and matches. She drew back, as the stove under the table she'd not realised was there, scorched her shins. She poked a cigarette between his lips. He sighed. She struck a match. Vukasin struggled to reach the flame, collapsed, the cigarette fell.

She lit the cigarette, touched his lips with a finger to indicate it was ready, and he sucked, eyes watering. Satisfied, she cupped her hands under his chin to catch the cigarette. She watched him smoke for a while, waiting till he paused for breath, before repeating, *'Kako vi ste?'*

With the cigarette between his fingers, he announced, 'I am blind.'

'You are a brave man.'

'Hvala.'

Thank you. For being brave?

He moved the cigarette in front of his eyes. 'I am blind.'

She placed a hand on his shoulder, as Colonel Petrovic had rested his, on Ivan's. It would be wrong to reassure that Audrey would bring his sight back, though she longed to. That was a difficulty with nursing, not making false promises.

'Koliko imate godino?'

When he didn't tell her how old he was, she wasn't sure he'd understood.

He smoked for a while before saying, in Serbian, 'I fight with my son, my father, my brother.' He twisted the cigarette between his index and middle finger. Smoke drifted between them.

'You fight well.'

Behind them, water was poured into a basin.

'We drove them back. They...our children. They...our women.' So many words she couldn't translate, she wished she knew them, but the shape of the sounds was unfamiliar.

The bandage across his forehead shifted and drops of perspiration dribbled down his forehead. With a handkerchief, she wiped the sweat, so it didn't run into his eyes.

She urged, 'You must keep calm, please.'

He spoke faster. He must think she understood. Her head was sticky under the cap and she stepped away from the heater. He gesticulated with his cigarette. She noticed he called those he fought alongside, 'brothers,' as did Colonel Petrovic.

Several minutes later, Audrey and Gladys joined her, on the opposite side of the table.

Audrey said, 'We need the lights over the cranium.'

'One either side,' added Gladys.

Ellen worked out how best to position the two stands. Each was built of uneven pieces of wood crudely hammered together. To move them was cumbersome; they looked fragile, liable to fall apart. The stand by Vukasin's head, only needed an adjustment of the bulb so the light shone on his head. Gladys, was dragging the other from the far end of the table, its bulb flickering and wobbling.

Ellen wondered when to remove Vukasin's cigarette.

Gladys snapped, 'Don't just stand doing nothing. You move that one to the other side.'

It would have been simpler to leave it where it was, but Ellen suspected Gladys wouldn't take advice from a newcomer.

Audrey was leaning over Vukasin, her hands feeling his head through the bandage.

As Ellen shuffled the stand behind his head, Audrey asked, 'What's his name?'

'Vukasin.'

One of the legs caught in a gap between the floorboards and Ellen wondered why one of the men from the regiment hadn't been asked to screw it together so they didn't have this problem.

Gladys said, 'I'm taking the patient's cigarette and will throw it in the bucket outside. Obviously, at home he wouldn't be allowed to smoke in theatre, but it's different here. We have to get used to that.'

From the entrance, Gladys shouted, 'Miss Frankland. I am disinfecting my overshoes even though I only put a toe outside. That is because you can't be too careful.'

With the lamp stand in place, Ellen glanced at Audrey wondering when Vukasin would be given anaesthetic. She'd heard they used ether, but she couldn't see any containers. She walked round to Gladys' lamp to manoeuvre it so that it stood opposite hers.

'How old is he?' Audrey leaned over Vukasin, examining his face. At the same time Gladys called, 'Miss Frankland, hurry with that lamp.'

The stand wobbled as she pushed and pulled it across the floorboards, careful not to disconnect the flex. The bulb burned through her cap into her scalp; she was sticky with sweat and anxiety. She'd be relieved when they got started.

'Is he your age?' Audrey prompted.

He didn't look twenty-one. Indignantly, Ellen said, 'He's got a son fighting.'

'He'll have witnessed more than we can imagine.'

'Poor man,' Ellen agreed twisting the lamp shade so the light fell across his bandaged head. His eyes were closed and she was reminded of the boy soldier. Rose had said she would get over it. Audrey's hands rested on his forehead, her stillness reminded Ellen of her father serving Eucharist. A prayerful attentiveness.

Gladys called to Ellen, 'You have to direct the light over the patient's head.'

That was what she'd done, wasn't it? She pushed the stand closer to the table, careful that its feet didn't obstruct Audrey's movements. The lamp shuddered, the beam fell, not over Vukasin's skull, but on the sheet to one side. She groaned.

Gladys raced from the far side of the tent, hoisted herself onto the edge of the table and narrowly missing Vukasin's neck, steadied the bulb so the light fell directly. Relieved, Ellen stepped back, but no sooner had Gladys stumbled to the ground, than the bulb jolted to its original position.

Audrey said, 'Let Ellen do it. It will be experience for her.'

Ellen twisted the stand till its feet were tucked under the operating table and its central post rested against the instrument pockets. Her legs were scorching. She tightened the clamps holding the flex in place, and angled the bulb to shine over Vukasin's bandage. Beads of sweat sprouted across his forehead.

Audrey leaned over him. 'We are going to operate. First, Nurse will remove the bandage.'

Ellen blurted, 'What about the anaesthetic?'

On the opposite side of the table Gladys began to unravel the bandage, raising and lowering Vukasin's head.

He roared, 'Help!' and reached his hands to snatch the bandage. Not able to remember any reassuring Serbian phrases, Ellen said in English, 'Keep calm.'

'Hold his hands down, will you?' Gladys said.

Ellen couldn't move.

'Be careful,' Audrey said, 'There could be leakage.'

Gladys unwrapped more slowly. Ellen was shivering. Surely, they had something to ease his pain. He had a head injury. She ought to have asked more questions before she'd agreed to assist. As Gladys tore off the final piece of gauze, the wound began to bleed.

'Take a breath of fresh air,' Audrey said to Ellen. As she scurried to the door, Gladys called, 'Don't forget to swill your shoes.'

When Ellen returned ten minutes later, Gladys was cutting off Vukasin's hair in chunks while Audrey stood at his feet.

'Fetch me a bowl, will you?' Gladys asked.

41

As Ellen hurried towards the wash stand, where she'd seen them stacked, Audrey was saying, 'Would you like to fight, Gladys?' It seemed an odd question. She must have misheard.

'My Harold isn't very good at writing,' Gladys said.

Ellen skidded on the floorboards in her haste to grab a bowl. She marvelled that Audrey and Gladys could chat as they prepared their patient, as though they were doing no more than trim his hair. Outside, having a cigarette, she'd decided to ask about the anaesthetic, if there was none, she would leave. To witness such pain, was too much.

Gladys snorted when she handed her the bowl. 'That's not big enough. It's for his hair.' Sweat streamed down her forehead; she stank of sweat. Audrey, standing at the foot of the table, arms folded, was talking about her and Ellen going to Jevo for a day, asking if Gladys would like to join them. Colonel Petrovic had arranged for a lieutenant to drive them.

'Thanks for the invite, but no. There's nothing there. Just a street.' Gladys handed Ellen the scissors. 'Put them in the washstand when you fetch another bowl. Afterwards, I'll show you how to wash and sterilise them.'

Back at the operating table, Gladys asked her to hold the bowl while she shaved Vukasin's head. 'The men are brave,' she said, 'I like the men.'

Blood and juices from his scalp oozed onto the sheet. Ellen's knees shook. The bowl wobbled in her hands. Water splashed onto Vukasin's cheek. She smelled disinfectant. Glady's face blurred, her body, a green fuzz.

Ellen drifted towards her, till Audrey snatched the bowl. 'Take another breather.'

Ellen steadied her hands, swallowed. 'Where's the anaesthetic? she asked.

'At the railway station. We ran out two days ago.'

If Vukasin had to endure the pain, she must be there. 'I'm fine now,' she told Audrey, returned the bowl.

Audrey seemed to be shouting, 'Dying on the battlefield must be appalling. The pain, the noise of guns, the screams of other men.'

Gladys glanced at Ellen before continuing to shave, crouched over Vukasin's face as she drew nearer and nearer to the wound. She wiped the edge of the razor on the towel.

Ellen didn't want to talk about death either. 'The soldiers are brothers,' she said, 'They support each other.'

'They may have to fight,' Audrey said, 'but not women.'

Gladys was dabbing blood with a wad of lint. There was a peculiar smell Ellen didn't like. She would tell Matron she didn't want to come in a theatre again.

It took Gladys twenty minutes to clear the area around the wound. The fragile flesh parted. Ellen clenched her hands so tight, she felt dizzy, terrified he would die.

Audrey spoke through her mask to Vukasin. 'We're going to remove part of the frontal lobe. It will sound worse in your head than it is. Nurse will assist by giving you a bandage to bite on. We'll remove as little as possible, but I want to ease the pressure.'

With a flick of her head, she looked at Ellen, then back at Vukasin. 'You look deathly. Have a cigarette and come back. We can manage.'

Ellen shook her head. Her temples thumped. She longed for cold air on her cheeks, to smell the earth outside, feel strength return as she walked through rows of tents, crossed the courtyard, back to her room. She steadied herself on the edge of the table.

Now he stank of sweat and urine. The smell of disinfectant was less strong. Gladys passed Audrey a small saw, which she drove in short strokes. Vukasin's head juddered.

Ellen crouched by the side of the table, slipped her hand under the sheet. A broad strap had been fixed to hold his arms by his side. He smelled of shit. She slid her hand along the rubber sheet till she touched a finger. She squeezed it, murmured in Serbian, 'You are a brave man. Your father and brothers are proud of you.'

His breathing eased.

Two hours later Gladys lowered a piece of gauze across the wound, which now extended across the skull. Blood flowed beneath it, and she placed a roll of lint over his eyebrows, as she removed the bandage he'd been biting on. He grunted as his mouth open.

'Shall I see if he wants a cigarette?' Ellen's throat was so dry, her voice squeaked.

'He's tired. Gladys will wash him and make him comfortable before he sleeps. We'll take a stroll outside.'

Gladys was collecting the razors, scalpels and dropping them in a bowl. 'You go with Doctor. I'll show you later how to disinfect.'

Ellen's body ached. Her joints and muscles stiff, not only with the physical effort of crouching, but also with the mental effort of willing Vukasin to recover, and of not fleeing herself. She followed Audrey as vigorously as she could.

Outside, relishing the breeze on her cheeks, Ellen pulled off her cap. A light covering of snow had fallen, and she was enchanted. The path and grass around the tent were completely white. Snow had settled on ridgepoles, guy ropes, tree stumps. The striking of the quarter hour on the courtyard clock was muffled, the world slept.

Audrey said, 'You did well. You'll make a good nurse.'

No point repeating that she didn't want to be a nurse, her experience on the ward had confirmed that.

'Do you feel all right now?'

'I'm fine.'

'We'll have no more talk of becoming a soldier.'

Audrey never listened. Didn't understand that her uncle, killed in the Boer War, had been her childhood hero. She thought of the boy-soldier. The down on his cheeks and across his chin. She wished she'd been able to give him water, moisten his lips.

Audrey snapped, 'I said, we'll have no more talk of becoming a soldier.'

It occurred to her that Audrey was being silly. She'd already apologised for her mistake, though there'd been no need. She wanted to lie in the snow, feel the earth on her back, the stars looking down on her.

She asked, 'Will he live?'

Chapter Four

North of Sarajevo, Bosnia. October 1914

It was approaching eleven when Stefan and Rajko reached the clearing to inspect Glisic's unit. The orderlies tethered the horses. Stefan removed his mackintosh and began to brush the mud from his greatcoat and trousers. He ordered Dragan to polish his boots, rub them till they shone.

Rajko removed his cap, dabbed his forehead with a handkerchief and adjusted his cap.

Glisic and his men were gathered in a shelter that lay in a hollow several metres below ground level. Stefan hoped there was a fire. All morning, rain had dripped between his neck and the collar of his raincoat, slipped through the stitching on his gloves.

His boots cleaned, he crossed the clearing and looked down at the shelter, relieved to see a fire, around which ten officers were gazing up at him. The dug out was well built. Hollowed from roots of a fallen beech, it was the height of a village dwelling. Wooden posts and sandbags shored up its earth walls and a neatly constructed brushwood roof covered one third of the area, sleeping quarters for off-duty officers. He looked again. The ground was well swept and in addition to the men around the fire, another sat on a tree trunk as though posing for a photograph.

With a sigh, he took the cigarette Rajko offered, the first sign of goodwill all morning. During the ride, Rajko had seemed morose, not replying to Stefan's observations that the men were exhausted, ammunition in short supply, greatcoats, waterproofs and boots unavailable.

He dragged on the cigarette, peered down trying to make out Glisic, whom he'd met at Military Academy as a student, though Glisic was several years older. A good-natured buffoon with a squashed nose on a clown's face, he was apt to be silent during strategy discussions at regimental meetings. Only when Stefan concluded, did he speak. Something pithy, perhaps philosophical.

'Our confidence never waivers,' or 'Only those whose love for our country knows no limits, can act with the needed courage.'

Rajko described him as empty headed, but there'd never been any adverse reports.

Below them, the orderlies were loading logs onto and around a fire.

Stefan threw his unfinished cigarette to the ground and began to climb down the ladder. The three officers to the left of the fire were watching. Closer to the wall of the shelter, the man seated on the tree trunk with his hands behind his head, opened his mouth to catch droplets of rain. Glisic faced his officers, his back to Stefan.

As he drew nearer to the ground, he realised what was different about this dug out. The ground sheet was well swept, maps pinned to an easel, cartridge belts, helmets, jackets and boots stacked in order. Even as he was thinking that it was reminiscent of a monks' retreat, it struck him there was no shortage of equipment. Elsewhere the constant complaint: no weapons, no boots, no jackets.

And then, as Stefan jumped to the ground, Glisic whirled around, clapped his gloved hands, 'Colonel Petrovic! Glad to see you again, sir.'

With outstretched arms, he turned back to his officers. 'Well, boys. Colonel Petrovic has come to inspect.'

Two older officers stood on either side of what was, by his youth and rank, a student officer. Stefan opposed the government's decision to deploy these young men across the army; he'd not seen anything to suggest he'd been wrong. This corporal looked eighteen.

Stefan and Glisic shook hands, and as Rajko reached the ground he greeted Glisic, too. The latter was short for a Serb. Rajko, despite pain, held himself proudly.

The wind moaned through the trees. Leaves fell, mingling with the rain. Rajko began to swagger towards the covered area, waving his stick theatrically. He appeared to be enjoying himself.

Glisic cleared his throat.

After a brief silence, Stefan said, 'You will introduce your officers, Major.'

Glisic glanced at the three men to the side of the fire, before taking a step or so towards the tree trunk.

'Lieutenant Vasic. Your attention, if you please.'

Vasic looked up, removed his hands from behind his head at the mention of his name. He peered at Glisic, who'd moved within a foot of him, then at the fire and finally at Stefan. He was frowning and Stefan saw that his face was an ugly grey; black tangled curls protruded beneath his cap, and a large bruise extended from the left cheekbone to his jaw.

Glisic turned to look at Stefan, smiled before returning his full attention to Vasic. He said, 'Colonel Petrovic has come to inspect the unit.'

Vasic unfurled. His uniform was crumpled. His boots caked in mud. A drop of blood trickled from his mouth down the stubble on his chin. He appeared newly arrived from the battlefield, though that was impossible. Nonetheless he was wounded, and should have been picked up by the medics. Stefan could see no reason why he was sitting in the cold when there was shelter behind him.

'At ease, brother,' Stefan said. Vasic collapsed back onto the tree trunk.

'What is wrong with Lieutenant Vasic?' Stefan asked.

Glisic nodded. 'We've been listening to the General's most encouraging report on the latest situation.'

'Will you make the introductions, Major?'

'Yes, sir. In the far corner we have Borivoj Vasic, 3rd Platoon.'

'Let's begin with these officers,' Stefan said impatiently.

For a second Glisic hesitated, then with a clap of his hands began with the senior officer, Lieutenant Bratanic. Stefan judged him impressive at over six and a half feet, broad shouldered, tidy uniform and polished boots. Yet, when they shook hands, Bratanic averted his eyes.

Skerlj, the student corporal, also in full uniform, was wearing *opanki*. As Stefan recalled, students were allocated boots when they left Belgrade and there were plenty in the store. It was the older seasoned soldiers who preferred the light sandals, arguing they could move faster, had greater flexibility, but not in this weather, not when rain threatened to turn to snow.

Lieutenant Tomasic was small, wiry and looked at him head on. Trustworthy. Stefan chatted to the officers, found out which village they came from, how their men were doing, before turning back to Vasic. Something needed to be done for him. Rajko, who'd left the shelter, was standing, still as a heron, next to Stefan.

Stefan walked across to the tree trunk, to where Glisic had stood earlier.

'Rank?' Stefan asked.

Glisic replied, 'Lieutenant.'

If the man didn't know his rank, he was in a very bad state.

Vasic was scratching under his cap with his fingers so that more and more of his hair began to flop over his face.

Stefan had another go. 'Where are you from Lieutenant Vasic?'

His eyes met those of Stefan who was encouraged. Perhaps he was not as ill as he appeared.

'I'm not quite sure. It's been confusing with the rain not stopping. Except for the snow. We've had all weathers.'

Stefan repeated the question, getting the same answer.

Glisic had stepped to Stefan's side. 'Lieutenant Vasic helped take the Austrian trenches on the east line, but lost half of his men. Did well.'

Vasic touched and re-touched his gun holster.

Stefan said, 'He needs to see the MO.'

'There's nothing he can do.'

'That's an order, Major.'

Bratanic cleared his throat. The student officer licked his lips.

Stefan said, 'You'll have heard that the General has ordered a further two days rest. He's keen to know the battalion's requirements.'

Glisic pulled a packet of cigarettes out of a side pocket in his greatcoat. 'We have been listening to the eloquent words of our Commander's report. He never fails to be an inspiration. He tells us we are holding the line.'

Stefan glanced at the boots Rajko had lined up at the entrance to the shelter; he lost count at five pairs. Bratanic was kicking the ground, the student officer holding his breath, only Tomasic was looking directly at him.

Glisic said, 'This is the victory our glorious General promised.'

'It is too early to claim victory.' Stefan made sure they all could hear him.

Vasic shifted his arms from round his head to around his knees. The tip of his boots grazed the ember edge of the fire. 'It has rained every day. Rain or snow. Rain and snow.'

Bratanic muttered, 'Motherfucker.'

Vasic began to rock to and fro. 'It has rained every day,' he seemed puzzled. 'Rain and snow. Rain or snow.'

'Before I leave to inspect the front line, is there anything you need in order to get back into action?'

'We've insufficient officers,' Bratanic spoke quickly, 'and when we get them they're inexperienced. Eight student corporals a week ago and they didn't bring a single weapon. Not a fucking one.'

'Corporal Skerlj has both a pistol and a rifle,' Stefan pointed out.

'Show him.' Bratanic said. 'Go on. Show him.'

The student was looking at Glisic.

Bratanic snatched the handle of the pistol and marched over to Stefan. 'We took an Austrian Männlicher from a prisoner and a 9mm Steyer-Hahn automatic.' He opened it up. 'Both without ammunition.'

Stefan said, 'Major?'

Bratanic flung the pistol over to the student, who caught it with one hand, replaced it in the holster.

Glisic threw his cigarette stub towards the fire. He beamed, 'We are Serbs. We will fight with sticks.'

Such exhortations were admissible in a battle, but not now. When he'd been a major, he'd have been furious his men hadn't got the ammunition they needed.

'Let me know what's wanted and I'll do what I can before the counter-attack,' he spoke angrily. He couldn't understand why there were so few officers. Matching ammunition to weapons was proving a common problem, but he'd have noticed a lack of officers in the lists.

Glisic folded his arms across his ample chest. 'I tell our young corporal here that these are stirring times. It is when we Serbs face defeat, we discover pride in ourselves and in our country. Young men are faced with new sensations.'

Bratanic spat on the ground. 'Fucking sensations.'

Stefan could sympathise.

With a glance, Bratanic said, 'Excuse me, sir. Call of nature.' He hurried without looking at Glisic and clambered up the ladder to the top of the hollow. Mud showered behind.

An orderly was adding yet more logs to the fire. Vasic appeared to doze. For a moment, war was far away. The sound of artillery fire was subdued. As Stefan watched Bratanic move into the pine trees, blue clouds surfaced among the grey. Birds were singing. Here they were sheltered from wind, protected from fighting.

The student officer was frowning. Tomasic gave Stefan a slight smile. Glisic lit another cigarette and threw the packet towards Stefan who passed it to Rajko without taking one.

With a 'Thank you, sir,' Rajko tucked the packet inside the pocket of his greatcoat. 'Plenty of fags, as well,' he commented to Stefan.

Glisic continued, 'Serbia is fighting for justice.' He raised his arms, waving them above his head. Stefan worried the man had become a little mad.

He addressed his question to Glisic. 'Is this what your men think?'

After a short silence, Tomasic said, 'Lieutenant Bratanic is correct. We have nothing to fight with, sir.' He was fiddling with a button on his tunic jacket.

Stefan said, 'You've equipment over there. You're better equipped than many battalions I've seen.'

In the distance, Bratanic was peeing among the trees.

Glisic gave two short claps with his hand. 'Corporal, Serbs, naked and barefoot, without artillery protection, without food for days on end, our people give their lives on every hillock, every meadow from here to the Drina. Why? Have your studies not helped you? Would they do that, if they were not fighting for justice?'

Tomasic grunted and began to speak, 'We can't fight without...' He paused for an instant. Twigs cracked as Bratanic stomped through the undergrowth.

Glisic spoke over Tomasic, 'We fight for freedom. We are a people who love freedom. That is why.'

Stefan was weary of politicians' rhetoric. Too late he recognised Glisic mimicked their empty words, when he philosophised at the end of regimental meetings.

Tomasic insisted, 'We can't fight without weapons.'

Having climbed down the ladder, Bratanic strode back to his fellow officers, saying, 'We can't always provide our men with food.'

'When did you last receive rations?' Stefan said, increasingly exasperated.

'A loyal Serb can live without food. He fights with his soul.'

Bratanic guffawed, 'You came for information, Colonel. The men have little food and few weapons.'

Stefan hoped Glisic would give a straight answer. 'Have your supplies arrived?'

Glisic was jumping up and down, his cap askew. He shouted, 'The victor is humiliated more than the victim.'

Rajko was tapping his stick, against the side of his boot.

Stefan was ashamed. In his need for diversion at crucial meetings, he'd not picked up Glisic's shortcomings. An error of judgement. As though addressing a child, he said to Glisic, 'We're fighting to survive it's true, we're fighting for freedom and justice, but we can't without officers, food and equipment.'

'Other countries are greedy.' Ignoring Stefan, Glisic addressed the student officer, 'We must not be like them. We mustn't fight for what we can get out of war.'

Stefan said to Bratanic, 'Lieutenant, please telephone for the supplies you need. Tell them the order is priority, and made on the orders of Colonel Petrovic.'

Bratanic and his orderly began to assemble their kit.

Glisic rubbed his hands up and down the side of his tunic jacket. 'Serbia will live as long as there are people prepared to die for justice, or freedom, or truth, or beauty.'

'Damn you,' Stefan shouted. He recalled, Glisic came from a military family; his father and younger brother were high-ranking officers.

'Major, you are to take leave, temporarily relieved of your command. Major Kostic will accompany you to headquarters.' Glancing at Vasic, he said, 'And Lieutenant Bratanic, arrange for medics to pick up Lieutenant Vasic as a matter of urgency.'

He would leave it up to Rajko to ensure he'd sufficient men to transport Glisic safely, in the meantime he would continue his plans. 'Corporal,' he said to the student officer, 'I'd like to see the front line trenches.'

It took Stefan, Skerlj and their orderlies twenty minutes to trudge through the trees, to reach the main communication trenches. Initially built by the Austrians, the trenches were deep, well shored with sandbags and timber. Though it had stopped raining, the north-easterly wind chafed Stefan's face, chilled his ears and nose. He wouldn't want to be serving on the front, and was glad promotion had freed him from that duty. Their journey was slow, roots tripped them, and at intersections Skerlj checked and re-checked their position on the map.

Despite brooding over Glisic's shortcomings, Stefan's optimism returned. The morning's work had been necessary. Vasic would be taken for whatever medical help was available (at least he would be away from the war that was causing him anguish), and Glisic would be given time to recover and learn a lesson. Gradually, Stefan began to sympathise with Glisic. Vasic was unlikely to recover; his career was over. Glisic was only trying to protect him. Wasn't his treatment of Rajko similar? After all, Rajko ought to be leading a unit, but Stefan had included him in the inspection team.

As they tramped single file, through a connecting trench in the woods, Stefan peered beyond Skerlj to work out if they were approaching the front line, but it was overcast and difficult to see. Shapes loomed, retreating when they moved into the light. By the time they reached the cleared ground, Stefan estimated they'd covered about two kilometres. Examination of his wristlet, told him it was already two o'clock.

It took another half an hour before Skerlj called, 'We're here, sir.'

Crouched on a sandbag, Stefan glanced across their line of trenches and barbed wire, to those of the Austrians. There was no activity. They'd seen little as they'd travelled. The occasional unit, but largely medical teams scooping up the wounded and dying. They'd met a column of soldiers whom Skerlj informed him were travelling towards a dressing station, a former miner's cottage, less than a kilometre away. The irony that Vasic was so close to help saddened Stefan.

Stefan smoothed the lapels of his greatcoat, ensured that the peak of his cap was straight. In uncertain situations, appearances were particularly important.

Skerlj flattened himself against the wall built up with sandbags, so Stefan could pass.

Stefan said, 'Stay close, Corporal.'

As Stefan strode on, a rat slipped across his boot. He hated them. Then another. The hairs on his arms stood; he shivered.

'Who's the officer-in-charge?' he asked.

'Corporal Djaja. He came out with me.'

Stefan's feet sank a centimetre or so into the mud. The trench was too shallow, little more than a meter deep; it couldn't have been attended to for some time. Water covered his feet, rising almost to the top of his riding boots and he pitied Skerlj in his *opanki*. He began to wonder if it had been abandoned, till immediately ahead, in a hollow within the trench wall, he could make out the form of a cowering man.

'On your feet, brother. Colonel Petrovic to inspect,' Stefan announced.

The man was motionless.

Stefan stepped closer. The one man was a huddle of men, squatting in the mud. The stench of rotting flesh, urine and excrement gutted him, and he put his hand over his mouth to keep down bile. He felt shocked that men from his regiment had allowed themselves to get into this state. He stretched a handkerchief over his mouth and nose.

He asked, 'Where is Corporal Djaja?'

The man nearest groaned.

'Corporal Djaja?' Stefan repeated.

A hand clasped his knee. Stefan shuffled forward. The soldier's face was grey, his eyes half-shut. He moved his hand towards the distant, far end of the trench. 'The bugger without a head.'

Stefan shivered. *The bugger without a head.*

'How long have you been here?'

The soldier said, 'Sorry, sir. Hole in gut.'

From within the group, a voice screeched, 'We drove off the motherfuckers. We forced them out with our bloody bayonets.'

The man with the stomach wound whispered, 'We've been abandoned.'

'No medics?'

'No, sir.'

'Food?'

'Nothing for days.'

Stefan turned back to Skerlj. 'Make a note of names, rank, injuries.'

A man prodded him. 'Are you wounded?' Stefan said.

'Yes, sir.'

'What...?' Stefan began.

The man with the hole in his gut struggled to speak, 'The miserable fucker ...said ...the Austrians didn't kill us...'

'He poured the bloody wine away,' said someone else.

Stefan couldn't place where the man was speaking from, but he could feel the pain in his voice. Nor could he work out what had happened. What had wine to do with it? It made no sense.

He waded on, his head hammering. The platoon had to be evacuated, Djaja replaced if they were to be ready for the counter attack. The trench needed to be dug more deeply, the water removed. Pulses in his forehead throbbed. It was bad enough Vasic hadn't been sent to the medics, but here was a whole trench of forgotten men. He'd not come across anything like it. Men could be abandoned in a rapid retreat, all kinds of dire things happened during action, but there'd been no activity for several days.

He stumbled back to where Skerlj was still taking the names of the first group of men. 'Do you know what's going on, Corporal?'

He sounded defiant. 'They're all wounded, sir.'

'Get the details and I'll send an officer to evacuate the trench,' adding, 'and when you've got their names, distribute the bread from my haversack. It's not much, but the best we can do for the moment.'

Moving on to the middle of the trench, dead and wounded lay side by side. The air above the trench stank of stale explosives. He waded on through bodies and body parts, determined to see what remained of Corporal Djaja.

As the sun began to fade, he couldn't see where the trench ended. He paused, to allow himself to absorb the horror. Glancing at what appeared to be a corpse, he saw a movement.

The hairs on his arms prickled, but he peered closer, poised to straighten if indeed it was a rat, or several. Under the tip of a cap, large eyes met his. Stefan reached down to touch the man, not knowing which of them was shivering the most.

'Name and number.'

The soldier pointed to his throat, and mimed a knife slicing through it. Stefan touched the man's jaw line. Felt its bone, the stubble where he'd not shaved. Gently he lowered his fingers towards the neck. He was no medic, but knew that traumatised men sometimes lost the power of speech, sometimes imagined wounds.

Skerlj waded towards him. He said wearily, 'They don't answer, sir and I can't always read their tags.'

'Get the names of those you can, and pick up any weapons. God knows what Corporal Djaja thought he was doing. If I'd got hold of him, he'd have been court-martialled.'

'That's not fair, sir.' Skerlj broke off, unable to contain gulping sobs. Embarrassed, moved, Stefan waited. 'He didn't want to come out here. He'd not seen a real trench before, not in a proper campaign.'

'His duty was to his men,' Stefan said firmly.

'What about Major Glisic's duty to us?'

'Be careful what you say, Corporal.' The lad was understandably overwrought, but he didn't want him on a charge.

'Two officers, and they were experienced unlike Djaja, joined the Austrians, took men with them and Glisic expected a colt to sort it out. That's not reasonable, sir. Not the way I look at it. And now he's dead.'

'You're saying that Major Glisic sent your friend, Corporal Djaja, to command a trench, previously led by officers who'd deserted?'

'Yes, sir. They'd gone before we arrived. Bratanic said they deserted because they thought we were done for, and Major Glisic refused to send trench weapons or food after that. Just Djaja. He'd no chance and I was bloody glad it wasn't me.'

'Why didn't any of the other officers say anything? They could have reported him.'

'I don't properly know, sir. I was scared, sir, coming out here. All the students were. But from what the others said, Glisic was mad, but well liked by, well, you know, High Command. His father's a General.'

'His father's well-respected, but not a General.'

'I don't know, sir. He said the men wouldn't be relieved till they started to act more like soldiers. He was like that. He took my boots because I complained my feet were bleeding. He said a good soldier would fight bare foot for his country.'

Stefan wasn't sure what to make of Skerlj's story; it would have to be investigated. In the meantime, he would do what he could for these men.

'Get the names as best you can. I'll carry on here.'

As Skerlj sloshed back down the trench, Stefan pulled out his flask, removed the top. 'Have a drink, brother,' he said to the dumb soldier. If he could swallow, he might survive. The smell of *rakija* obliterated that of death and Stefan was relieved to hear the glug, the sound of the man swallowing two long draughts.

56

Taking his flask back, he said, 'Well done.' He would have allowed him the lot, but there'd be other wounded.

Stefan didn't want to continue to the end of the trench. He didn't want to see Corporal Djaja's corpse. Yet, he'd to mark the fact the youngster had given his life for Serbia, whatever the circumstances.

He came upon the body suddenly, stumbling into the legs, almost falling over it. The smell of excrement burned his nostrils and throat. Reluctantly, his fingers touched the edge of a shoulder strap, the brass buttons. He didn't want to feel where neck had parted from head, and swiftly moved his hand down to the shoulder blade. The body stirred beneath his palm. He waited till he'd stopped trembling.

Skerlj had said they'd come out together. He would ask him what Djaja was like, if he knew the family. Stefan would write the letter himself. Glisic, Goddamn him, would be in custody. He could think of no greater crime. He'd write to Djaja's parents, 'Your son died a hero... he was loved and admired by his platoon, his sacrifice has not been in vain.'

Behind him, he heard Skerlj asking men their name and rank. Cold seeped through the earth ramparts, from the water in the trench bottom. More than ever he craved peace. It occurred to him to pray. He prayed Serbia would repulse the Austrians so the young man's death hadn't been wasted.

'A loyal Serb can live without food; he will fight with his soul.' Stefan heard Glisic's words again. He should have sent Vasic for medical help. Skerlj had arrived with boots and they'd been taken away. It was evident that the absconding officers had no confidence in his leadership. A damned idiot.

It was dark, by the time they'd noted the names of the four dead, removed their bodies from the trench and shared out bread and *rakija*. When they left, they promised medics would be along within the hour. Stefan thought the worst thing was that Glisic didn't report the desertion. He'd told no one, presumably, to protect his reputation.

While Skerlj was looking at the map with his electric torch, Stefan said, 'There'll be a court martial.' That would get to the truth and, if Skerlj was correct, the man deservedly shot.

Skerlj folded up the map, tucked it into his trouser pocket. He spoke slowly. 'He didn't want to go out there, but Major Glisic said it would be good experience. He said that in the Turkish campaign, one soldier armed with no more than a stick, held a trench for several days till reinforcements arrived.'

'Did the Major ask for reinforcements?'

'I don't know.' The lad was close to tears again. Stefan didn't want him to break down. Within the next day or so, he could be leading action.

Stefan adjusted his knapsack. 'My feet bleed. You're not the first to have bloody feet, but we'll make damned sure you get your boots.'

Chapter Five

November 1914, south of Sarajevo, Bosnia

It was snowing heavily as Stefan, Rajko and their orderlies reached the brushwood stockade where they were to spend the night. At the gate, a servant greeted them. He explained the officers would be accommodated inside, the orderlies on the veranda.

As Rajko dismounted, Stefan noticed his left leg crumple under his weight. The knee was becoming increasingly troublesome. While Dragan followed the servant with their horses, the burly Jovan helped Rajko stand. Stefan brushed snow from his shoulders, shook it from his cap, before picking up the pannier of personal papers and walking stiffly up the newly cleared path. He would stretch out in front of a fire, relax before bedding down.

Stefan had asked permission for the regiment to rest overnight, following Tomislav's orders to return full speed to Serbia. Morale was low, the stop would lift spirits after their defeat outside Sarajevo. Leaving his men to camp close to the road, Stefan and Rajko had plodded on horseback through frozen forest tracks.

A wooden spade leaned against a veranda post. Flakes of snow flashed in the light of a hanging lamp. Stefan pulled the bell rope.

A tall man dressed in homespun trousers and a sheepskin jerkin opened the door.

'Andric Kovacevik welcomes you, Colonel Petrovic.'

Having shaken hands, Stefan followed his host into the house. He was back home. The earth floor strewn with woven rugs, the beams across the ceiling festooned with bunches of paprika, bundles of onions, hung with joints of dried meat. The white walls, decorated with colourful tapestries and plaited stems of vines, reminded him of the way Stamenka used to adorn their living quarters.

When Rajko joined him and the door shut, they were led to three-legged stools in front of a stove, its doors open. Lighted candles fluttered in alcoves.

Stefan was exhausted. The troops had marched slowly on roads of slush and mud. The road out of Sarajevo had been passable, but in the pine forest, the snow, seven or eight inches deep, their horses had stumbled. Cold penetrated his greatcoat.

Andric's wife appeared with the customary *rakija* from behind the blanket, separating the kitchen from the living area. On the hospitality tray, warm bread and black olives. Stefan limited himself to two glasses of beer with the large helping of chicken and vegetables, determined to make conversation for as short a time as was polite.

When the dishes had been cleared away, Andric opened a bottle of red wine, its vine grown over the veranda. Andric declined to sit, standing between guests to pour. Rajko gulped urgently, while Stefan put his glass on an alcove shelf next to a candle.

Stefan asked, 'Do you have children?'

Andric squatted on the floor, the bottle of wine and his glass on the rug. He wiped his mouth with the back of his hand.

'Two girls,' he said softly.

Stefan felt sorry for him. Not to have sons was a burden for a man who worked on the land. 'You don't have sons?'

He'd been thinking of his lad, as he'd ridden among the cavalry. Had they been a poor family, thirteen-year-old Mitar would be working, not attending school. In the silence, Stefan reflected on Mitar in Belgrade. He didn't have the making a soldier, apt to be solitary, wandering by the river Sava reading poetry. He'd tried to encourage him to play and fight with other children so he could look after himself, but the boy spent too much time with his mother and grandmother.

Andric leaned towards Stefan, his voice low, 'We do not speak of them. My wife says she has no sons.'

'I'm sorry.'

'It's worse than that.' Andric clenched his hands.

Rajko's eyes flicked open. He re-positioned his back more firmly against the wall. His breathing slowed, as he drifted again to sleep.

Stefan waited. Snow stirred on the roof, thudded onto the veranda floorboards. Dragan stopped playing. A burst of laughter between him and Jovan. The sharp notes of the flute restarted moments later. From the kitchen the questioning voices of little girls, the steady replies of their mother.

Andric addressed the mat. 'My sons joined the Austrian army.' He whispered, his hand over his mouth, 'They signed up with Emperor Franz Josef.'

'Ah.' Stefan tried to sound sympathetic; he resisted the temptation to respond that Bosnians did what was needed to survive. Under the Turks many converted to Islam, under the Austrians, sons betrayed their country. But even as the thought arose, he remembered if he'd had the courage and the opportunity, he would have taken his family to the safety of England.

Andric went on, 'The Austrians are harsh. They charge high taxes for things we don't want.'

'What "things"?'

'Roads, where mule-tracks have served for hundreds of years, schools that teach our children to abandon the land we have struggled for.'

'It is hard.'

He began to unbutton his boots. 'We must rest, my friend,' adding, 'You have treated us well.' As he slipped off his tunic jacket, he said, 'Please thank your wife.'

Andric laid the jacket across the bed under the window. 'You will take my bed, of course, sir.'

'Not drinking, brother?' Rajko asked when Stefan crossed in front of him.

'We have a long journey tomorrow.'

'I'll drink to that!' Rajko held his empty glass towards Andric who had turned to leave.

As officer cadets, Stefan out drank his friend, but not now, not after Bregalnica. Following that battle and being wounded, he slept less soundly after a drink, more liable to nightmares. Instead of being amused by Rajko's drinking as he used to,

Stefan was now embarrassed. The day following the celebration in the Karakjodj, Tomislav's adjutant telephoned to complain of Rajko's behaviour. Stefan didn't blame Rajko for returning to the restaurant, of making the most of the free drink, but he'd had to be restrained from fighting, carried to the motorcar, returned to barracks. At thirty-five Stefan considered them too old for such antics. Nonetheless, he recognised it was he who'd changed.

Rajko smiled at Andric, then Stefan.

'You need to relax more,' he chided.

Topping up Rajko's glass, Andric said, 'When you're ready, sir, I'll make up a bed of homespun and straw. I'm only sorry I don't have a bed for you as well.'

Rajko's eyes closed as he balanced on the stool, slumping over his stick. With a jolt, he slipped to the ground.

'Bugger.' His face whitened.

Andric got to his feet. 'Lean against the wall, sir, where it's warm. You are brave men and I thank you for what you've done.'

He shouted to his wife on the other side of the dividing blanket. He asked for bedding and she returned with blankets, straw and cushions, some covered with shot silk. Stefan commented they were of too high a quality to be placed on the dusty floor near the fire, but she said they were of no importance. She asked if they needed more logs, if the room was too dark, should she light more candles? On the veranda Dragan began to play his flute.

Andric ushered her into the kitchen, as if her kindness might upset his guests. Stefan told him to take the wine, they were going to sleep. Their host withdrew immediately.

He was awoken some time later, by the sound of hooves, men's voices, Andric's servant calling to strangers entering the gateway.

Stefan reached for his holster. If necessary he would waken Rajko. Frowning, Andric was on his feet. 'I am not expecting other guests. Excuse me, sir.'

Stefan began to re-fasten the buttons on his boots. The flute playing stopped. Dragan's, 'Good evening, sir.'

Stefan was puzzled. Andric's home was small and no other officers were expected.

His host reached the door, opened it. 'Who's there?'

Leaning on his haunches, Stefan saw a lantern, the silhouette of the servant.

'It's a Serb. A General. Stavisto,' Andric reported.

'Damn,' Stefan muttered. Rajko hadn't stirred. Stefan kicked him, finished lacing his boots and snatched his jacket from the bed. A cold wind blew through the door. In the candlelight, flurries of snow flew onto the rug.

Stefan leaned astride Rajko, grabbed and shook his shoulders. 'The General's here,' he urged.

Rajko raised his head. 'Bugger.'

Stefan straightened. Typical of Tomislav, to arrive without warning. He would argue, it maintained morale if troops saw that their leaders were more than strategists, that they shared in the action on the ground.

Andric's wife appeared from the kitchen wrapped in a knitted blanket. Her hair was piled in two thick plaits across her head, her face, a weary grey, her eyes shrunken. How would Stamenka have reacted to being woken in the early hours, while officers occupied their living room?

'I am sorry, ma'am,' he said, 'It's another of my compatriots.'

She put her hand to her mouth. She's frightened of us, he thought. 'Don't worry.'

After Andric and his wife had welcomed Tomislav, the orderlies retired to the veranda. Rajko returned to his bed, curled into a ball and, without covering himself, began to snore.

Andric fetched another bottle of wine, an extra glass and retreated behind the blanket. Tomislav leaned against the wall alongside the oven, his legs stretched out.

Stefan sat on a stool and poured the wine. The logs crumbled, flared. He stood to pass Tomislav his drink. Tomislav didn't reach for it, but stared into Stefan's face. Stefan held the gaze. After a moment or so, irritated, he crouched and placed the glass within reach, too tired for games.

Tomislav drank, dabbed the corners of his mouth with his knuckle.

'Do you remember "the professor"?' Tomislav removed a leather tobacco pouch from an inside pocket.

Stefan remembered. At Military Academy, they used to sit late into the night, drinking and smoking in the common room. Tomislav, the most senior lecturer, used to tease 'the professor' because he wrote long letters home to his girlfriend. Dead now, along with most of his men, but why mention him?

'Killed at Bregalnica,' Stefan said.

The victory had been hard won. Hundreds of deaths. He suppressed the memory of being carried by stretcher through the streets to the casualty station.

Tomislav said, 'You and he were the bravest of that generation of officers.'

Stefan didn't agree. Neither of them was 'brave'. The 'professor' became a hero in the manner of his death, leading his men into action, rather than by directing from a distance, as he usually did.

'Reckless' was how one in his unit described him, unnecessarily visible to the enemy.

Stefan rolled the wine round his glass, admired its skittish, swirling motion, wondering where this was leading.

'We have always been frank with each other despite our difference in age.' Tomislav selected a few strands of tobacco from a tin and rolled them along a cigarette paper. 'How is Stamenka?'

'Well. And Louise?'

'Well also, but worried about our sons.'

'They're safe?'

'Thank God. My daughters too.'

'They're valiant women.'

'I sometimes think it is harder for nurses, but perhaps not as hard as for those left at home.'

Tomislav licked the edge of the cigarette paper, and ran his finger along its length. While he tweaked stray ends, he asked, 'How do you think we are doing?'

Had Tomislav travelled out of his way for reassurance? 'We're making an orderly retreat.'

'You are right, and our men are resilient.'

'The conditions are difficult.'

'Sleep will energise them.'

The stiffness between them hadn't existed before the war.

Stefan got to his feet, picked up the candle from the alcove and carried it across to Tomislav. The flame shivered, flowered blue. He cupped his hand around it, moved it towards the cigarette. Their faces were a breath apart, and Stefan's legs ached as Tomislav refused to inhale. Eventually he leaned forward. The edge of the paper flickered; a twist of burning tobacco fell to the floor. Tomislav sank back against the wall.

'Why was Major Glisic removed from his post and questions asked about his competency?'

Stefan responded without thinking. 'He neglected his men.'

'Men need faith in their leaders, without faith they will not die for their country. "The professor" encouraged his men to die, by his bravery. Like your friend here.' He pointed to the snoring Rajko. 'Like you.'

Stefan couldn't follow the reasoning. Rajko and the 'professor' had led their units from the front. Glisic was protecting his reputation. Had Glisic's father raised objection to his son's withdrawal from his post?

'He lost the confidence of his officers,' he insisted.

'To question his competency on the eve of battle, reduces men's faith in their leaders,' Tomislav retorted.

'Hell! He sent a student to deal with a mutiny. Glisic won't be asked to account for himself. Is that what you're saying?' His shoulders tensed, as he clenched his fists.

'Remember you are talking to a senior officer, Colonel.'

Stefan stared into the stove; the heat burned his shins. Sparks struck the rug, fizzling out. From the kitchen, children giggled. He wanted to punch Tomislav, force him to investigate what witnesses had reported.

Tomislav said, 'Glisic was acting out of character. He'll be sent to South Africa. A couple of months in the sun recuperating from battle trauma, and back to action thereafter. We need capable officers, if victory is to be ours.'

'Victory,' Stefan observed dryly.

'Colonel, our people wanted us to rid the country of the Austrians and indeed, we've the admiration of the world for doing so.'

Stefan ground his boot into the earth floor, leaning towards Tomislav, who, to his annoyance, appeared as relaxed as though on holiday. He spat, 'It's our men who pay the price. They leave their homeland and return in sadness.'

'Do not lose your temper, Colonel. You know as well as I, that Austrian scoundrel, General Potoriek, was claiming he'd defeated us; we had to show he was wrong.'

'So we slink home.'

As he spoke, the blanket was pushed aside. He was relieved at the interruption. Andric's wife was giving instructions to two children who stepped across the floor, their bare feet lightly touching straw and rugs. Dressed alike, in knee length brown tunics, their eyes downcast as they shivered in front of their guests.

The smallest girl held out a plate of apples to Stefan. Goose pimples on her arms. The other child pushed a dish of plums towards Tomislav.

From the doorway their mother said, 'Ask the gentlemen to help themselves, Ljubi.'

'Would you like a plum, sir?'

'Would you like an apple, sir?'

Stefan stroked the girl's cheek with a finger. 'You are beautiful. Thank you.' The family needed the fruit. He selected an apple and the child moved across to Tomislav who took two.

Tomislav said to Ljubi, 'My grandfather had an orchard when I was a boy, and I used to help him pick them. Is that what you do?'

'My grandfather is dead, sir.'

Tomislav nodded. 'You help your father and mother.'

'Yes, sir.'

'You are good girls.'

'Come on, now! Ljubi and Milica! The gentlemen wish to talk, and then sleep so they can save our country.'

After the children left the room, Stefan slipped the apple into a pocket. He would eat it during his journey tomorrow.

Tomislav said, 'You see, I am right about the people and yet I ask, "Have you lost heart?"'

'Because I despise the behaviour of an officer?'

'For over-reacting. Glisic is rock solid, you know him from Military Academy, he's loyal, able. What you saw was shocking, but you're not a recruit. Mistakes are made. If men think an officer like Glisic is to be doubted, what does it say for the real rascals? Those we'd never have appointed, except there's a bloody war.'

The logs on the fire shrank. He'd be glad when they were back in Serbia. They needed time not only to rearm, but to recover the sense of who they were, what they were fighting for.

His voice was low, angry. 'You've seen the feet of the soldiers in *opanki?*'

'Boots are ordered.'

'The bullets the French sent are the wrong size.'

'A fresh consignment will reach you before Chekoj ridge.'

'We are to attack the ridge?' Stefan was taken aback, he thought it impregnable.

'Take your best men. It's an important position.'

'Have our engineers built pontoons in readiness?'

'You are anticipating defeat. It is leadership, which provides men with morale. Where there is a lack, there hides an officer who has lost heart.'

So, ill equipped, they were to attack the Austrians. Stefan hoped the Austrians were as unprepared; expected no more action in Bosnia.

Tomislav finished his drink. 'If you will excuse me, I will take to my bed. I doubt to sleep. I must think how we are to outmanoeuvre our wily enemy.'

'Bullets, sir. Of the correct size.'

Stefan wasn't the sort to waste time regretting the pleasure of a comfy bed. During campaigns he slept outside, wearing uniform and greatcoat, curled in a nest of twigs, undergrowth and moss. Ready for sleep, he arranged rugs in front of the fire, rested his head on cushions, his body covered by his greatcoat. The scar on his thigh ached and though tired, his mind roamed over the conversation with Tomislav.

There'd been a time, just before the fighting began in 1912, when he'd believed they were friends. They'd met outside work at the Academy for a drink, exchanged books, dined with their wives on several occasions. When the war against Turkey began, Stefan was sent to Macedonia and Tomislav remained in Belgrade. Though Stefan's promotion followed victory at Bregalnica, Stefan considered their ties weakened, only when Tomislav was made General of the Sixth Army. He'd telephoned his congratulations, his feelings mixed. On the one hand, excited at an able strategist being at the helm, yet angry, anxious his friend was fooled by politicians' words.

He pulled the cushions into his neck to minimise the draught. It was difficult to banish Tomislav from his mind. Tomislav bit into an apple and when he stopped chewing, he sighed. Evidently, Tomislav doubted Stefan's capacity to encourage his men. He'd questioned Stefan's judgement. He'd travelled out of his way to say so. The injustice rankled. He ached from the day's ride, though he shouldn't complain, when many of his men had slogged through mud and slush on foot. And he was beginning to mistrust Tomislav. Why? Why couldn't he summon some enthusiasm for this war, this new role? Why did he yearn so much for peace?

Rajko stirred. Now and again he grunted.

Stefan remembered years ago, 1906? 1907?, helping Rajko fix a metal rim on an artillery wagon. Why were they doing it? He couldn't recall. It had been summer. Stefan came across Rajko at the blacksmith's in Jevo, stripped to the waist instructing the blacksmith how to light the fire. He called Stefan over to give a hand and Stefan hadn't hesitated.

The embers of the stove burned his cheeks. Perhaps that brought back the memory. That and the smell of wood smoke. Stefan had removed his tunic jacket, kept on his shirt. Rajko was skinny in those days, his moustache thick, his face clear of the tiny frown now present between his brows. Stefan was wearing his cap, but his face scorched as they'd grasped the metal rim between huge tongs and carried it across the forge to the wooden wheel. Even now he smelled Rajko's hair and brows singe. Rajko swore, not in anger, rather in pleasure at his physicality. And yet, no women. He never went home to his wife, never paid for gypsies, whores or ladies. They'd flung water over the metal, doused the flames on the wheel as it burned. Rajko poured a bucketful over his head, his face rippling with mirth.

Stefan's throat was dry. Wine didn't suit him as it had. To attempt Chekoj ridge was suicide. Again snow rumbled down the steep roof and collapsed onto the veranda floor. He fell asleep to Rajko's laughter. The sound of a summer breeze fluttering the branches of trees, light and dark flickering like water over stones.

Chapter Six

Chekoj Ridge, Bosnia,
close to border with Serbia, November 1914

Three days after his encounter with Tomislav, Stefan and his special unit set up camp in an abandoned village, Kula Grad. The building of shelters for the men disclosed fields of maize that hadn't been harvested in September, the villagers having fled. The schoolmaster's quarters, the only building with glazed windows, was set up for Stefan's use. The schoolroom became the officers' mess, their quarters the stone dwellings villagers had shared with their animals.

Shortly after five that afternoon, Stefan read out his detailed report on the field telephone to Tomislav's adjutant. He explained the reasons behind the choice of encampment, his decision to make two separate attacks: the first would get into position during the night, ready for action at dawn.

While he waited for Tomislav's response, he nursed a beaker of lime tea at the table. He raised his greatcoat collar against the draught blowing between gaps in the window frame and stone wall. On the other side of the partition, men chattered, occasionally bursting into laughter. What sounded like fragments of ice, hit the pane and he fought a sense of foreboding.

Tapping the table, Stefan examined the situation as objectively as he could. The Austrians held all the positions in Bosnia, threatened Belgrade from the north and, having crossed the river Drina, were about to attack Kuriacica in southern Serbia. Even if his men regained Chekoj Ridge, it would be pointless if Kuriacica fell.

On the first ring of the telephone, Stefan picked up the receiver. The line crackled, as it often did, but then went dead. He prayed they wouldn't be disconnected. He was relieved, when Tomislav's adjutant announced the General was ready to speak.

Tomislav began, 'You stand by your decision to attack at dawn, Colonel?'

'Yes, sir. The element of surprise is our best tactic.'

'Tell me, what do you think of your chances? Total frankness, Stefan. Total frankness.'

Stefan prevaricated. 'Morale is high, despite atrocious conditions.'

At the last regimental meeting, he'd spoken of Tomislav's pride in their success in Bosnia, the way they had challenged the mighty Austrian Empire, how Europe was full of admiration and the Austrians had learned never to disregard Serbia again. The officers' backs had straightened, they grunted approval.

Stefan said, 'The men hate the Austrians.'

The schoolhouse door slammed. The line faltered. He held the receiver close to his lips. 'They will fight to the death.'

'Well done, Stefan.'

'Thank you, sir.' The admiration he'd felt for Tomislav at Military Academy was returning. 'If we can break onto the western ridge in the first assault, we'll back it up with a second.'

'Once we've secured Kuriacica we can provide a full battalion.'

Stefan curbed the temptation to point out, that an extra battalion might make all the difference that coming night. 'We'll do what we can, sir.'

'You're not leading a unit, are you?' Tomislav asked.

'No, sir. I'll remain below the ridge to decide when to co-ordinate the second attack.' If they failed, he would delay the next attempt to the following day.

'You do well to remain where you are. As you say in your report, you have capable officers to lead the platoons.'

'Officers and men are volunteers. All brave. Lieutenants Nis and Kojic on the right and left flanks and Major Simic and Captain Lutovac in the centre.'

'What of Major Kostic?'

'Not yet fit, sir.'

'What! Our most distinguished officer. Has the MO certified him?'

Stefan was prepared. 'I've taken the decision for him, sir. He'd be killed within the hour.'

'You're not running a kindergarten. I want him there.'

Tomislav slammed down the telephone. Stefan stared at the remains of his tea. The inside of the beaker was stained, leaves stuck to the sides. The perfume of lime blossom reminded him of drinking tea on Bulevar Foccicia with Stamenka, Mitar playing under the table. With one finger he squeezed the green leaf. Rajko's knee wouldn't last an hour's hard climb. He suspected Rajko didn't care if he died in battle, it was preferable to a risky knee operation. Yet Tomislav was right, he was behaving like an overprotective mother. And if Tomislav knew, so did his officers.

He pushed back his chair, his body raging with cold sweat. He approached the fire, lit a cigarette. Rajko was a true patriot. Brave, single minded. The long drag hurt his throat. He coughed, threw the cigarette into the flames. He shouted to Dragan for his gloves.

The dwelling Rajko shared, had previously been inhabited by a family and their animals. Rajko, in the far corner, was asleep in his undergarments, stinking of alcohol. During the morning's ride, he'd been sober, but several hours had passed. The smell of animal shit permeated the tiny room. Jovan shook his officer, as Stefan crossed the floor. For a moment, Stefan gazed down at his friend, this the man whose actions on the battlefield had earned the gold Obilich. He snatched the bowl from Jovan and flung the contents over Rajko's face. With a sharp crack, the bowl bounced where Stefan dropped it.

Rajko sat up, water dripping from hair, face, chest.

'You have two choices my friend,' Stefan announced, 'Retire on full pension…'

Rajko wiped his face with the back of his arm. His teeth were coated with a greeny-yellow scum; his lips cracked.

'Or consult the MO in Jevo about an operation.'

'I'd rather die,' Rajko muttered.

'You choose retirement?'

'No, sir.'

Stefan was reminded of his father, lying in the gutter outside the homestead or in the courtyard by the well where he went for a swill after waking. He'd never felt sorry for his father. Sympathy wouldn't be much use to his old friend either.

Rajko shook his head. The left knee was twisted out of alignment. Jovan shuffled. Sighed.

'The drinking will have to stop.'

'Very good, sir.'

Moments later, Stefan entered the crowded schoolroom transformed into a church. Men and officers crowded around the altar table, as Stefan squeezed through them to join the priest. His eyes itched, sore from days of exposure to the easterly wind, and the smoke in his quarters. He shut them, not needing to see the candle, brass bowl of holy water, twig bearing fresh growth and most sacred of all, the regimental cross. All had been precious since childhood.

Behind the single lighted candle, the priest held the Bible in both hands. His lips worked in prayer. He replaced the holy book. Between his finger and thumb, he raised a sprig of pine. On the outskirts of Sarajevo, the priest had fought alongside the men, but not here, under the steep sides of Chekoj ridge, though he'd volunteered, this assignment needed young or skilled men.

Stefan could think of nothing but the attack. If the sky remained cloudy, there was a chance they would recapture the guns. Whatever the conditions, the men were motivated. They were rested after the march from Vlasenica. During the past few hours they'd eaten well, mended their tunics and trousers and darned their socks. Experience mattered on a foray like this, but, sadly, newly promoted officers like his cousin Mikaiho, enthusiastic but untrained, didn't use their wits, had never learned to heed advice, whether from Stefan or other veterans.

The priest kissed the cross and laid it over the wooden bowl, before walking to the line of soldiers in front of the table. He halted in front of each, sprinkled water over every uncapped head. He held the cross, glinting in the light of the candle, for all to kiss. Courage was not enough. If it was, Stefan would have led a platoon himself. He wasn't innately brave like Rajko; he led the action because he thought it wrong to expect his men to do what he wasn't prepared to.

When it came to Stefan's turn to kiss the cold cross, he prayed his cousin would return. Despite Tomislav's confidence in Mikaiho, most of what Mikaiho did ended in disaster. Shepherd, builder, woodman. He went with any woman who would have him, was even suspected of rape, though he'd denied it. His widowed mother arranged marriage to a twenty seven year old no one wanted, hoping Mikaiho would settle down. Tomislav had rewarded his action during the battle at Bregalnica, but Stefan was worried that Rajko was right. Becoming a capable lieutenant, was beyond Mikaiho's abilities.

As Stefan's lips left the brass, he hurriedly remembered to pray their attack would bring honour to Serbia.

Several hours later, Stefan again stood by the side of the priest, this time in the lee of the ridge, as the first of ninety soldiers departed. Each man wore on his shoulder strap, the star of the Jevo regiment. Each was hunched over his knapsack. Excited, nervous in his own way. Stefan addressed some by name: Danilo and Kajafa, student officers, Hadijic known as the Cross-eyed one, Bogdan, a carpenter, the factory workers from Nis, Stretan, Misho, Mikaiho (his cousin) and another Danilo. All from Orasac.

At Military Academy, he'd lectured on the qualities of leadership on the battlefield: witness, co-ordinate and where possible direct. Tonight, his job was to wait. Though hard, he was safe; his men's lives were in danger. Tonight he'd to leave the action to others. In the morning, he would face the survivors, knowing he'd risked nothing.

Conditions weren't in their favour. Though the early evening blizzard had stopped, snow marked out the men as they climbed. Most were hardened soldiers, but ill-equipped. Five greatcoats among the ninety. A few woollen capes, though most were homespun, a handful of tweed tunics. Action should keep them warm. Tomislav had promised boots, but not till they crossed the Drina. Most men were wearing the leather *opanki*. The snow was deep on the ridge and they could suffer frostbite.

When they were out of sight, he listened to the roar of the Drina, the wind stirring the pines, the hooting of a snowy owl.

Later, he climbed to the top of a windswept hill on the edge of the wood. He felt his face blanched by the easterly wind. Beneath him, on the road to the river bridge, embers glowed where men from other regiments, wrapped in their tents on the roadside, slept around small fires. He thought of Stamenka, disappointed that he'd not received letters from her, but there could be many reasons, including that he, unusually, hadn't written to her, feeling a breach, no longer knowing what to say. Remembering her, he worried that they would lose Kuriacica, that Belgrade would be under attack. He shivered.

At three in the morning, he returned to camp. The ground vibrated with the pounding of big guns. Other men joined him. He returned to the ridge: the shrill flight of shells, the familiar firework flashes against the snow, the dark sky. He strained to hear his men's rifles. He heard their whistles. He wasn't sure if he heard rifle fire or Mikaiho's grenades, or smelled the cordite. More volleys from the field guns. More rifle fire? He wasn't sure. He stamped his feet, clapped his arms against his sides. The medical detachment would pick up the wounded as fast as they could, but many would have to wait. He prayed for Mikaiho, Stretan, Danilo, for each of the men whose hands he'd shaken.

At daybreak the artillery guns which had been firing non-stop for half an hour or so, roared a final crescendo. He longed to know what was happening, though he tried to hide his anxiety by walking. He strode to the top of the hill, where he'd stood last night, he inspected the camp, he paced the track along the Drina, but as time passed, he moved inside the schoolroom to be close to the telephone.

Just before noon, the losses were reported. His hand trembled as he received the call. All the men who'd attempted the direct attack on the ridge, slaughtered. They'd been the first to be blessed. Stefan had voiced their names, shaken their hands. He wouldn't see them again. He pictured the priest, shuffling along the row, holding the cross and whispering his blessing.

Half the column which attacked the right flank, killed before they got into position, others fought on before being struck down, most who remained, wounded. There was no news of the men who'd attacked the left flank. No word of Mikaiho. The scouts were optimistic they would reach the ridge, and inflict damage to the artillery. Stefan wasn't as optimistic. He postponed the second assault.

After listening to the report, Stefan gave orders for the engineers to move down the river, and build a pontoon to transport the wounded during the next couple of nights.

As the sun rose, Stefan returned to the foot of the ridge. Fighting was easier than this. A sort of paralysis affected his body. His bones set like those of the old.

He scanned the remnants of his unit, as the first few staggered through the mud and snow. He longed to wrap his arms around these sons of Serbia, these weary men, but he could barely move his jaw and pronounce, 'Well done, brother.'

Was Mikaiho among them? Stefan's flask of *rakija* was empty, his throat tobacco dry. He examined each face. No Mikaiho, but Salko from Uzice who looked forty though only twenty-three. His brown eyes, which had glistened like honey, were now full of tears. Salko, who'd boasted that at Sarajevo, he'd killed two Austrians with his bare hands after he lost his bayonet. Stefan found it hard to breathe. No Mikaiho, but Osmananga, as wiry as a lizard, who called out in his sleep for his mother. Danilo, the candle maker from Orasac. Blood seeped through the bandage, medics had wrapped round the top of his arm. The arm hanged, the other dragged his rifle. Still no Mikaiho. One man after another. Unshaven, ragged, mud-stained.

It was several hours before Mikaiho returned. Stefan didn't immediately recognise his cousin, carried into camp between two privates. A blanket covered his shoulders. The black moustache on a sunken face as frozen as the distant mountaintops. Lifeless eyes. Dumb, he didn't speak for twenty-four hours.

Below, on the track through the village, Stefan heard the rumble of Serb gun carriages, the march of infantry, the bells of oxen. It would take the regiment days to cross back into Serbia. Stefan told Tomislav he'd decided against a second attack that night, would try again tomorrow. Without reinforcements, he considered the effort pointless. More Serbian blood melting the snow. Behind him, on the ridge, wolves howled.

By mid-morning, the sky was as blue as Stefan remembered when he'd huddled as a child with the sheep, in the stone folds on the hillside outside his village. Yesterday's snow-laden clouds had shed their loads and the mid-day sun shone. Stefan leaned against the stone wall, which surrounded the schoolhouse. He pulled out the flask from the pocket of his greatcoat, and unscrewed the top. Behind him those not involved in this night's action, were moving on. The camp was being dismantled, leaving only the basics, skeleton kitchen, medics, as few engineers and support personnel as possible. A soldier swore, urging on the team of bullocks, dragging the first of the kitchen wagons. If the animals stopped, however exhausted they might be, the war train could get stuck. There was little conversation among the soldiers. Tunic and trousers, wet from yesterday's snow, had frozen on their bodies. Icicles melted on the rims of their service caps, defeat sounded in the slap and slither of *opanki* soles.

Stefan drank from the flask. Somehow he'd to encourage the unit attacking tomorrow tonight. Somehow he'd to overcome his desire to disobey orders, and refuse a second assault. Tomislav had been furious the MO decided Rajko wasn't fit to fight. *Rakija* burned his throat. He listened to the horse slurping from the leather bucket Dragan was holding. He wanted to drink the horse's water. His throat was on fire. He scooped a handful of snow into his gloved hand, formed it into a ball and flung it over the heads of the men, towards the trees on the far side of the track. He didn't see or hear it fall. His feet were numb.

His cousin was standing in front of Dragan, watching the horse drink. Mikaiho, having lost his greatcoat during the attack, stood in his tunic and trousers, as straight as though held upright by invisible thread attached to the sun. The mud and blood had been brushed from his uniform, but the right sleeve was ripped off at the shoulder, revealing the shirt beneath. There'd been no time for repairs. He was twenty-six; at that moment, he seemed a mere boy, who ought to be at home helping his mother harvest plums and apples. Stefan wanted to urge, command Mikaiho to stay by his side and keep out of the fighting. Insist, this is not for you, brother.

The sun, high in the sky, bounced off the silver flask. He could no longer hear the horse slurping or Dragan ripping the bread into pieces for them to share. He was back waiting, watching his men return from battle.

He screwed the top back on the flask and became aware of sound of the horse drinking.

Tomislav's Sixth Army held Kuriacica. The Third Army was holding back the Austrians, south of Jevo. Would it be enough to give his men hope?

Chapter Seven

Dobro Majka, December 1914

It was nine thirty by the chapel clock, as Ellen strode across the courtyard to meet the soldiers who were to take her and Audrey on a ride to explore the countryside. Most of the men she nursed were poorly clad. These two were impressive, their uniforms pressed, their boots polished; they'd the military air she expected. The one with campaign medals on his tunic pocket dismounted, saluted. He resembled an English officer. Dark moustache, hair just showing under his field cap and when she extended a hand, he introduced himself as Lieutenant Nis, his orderly as Corporal Mitrovic.

The latter also was smartly dressed in full army uniform, but when he smiled, revealing pointed incisor teeth, Ellen remembered him from the *kafkana* where she'd had coffee in Jevo with Audrey. He was skinny, in the way many of the wounded were, though she was learning not to judge. Nurse Rose explained that a lot of soldiers, including officers, were in bad physical condition even before the war.

'*Dobar dan.* I am waiting for Dr. Eyres,' she said slowly in Serbian.

'You choose your horse from the stables,' the lieutenant replied in English.

Irritated that she couldn't speak his language as well as he spoke hers, she strode past him, slowing to tread more carefully when the ground became tacky. Back home, a shelter like this, its wooden posts supporting a roof of twigs and small branches, wouldn't deserve the description 'stables'. Straw was spread thinly over puddles. The smell stung her throat, as she leaned over the gate to the stall, to examine one of the horses. She stretched to stroke its nose, but it didn't nuzzle like her horse, Prince.

The men stood behind her so that she felt hemmed in.

Lieutenant Nis said, 'That is Danica. She is a good horse.'

Ellen, mindful that Audrey wasn't an experienced horsewoman, turned to the opposite stall. The men moved aside. The second animal was shorter, she gazed untroubled when Ellen reached over the gate to pat her rump; she looked easier to handle.

While the men got Danica ready, Ellen wandered back to the courtyard, busy with orderlies unloading patients from the mule ambulance. What had delayed her friend? She kept glancing towards the gate into the orchard. Every now and then, someone entered the back door to the main building leading to the ward where she worked. She eased her restlessness, by picturing Rose in the narrow aisle, bent over the medical trolley or hunched over a patient, the high wooden desk lit by the oil lamp, its register of names, daily added to and deleted.

And Audrey was right. Seeing more of a peaceable Serbia would do them good. They would enjoy a few hours away from the smell of blood, disinfectant, gangrene, forget men crying, calling out in an unfamiliar language.

When the gate to the orchard clicked, Ellen presumed it was Audrey; she prepared to tease her for being late. But it was Nurse Gladys who ambled through the courtyard, ignoring orderlies unloading a wagon and waving as Ellen hurried across. Gladys never moved with speed. She put one foot on the cobblestones, paused to ensure she wouldn't slip on ox dung, before moving the other. Typical of Gladys, though it wasn't raining, she wore a sou'wester and mackintosh.

'What's the matter?' Ellen asked when they were level with each other.

Grace raised the brim of her hat. 'Dr. Eyres said to tell you she can't make it. The Serb MO has brought an unusual thigh wound and wants Doctor to have a look. You'll be all right on your own, won't you?'

Ellen was doubtful. 'No chaperone?' Matron insisted when they went into Jevo or for a walk in the woods, they went in pairs. She assumed Audrey expected the same.

'If you don't mind. She's awfully busy, you see. It's not often these Serbs admit they don't know something, so she wants to co-operate.'

'If Audrey says it's allowed, I'll go. The men are getting the horses ready.' Behind her she could hear Lieutenant Nis and Corporal Mitrovic talking. No harm would come to her. At home, she rode unaccompanied and regularly stopped to chat to male riders. Nonetheless, she was disappointed. She'd been looking forward to telling Audrey she would soon be transferred to the mule ambulance. She turned from Gladys towards the field where the bells on the halters of the grazing oxen tinkled. It was regret she felt, not apprehension, she scolded herself, sad the day wasn't turning out as she hoped.

As Ellen joined the men, Gladys called, 'Miss Frankland!'

Ellen looked back. Gladys waved, 'Bye!'

In the fields around Bakewell, a ride gave Ellen chance to think, work through problems. As she trotted behind Lieutenant Nis, her thoughts returned home and in particular to Edward. When he'd driven her to the boat at Southampton, he had admitted he was a poor writer, but promised to make an effort. His now weekly letters were brief. He complained much of hers were obliterated by the black markings of the censors, and those that weren't, 'upset his mother'. She was beginning to wonder if it was Edward who didn't want to read about the realities of war. After all, her letters weren't intended for his mother.

The scenery differed little from the short walks in the forests around Jevo. The paths were just as narrow, layered with leaves, the trees a mixture of beech, oak, chestnuts and several varieties she didn't know. The smell of thyme, the taste of decay, the sudden flurry of wind, the two-tone call of the great tit were becoming familiar.

After half an hour, they moved into a deeper wildness of larger trees, briar thickets and wild blackberries. Habitation ceased. The one house they passed was two storeys high, but its windows, upstairs and down, were shuttered and there was no smoke from the roof. She wondered if people lived there only during the summer. She couldn't formulate her speculation into questions in Serbian. Nonetheless, she would soon improve. Matron had agreed to more lessons, along with additional First Aid training, in preparation for her job.

The tops of the trees scratched a blue sky, its primrose sun. It was becoming darker. Danica's hooves squelched through the sticky earth. The smell of pines mingled with rotting leaves and twigs. In the distance an animal crashed through the undergrowth. Even if Audrey had been with her, they wouldn't have found it easy to talk because they would have had to ride single file. Nonetheless, quite apart from her company, she would have liked the chance to boast of her transfer. She'd explain that she could become useful, might be able to save lives because she was working close to the front line.

She estimated they'd been in the forest for over an hour, when she caught up with the officers, who had dismounted, slightly off the path. One horse was tethered, the other grazing among the trees. The corporal was opening the pannier.

Lieutenant Nis said with a gentle smile, 'We will soon arrive. Many foreigners admire the little church.'

She'd expected him to apologise for the dismal route so she nodded politely, but without enthusiasm.

'We will eat, while he goes first to the village,' and pointed towards the corporal who was carrying something wrapped in newspaper, towards them. As the corporal placed the parcel on the ground, Ellen smelled chicken and her mouth watered. Having jumped down, she hung Danica's reins over a low branch, instructing her, 'stand still.'

The corporal unwrapped four chicken legs, before taking one, saluting and ambling in what Ellen took to be the direction of the village.

'Your horse!' she shouted after him.

When he didn't turn back, the lieutenant guffawed, mouth wide, head back, 'He does not like horse.'

Ellen was worried the horse would stray, but said nothing. She hoped they knew what they were doing.

While she was taking off her gloves, the lieutenant bent down and picked up a chicken leg on crumpled paper. He handed it to her. He stood formally several feet from her till she began to remove the skin. It smelled deliciously of garlic and paprika. Tearing off a piece with her teeth, she began to chew. When she glanced up, he was leaning against a pine trunk, staring up at the sky tinged with drifts of smoke. He helped himself to a piece of chicken. She liked the way he ate, in small bites, wiping his mouth after each, particular that grease didn't stick to his moustache.

For several minutes, they ate in silence.

When she had almost finished, she asked, 'What is this, in Serbian?'

'Chicken.'

'In your language.'

'*Piletina.*'

'Pee let ia.'

He laughed. 'No.'

After several attempts, he said, 'Good.'

'This is beauty spot,' he said slowly.

Pointing to the tops of trees, she commented, 'Dark.'

'You don't like "dark"?' He pulled at his moustache and out of courtesy she replied, '*Srbija je divna zemlja.*'

'Serbia is beautiful,' he agreed.

When the corporal returned after some ten minutes, Lieutenant Nis excused himself and went to stand next to him. They talked, shoulder to shoulder, in low voices, though Ellen could detect neither excitement nor panic. At home, she would have asked what was wrong. Something to do with the smoke, she thought. Only her poor Serbian stopped her. And the tiniest tremble in her stomach. Danica shuffled and Ellen stroked her neck, murmuring reassurance. A leaf fluttered in front of them. She would like to have read Lieutenant Nis' expression, but his face was averted.

The muscles in her buttocks and thighs ached. It was months since she'd ridden. She decided to stretch to release the tension. She raised her arms, swung them in an arc level with her shoulders. She began a series of gentle side bends.

A family of raptors flew ahead, squealing like gulls.

When she could bear the waiting no longer, she called out, 'Lieutenant, why have we stopped?'

The men walked towards her and Lieutenant Nis spoke in the formal polite way, he had when he'd greeted her. 'I am sorry, Miss Frankland. The enemy has been.'

He spoke rapidly to the corporal who glanced at Ellen, then back to the lieutenant before taking a step forward. When the lieutenant spoke more sharply, he sprinted across the track into the trees.

She asked the lieutenant, 'Has the enemy set fire to something?' She was strangely excited. The words from her History teacher came into her mind. Men, flowing hair, horned helmets, torching huts.

'Please. Wait with Corporal Mitrovic.'

'I am a nurse.'

'It is not a place for women.'

She was back to St. Thomas' hall, listening to Lady Alice, hearing the words, which had inspired her to join the Women's Medical Corps. Just as the phrase returned and she began to recognise its present significance, it evaporated.

The corporal was leading his horse through the trees, and she waited till he re-joined them.

The lieutenant said in a reassuring tone, 'Please wait here. My orderly will see that you come to no harm.'

The air felt autumnal. In the corridor of trees, it was difficult to see further than a few yards ahead. A sharp crack, like gunshot, startled her. The corporal didn't react so she presumed it was something innocent like a twig breaking. The sun pierced the distant smoke, and Ellen longed to see what Lieutenant Nis was doing.

The calls of the raptors became more strident.

The words of Lady Alice returned. The feathers on her hat had fluttered as she'd proclaimed, 'Wars will never cease till women see for themselves the tragedy of war, witness the cruel secrets behind the footlights.'

She jumped back on Danica so she could see. While she put on her gloves, she saw that the path turned steeply towards a ridge of taller, barer pine trees.

Corporal Mitrovica mounted his horse and drew it close to her, 'Lovely lady.'

She tensed, till she remembered Audrey's comment that he was 'a simple lad'. She told herself there was no need to be afraid.

The sun felt strong on her face. The wind rustled the leaves. She couldn't hear birds singing and wondered if they didn't sing during an afternoon. She smelled the damp earth, traces of thyme. The corporal began to fidget with his pistol. Perhaps she was making him nervous.

He reached to place a hand on her arm. She shrugged him off, more disgusted than frightened. He felt dirty, this placing of a gloveless hand, in some strange way, violating her. She didn't understand why: at Dobro Majka, far filthier hands touched hers. She had dressed stinking wounds, wiped soiled bottoms, been grabbed more suddenly and ferociously.

She was irritated she couldn't talk, find out what had happened. It wasn't her country and Lieutenant Nis was in charge, but she ought to be involved. What would Lady Alice expect? If the enemy had set fire to the village, she could administer First Aid, though she'd no bandages, no lint, only a handkerchief trimmed with lace. If Audrey had been with her, they could have worked out what to do. She could gallop back to Dobro Majka, and yet with no explanation as to what was wrong, what purpose would that serve? Nonetheless, she ought to discover what 'women' shouldn't see.

'Miss Frankland.' The corporal winked. He gave her the creeps.

She tightened Danica's reins. 'We will join the lieutenant,' she said firmly. She clucked and Danica took a couple of steps.

'No!' The Lieutenant grabbed at the reins, clung on for a few seconds, but as Ellen urged her forward and Danica gathered pace, he released his grip.

The track became narrower, the air colder. Danica slowed, her hooves unsteady on damp pine needles, slippery stones. As she followed the corporal into a clearing bounded by pines, she halted. Ahead: burned ruins of a row of houses, scorched trees. The smell of smouldering wood reminded her of bonfires her father made each autumn.

She had never stood in so desolate a place. The air tasted of death. Certainly the thud of her mother's coffin as it was lowered, had made her feel empty and isolated. But this was different. As though the spot embodied the place the dead resided. She was filled with a dread she'd never experienced.

She held back and the corporal led the way across the track.

The lieutenant was not to be seen. Dismounting, she led Danica to the ruins of the first house, while the corporal rode through an alley between the houses. One side of the dwelling was destroyed, its timber eaten by fire. Dust stung her eyes; she reached inside her breeches' pocket for a handkerchief. She remembered how a barn fire at home spread, so by the time the fire engine was summoned, and the labourers ran out with buckets of water from the yard tap, the wooden structure and grain were gone. However fast the men worked, once the fire had taken hold, they could never put it out.

She imagined flames catching thatched roofs, licking the struts and beams, burning mud daub, blackening stone walls. She dismounted and led Danica closer. The painted white stones at the front of the house were scorched; window frames and a roof beam had almost disappeared, and yet a wooden door, had collapsed, virtually intact, feet from the building. Some roof tiles sat on top of the stones on the ground, like peaked riding hats.

She gazed down the clearing to the remains of other houses. This was not something she could describe to Edward: - burned timbers, blackened heaps of stone. She walked two, three hundred yards, past a circle of twisted metal, past the skeletal remains of three houses. Her gloves were powdered with ash like the first flakes of snow. Dead leaves swirled in her path. In the distance, the call of the raptors.

She returned to where they'd entered the village. Catching a glint of light on the other side of the houses, she followed the track Corporal Mitrovic had taken. It took several minutes to persuade Danica through the alley. She paused, transfixed by a small, stone church, the sun on its white cupola. The lieutenant's horse was tethered to a post at the end of a white-pebbled path. She wanted to find Lieutenant Nis, so she roped the reluctant Danica next to that of his. Giving both horses a sugar lump, she began to examine the houses that encircled the church.

This was no accident.

She kept thinking of home. The area around the vicarage with its church, The Black Horse and the few houses along the lane, was of a similar size. What would old Mr. and Mrs. Williams do, or the two spinsters on the corner, the new family from Derby who'd moved to be nearer relatives? Run away? No. They'd try to put out the fire, someone would stay to fight. Maybe not if all the men were in the army. Would she? If she'd her pistol, if she wasn't outnumbered. No. She, too, would flee.

More scorched houses lay several yards further down the track, bushes burned to the ground. She dreaded knowing if people had died there. She stepped nearer. From behind the wall came a noise. If the whole village didn't appear to be deserted, she would have described it as a cough. She stepped nearer, handkerchief over her nose and mouth. She recollected an old soldier, at summer camp one year, telling them that's what they did when they came across an ambushed village in South Africa.

Holding her breath, she strode towards the burned out window. She didn't want to find corpses, perhaps of children, but she couldn't walk away. She peered over a stone wall about three feet high, slipped on charred timbers, caught sight of the remnant of an iron bedstead and what looked like firestones. At the sound of hooves, she swivelled. Corporal Mitrovic was riding towards her. She wondered where he'd been. His face was grimy, eyebrows plastered with dust, and he'd lost his cap. He stopped the horse a few paces from the house. His mouth worked before he spat. Too far away for the spittle to reach, she shrank. He spat once more.

'Damn you,' she said, frightened, shocked.

Relieved when he rode off, she held her breath as a man hobbled from behind the wall. He wore the homespun trousers and shirt that country folk wore. A flat hat fell over his face. She stared and stared at him for moments. She swallowed hard. This man had no eyes. Just red, blood-dried sockets. Under his arm, he held bagpipes. He was unshaven with an overgrown moustache. His nostrils flared.

'*Dobar dan.*' Her voice broke. She repeated the greeting. She searched for the Serbian words. 'Sir. We are with the Serbian army.' She wished Corporal Mitrovic was with her.

He shuffled forwards. His feet were bare and she was afraid he'd cut them. She repeated her sentence, automatically extending her hand. If she could get him on Danica, she could take him to Dobro Majka.

As she formulated, 'We are your friends,' she was taken aback when the corporal's voice sounded loudly behind her.

'You are bad piece.'

She flinched, hoping he wasn't going to spit at her again. The blind man stopped walking, and she didn't know what to do.

Turning to face the corporal she asked, 'Where is the lieutenant?'

He pointed in the direction of the church. It made no sense that the lieutenant should go into the church; she supposed he was a religious man. Nonetheless, she must tell him there was a survivor and ask him what to do.

'Excuse me,' she said, 'I am going to the church.' She ignored the corporal's frown, noticed his hands were shaking on the reins. He was frightened. It hadn't occurred to her. She'd an urge to apologise, but first she must help the blinded man.

She sprinted the few yards to the foot of the path leading to the church. The corporal may have shouted to her but, on the verge of tears, she didn't stop. At the door she glanced down to Danica and beyond, to the corporal and the blind man. The man hadn't moved, the corporal remained with him, watching her.

The wooden door wouldn't move more than an inch, however hard she shoved. She squeezed her boot into the gap and tried to inch her way around. Her belt caught on the metal door handle, and she snatched to free it. As she managed to poke her head inside, the smell reminded her of the ox-wagons loaded with wounded, the 'death carts'. She pushed with her foot, nudged the door a little, and slid through.

A cloud of flies swarmed towards her and she swatted them. Grey light slipped through narrow windows. The building was as cold and dank as a cellar. A candle was lit at the far end, where she made out the figure of Lieutenant Nis. In the poor light, she could only guess he stood under the dome, and beyond him, the altar protected from public gaze by a screen. This was the sort of church foreigners liked to visit.

As she stepped fully inside, she waited for her eyes to adjust to the gloom. Her soles stuck to the floor, a boot touched an obstruction and as she observed it closely, she saw one leg, then a second. One after another, the bodies formed a heap from the door along the wall of the church.

A cry wedged in her throat. The flies murmured relentlessly, however much she fanned them. She crouched, allowing her hands to feel the outline of a leg, its bones hard as sticks. With the tips of her fingers, she felt the weave of black skirts women wore as they'd worked in the fields. She ran her hand over the knitted stocking legs, touched the buckles on their *opanki*. She was hardly breathing.

When she opened her eyes, the bodies remained. Flies smothered the mouths, the eyes. One woman's head was hidden by that of another, so Ellen saw only arms stuck to her sides, her flat chest. The heap seemed alive. The stench was like that of an abattoir. Some of the faces were black, the lips swollen. Only one seemed out of place, white as a circle of paper. Ellen wanted to creep out of the church, ride back to Audrey.

She forced herself to move, edged her way round hands, feet and heads. She slipped now and again. She smelled excrement, must have stepped in it; it followed her. She felt she'd entered a tomb, brought to witness the process of decomposition. She squatted by the wall, her hands together, her fingers clenched. A piece of cloth lingered on her gloves. She wondered what her father would pray; she'd no words.

As she straightened, her foot released a ball, which rolled towards her boot, touched its tip and juddered along the floor. She bent to pick it up. It was the size of a tennis ball, made of some kind of material, packed hard with things resembling

89

pebbles. She thought of her sister's two little girls, and how she'd knitted each of them a multi-coloured ball stuffed with kapok.

Further into the church, Lieutenant Nis paced, smoked. With the ball in her hand, she walked to him and he paused next to the lighted candlestick. Two or three women's bodies lay against its feet. One of the women's skirts was raised, and Ellen reached down, pulled the skirt so that it covered the torn stockings.

Lieutenant Nis removed the cigarette from his mouth and threw it into the gloom. 'Miss Frankland,' he said.

She was reminded of her father's expression, the day her mother died. The muscles around his eyes, his mouth and his cheeks immobile. If she'd not known him, she would have thought him devoid of emotion. So it was with the lieutenant. She imitated his composure. She could cry when she was alone.

'I found a man, sir. He cannot see.' She didn't know what to say about the women.

The lieutenant gazed at her and she squirmed. He must have been trying to protect her from this.

'I'm sorry,' she said.

He didn't reply and she followed him slowly from the church, the ball in her hands.

Outside she was shocked the sky remained blue, that through the smoke haze the sun continued to shine. She waited at the foot of the steps, while the lieutenant walked over to Corporal Mitrovic who had tethered his horse next to Danica. A beetle crawled across her boot; it slipped down the slope over her toecap several times, before it clambered successfully to the top. The smells would not leave her. Austrian soldiers must have killed these women. Austrians were civilised. A bitter taste lodged at the back of her throat, which she couldn't swallow.

The corporal walked over, stood next to her, looking at his feet. She felt him shaking and she felt sorry for him. As she took deep breaths, determined not to cry, she thought Lady

Alice wouldn't expect women, or men, to witness such terrible scenes.

The blind man was sitting on the door, his knees drawn close to his chest. The lieutenant was bending down, talking to him and she was comforted. They would take him back to the hospital.

After several minutes, the lieutenant strode back to them. 'We must go.'

She countered, 'We can't leave the man.'

'We can do nothing for him.' The lieutenant hurried towards his mount.

Horrified, she dropped the child's ball and it fell and rolled towards the church steps. Through the blood she saw faint green paint.

'But Lieutenant, we must bury the women.'

'Their families will do that.'

There were no families. She was furious that she couldn't argue with him, wouldn't understand his answer to her questions as to where the families were and why the enemy had killed the women.

'They will return,' he added when she joined him to unfasten Danica.

By the time they reached Dobro Majka, the sun was sinking, the sky clouding over. As Ellen handed the reins to Corporal Mitrovic at the entrance to the stables, Audrey called her name. She shivered, folded her arms across her chest; she longed to climb into bed, curl round a hot water bottle.

Audrey stopped. The breeze blew her hair and she raised her hand, smoothing down her curls. She seemed to waltz, sidestepping two chatting Austrian orderlies. In the adjacent field, oxen munched grass. A fly lighted on Ellen's arm and she shook it, aware she'd not moved from the moment she'd heard Audrey's voice.

Audrey frowned. Ellen glanced down at the boots; they were covered with mud and ash. Excrement seemed to have stuck to them, for the smell jammed her throat. She remembered the toe nudging a stockinged leg and she suppressed a cry.

Audrey's arms were round her shoulders. Ellen released a sob. Audrey's breath touched her cheek; she remembered her mother's embrace, her eyes reading her face, the droop of her left brow, tiny broken veins in her cheeks.

Audrey stepped back. 'I'm sorry. You look terrible. What happened? Gladys should have come in my place. She didn't tell me. She wants to go home. I am sorry. It's my fault.' She apologised again and again, her arms first on her head, then waving up and down. 'It's such a blow. Gladys and I worked well together. Matron will be furious if it gets out. You didn't come to any harm, did you?' The door to the kitchen opened, the kettle was whistling. Silence as the door shut. 'It's mostly dirt. You look pale.'

Ellen tried to pay attention to Audrey who was shaking her head so her curls seemed alive. She went on for a long time, and Ellen yearned to sit down. She longed for a cup of tea.

'Tell me what went wrong,' Audrey said.

The sun disappeared behind the tents and though Audrey was looking at her, wanting a response, Ellen couldn't stop shivering.

'We went to a village. There were houses. A man.'

As she began to speak, Audrey glanced quickly behind.

Ellen saw the charred stones of the houses, the scorched timbers, Lady Alice's voice. 'I have seen the tragedy of war...' she began, searching for words.

Audrey was stepping back. Words gushed. 'Gladys is leaving at the end of the week. I've no one I can trust like you. Will you work with me?'

Ellen struggled to grasp the meaning. She managed a sentence. 'They blinded a man.'

Audrey wrung her hands. 'I am very sorry. I can see it's upset you, but Gladys should have come and she's thrown me into disarray. I needed a nurse, of course...'

'They burned their houses,' Ellen stuttered, but Audrey was asking a question to which she wanted the answer yes. Ellen knew the answer was no. She gave Audrey the answer she didn't want to hear.

Audrey's eyes filled with tears. Ellen couldn't make sense of them. Audrey was sensible. Controlled. Couldn't she grasp what had happened?

'I'm sorry.'

'It's all right. I just thought… It would have been good to work together.' Audrey turned and began to walk across the courtyard towards the gate.

Shaking, Ellen stepped towards the kitchen. The lantern in the window twinkled. In the distance, the clatter of hooves, the squeak of wagons' wheels. She hoped Gustav was in the kitchen. Having been discharged from the ward, he'd asked to work near her because she'd been kind. He would make her a cup of tea.

Chapter Eight

Dobro Majka, December 1914

At the entrance to the officers' tent, Stefan dipped his boots into the bath of disinfectant. The MO had dismissed the procedure as unnecessary, but Stefan was persuaded by Matron's argument that cleanliness saved lives. One of the tent flaps was tied back, rows of iron bedsteads, deep mattresses, cotton sheets folded over blankets. Officers in royal blue pyjamas were either lying or sitting against white pillows, each having a bedside table. A nurse pushed a trolley with a squeaky wheel past a trestle table in the centre of the ward. Compared to his experience of hospital after Bregalnica, this ward was orderly. Rajko was being well cared for.

No sooner had he stepped on the mat, than the nurse left her trolley to hurry across. 'I'm sorry,' she began, 'Oh, Colonel Petrovic! It's not visiting hours, but in your case…obviously… Have you come to see anyone in particular?'

'Major Kostic.'

'Very good, sir. He's just here by the door.'

At the foot of the bed, he was hesitant. 'He seems to be asleep. I don't want to disturb him…I'll wait a moment or so if I may.'

'I'll fetch a chair.'

'No, please. Carry on with your duties.'

The disinfectant had melted the snow on his boots, leaving puddles. He rested the book he'd brought on the edge of the bed, began to remove his gloves. He looked down at Rajko who lay on his back breathing through his mouth. The right leg of his pyjama trouser was rolled to the thigh, so his wound could be dressed. The bandage was wrapped neatly. No blood. As he pondered the bare lower leg, he realised he'd been afraid Dr. Eyres might have amputated it. He leaned closer. Sniffed. No trace of gangrene. He straightened, and turned his attention to Rajko's face. Considering Rajko had had the operation barely twenty-four hours ago, he looked well. White creases gathered around his eyes. He was shaved. Someone had trimmed the hair short over his forehead, so he looked like the lad he'd been at eighteen. They'd both been intense as young men, but Rajko more so; he'd been serious one moment, comic the next. The colour of the pyjamas contrasted with his weatherworn skin. And yet, God knew there were many times when he felt old, ready to die; and Rajko too, he was certain. Not that they ever said.

Rajko's chest rose and fell evenly. During a campaign, Rajko would cry out in his sleep, his hands wrestling with an invisible assailant, his breath in desperate bursts, hair sticky on his forehead. Drink perhaps released the demons. Now his hands rested by his side, the scar hidden, on his right palm, where he'd wrenched a bayonet from an attacker. Not a man with whom one associated jewellery, Rajko wore a gold ring on the fourth finger of his right hand. Flesh had swollen round it. Drink had caused the revelation many years ago that it had belonged to his father, who'd been shot outside their village by Turks, his body burned with the rest of the men of fighting age.

'Your chair, sir.'

'Thank you.' She was pretty in the manner of many English women, blood blanched from their skin, faces as unrevealing as a mask.

He knocked the bed with his knees as he sat down. He'd not known whether to bring a present, it wasn't usual between men. However, to offer nothing, particularly if Rajko had lost part of his leg, could be interpreted as lack of concern. He'd settled on a leather-covered copy of *Heroes and Legends of Serbia*. A book that would suit a patriotic Montenegrin who loved his adopted country. Of course, he would prefer *rakija*, but that could wait.

'Can I fetch you a cup of tea, sir?'

'No, thank you. I'll wait a few minutes. I expect he needs to sleep.'

'He'd a bad night. Miss Frankland sat with him.'

So, the operation hadn't been as straightforward as it appeared. Oddly satisfied, he leaned back in the chair. There was a draught. He would keep his coat on. To amuse himself, he began to identify the officers in the nearest beds. One poor fellow on the far side of the trestle table, looked as though he wouldn't make it, another letter, another grieving family.

'Got a cigarette, sir?'

Stefan stood up. Smoking wasn't allowed, not even among officers. 'Well done, brother. You're awake. They say you've had a bad night.'

'Not at all.'

'You look fine,' Stefan observed.

When Rajko closed his eyes, Stefan continued, 'Nice nurses though not as attractive as ours.'

'For pity's sake, colonel,' Rajko glowered.

Nonplussed, Stefan picked up his gift and handed it to Rajko, who was looking beyond Stefan, his eyes alert.

The book dropped on the bed and Stefan said, 'You might like to read it when you're feeling better,' but Rajko, was pushing himself up, trying to sit. Surprised Rajko was now beaming, Stefan turned to see who'd brought about the transformation.

Audrey was entering the tent, followed by Ellen. Stefan kicked his chair to one side, his mood lightening. He strode to greet them. They shook hands, but hurried on, one to each side of the bed. As he stepped out of Ellen's way, he smelled her perfume.

'Major Kostic, don't overdo it,' Audrey ordered.

'We'll help you,' Ellen added.

With their arms under his armpits, they raised Rajko upright, Audrey clucking, 'Remember you've stitches below and above your knee.'

Stefan watched as Rajko gazed at each of them in turn, like a fool in love.

Neither woman was in uniform. They were hatless, their hair coiffured, lips touched with colour. He glimpsed the pale blue skirt under Audrey's greatcoat. Stamenka could dress like this if she chose, but she refused to put up her hair, adopt European style clothes and insisted on wearing for special occasions, her hand embroidered national costume. Over her greatcoat, Ellen had slung a knitted shawl in reds, greens and yellows, such as old women lay across their beds, to keep their knees warm during the night. At first he thought it foolish, but the vibrant colours reminded him of Stamenka's early tapestries, and he decided it was stylish.

These women expressed a freedom, his wife could never imagine.

After assurances they wouldn't stay long, Stefan was persuaded to sit down. Apparently they were going to spend a few days with a French count who lived locally. Stefan had heard of him, but understood he was a recluse, a son having died of typhus several winters ago, his daughter moving to live with her Italian husband.

Audrey gave Rajko a box of Huntley and Palmer's biscuits. Her mother had sent it in the Red Cross parcel. As nearly every day someone received some biscuits, she'd brought hers for Rajko. It would tempt his appetite back.

Rajko was grinning, embracing the box, promising to think of Audrey at every bite. Perhaps it was the effect of the anaesthetic.

Though Audrey, without a doubt, was the prettier of the two women, Stefan preferred Ellen. Neither lacked confidence. They spoke as though their place in the hospital, in Serbia, was assured. Stamenka, born and brought up in the country, didn't exude a similar air of entitlement. And though he might appear at ease under the shoulder straps and buttons of his uniform, though he'd lived in Belgrade since eleven, he felt an outsider in the capital, perhaps because his father chose to live in a compound in the Turkish quarter. As he grew older, he became more alienated from his countrymen. Surely, age increased confidence?

The women were laughing at each other, at Rajko, at Stefan, and he did his best to appear jolly. He was glad to see them. The ward seemed happier. The officer he'd thought was dying, opened his eyes, listened to the exchanges. There was brightness in the air, as though the entire ward had been slumbering towards death.

Stefan stretched to see what Ellen was handing to Rajko, who seemed entranced by the small object in his hand. It looked like a whistle, the kind of thing he'd whittled out of a stick when a boy, but that was ridiculous. He couldn't imagine Ellen chipping with a knife.

'It's not much. I'm sorry. The men play them in the ward and it lightens us up. When I saw them in the newsagent's in Jevo this morning, I thought you might like one.'

Stefan was embarrassed for her. It was true Rajko liked to dance; he'd been particularly adept at the *kola* until his knee injury, but couldn't sing in tune and expressed irritation at beggars who played the whistle on street corners.

'I used to have one,' Rajko said.

Ellen nodded, as though she were familiar with his childhood. God knows, Rajko rarely spoke of it to him. Her sympathy, the patting of the blanket, must be an act. Convincing, if he didn't know Rajko so well.

Suddenly, Rajko picked up the whistle, winked at Ellen and began to play *Ruza, Ruza*. Stefan's favourite. He was back in Orasac, watching the village girls at the well. Nudging each other, giggling, glancing at him, a ten year old of no significance. He felt the stir of tears.

When Rajko finished playing, Ellen, Audrey, the nurses, even the patients clapped. Belatedly Stefan imitated them, diminished by the unsuitability of his gift.

The women began to say goodbye.

Audrey said to Stefan, 'Major Kostic will be discharged tomorrow.'

'So soon?'

'We'll have him out of bed this afternoon. Trauma is less easily dealt with. Major Kostic needs rest, of course, though psychological damage is best overcome by conviviality.'

He thought back to Glisic's abandoned trench. Its shadowy figures, the clutter of limbs, the stench. Was that what she meant by trauma? Rajko had faced no more gruesome incidents of war than anyone else; she must be referring to the operation.

'I suppose so, doctor.'

She continued, 'Even soldiers celebrate Christmas. We're having a carol concert and everyone's invited. There'll be wine and mince pies.' He wanted to explain that 25th December meant nothing to Serbs.

'We celebrate Christ's birth in January,' Rajko said. 'We'll have a party for you ladies. We'll show you how to enjoy yourselves.'

Ellen picked up his leather bound book, was smelling it.

Stefan remembered Christmas with Stamenka when Mitar was a baby. They're shared the Christmas Eve fast with his mother, his brother and their family and spent the rest of the evening by their own hearth. He'd played the *gusle*, Stamenka sung an accompaniment. She'd a strong, melodious voice. He'd a recollection of Mitar being older, of joining in the singing, but last year he'd not gone home.

When they left, Stefan laid his hand on the leather cover of the book, tempted to smell it as Ellen had done. He'd driven especially to Belgrade for something to help Rajko through the ordeal, wanting a gift that would last through his convalescence. Poetry, novels had been an option. Finally, he'd settled for a reputable history of Serbia. He could have saved himself the time, the anxiety (though he'd enjoyed a couple of hours browsing the shelves, wishing he was buying a book for himself).

With a sigh he turned to Rajko, who'd slid down the bed and closed his eyes. He tried to think of a jovial remark. *I'd love one of those biscuits. Play us another tune.* Nothing sounded right. He tried to pick up the conversation where the women had left it. *A party, my friend. Shall we have a party?* But Rajko seemed to have sunk into sleep. He'd been wrong to expect Rajko to thank him for sending him to the MO, which resulted in this operation, but that was the purpose of his visit, what he wanted.

'Any idea when you'll be home?' he asked.

'Home?' Rajko didn't open his eyes.

'Barracks.'

Women walked past, chatting. He longed for them to come in, to cheer them up as Audrey and Ellen had done. What was wrong? He and Rajko never sat in uncomfortable silence. He bit his tongue.

'Damn,' he muttered.

Eventually, he decided he would make one more effort. If there was no response, he could leave. He spoke at length about Mikaiho crashing his car. He didn't mention he'd taken it without permission, and was in the cells. When Rajko didn't respond, he half-rose from the chair.

'I wonder if officer training might help.'

'It'll make no difference.' Rajko ·spoke with surprising vehemence.

'He did well at Bregalnica.'

'Only because he's your cousin.'

That was unjust. The relationship wasn't something Stefan made much of, they'd different surnames, his uncle being on his maternal side.

Irritably he said, 'Dr. Eyres said wounds can be psychological as well as physical. You only need think of Glisic. Mikaiho was traumatised at Chekoj ridge.'

'Him traumatised? Nonsense.'

Stefan, uncomfortable perching, sat down. 'It will be nice to listen to the women singing carols.'

'It will.'

Stefan preferred men's voices. He and Stamenka had taken Mitar, when he started at the gymnasium, to St. Sava's on Christmas Eve. With Mitar holding his hand and Stamenka leaning against his other side, the smell of incense, the candles illuminating the darkness, the evening had been magical.

His voice shook a little. ' We could have a party.'

'Why the hell do you waste time on that useless cousin, when you never go and see your own son and wife?'

'And you? Jelena?'

'You're no better now than me.'

The operation had softened his head. Stefan hadn't seen Mikaiho in action. Other officers described the way he'd fought without a care for himself, not dissimilar to Rajko in his youth. Why would they record his bravery, if it weren't true? He wished he'd not visited his friend. He'd encouraged him to risk an operation so that he could fight lead his men to glory and he'd shown no appreciation.

After a moment or so, Rajko started to snore. Stefan picked up his book and left the ward.

Chapter Nine

Hotel des Balkans, General Staff Headquarters. Krusevac, October 1915

When Stefan drove from the barracks towards Jevo, the roads were packed with wagons. In the town, soldiers without limbs were begging on the pavement and, as they crossed the bridge to leave, a group of six or seven women boo-ed. Stefan ordered Dragan to stop. Stefan jumped out to offer reassurance. The women crowded round him, others began to join them. Like his mother and wife, they were patriotic, devoted to their families and afraid. If they hadn't recognised him, his promise that the army would fight to its final heartbeat, might not have been listened to. Their sullen expressions told him, they didn't believe him.

Back in the motorcar, he dozed.

His mind skittered through memories of other journeys: his mother and father, sitting side by side on the wagon taking them from Orasac, the rattle of stones against the wheels, the chatter, the laughter and teasing of his brothers and sisters as they lay on the floor among furniture...His, bare feet extended around the neck of a young ram, he was riding as a dare, the shouts of his friends, his giggles ...The whistle of shells in flight over gorge and valley...The wail of a cat, the roar of a train, the howl of the night wolf...His body clenched on a stretcher, the slap of the bearers' *opanki* sandals on cobblestones, the throb of his wound, the blood carrying fear to his heart. Peasant girls huddled, as they carried water jars. One of them, eyes like stars, reminding him of Stamenka...Women's screams. Though he resisted, the name of the village came to him. Kadavsic.

With relief he jolted awake to the *clack clack* of wipers. His scar ached, he rubbed it.

He'd been surprised by Tomislav's summons to General Staff Headquarters at Krusevac. Other than at formal meetings, they hadn't spoken since the Bosnian campaign.

Tomislav would have updated more senior officers. It was true he and Tomislav went back many years, but why now?

It was dark by the time an orderly showed Stefan into Tomislav's quarters. The blinds were closed, light glowing from the embers of a fire and an oil lamp hanging from the ceiling. By the door, the narrow bed was made up, Tomislav's greatcoat folded across it.

Tomislav could have been in his study at home and not a dilapidated hotel room adapted into accommodation for a general. A lighted candle in a holder was perched on top of a pile of books, and Tomislav, sitting on a wooden chair, his head bent, was reading. Though in full dress uniform, his tunic collar was open, and around his neck, the white silk scarf he'd worn at Military Academy.

Tomislav slammed shut the book, blew out the candle and walked to embrace.

'Good to see you, friend.'

As Stefan shook rain from his cap and gloves, his fingers burned, circulation returning. He unbuttoned his greatcoat.

The orderly asked, 'Drink, sir?'

Stefan was relieved when Tomislav said no. Of late, nightmares woke him around three; if he drank he dozed for no more than an hour.

'Lime tea will suit us,' Tomislav said.

During this war, Stefan had drunk more tea than alcohol. After Matron had discovered he disliked Indian tea and cocoa, which even politeness prevented him from taking more than a sip, she'd offered lime tea. So they came to enjoy the occasional afternoon discussing work.

While the orderly placed Stefan's greatcoat across the bed, Tomislav unfastened the shutters in a series of clatters. It seemed the wrong time of day to be opening them, but rubbing his hands, Stefan was content to observe.

Tomislav instructed the orderly to position two chairs to face the night sky. Stefan felt a stage set was unfolding. Tomislav gestured for Stefan to sit down.

Tomislav didn't look at him but sat, hands on knees, reminding Stefan of old King Petar in photographs, recording his presence for posterity, or perhaps demonstrating he wasn't dead.

Tomislav considered himself a poet, and perhaps saw more than a dark sky, but Stefan, feeling a draught from the window, would have preferred to warm himself by the fire. He wondered whether to initiate the conversation, but after a moment, decided to wait. Tomislav had summoned him so he listened to the crackle of the logs, smelled the extinguished candle and tried to quell growing apprehension.

Tomislav muttered, 'Quite like old times.' His face seemed longer, the line of his nostrils, sharper, more severe.

Tomislav put a finger over his lips, leaned close, whispered, 'We're to be dismembered, like a pig. Italy is to have Dalmatia and Istria....' He sank back into his chair, blinked back tears, before continuing, 'Rumania gets Banat ... Bulgaria wins Macedonia.'

'Dismembered like a pig,' Stefan distrusting the colourful words, couldn't help be moved by Tomislav's distress.

'And Russia?' Stefan asked, anticipating further bad news.

'She...urges us to accept Bulgaria's offer. Good advice if she's not to fight alongside us.'

Two years ago, Serbia had won Southern Serbia. Now it would revert to Bulgaria. The escapade into Bosnia, the victory at Kolubara, for nothing. Their men had died for nothing.

'Why do you want to see me?'

'We are friends.'

Stefan wasn't convinced. He said morosely, 'Without agreement on the British loan, we've nothing to fight with.'

'Serbs fight with whatever is to hand.'

That was how Glisic talked. Stefan was about to argue. As he bent forward, his knee touched Tomislav's, and he withdrew. What did it matter? They were finished. The British and French he understood, but not the Russians. He was disappointed. Did they fear Serbia would become too powerful, would forget from whom their success came, did they prefer Serbia weak?

Tomislav twisted the fringe of his scarf between his fingers. 'Why should we be the only country to adhere to the terms of a treaty? The Bulgars won't.'

Stefan nodded, remembering that a year ago he'd wanted to capitulate to Austria's demands, but not now when the men were exhausted and dispirited. He rubbed his palms along his thighs, with a shrug, 'It's out of our hands.'

He pushed back the cuticles on his nails, half listening to men's laughter rising from the mess downstairs. Maybe, the pains in his stomach, his restlessness, were linked to this dread.

Tomislav sighed. 'If we can hold out for two, three, maybe four weeks,' Tomislav went on, his eyes brimming.

Stefan turned away. They both knew Belgrade could hold for one, possibly two days. German planes were reconnoitring. An attack was imminent.

He offered, 'I'll lead a unit to defend Belgrade, sir,' at the same time as wondering how he could ensure Stamenka's safety. There might yet be time.

'I knew I could depend on you.'

'There'll be no shortage of volunteers.'

'It'll give the army time to retreat,' Tomislav whispered so quietly Stefan had to crane his neck. They were children telling secrets in the dark.

'Retreat?'

'The men must not informed. Not yet. It's in the hands of the politicians.' Tomislav removed a handkerchief from his pocket, blew his nose.

'The army is to abandon its people. Is that what you're saying?'

'The government refuses to surrender. When it transferred to Nis, the move was temporary. The Assembly has decided the government, the army and its cadets will depart for Corfu.'

It was a bold move. There was no virtue in soldiers being taken prisoner, for how many would survive? The removal of cadets would prevent the Austrians and Germans murdering Serbia's future. Even so, how would his men react, the crowd of women in Jevo. It stank of cowardice, betrayal.

Behind him, a spark snapped like gunfire. If only he'd recognised his unease for the warning it signified. When he'd gone home, as duty required, to celebrate the family Sava day, he'd not stayed overnight. He understood now, that he'd not wanted to admit the possibility of defeat to Stamenka, something he'd feared since war had begun.

There was a tap on the door. The orderly entered carrying a pot and two beakers.

Slowly Tomislav rose to his feet. 'Leave a guard at the door. Rest for a few hours. Come back at sunrise. We'll look after ourselves.'

When the door closed, Tomislav said solemnly, 'I am aware as never before that we may never see each other again. Allow me to pour.'

Embarrassed, Stefan said, 'Thank you, sir.'

While Tomislav moved stiffly towards the table, Stefan stepped over to the window and looked down to the street, lit by tiny oil lamps set in the recesses of house walls. In the doorway opposite the hotel, a man wrapped in a sack, slept. The man had woken when Stefan's motorcar stopped by him. Stefan had murmured reassurances and the man returned to his sleep.

Tomilslav said wearily, 'You have provided for your wife and son, my friend?'

Stefan snapped, 'Of course.'

Over the past few months he'd spoken to Matron about Mitar finishing his education in England. He was too young to be evacuated as a cadet. The need to remove his family from the city was urgent; otherwise they would pay for his prevarication.

'Stamenka and young Mitar have left Belgrade?' As Tomislav poured, the fragrance of lime filled the room.

Stefan said quickly, 'Not yet.'

For a second, Tomislav's hand stopped, but as he continued pouring, he said, 'I want your cousin in charge of the evacuation of the cadets.'

'It's a big responsibility.'

'He did well on the mule-ambulance.'

Apart from asking permission to marry Miss Frankland, who'd been moved, transferred to the main hospital. At least he wouldn't be fighting. Rajko had been right; officer training had done no good. All the officers reported he was fragile, lived in a storybook world where he was a giant who defeated his enemy with Prince Marko's sacred lance. The prospect of battle sent him back to the safety of his imagination.

'It may suit him, sir,' Stefan said doubtfully.

'He's not a warrior.'

Tomislav held out the beaker. 'Let me be frank. Politicians are fickle.'

'We both know that, sir.'

'In time, you'll replace me. You're not as outspoken as I am, and you love the men. The politicians dare not ignore that.'

Stefan went to the table and took the beaker. His hands were sweating. His stomach lurched. He placed a hand over his mouth and swallowed hard. He hoped it was too dark for Tomislav to see his expression. Dare he admit, that to be general, wasn't what he wanted? That he craved peace, as others craved victory.

'One day, my friend, I hope to hear you have become General Stefan Petrovic, but you must regain your passion for Serbia.'

Stefan shrugged. 'Thank you, sir.'

'This is not a time for doubts. We can argue about strategy and politics when the war is won, but now we *must* believe we're doing right.'

Tomislav returned to the chairs by the window. 'Louise will be joining me the day after tomorrow. I will make arrangements for her motorcar to pick up your wife and son.'

Stefan didn't move, ashamed by the implication, murmured,' Thank you, sir.'

'Make sure you go home and prepare her. They'll need warm clothes in the mountains. Stout boots for the lad. The journey will take three weeks in an inhospitable Balkan winter. So explain to her.'

'I appreciate it, sir.'

'You never know, Louise might show her yet how to be an officer's wife.'

The urge to vomit was not going to disappear. 'If you'll excuse me, sir,' he gabbled.

After being sick, Stefan returned, ready to return to barracks. Picking up his greatcoat, he said, 'I will leave straight away to say goodbye to Stamenka.'

Tomislav remained seated by the window. 'We will watch the sun rise, my friend. It heralds a new beginning for Serbia.'

Stefan stood uncertainly by the bed, wanting to put on his greatcoat. He might never see his wife, son or mother again. He also needed to prepare his officers. Tomislav didn't turn. The embers, in the fire, spurted, dying strongly. Despising his lack of resolve, he moved to Tomislav's side.

Yet, as dawn broke, he felt all would be well. Tomislav wanted him to lead the defence of Belgrade. Louise would take care of Stamenka. There was no need for concern. He would write her a note, explain the situation, tell her he loved her, so he could concentrate on preparing his men.

His mood shifted again on leaving Tomislav. Ill-at-ease in the bustle of the Jevo where fresh trenches were being dug, allied flags removed, he was full of despair. Faced with a campaign meeting, the note he gave Mikaiho to deliver to Stamenka was short and factual.

At regimental headquarters that evening, the campaign maps were folded and tucked under the conference table. Black arrows marked the regiment's route from Jevo through Krusevac to join the First, Second and Sixth Armies at Nis, from where they would prepare to march south, to defend Kossovo. The blue arrows delineating the German and Austrian attack across the Danube and Sava rivers, indicated the small unit Stefan was to lead north to delay the fall of Belgrade.

Red wine, dark as blood, flowed in the light of chandeliers and candelabra. Stefan poured himself a small glass, before passing the decanter to the officer next to him. The curtains of the library shut out the drama unfolding in the barracks. The officers were wrapped in smoke from the blazing fire, hidden within the fog of Austrian cigars. For an hour, they were cut off from the rumble of departing gun carriages, the bombardment of their beautiful white city. They were removed from overloaded wagons of government officials and their families.

Stefan's meeting with Tomislav seemed longer than twelve hours ago. During the vigil he had nodded off. When he tried to picture a Serbia without its soldiers, he visualised pastures, orchards and fields where old men smoked, children played, women tilled and worked the land. And what of the soldiers? The unease he'd felt at the outbreak of war was replaced by images, not of soldiers in uniform, but of wounded men lying on palisters on the shores of Corfu attended by women like Matron, in white robes and headdresses.

Business concluded, the men relaxed. In the courtyard, a motorcar engine was being cranked, its ignition refusing to spark. More wine was poured, cigars and cigarettes lit. Stefan glanced at Rajko. He wanted to remain with his old friend, with these men, their future stilled within the library walls. He pictured Stamenka kneeling on Mitar's bed, a pile of his jumpers, socks and gloves knitted by his mother. He saw her face turn to smile as if she knew he was watching, her lips parted for a kiss.

An officer was saying, 'We are Slavs, yet even the Russians are afraid of a Slav state.'

Inevitably, they were discussing the possible terms of an armistice.

'What will we do if our allies fail us? We're too small to fight both the Austrians and the Germans,' Mikaiho said. He'd returned from Stamenka with nothing to report.

Stefan raised his hand for attention. His cousin provided a good way to start. He leaned back in his seat, stretched his legs, speaking as though he was reassuring a student officer.

'Brothers, you are wise to voice concerns about the future. On the one hand, against the odds, we defeated the mighty Austrian Empire at Cer, at Kolubara, so we fight on, honouring all those of our brothers who died in combat...' His boots touched the edge of the maps under the table.

He took a breath, determined his voice wouldn't crack, 'We have set an example to our people. We must, wherever we can, face the enemy head on.' He was sounding like Glisic.

The men were silent. 'Brothers.' He cleared his throat, straightened the lapels of his tunic jacket. Somehow he'd to make it clear they were facing disaster, and yet maintain hope.

'The odds, brothers, are against us. Our beloved city faces occupation. Our men are brave, but we're short of weapons and ammunition.' These officers would have read in the *Echo* that the Russians refused a further loan, unless the Serbs agreed to Bulgarian demands. 'Our hope lies with our allies. It is true that the British and French have landed at Salonika.' His voice strengthened, 'Against the odds we've defeated the Austrians, and when we defend ourselves, as we must in Belgrade, we honour all those who have died in battle.' In the days to come, when the politicians announced the retreat of the army, his men might recall that he didn't speak of regaining Belgrade.

He glanced at the rows of books along the shelves between the casement windows. He could think of no examples of heroes, instead a passage from Ecclesiastes came to mind:

For everything there is a season,
and a time for every matter under heaven: …
a time to kill, and a time to heal;
a time to love, and a time to hate;
a time for war, and a time for peace.

He went on slowly, 'In Belgrade, civilians are ready to fight alongside and help push back the invaders.' He must prepare them for defeat.

In the reception area outside the library, a guard shouted a command. There sounded to be a scuffle, an argument going on. A woman's voice.

'We are at a crossroads in our history.' He paused, discomforted by the noise outside.

Another guard called out. A crash. A bench maybe?

He paused, distracted by the rapid knocking on the door. The men were no longer paying attention. He tapped the table with the edge of his fingernails. After a second, he resumed. 'The British and French cannot reach us in time…' Among the communal gasp, he thought he identified that of Mikaiho. He knew it was impossible to single out his cousin's consternation, but he worried how the army's retreat would affect this man, who identified so much with victory. Tomislav's suggestion he be put in charge of the cadets' withdrawal was inspired.

Again, a beating of what sounded like fists on the wooden door panel.

'See what's going on, will you, Major?' he asked Rajko.

Rajko picked up his stick and walked to the door. As it swung open, one of the candles in the candelabra blew out. An orderly got up to re-light it.

'What's going on?' Rajko shouted.

A woman with an English accent said, 'Sir! I must speak to Colonel Petrovic.'

Rajko stepped to one side so Stefan could see the woman, riding hat askew, wearing a mackintosh. For a second he thought it was Miss Frankland, whom he'd spoken to, at Rajko's bedside, almost a year ago.

'The colonel is in conference, ma'am.' Rajko began to close the door, saying to the guard, 'See to it that we're not disturbed again.'

The door slammed. A scream echoed round the reception area and Stefan stood up in exasperation. Rajko returned to the door, opened it again and shouted, 'That is an order, Private.'

What the hell was a woman doing in the barracks? The medical unit had no instructions to move. When the Austrians occupied Jevo, it would be sent back to England. He'd informed Matron of this in confidence.

The guard said to Rajko, 'Sir, she refuses to leave the building.'

It would be hard to concentrate with an argument going on. 'Let her go,' Stefan instructed.

As the guard released her, the woman swivelled round, skidded back into the room, almost slipping to her knees. There was a roar of laughter. She looked round, adjusting the peak of her hat so it lay in the middle of her forehead. It *was* Miss Frankland. He was embarrassed on her behalf. She straightened her belt. Her face, garments, boots were splattered with mud. A twig stuck in her shoulder straps. When Matron heard of this behaviour, she'd be reprimanded without doubt.

Nonetheless he was pleased he kept order at every stage of his meetings. His men's jackets were fully buttoned, they sat straight-backed though they'd been drinking, unlike in some regiments where drunkenness was normal.

Ellen marched, arms swinging, between the bookshelves and the backs of men's chairs, to where Stefan was standing. Irritated by her audacity, Stefan ordered the men to be seated and the guard to resume his duties.

In English, he said, 'It is late.'

'I am sorry to disturb you, sir.'

'It is late,' he repeated.

'Yes, sir. We met at Dobro Majka.'

'Miss Frankland. It is late and we are in conference.'

Her hairpins were slipping, strands of hair fell onto her collar. If she could see herself, she'd scuttle from the room. All the women in the medical corps were particular about their appearance.

'I am sorry to disturb you, but I wish to speak to you on a matter of urgency. I understand you're leaving tonight. I'm happy to wait till your conference is finished.'

In Serbian, Stefan asked Rajko if he knew what the problem was. Rajko shrugged. She'd told the guard it was a personal matter. Stefan hoped she wasn't pregnant with Mikaiho's child.

'Where is your chaperone?' he demanded.

'We don't have chaperones in Serbia, sir.'

An officer poured himself more wine. Comments were exchanged between the men. Stefan had no wish to be left alone with this woman. He couldn't understand why he'd ever found her attractive, why he'd been keen to meet her again, hoping to encounter her on his visits to Matron. Nonetheless, he sensed she brought trouble. Anyone associated with his cousin seemed tainted.

'Lieutenant Nis. If this young lady is to speak to us on an 'urgent matter', she must be searched.'

Mikaiho was sitting upright, his back to the fire. Stefan was uncertain whether his disinterest was genuine or if he was acting.

Ellen said, 'Tell them about the woman soldier, Mikaiho.'

They were on Christian name terms. Mikaiho flushed. He walked rigidly round the backs of the chairs, his eyes lowered. No one spoke. Rajko raised his eyebrows.

Mikaiho stood an inch or so in front of Ellen. He preened his moustache.

'Tell him. Please, Mikaiho.'

'Raise your arms.' Mikaiho said sulkily.

Ellen turned to Stefan. 'I don't need to be searched, do I, sir?'

'We are at war, Miss Frankland and there are enemies everywhere.'

'You know who I am.' She sounded indignant.

'Do you have papers?' Stefan said.

'I don't have them with me.'

'Then you must be searched.' He was teasing her, using her to amuse himself and his men. Mikaiho again asked her to raise her arms. One or two of the men tittered. Mikaiho placed a hand on the top of her head. Her hat slipped to one side, more hair escaped.

'Excuse me, miss,' Mikaiho said.

'Is this really necessary?' she said to him. Her face was red as she pushed the loose strands under the hat.

'Raise your arms, please.' Mikaiho ran his hands from the tip of her gloves down her arms to her waist. Stefan judged Mikaiho hadn't touched her before.

She stepped back. 'I have this.' She unbuttoned her mackintosh, pushed her hand around the waist and after a moment produced a small pistol. 'For personal protection.' She placed it on the table in front of Stefan.

'If you please, miss, raise your arms.' Mikaiho's mouth was twisting into a leer. Stefan began to regret his decision. Glisic's words came back to him. *The victor is humiliated more than the victim.*

Down the length of the table, the men drummed their fists as though marching. The pace quickened till they clattered to a halt, falling out of line. It was the sort of caper they got up to in the mess when someone made a mistake. Ellen straightened her shoulders and closed her eyes. Mikaiho was some six inches taller than Ellen and his hands running along the front of her mackintosh sounded like the rhythmic stroking of a horse. The woman smelled of the misty, autumnal evening. Mikaiho's hands stopped at her waist. He fumbled between the belt and the body of the mackintosh. A log collapsed on the hearth, breaking the silence. An orderly hurried to the fireplace.

'Get on with it, Lieutenant,' Stefan said irritably.

Mikaiho skimmed the skirt of the mackintosh. 'Turn around, Miss.'

'That'll do,' Stefan said. She'd need to be a contortionist to reach a weapon in the middle of her back.

Mikaiho said, 'Nothing, sir.'

As he strode back to his seat, Stefan said to Ellen, 'You are foolish to be unaccompanied.'

He picked up the pistol and held it in the flat of his hand. The men laughed. He turned it over, no longer at ease with himself. She wouldn't come here if she were pregnant, Matron would be the person to tell.

'It is because of the war I want to speak to you.' She placed a trembling hand on the edge of the table.

'Men do not behave as they should at time of war. A pistol is useless.'

'Yes, sir.'

'What is this matter of urgency?'

'I prefer to speak to you on your own.'

Stefan couldn't work out if her face was flushed because she was embarrassed, or because of the heat. Outside a voice called, '*Laku noc!*' Footsteps echoed and re-echoed in the entrance hall.

Everyone was watching Stefan. Once more he enjoyed her discomfort. 'I am waiting, Miss Frankland. This matter of urgency. Let us hear.'

Ellen flung back her shoulders and held his gaze. She said, 'I'd like to enlist in your regiment, sir.'

To stop himself from laughing outright, Stefan rubbed his chin. He repeated in Serbian for the benefit of those who didn't understand English. One or two men clapped. Her interruption lightened the atmosphere, he was going to make the most of it.

She went on, 'I am ready to fight for Serbia.'

Stefan translated, his voice registering his amusement. One or two men muttered to each other.

'I've been trained to use Mauser rifles.'

For a moment, Stefan was impressed. He translated, 'She shoots with Mauser rifles.' He rubbed his hands together. Once more the men drummed with their fists.

'I am a founder member of the Women's Yeomanry Corps and we were trained by the army…'

Stefan smirked at the idea of women in grey dresses and white aprons on the march. The room filled with laughter. He glanced at Rajko, who listened unsmiling.

Stefan cleared his throat. 'We are in desperate need, Miss Frankland. Our country faces enemies from every side and your government sends us an orderly from the Women's Medical Corps. Will there be others? Will other women in the corps, volunteer to fight for us?'

The volume of laughter increased. Ellen turned to looked at Mikaiho who was leaning in his seat, mouth open in a guffaw.

Her reply was directed at Mikaiho, 'I understood the Serb army accepted women.' There was no mistaking her anger. Mikaiho blew his nose. She faced Stefan, said, 'Sir.'

Stefan gestured for silence. 'It is enough. We've had our fun. We'll let you return to Dobro Majka, but you must not be unaccompanied. Major Kostic, will you ensure Miss Frankland gets back safely?' She might talk to him, give him some idea as to what lay behind her offer. Mikaiho had something to do with it.

'You'll be driven to the hospital. That will be all, Miss Frankland.'

Ellen did not move. 'What about my horse, sir?'

Didn't she know, the barracks had stables? She was more foolish than he'd realised.

Mikaiho jumped up. 'May Miss Frankland have her pistol, sir?'

'I think we can allow our lady-soldier her arms, don't you? And, Lieutenant, will you fetch my motorcar to the front of the building?'

Ellen picked up her pistol without looking at Mikaiho. The men stood up as she marched out, Rajko following.

At the door Mikaiho paused. Stefan wondered what had passed between him and Ellen during their time on the mule-ambulance; he was beginning to see his cousin through Rajko's eyes.

As the door closed Stefan, remaining on his feet, sighed. 'Well, brothers.' While he waited for them to settle, he prepared to address them again. The diversion had lifted the mood. The orderly added more logs to the fire, which together with the heat from the candles, made the room particularly hot. A slither of sweat slid between his shoulder blades. He'd telephone Matron and ask her not to treat Ellen harshly. It was true some women fought alongside their husbands, but it was rare. Not like the Russians, who'd a battalion of women soldiers. The front door banged.

He rested one hand on the table, looked at each officer in turn. 'I will be as straight with you as I am allowed.' He paused to make sure everyone was listening. 'Our prime minister has sworn Serbia will never surrender. Our allies, though they have reached Salonika, will be too late to help defend Belgrade, or Nis. The battle in the south against both the Bulgars and the Germans is one that, eventually, we will lose.'

He took a deep breath, 'What I want to say to you brothers is this: that young woman was misguided, but she has our spirit, the spirit of Serbia. The citizens of this country, will defend their right to live in freedom in their own land.

'I cannot foresee the future, other than to say, that in the hard times ahead, we must remember the fight to defeat our oppressors may be long, but one day, because we are Serbs and we love freedom, victory will be ours.'

He watched the receptive faces.

'Brothers, let us fill our glasses.'

Last night he'd drunk tea with Tomislav. He remembered Tomislav's bowed head, as he now watched Bratanic, at the far end of the table, hold out his glass for an officer to fill. Wine glugged. Stefan waited until all the officers and orderlies had full glasses. He raised his hand to indicate they should get to their feet.

With glass high, he quoted the first line of the national anthem. The men knew *Mars na Drina* well enough. They often marched to the beat of its rousing words, but Stefan spoke softly as though to an old wounded soldier on the verge of sleep. 'To battle. Go forth as heroes.'

'Serbia!' the men said in unison.

Stefan put down his glass and shook the hand of the officer on his right, clasped his shoulders, as he and Tomislav had at dawn. 'Well done, brother.'

After officer embraced officer, orderly held orderly, Stefan watched from the head of the table, the toes of his boots touching the maps. He waited while they filed out of the room.

Only when he was alone, did Stefan crouch and pick up the maps, placing them one by one on the table.

Stamenka. What would happen to her? He remembered the shy touch as they'd held hands on the day of their engagement, in front of the walnut tree that was her dowry.

'Is it enough?' she'd asked.

'Of course.'

He had enfolded her in his arms. She leaned against his chest and he felt the softness of her breasts, the beat of her heart. He liked the way she clung to him. He stroked her hair smelling of rosemary and thyme and wished then, as he did now, that he'd the words to express his love.

He picked up his gloves, flipped them against the edge of the desk. She'd have finished packing. She'd only ever travelled as far as visiting her parents in Orasac. Mitar had never lived anywhere but Belgrade. He would miss his school friends, his grandmother. He wished he'd made more effort with his note.

Chapter Ten

Jevo regimental Headquarters, October 1915

Ellen strode out of the library, past the bench where she'd been instructed to wait when she'd first arrived, past Rajko addressing Mikaiho. The moment Rajko finished, she would leave. Turning her back on them, she waited under the Venetian glass chandelier, fidgeting with the buckle on her mackintosh belt. Mikaiho should have refused to search her for he'd misled her. Her glance fixed on the statue of the angel at the side of the banisters. She admired its haughty air, its poised sword.

To gallop back, would suit her mood. The traffic would have eased. Her journey to the barracks had become an ordeal, not the canter she'd envisaged. Priority had been given to army traffic: gun carriages hauled by teams of oxen, rows of cavalry and infantry, wagon upon wagon of ammunition, food, weapons and equipment. On a track pitted with axle-deep holes, Danica had struggled.

Rajko's cane clipped the marble floor, as he approached. She'd neither seen nor heard Mikaiho leave. Transferring his cane, he shook her hand.

'Major Kostic, ma'am. We wait for Lieutenant Nis to bring the colonel's motor car to the front of the building.'

'I prefer to return on horseback.'

'That is not acceptable to Colonel Petrovic.'

Sidestepping him, she dashed for the door. Surprised at how quickly he sprang to bar her way, she protested, 'Sir,' but he stood resolute. 'I must ride back to the hospital,' she added. The sooner she reached Dobro Majka, the sooner she would sink into bed, hide under heavy blankets.

'Miss Frankland, I have my orders.'

Resigned, she gave in. Her arms and shoulders ached, as though they'd been pinned between presses. They stood side-by-side like strangers in a queue at the bank. Sycamore leaves brought in on boots blew circuitously in the draught. Ellen watched the twisted door handle, waiting for Mikaiho to open it. The smell of drains, which permeated the hall, reminded her of the cesspit and the colonel's belated covering of it with a wooden lid. She banished Matron and the colonel from her mind, aware of Rajko's brooding presence, his cane grinding into the mosaic tiles.

In the distance a horn blared. Rajko dived for the door, dropping his stick. As they both bent to pick it up, Ellen apologised.

When Rajko opened the door, rain cascaded over his boots and cap. The air smelled of woods, earth, metal. Wind howled across the courtyard and Ellen pitied Danica.

Through the downpour, she discerned flashes of the motorcar's lights and drew down her hat, preparing to leap down the steps. Rajko held up a hand like a policeman. She stepped into the deluge unable to resist the urge to escape. Rajko stretched an arm in front of her. Again, she retreated.

From the step, his hand round his mouth, he bellowed, 'An umbrella, Lieutenant.'

A roar of thunder followed his words. Mikaiho would never hear. Rajko stepped back inside, saying sadly, 'He is idle.' Rain trickled from the tip of his cap onto the ground.

Ellen wanted to be outside where water danced like diamonds along the cobbles, the roofs of motorcars, across steps and balustrades.

She sighed. 'My poor horse will be perished.'

He spoke quietly, 'We will feed and stable her and a lad will return her in the morning.' He tapped the cane. 'Though he is Colonel Petrovic's cousin, the man is useless.'

He moved back onto the step, raised his arm, shook his stick and shouted. Eventually Mikaiho noticed, sprang from the driver's seat. Ellen thought it wiser to forget the umbrella. Rajko's cap and shoulders were soaked. A few more splashes were immaterial to both of them. There was more gesticulating and hollering, and Mikaiho slammed the car door and lifted the boot lid.

Momentarily satisfied, Rajko returned to the hall, shook water from his cap revealing a mass of black curly hair. She was back by his hospital bed, holding his hand after his nightmare, delighting in his recovery. Bad dreams were commonplace for a soldier he'd told her.

He spoke as though shouting had damaged his throat. 'He will bring you an umbrella.'

'I am sorry to put you to this trouble.'

'That villain is trouble. You are an angel in comparison.'

She doubted Matron would regard her as an angel. Or Audrey. To distract herself from such thoughts, she shifted so she could see Mikaiho, who seemed to have difficulty in locating the umbrella. The boot wasn't large. She wondered if he was being deliberately awkward. When at last he tried to put it up, in whatever position he stood, it turned inside out. For the first time that evening, Ellen was amused. If he was acting, he was good.

'A moment, I have an idea.'

Rajko turned into the hall and shouted to one of the guards who'd resumed his position on the bench. 'Corporal, please fetch me my cape.'

The man marched across the floor, his steps becoming fainter. Ellen sheltered well inside, while Rajko leaned on his stick and watched the storm. 'Colonel Petrovic has faith in that fool, but he is lazier than any man I know.'

Ellen wondered if Rajko was jealous of the lieutenant, for on the mule-ambulance Mikaiho hadn't been lazy. He'd been disorganised, but listened and followed her advice. On occasion he became ill tempered, sulky, though on the whole he was good-natured.

'It is a bad night,' she said.

'He is lazy whatever the weather.'

Rajko replaced his cap and strolled towards the library. She noticed he didn't put weight on his knee. Audrey had told her they'd been unable to remove the pieces of shrapnel. At the library door, Rajko listened for a moment before rejoining her. He glanced at his wristlet.

'I'm sorry to have kept you from your business,' she said.

'It is a great honour to be a soldier fighting for Serbia.'

'Yes, sir.'

'It is too hard for a woman. They make better nurses.'

She didn't know how to reply to what seemed a generous observation and was spared a response because the guard returned with a black oilskin cape.

'Allow me.' Rajko held the cape over their heads, his stick at right angles in front of him. On the top step, a gust of wind lifted the cape and an ocean burst upon them.

'Miss Frankland, if we walk side by side and I hold the cape, we will keep dry.'

Ellen doubted it. 'Shall I hang on to this corner?'

'Thank you, ma'am.'

She grabbed the top left hand corner; her fingers slippery, she drew it close to her head. They edged along the first step. Out of courtesy, she kept pace with him. The cape flapped, flung itself in their faces, flipped behind. As they descended, the rain slackened, but Ellen was as wet and cold as the rain itself. Water that had collected in her macintosh cuffs overflowed down her legs.

Mikaiho remained fighting with the umbrella, till he spotted them approaching, when he had flung it into the boot, and raced to the front seat. She didn't know why. He'd been asked to fetch, not drive the motor car. Anger towards him surged, surprising her.

Rajko tapped the window. 'Open the door for the lady.'

Mikaiho hopped out. She was pleased he was drenched and sulking. They shuffled back a step, so he could reach the door handle. The cape swirled as Ellen let go. Rajko trapped it on the roof with his stick. Mikaiho bowed from the waist as Ellen slid onto the back seat. She wanted to kick him.

Rajko instructed, 'Shut the door for Miss Frankland.'

Exhausted, Ellen squeezed the hem of her culottes. Mud stuck stockings to her legs and ankles and she rubbed them with a handkerchief. She smelled of ditch water. Rajko slammed his door, accelerated from the building, along the drive. She closed her eyes.

Sinking into the upholstery, Ellen gripped the seat. She wished she'd never met the woman soldier yesterday, wished she'd not listened to Mikaiho. So much had been going on. They'd learned that an Austrian attack was imminent, that the country would soon be occupied and that on the orders of Colonel Petrovic, the wounded who could walk, were to be discharged. At the same time, she was helping the injured from the mule-ambulance to the admissions tent. The men were despondent, some weeping.

And Mikaiho had interrupted her.

'You have dreamed of being a soldier, Miss Frankland. Today, a woman soldier is here.'

Ellen was curious.

'She will tell you what it is like,' he insisted.

The woman soldier sat in a queue of new arrivals, squashed between a man with crutches and an ashen-faced boy. Her head and back were bowed. She wore no cap, her matted hair was roughly chopped above her ears. After Mikaiho had introduced them, he moved away.

As she did when she felt uncomfortable, Ellen pulled out her case, fumbled for a cigarette. She was conscious her boots were polished, the woman's soles worn to bare feet. A year had passed since she'd spoken of her girlish fantasy to Mikaiho and she'd witnessed too much pain in the meantime to consider being a soldier.

She crouched, peering into a weather-beaten face. Buttons were missing from her oversized jacket, the trousers ripped and bloodied above the knee of her wounded leg.

'*Dobar dan.*' Ellen spoke hesitantly, offering a cigarette.

Calloused hands waved it away.

'Are you wounded?'

The woman closed her eyes.

'Can I help you?'

Maybe the woman couldn't understand her pronunciation. Ellen squatted nearer.

Politely she asked, 'Are you waiting to be admitted?' There was no point in asking more, though she was curious as to how she'd become a soldier among all these men.

Ellen glanced at a foursome playing cards by the tent. They smoked between contemplation of the cards.

She straightened. 'The doctors are very good.'

'English.' The woman's lips twisted as though she was spitting.

'One is English, but there are surgeons from the regiment.'

The woman's face was screwed up. 'Serbs hate the English.'

Disbelieving, Ellen glanced at the card players. The men praised them, thanked them. Nationality didn't seem an issue.

The ground shook. Now and again, small earthquakes, indistinguishable from the rumble of artillery fire, affected the medical unit. A few yards away, by a tent corner, a soldier moaned. Behind him, the tent shifted like a sheet on a washing line. As his cries continued, still holding the cigarette, she climbed over legs and bodies. His head swayed. Ellen stood over him. Uncertain. Even after a year, she hated the men's pain. Perhaps, she could reassure him he was safe.

The more he groaned, the more Ellen longed for him to stop. She glanced back at the woman watching her. It felt like a test. If she passed, the woman would like the English. The man pointed to his chest, over and over again; he picked at his shirt with his fingers. Blood trickled from a swollen upper lip. His lower jaw appeared dislocated, his tongue protruded.

'What does he want?' she asked the man next to him.

He didn't answer.

Crouching, she asked if he'd like a cigarette. Stemming tears, she stroked the back of his hand.

'You have done well, brother. Serbia is proud of you.' He continued to groan and after a few moments, she lit the cigarette and gave it to the next man.

Feeling helpless, she walked back to the woman soldier, with the intention of wishing her well, before going back to the courtyard for the next patient.

Curiosity prompted her to ask, 'Why do you hate us?'

'The English!' She spat on the ground.

'Where is your husband?'

'My husband is a good man, but in the confusion of fighting, I lost him.'

Relieved that the woman no longer spoke of hatred, Ellen persuaded her to print her husband's name. She promised to look for him on the admissions' list so they could be reunited.

Later, as Ellen and Mikaiho were drinking tea in the courtyard, she asked him why the woman soldier disliked the English.

He explained, 'It is because the English promised to fight alongside us, but are slow to come.'

It was hard to understand. The English had been vociferous allies at the beginning of the war, but fighting on other fronts now seemed to be taking preference. She felt ashamed, wondering how widespread the antagonism was.

Mikaiho preened his moustache, 'This is your chance, Miss Frankland. My cousin will enlist you so he can boast he has an English woman fighting for Serbia.'

Even as she shook her head, she was rehearsing her military training: top horsewoman in the Women's Yeomanry, good marksman, superior to many of the men, elementary rifle drill and signalling. She would be a hero like her uncle.

Mikaiho said proudly, 'Every regiment will call you "Serbia's Joan of Arc" and my cousin will be a great General.'

Flattered, she pictured black boots, polished buttons as she marched in a column under the Serbian flag.

'I will speak on your behalf. I will tell you when to approach him.'

Fool that she was, she'd misunderstood when Mikaiho boasted he was to attend a vital regimental meeting, presuming he'd spoken to his cousin.

Ignoring Ellen's request to stop in the courtyard, Rajko drew up at the front of Dobro Majka. She would have to run through the cloister, along the side of the building and hope she'd not be noticed.

Fortunately, the rain had stopped, the wind blown itself out when Rajko held open the motorcar door. She shivered. Goose pimples pricked the nape of her neck. Rather than illuminating her path, the spluttering headlights distorted it. Rajko, leaned against the driver's door, offered her a cigarette. Delicate black hairs shone on the back of his hand.

She declined, ready for the privacy of her room where Gustav would bring hot water, so she could retire early. 'Thank you, sir, for your kindness.'

Smoke drifted between them. She guessed it was close to eight, so her friends would be crossing to the mess for cocoa.

She mustn't be seen. A wagon of wounded men rattled through the gate.

'Do you want to be a soldier in the Serbian army, Miss Frankland?'

'I was wrong, sir.'

'It is the greatest honour a country can grant its citizen.'

'Honour' had never occurred to her, though she supposed it was implicit in her uncle's heroism.

Rajko went on, 'I will tell Colonel Petrovic the fault is not yours.'

'I was silly.'

He took a drag of his cigarette. 'To the men, you are their "angel".'

'No, sir.'

'You do not look an angel.' He smiled, 'but you asked the colonel if you could serve as a soldier in the proudest of Serbia's regiments.'

Her feet squelched inside her boots as she squirmed, for however briefly, it was what she'd wanted. Now, she wanted to hide, not explore the reasons for getting in this mess.

'My suggestion is, that for a few moments you act as if you are a soldier.'

She was puzzled.

'When you held my hand, during that night you were not on duty, I expect you were tired. You may have been hungry or bored with so many sad stories.'

'No, sir,' she said quietly. He'd described his nightmares, always of his mother raped by soldiers while he, a five year old, watched from the hayloft. Many men witnessed similar events, he whispered, wiping his eyes.

Through cigarette smoke, he spoke intensely, 'You looked the part.'

She ran a hand down the sleeve of her tunic.

'Miss Frankland, you can slink from here or you can act like a soldier.'

'That's impossible.'

'Colonel Petrovic makes a point of brushing his uniform after battle, straightening his cap, wiping his boots.'

She supposed she could rub as much mud off her boots as possible. It would do no harm, particularly if she met Audrey before she'd time to wash and change. Pulling out her handkerchief, she bent down.

'Please! I have newspaper.'

While he unlocked the boot, she remembered bedraggled soldiers returning to barracks. The wounded rarely looked smart. Yet, on one occasion, she'd arrived at the barracks as Colonel Petrovic, covered in mud, was helped from his horse. His orderly had brushed his hat, his boots, removed his muddy greatcoat, so the colonel entered the building relatively clean. A touch exaggerated; nonetheless, she grasped a good impression mattered.

The leather yielded to her rubbing; the mud less thick. She glanced at Rajko's boots in the headlights. Ashamed of what she must look like, she wriggled her toes inside her soaked stockings. The women's corpses in the burned out village came into her mind along with the smell of the candle wax. She'd an urge to understand.

'It is not good for you to be a soldier,' he insisted.

Her mind remained with the women, as she twisted to scrub the muck from the back of a boot. The newspaper stank, as she attacked the other. Crumpling the paper, she gave the leather a final polish before handing it to Rajko.

While he put it back, she examined her culottes. She made a half-hearted effort to smooth the creases with the palm of her hand, but was wasting her time. No wonder the men laughed. How could she expect Mikaiho to speak up for her, when she was dressed like a tramp? She adjusted her belt so the buckle was in the centre.

Rajko handed her a clothes' brush. The wooden handle was worn smooth, faint colours in what may once have been a pattern. The bristles were soft, she doubted they would make much impression. She flicked at her left shoulder. A twig stuck in the bristles.

'Oh,' she gasped.

'Allow me.'

Rajko's hand was light on her shoulder. He gave the macintosh hem a slight tug, first on one side, then the other.

The strokes were hard. Her eyes filled up. She took a deep breath, slowly exhaled. When he handed it back, her throat was tight. Briskly she brushed her chest, aware of his eyes on her.

'Now, your hat.'

When she removed that, she was horrified to see that the stitching of the WMC badge was loose on one side and had disappeared altogether along the lower edge. Debris was trapped in the rim. She shook it, pulled out bits.

'Lieutenant Nis is not the man for a lady like you.'

She flushed, laughed. Relieved. 'I am engaged to be married.'

She began to brush the crown. Mikaiho had taught her Serbian, encouraged her to be a soldier because she'd confessed it was a childhood dream, but she wasn't as close to him as the wounded. Their pain, their vulnerability awoke a feeling in her, a willingness to give them the affection they needed.

She began, 'One day we went riding, Dr. Eyres should have come, but couldn't at the last moment... we came across a village...' She frowned, flattened the badge with her index finger.

'You and Lieutenant Nis went for a ride?'

'And his orderly...'

'Miss Frankland, I want to understand. You and Lieutenant Nis went for a ride.'

'Dr. Eyres arranged it with Colonel Petrovic, to discover the countryside, but at the last moment she couldn't come. His orderly was there...but we came to a village and the village had burned down. There was a man who had no eyes,' she made a circular gesture with her hands, 'and then...'

Still hanging on to the handle, she started to pass him the brush, '... I went into the church...'

'With the lieutenant?'

'He was already there. I could not push the door at first, but then... then I saw the bodies...' She clammed her lips tight, pressed a hand over her mouth. She mustn't cry. She shouldn't have spoken of it till she'd got home, back with

Edward, but she guessed Rajko would understand and could explain.

'Did Lieutenant Nis take you to this village?'

Pointing to the ground with the brush, she went on slowly, 'They were women. Their corpses lay in a heap by the door and near the candles where Mikaiho was standing. I wanted to bury the women, or ask soldiers from the barracks to dig their graves.'

'What was the name of the village?'

'He said the villagers would bury them.'

'He is worse than I thought.'

'It wasn't his fault.'

'Do you suppose Colonel Petrovic would suggest an officer show you such a place?'

'He didn't know it was there.' She'd kept silent for too long. It mattered she gave voice to those poor women.

Rajko threw his cigarette on the ground. She wasn't sure, but thought there were tears in his eyes. He didn't move.

She asked, 'How did it happen? Who killed them?'

'Have you heard of Shabatz?'

Some of the men talked of the border town, but she wasn't sure whether or not to believe the stories, which sounded too dreadful to be true. 'They say the people were murdered by the Austrians.'

'It was in revenge for the murder of their Archduke. What you saw was evidence of a revenge attack. Some villagers will have escaped, which is why Lieutenant Nis told you the women would be buried.'

She remembered Rajko's mother. Perhaps the women she'd seen had also been raped. She'd adjusted their skirts so that their bodies were fully covered.

'The brush, ma'am.'

She released it, forcing back tears.

'Have you a comb?' he said.

With shaking hands, she unfastened the button of her breast pocket. It had never occurred to her that the women had been raped. Gently, he took her hat from her. Her fingers scrambled in the pocket unable to locate the comb.

'Did you tell Matron?'

'One of the nurses should have come with me instead of Dr. Eyres. It was meant to be a treat. She didn't, because she'd wanted to talk to the doctor, and she'd end up in trouble, so I said nothing.'

'Did you tell your friends?'

'They might have become frightened.'

'There is no reason for the English to be alarmed. It is Serb women who're punished. However, I advise you to avoid Lieutenant Nis.'

With a sigh, she extricated her comb. Pulling out hair pins, she wished now she'd questioned Mikaiho. Tangles snared the comb and it took time for her hair to fall loose on her shoulders. She wondered if the men had fled, or if they'd been away fighting. And they were soldiers. Enemy soldiers had raped and killed women.

Taking the hat from Rajko, she said, 'It was a terrible thing to do.'

'You understand why it is hard for a woman to be a soldier.'

She twisted her hair, snapped her hat on as securely as she could without a pin. On the other side of the cloister, in the courtyard, orderlies were shouting to each other as they unloaded the wagon.

She put out her hand. 'Thank you, sir.'

'It has been my pleasure.'

As she walked through the cloisters in boots, stockings and socks that were still wet, she determined to be dignified. The escapade had been a disaster, but some good had come of it.

The next morning while Ellen was having breakfast, Matron's orderly told her to report at eight sharp. The other girls asked what was going on, but Ellen didn't tell them. She ate her porridge and drank her tea as though she wasn't worried. Audrey ignored her.

Though it was dark, birds were singing as she approached Matron's tent. At the entrance she called out, 'Matron,' more loudly than she intended so she sounded as though she was giving an order, rather than keeping an appointment for a reprimand. She'd no idea what to say. She'd avoided trouble at school, pitying girls who waited outside the headmistress's study.

Though yesterday's storm had stopped, the wind had picked up, threatening to whip out the guy ropes. She hesitated, not knowing whether to walk straight to the table or to wait. At least she hadn't been summoned last night. When she saw the mud on her face in the looking glass, she was further dismayed at how she must have appeared to the officers. Wiping her boots on the edge of the reed mat, she waited for Matron to speak. She was sitting at a table on a yellow painted chair with a sheepskin draped over her shoulders. A paraffin heater stood at the far end, next to the camp bed. Matron covered a letter she was writing with blotting paper.

She demanded, 'Where is your hat?'

Trying not to appear intimidated, Ellen managed a smile, pushed back her shoulders. 'My hat, ma'am?'

She'd washed her hair, but the hat was beyond repair, she'd have to apply for another. 'I'm not on duty till half past eight, ma'am.'

Matron spelled out each syllable. 'You are seeing **me** and that is being on duty. Is that understood, Miss Frankland?'

Ellen took a step backwards. She would have to borrow one. 'I'm sorry, ma'am. Shall I fetch it?'

'Not now. Remember for the future. I don't have time to waste, even if you do, or so Colonel Petrovic tells me. Come. Stand in front of me.'

Ellen inched forward.

Matron picked up the lantern on the table and held it in front, slightly to the side of her, as though trying to see Ellen more clearly. Ellen peered into the depth of the tent to the unmade camp bed. Books and clothes were scattered across it. A dressing gown trailed over the wooden locker. Matron didn't tolerate that level of untidiness in their rooms.

'Look at me when I'm talking to you.'

Ellen glanced at Matron's narrowed lips, the expression in her eyes, difficult to make out. Matron put the lantern to the right of the blotting paper, her finger catching the edge of a silver photograph frame. 'Right up to the desk.'

When Ellen stood so close her tunic jacket touched the desk, Matron said, 'Now! Miss. I am waiting for an explanation.'

Ellen shuffled. This was worse than Colonel Petrovic laughing at her. In desperation she tried to distract herself. She wondered who the photograph was of. Grace who knew Matron from their days at St. Barts' said she never walked out with a man, not even when she was young.

'I'm sorry, ma'am.'

'What are you sorry for?'

'I will return home straight away.'

'That will not do at all. I took you on against my better judgement. You come from a privileged, protected background. If Lady Alice hadn't pointed out you were recommended by Dr. Eyres, I wouldn't have considered you. Spoiled, with no nursing experience, turned down by the Women's Yeomanry. What on earth did you think you were doing?'

Stung by the injustice, because she'd been too young for the Women's Yeomanry, she said, 'I'd some time off.'

A group of women walked past giggling. Ellen blushed. The worst thing was, everyone would know. They would cluster around, just as they had when she'd been sent to St Catherine's as a weekly boarder after Mama died.

'It is wholly unacceptable that you approach the Colonel. Why did you ask to become a soldier?'

'It was wrong.'

'Answer my question.'

'My uncle died a hero in the Boer War.'

'Did you wish to die, or be a hero?'

'Serbia will be occupied and the men talk of how we, the English, have let them down.'

'Do you still wish to be a soldier?'

'It was an impulse. I felt sorry for the woman soldier whose husband was killed, I think.'

'Colonel Petrovic says it was a schoolgirl prank. It's very well wanting to be heroic, but hard work is damned more effective. You're a good worker. You've proved a reliable orderly. Of course, the men like you. You're young and attentive, but beware of your emotions, miss. They let you down.'

'I'll go home.'

'You'll write to Colonel Petrovic and apologise. I suggest you do the same to Dr. Eyres who's most distressed. In future, you'll not fraternise with any officer unless in the course of your duties. Is that understood?'

'Yes, ma'am.'

Ellen looked at the grooves on the desk. Of course, she'd known it was wrong to go to the colonel, but fraternising she interpreted as kissing, being intimate. Not for one moment had she thought chatting to the officers was fraternising. She, and most of the other women, talked to them.

There was a stirring behind her and the flame in the lantern flattened. An Austrian orderly, wielding a tray, stormed in, dropping the tray on the table with a clatter, knocking over the photograph frame. The teacup rattled in its saucer, and tea from the pot spilled onto the plate, wetting buttered slices of bread.

Ellen suppressed a giggle.

The orderly spoke in German. 'Shall I fetch another cup and saucer for the lady?'

Matron frowned.

Ellen translated.

The orderly looked at Ellen for the reply. 'She says, "No thank you."'

He bowed and reversed out of the tent. Ellen righted the photograph frame, managing to glimpse two formal rows of boys and girls with what she took to be parents in the centre of the front row. She half-expected Matron to shout at her.

'As you continue your duties, use your intelligence as well as your emotions. That will be all.'

At the door to the tent, Ellen listened to the wind whistling through guy ropes. She would be better off at home. She longed for Edward's arms around her, for him to reassure her all was well, but, of course, it wasn't. And how could she avoid talking to the men? It was part of her job. Bare headed, she shivered. She ran towards the operating tent. She'd time before she went on duty to apologise to Audrey.

Chapter Eleven

Courtyard in Dobro Majka October 1915

Cloud hung like a shroud over the courtyard, the buildings and the encampment, mist settling on the windscreen as soon as the wipers were switched off. Stefan adjusted his cap while Dragan walked round to open the door. As some wagons arrived from the front line, others were carrying patients back home. Oxen and bullocks stirred between shafts, sniffing the air. Orderlies called to each other in their different languages, some keen to unload, others slow, smoking, anxious to pick up news about the fighting, the casualties, the whereabouts of the enemy.

As Stefan stepped onto the courtyard, he was thinking of Stamenka. Since the telephone call last night from Tomislav's adjutant, he'd pictured her over and over again, at the foot of the steps to their house, wearing the peasant dress she insisted on, her hair pulled from her face, lips in a line.

'No, Louise. I cannot possibly leave my mother-in-law.' Spoken, no doubt in the accents of the country.

And if Stefan were to question her, she would assure him the priest told her to be loyal to her mother-in-law, or some neighbour, who'd once broken with tradition and a calamity had befallen her. Surely, all that mattered was that he'd arranged for her and Mitar to be removed from the fighting? It was true the American journalist was also to include Stefan's mother, but his brother, who lived in the compound, would ensure she was taken to their home village. And what would Louise think, who'd travelled out of her way? She'd always been kind to Stamenka, encouraged her to try on elegant French dresses, to read novels in addition to the Holy Scriptures and Serbian poetry.

If duties had permitted, Stefan would have driven through the night to reprimand his wife. Yet, he was not to be thwarted. He would do his utmost to persuade Matron, Ellen and Audrey to take his son. The government had organised the evacuation of cadets to Corfu. If the women would accompany a small unit, Mitar could be included. Foreign women would accomplish what Stamenka refused.

Dragan slammed the door shut. Despite the drizzle, there was a keenness to the air Stefan loved. Having ordered Dragan to give a final polish to his boots, he took a deep breath, eyes on the entrance to the kitchen, his thoughts on the request he was about to make.

Dragan said, 'They're returning to Orasac.'

Normally Stefan would turn, acknowledge his men, wish them well. This afternoon, he'd other priorities.

As Stefan stepped into the kitchen, a prisoner-of-war was throwing logs on the stove in the corner, as though stoking hell. The room was warm, Stefan presumed from the baking, a batch of bread stacked on the counter. The poor light from the window was supplemented by candles in alcoves and lanterns, one hanging from the ceiling at the far end of the room near the pantry, the other above the long wooden table. Dragan banged the door shut, clinking the crockery on the rack.

Seated at the head of the table, Matron invited him to sit to her right. He handed Dragan his cap. He was surprised he'd become fond of her. She reminded him of ash saplings along the hedgerows. Resilient. Able to survive despite competition. Though she was dressed in uniform, Audrey and Ellen wore the day clothes in which they visited Rajko a year ago. All three looked cheerful. He felt outmanoeuvred, didn't know why.

Ellen was unrecognisable as the woman who'd interrupted his campaign meeting two days ago. Her dress was almost certainly silk. He'd bought one of a similar material for Stamenka when they were first married. Ellen's waist was much narrower than her uniform suggested. A panel of cream lace accentuated the low neckline. His anger with Stamenka reignited; she could have looked equally striking. When she'd not approved of that first dress, he'd asked Louise's advice and treated her to one a little more modest. Honey-coloured silk with embroidery on the bodice, tight waist to accentuate a soft, flowing skirt. But no, she spurned that, just as she turned aside the military escort.

He removed his gloves and unfastening the greatcoat buttons, concentrated on what to say. He needed to persuade the women to delay their return home for two or three weeks. Matron and Ellen would agree he was almost sure; Audrey he found less compliant.

Dragan helped him remove his coat and lay it across the opposite end of the table.

Matron said, 'Is the evacuation of the army going well?'

The situation felt unreal. He could only use empty phrases like those of Glisic. 'The men are grateful for all that you have done,' he said.

Matron was frowning. 'We're putting on a final concert for the men.'

It explained the informal wear. 'Very thoughtful,' he responded, hoping he'd not be expected to attend.

Matron continued, 'It's hard to credit the Austrians will kill wounded men in hospital. Some are too sick to move, as you know.'

'We're their enemy, ma'am,' he said.

Ellen nodded and he turned away, afraid his fascination might be noticed.

He took the chair Matron had indicated, facing Audrey and Ellen.

With fingers under her chin, Audrey said, 'The men can't grasp the basics of medical care. Cleanliness is vital in the early stages of amputation. They won't get that at home, will they?'

He disliked her tone of superiority and yet yearned for Stamenka to sound a little like her.

The orderly was adding another log to the stove.

Stefan said, 'The orders come from the government, Dr. Eyres, and are for the men's benefit. The enemy can be ruthless.'

Of the two women, Audrey, looked the most English. Her skin was white as though she didn't see daylight, her hair drained of colour like corn stubble. She was slight, appearing less hardy than either Stamenka or Ellen; yet capable of amputatations.

She went on, 'No doubt you'll say that it's beyond your jurisdiction, but in my opinion it's wrong we're not allowed to remain. After all, the Women's Medical Corps has no political affiliation.'

Their unit was British for God's sake. Dobro Majka treated his regiment, other military or prisoners-of-war when necessary, but he didn't argue, uttering platitudes about their 'devotion' and the Serbs being 'forever in their debt', while praying they would agree to his request as soon as he voiced it.

'You'll be glad to return home,' he began. He was disappointed when Ellen responded with enthusiasm that she would. Two days ago she'd volunteered to join the army; she'd have no leave for at least a year.

'Shall we have tea, ma'am?' Ellen said.

Matron addressed him, 'Gustav is making lime tea. Is that to your liking, Colonel?' Her eyes were watchful.

'That will be delightful.'

Ellen moved from the table and took porcelain teacups and saucers from the shelf above the draining board. She moved with the grace of a lady.

With an effort he turned to Matron. 'And you, ma'am, will you be pleased to return to England?'

'I'll never forget these times. I confess when we came out here I thought, forgive me Stefan, Colonel… that you, the Serbs, were a primitive people, but no, that was my ignorance. I have learned to admire the brave soldiers who suffer their losses with smiles.'

She'd come to love them, so might be persuaded. He glanced at Ellen placing cups and saucers on a wooden tray. Strands of hair lay on her neck beyond the confines of her combs. He wanted to stroke her neck. Mikaiho had asked permission to marry Ellen, now, he could understand the attraction.

'I think not all?' He raised his eyebrows at Matron. She'd told him, in confidence, how Sibin, a patient with a high temperature, had locked her in the pantry, how she'd panicked because she was claustrophobic.

The fragrance of lime reminded him of childhood, his mother drinking tea in front of the fire with a sister or one of the village women. Damn Stamenka. It wasn't his fault the car couldn't take his mother and he'd been sure Stamenka would go, that it would make up for the American journalist not turning up. Damn, damn, damn.

He allowed himself to feel a regret, he usually suppressed. Surrounded by these women, he admitted, acknowledged that the sixteen year old he'd married hadn't become the wife he wanted. Was that the root of his unease, this state of mind, which yearned for peace? Was it that simple?

He said to Ellen, 'Allow me.' Stumbling to his feet, he strode across the kitchen and picked up the tray.

'Thank you, Colonel,' she said, 'The cups are rather full.' She spoke in Serbian, her accent more German than Slavic, but a good effort nonetheless.

He held the tray level as he walked, lowering it in front of Matron. He sat down while Ellen placed a drink in front of each of them, passing the tray behind her head to Gustav, before rejoining them.

'Why do you wish to see us?' Matron said.

'Before you got here, we were trying to guess,' Audrey said, 'but we haven't come up with a thing.'

Stefan smoothed the lapels of his tunic jacket. They wanted to help; it was a step in the right direction.

Matron removed her spectacles, rubbing them with a white handkerchief. Audrey leaned forward, her chin resting on the edge of her fingers. Ellen pushed her chair away from the table and fiddled with a turquoise comb in her hair. He hesitated.

'I am thinking of the future,' he began.

'The Austrians must give assurances that patients will be treated as though they were their own,' Matron said firmly.

'Assurances may be given, but when you and our army have departed, who will ensure the Austrians keep their word?'

'Nor must we forget the wounded who're leaving,' Audrey interrupted, 'Did you see the wagon in the courtyard, Colonel?'

He didn't want to think about them.

'The point is,' he ploughed on, 'when the enemy crosses the river, no Serb is safe.'

He slapped his hand on the table, tea spilled, spoons rattled.

Matron removed her spectacles, wiped them again. 'Colonel, are you exaggerating a little? It is a difficult time.'

Was he? If it got him what he wanted he would, but the women were unaware of the barbarity of the enemy.

'Ma'am, I want to tell you about our cadets. The government has a plan to get them out of the country.'

Audrey sniffed. She reminded him of a snuffling boar in the woods around Orasac. She said, 'If that's the case, I'm surprised you don't agree to Austrian and German demands.'

'That's in the hands of the politicians.'

He picked up his cup, savouring the fragrance, glancing over the rim at Ellen.

As he sipped, Audrey said, 'I cannot believe that either the Austrians or the Germans will murder Serbs in cold blood, that's what you're saying, isn't it?'

Ellen's voice shook. 'Why not? They killed the people in Shabatz.'

Even though she was on his side, he didn't want a discussion about the rights and wrongs of revenge killings. He glanced towards the open window, drawn by the sound of voices. The lower pane was steamed up, but through the mist, single droplets chased each other. He thought of his men returning to Orasac.

Audrey twisted to face Ellen. 'Shabatz, Ljubovia and the rest were wrong. Of course, of course. I know innocent Serbs were killed, but I don't accept that a victorious army will do such things.'

Quietly he said, 'I have a son.' He'd their attention. Even the orderly loading a trolley with beakers, stopped.

'Thirteen-year-old Mitar,' Matron said, 'He's not in danger, is he?'

Audrey tapped the edge of the table with her fingers. 'Where does he live? Can't his mother keep him safe?'

Stefan pressed his fingers together. 'You've served Serbia well, and I've no right to ask you to do more, but yesterday my

138

friend, General Stavisto, sent a military escort to accompany my wife and son out of the country. I'd written advising her of this. The General's wife, who is known to my wife, was in the motorcar.' He looked at Matron. 'My wife turned the vehicle away.'

Scratching her cheek, Matron asked, 'Was she frightened? Perhaps your letter didn't make the situation clear. It can be difficult for women cosseted at home.'

He barely gave her the chance to finish. 'What explanation did she need? We're Serbs, war is part of our lives. For you, it is hard to accept, but it's been our reality for centuries.'

The breeze gusted chill through the window. Men's voices urged oxen to move, hooves clattered and the wheels of a wagon creaked. He ought to have spoken to his men. Misjudgement caused by anxiety.

Stefan leaned back. 'Mitar, my son, is too young to be a cadet.' He pictured him last summer, dark and scrawny like Stamenka's father, walking between them. A dreamer, not a soldier. If he'd been alone with Matron, he could admit he wanted his son included in a legitimate unit so he needn't discuss the matter with Tomislav.

'Maybe your wife didn't want to leave you behind,' Ellen said. Her eyes, their pupils black, met his for a moment. Goose bumps pricked his spine. She picked up her teacup.

'A soldier's wife accepts her husband may not survive, what matters, is my son.'

Cocooned in his greatcoat, Dragan appeared to have nodded off. The trolley squeaked, the crockery rattled as the orderly began to push it. Ellen's chair legs scraped as she got up to open the door. Stefan took a deep breath in an effort to stop the pain in his stomach, aware he'd to watch his words as carefully as a politician.

'He'd be safer with his mother,' Matron said.

Ellen shook her head. 'I doubt it. The women in Shabatz were killed along with the men. I heard, sir, the women were violated.'

'Now you're being melodramatic. We're talking of the Austrians and Germans.' Audrey glowered at each of them.

Another strand of hair tumbled onto Ellen's shoulder. He swallowed. 'It's true women are violated.' He began strongly, much as he used to at Military Academy when leading a debate. 'I'd rather my wife ...' His hands began to tremble. '... was dead, than an enemy touch her...her body.' It was easier to focus on Matron who was sympathetic. 'But it's not our fear that our city will be treated like Shabatz. The enemy chooses one village, maybe two...' Barely able to whisper, he carried on '...for their reprisals. However, as far as my son is concerned...'

'So, you'd like us to take your son out of the country along with a unit of cadets?' Audrey spoke as though a nasty smell filtered through her nostrils and the effort of speaking increased its intensity.

'His mother refuses?' Matron said.

'She wishes to remain with my mother.'

Matron nodded. 'She has a kind heart. However, you are understandably worried about your son and would like Dr. Eyres and Miss Frankland...'

'And you also, ma'am.'

'I'm afraid that's out of the question. My youngest brother, from my mother's second marriage, has enlisted and I'd very much like to see him before he sails for France.'

'It would be wonderful if you could persuade him not to go,' Audrey said, 'He's only eighteen.'

He'd forgotten the brother. From what Matron told him, she was both protective and proud of her brother's patriotism. Audrey didn't understand. 'I'm sorry,' he said sadly. The bile in his stomach stirred and he pressed with his arm to calm the agitation. 'It will take two or three weeks to take Mitar and the cadets out of Serbia, through Albania to the port of Durazzo to sail to Corfu.'

'How many cadets?' Audrey asked.

'Thirty.'

'Will it be dangerous, sir?' Ellen said.

And she'd volunteered to be a soldier. 'Women are better than men in these situations,' he said.

Ellen shook her head and turned to look out of the window. He didn't know what he'd do if they refused.

140

Ellen said to Audrey, 'I was looking forward to seeing Edward, and you'll be pleased to be back in Glasgow with Douglas, won't you?'

Audrey said, 'We're talking of two or three weeks.' In profile, there was a heaviness around her jaw, which accentuated her determination and again he wished Stamenka were more like her. She went on, 'We'll find it hard at home after this freedom.'

'We've no experience of cadets or thirteen year old boys.'

'You'd no experience of bringing men from the casualty station by mule, nor of an operating theatre. You won't get a chance like this once you're married to Edward.'

He began to feel more optimistic, searching for a way to develop Audrey's support. This Ellen was very different from the one two days ago. Something had affected her and he didn't blame Mikaiho despite Rajko's report. And yet, if she were his wife, he'd not allow her on such a venture.

A picture of Stamenka shaking her head at Louise, her, 'No thank you,' as she turned her back on the motorcar impelled him to continue, 'You once asked to join our regiment, Miss Frankland and that was inappropriate, but it made me think you were on our side.'

Audrey interrupted Ellen's attempt to speak. 'The least said about that the better, but I, for one, am game. Where will we sleep?'

'The cadets are used to bedding down in fields, in hedges.'

'Well, we're not.' Audrey tapped the table with a finger.

'You're interested? That's eased my mind.' As he looked into Ellen's eyes, he doubted his ability to push her further. She was meant for an English drawing room, not a war zone.

'Edward wanted me to go home last Christmas.'

Damn Stamenka, putting him through this. Why couldn't she do as he told her? He'd take Mitar himself. Mikaiho could stay with him during the fighting. No. Mitar mustn't be anywhere near trenches.

Looking at Ellen's hands, he said, ' It was you I was counting on. Matron and Dr. Eyres are the best in their fields, but you've inspired the men. You've learned our language. The men boast of their teaching and your learning fast. I don't intend to embarrass you, ma'am,' he turned to Matron before continuing, 'but they know you disarmed Sibin. He'd an axe, hadn't he?' He hoped Matron wouldn't be upset at his breach of a confidence.

'A meat cleaver. It was small and he was delirious.' Ellen shrugged.

'He's taller than me. Broad shouldered and mental.'

The tap dripped. No one spoke till the door banged when the orderly wheeled back the trolley.

'You asked about danger. I'm not about to send my son to his death. I know the fathers of the cadets, I'm responsible to them. Further more, I'm indebted to all the women in this hospital. You're our allies. Even if I was the most hard-hearted of men and considered only the Serb cause, nothing would cause it more damage than two British women killed in a foolhardy escapade.'

It occurred to him, Mitar might not like these women. That he might miss his mother. To his knowledge, the boy had never slept outside the family bedroom. He brushed aside concern that he was making a mistake. If Stamenka wouldn't, he'd take responsibility.

'It's up to you, Miss Frankland. If you want to be reunited with your fiancé as soon as possible, please say no. There may be others who can help,' Matron said.

Audrey snapped, 'He spoils you.' Addressing Stefan, she said, 'Edward didn't like her descriptions of the wounded. He asked her to spare him the details.'

Spending a year in a military hospital didn't sound like spoiling. Certainly, he thought, she needed a proper man, not someone who flinched at description. 'Well, I don't know. Perhaps, ma'am, as you say, there may be other women.'

'I'm sorry, sir,' Ellen said. 'I was foolish to volunteer as a soldier. I've thought about my reasons and they're complicated, but I've reflected on what's demanded of the men, and how comfortable my own life has been in comparison. I just don't know if I'm strong enough to do as you ask.'

Matron sipped her tea.

Audrey said, 'What on earth do you mean, "strong enough"?'

He said, 'The lads will do all you ask. If you can get hold of tents for yourselves, you can sleep comfortably. Or perhaps, you're thinking of the walk each day?'

'The woman-soldier was resilient, sir.'

Rajko had mentioned her. 'She wasn't born that way. She became "strong" because she loved her country.'

Putting down her cup Matron said, 'I agree with Colonel Petrovic, you've qualities that make you suitable for the challenge, but, be that as it may, you're at liberty to say no.'

Audrey said, 'We can arrange our own transport. Do you think the Berry hospital will help, ma'am?'

'They may have tents. We can provide medical supplies, some food, blankets.'

'Come on, Ellen!' Audrey said.

'You know the terrain, sir. You know your son and the cadets. Will they allow foreign women to take them away from their homes?'

He'd nearly got her. 'Mitar speaks English and some cadets have been outside Serbia with their parents. They've been on military camp.'

'Do you think your wife would travel with us?' Ellen asked.

'Sadly, she won't leave my old mother.'

Audrey sniffed again. 'Colonel, Ellen is distressed because Serbia is losing the war.' She placed a hand on Ellen's arm, 'You'll feel happier if we do all we can to help. In two weeks time, we'll be in Corfu. Edward and Douglas can wait two weeks.'

'I'm sorry to make such a fuss, sir, but just one further thing.'

'What's that?'

'Mitar's mother must agree.'

Stefan didn't know whether Stamenka would give permission and he'd no intention of asking her. 'Of course. I understand.'

'Very well, I'll go.' She sighed. 'It will be an adventure to tell Edward.'

*

143

Rain was streaming down the sides of the wagon, when Stefan returned to the courtyard. The men had improvised shelter by piecing together tent canvas, an oilskin cape and an army mackintosh. Two years ago, wounded, lying on a stretcher, worried he would be thrown to the ground, he was transported through cobbled streets to the hospital. He recalled the pain in his thigh, fear of losing his leg, felt it again.

A moment later, he was shaking the left hand of Danilo, a student officer. 'Your family will be glad to see you.'

To Hadijic, known as the cross-eyed one, 'Serbia is proud of all her sons.'

Hadijic shook his head, 'What use will I be when I can no longer carry hay?'

To Bogdan, a factory worker in Nis, 'You have done well, brother.'

'I hear Nis has fallen, sir.'

'We're not yet defeated,' Stefan said.

To Sibin, the infamous Sibin, 'Your family will be glad to see you.'

Sibin turned away and Stefan couldn't blame him. A liability now. Thank God, his own wound had healed.

Chapter Twelve

Belgrade, October 1915

Stefan could see neither moon nor stars as he climbed the familiar road from the park, through the new cemetery and up to the bluff above Kalemegdan fortress. It was a favourite walk, which he'd first taken with his father, later with Stamenka, and more recently with her and Mitar. It was foolish to be out on the eve of an attack, but he needed to think. It was a good place to start, among the spirits of the dead.

Wanting to be alone, he'd put on his mackintosh and tucked his electric torch into a pocket, insisting Dragan remain in headquarters in the army chapel at the foot of the fortress. They'd walked miles during the course of the day so Stefan could examine the most effective defensive positions with his engineers. Dragan, physically tired, was persuaded to retire.

Stefan paused to watch candle flames rising and falling on a gravestone some yards away, where two women kept vigil. Their voices soothed. Squeaking bats scooped tracks through the shadows. As a child he'd raced through the cemetery, afraid ghosts would waylay him. His father had explained such fears were women's superstitions. He continued on, thinking of his wedding night, the last time he saw his father.

Stamenka was undressing behind the screen, while his father in the adjoining room, began a drunken assault on his mother. Bellows of rage. Slashes of belt on flesh. Her pleas, sobs. Incensed with shame and fury, Stefan strode into his parents' room, wrestled for the belt with his father, before dragging him across the courtyard and dumping him outside the gates. That his father never returned, justified his behaviour.

As the ground rose, Stefan's pace quickened. The air smelled damp, earthy. He'd never expected to miss his father, didn't for several years, but as he grew older, so had his appreciation. His father had taught him to enjoy commercial Belgrade with its cigarette, silk, soap and candle factories, its sawmills, the stink from breweries and slaughterhouses built by the English. A village boy, Stefan viewed cities with suspicion, but his father led him along the quays, the Customs House, the Turkish shops. He skipped behind his father, among the smells of the charcoal brazier in front of the *kafkana*, watching camels loaded with cotton from the East, donkeys laden with salt from Roumania, pigs and horses for export.

Leaving the cemetery, he began to climb the hill. In the distance, a wagon rattled along cobblestones, defying the curfew. Why had Stamenka disobeyed him? He'd been humiliated when Tomislav's adjutant telephoned. Detected pity in the man's, 'She wouldn't leave your mother.' At Stefan's next meeting with Tomislav, the General joked, 'It's the first time a woman's refused to ride in my motorcar,' waving aside Stefan's apologies. Nonetheless, the incident reminded him of the evening at Andric's homestead.

As he left the last of the gravestones, the steep, cliff-side path became bounded by a wall, an iron hand rail inserted at intervals. He skidded on loose stones. He resisted the temptation to pull out his electric torch. No point in drawing attention. The velvet air calmed. The distant voices of men carousing, probably soldiers, took him back to accompanying his father to St. Petka's, the ancient church within the fortress, listening to the monks' chanting, feeling they must have grown old with the stones, that they remained singing forever.

After a while, Stefan paused to look back. The centuries old citadel dominated the darkness. How many times had it been destroyed and rebuilt? Powerful German guns wouldn't be the last to attack. If he were to be killed in battle, he would choose here, Belgrade, the city in which he became a man, rather than the heroic Field of Blackbirds in Old Serbia.

He stepped onwards.

Beneath him, the rush of water where the Sava and the Danube met, resonated strong and tumultuous. As a child, Stefan felt out of place. His father settled in the Turkish quarter because he was a craftsman and its vitality suited his business. Their relatives in Orasac considered the Turks hated oppressors, even though the Serbs had been an independent nation for several years. He didn't want Mitar to suffer that disorientation.

He walked slowly, enjoying the peace. The shadows shifted and the path veered sharply so the easterly breeze now brushed his cheeks, ruffled his hair. The Cathedral clock struck ten.

If only Stamenka had accepted Tomislav's generosity. He remembered the texture of her hand on the afternoon of their betrothal. Soft, a little sweaty, as she wrapped her fingers around his so he felt her bones, imagined her flesh caressing his, when the time came. They strolled in the shimmering autumn light to the end of the village, where she showed him part of her dowry, a walnut tree. They ambled further, he swinging their arms in time to the love song, *Ruza! Ruza!* dancing in his head.

'Have you been to the city?' he asked.

'I have been on a train.'

'We'll sell your tree and we'll build our house in my father's compound.' He didn't tell her they lived among Turks, not wanting to alarm her.

'Will we have children?'

'Would you like that?'

'Many.'

He'd been careful they didn't have one every year like his mother, who grew exhausted, losing more than survived. But their first son, Dusan, had died after four days and Stamenka had several miscarriages before the birth of Mitar. Their daughter died of typhus at eighteen months, just before the first campaign against the Bulgars in 1912.

Last summer in this place, he'd stretched his hand for Mitar to hold, but the boy lowered his eyes, skipped past him to walk with his mother. The rebuttal clouded Stefan's day. The ride on the tram, the stroll through the zoo, the buying of Italian ice cream from the vendor in front of the clock tower, counted for little in the midst of disappointment. He drew apart from them, pretended to admire the river below.

In the evening when the child was in bed, Stamenka explained, 'You're a distant figure to him. You've been away a long time.' He wanted to weep.

For the last few metres to the top of the slope, he concentrated on keeping his feet on the path. A fall wouldn't be fatal. To be wounded by an enemy bayonet was heroic, to be carried out of the city on a stretcher because he lost his footing during an unnecessary walk in the dark, madness.

At the summit, on the bluff where he'd stood with Stamenka and Mitar that summer before the war, he stopped. His breath whitened the darkness. He crouched, picked up a stone, felt its edges through his gloves before throwing it down towards the river. Not far enough. Three more stones. The last needed the deep rotation of his arm before he heard the splash of the Danube. He smiled as he stood facing north, looking beyond German guns, to the Panonian Plain where Europe began. He prayed that one day, his son would experience the peace he yearned for.

Beneath him the silver shadows of the Danube; its water lapping the sandy banks; the occasional drop of rain on his face. On the opposite bank, the lights of the gunboats, the thud of artillery being manoeuvred into position. Heavy rain might hamper the Germans for a day at most; for his men, it would make the digging of trenches more treacherous, the walls more liable to collapse, the base to fill with water.

For ten minutes he listened to the wind raising the waters, smacking the quayside, stirring the bare branches of birch and chestnut.

The next day, the setting sun coloured the old walls of the compound a steely white, as Mikaiho drove across the courtyard of Stefan's home. Stefan wound down the window and ordered the boy, who was about to close the gates for the night, to wait till he left. The cobblestones were black after the day's rain, though by now it was clear and the cold wind blew straw in waves from the stables.

Having stepped out of the car, he instructed Mikaiho to keep the engine running. He straightened his cap, smoothed the lapels of his greatcoat. He must appear businesslike; mustn't digress from the task. There was no activity in the courtyard. Oven doors closed. His mother would be in the old building with Woislav and his family. The windows to his house were shuttered. He whistled the barking dog in its kennel to be silent.

On the landing at the top of the stone steps, he heard Mitar chattering. When the boy was seven or eight, they were close though Mitar spoke little. Stefan felt it a companionable silence. As he opened the door, he smelled lavender and polish. The candles, in the alcoves and on the table, shrank in the draught. He slammed the door. Ashamed, he realised he was trying to frighten Stamenka. Sweat ran across the furrows on his brow and he brushed at it with the back of his gloved hands.

Mitar sat on one side of the long table, his mother at its head, on a low stool by the side of a tapestry loom. They looked up as he stood without moving. He wanted to whisk the lad into the car. No fuss. No argument. Stamenka gazed at him, her hand cupped over her mouth, her tapestry needle gleamed on her cheek. Stefan couldn't decide whether to remove his gloves or put them on the table as usual. He kept them on. Mitar who appeared to be whittling a dragon's head, dropped his knife, which clattered to the floor.

In a shaft of horror, Stefan knew that in a few days time a German officer could be poised where he was standing, wearing a greatcoat, boots and cap, feeling his revolver in its holster with his forearm. Stamenka's hands fell to her lap, though she continued to stare at him. He cleared his throat.

Last night he'd intended to come home to sleep, for though Tomislav's car was no longer available, he thought he could persuade Stamenka to let Mitar leave Belgrade with the cadets and suggest she and his mother went back to Orasac. Instead, after his walk, he talked and ate apples with Tomislav in his quarters before taking breakfast at the *kafkana*. The day had been spent preparing his troops for their part in the defence of the city.

During the drive, he'd considered several ways of telling Stamenka their son was to leave Serbia. He contemplated instructing Mikaiho to remove him, so he needn't face her. He thought of ordering Mitar to the car without any explanation, but worried the lad would refuse, wait for his mother's permission. Though he was doing his best for the boy, a part of him was taking revenge for her disobedience.

'The enemy is on the other side of the river,' he said as he marched down the length of the table, the heels of his boots resounding on the wooden floor. He stopped at the back of Mitar's seat. The child's hair almost touched his shoulders. The women must cut it, or the cadets would tease him.

'We are good people.' She fiddled with her tapestry needle.

'The government has left the city. I wrote to you.'

'Your mother says the army will save us.'

'What does my mother know! The army is leaving the country. Only a few units remain.'

He saw Mitar sneak a glance beneath half-closed lids, before jumping from his chair and scrambling under the table for his knife. Stamenka's shadow flickered on the table where he'd sat.

'I've brought the motor car.'

'I didn't get a letter.'

She was lying. 'The lad must come with me now. The Germans won't be long.'

'You sent a car, but Louise said there was no room for your mother and we'd no time to prepare.'

'It was General Stavisto's car. You should have been honoured he was prepared to have you driven all the way to the coast. You would have been with Louise. That was better than the American journalist.'

Mitar picked up his knife and was looking at his mother.

'He's not ready.' She half-rose from her stool.

'He must come as he is.'

'Give me a few moments to pack.'

He strode at her, shouted in her face, 'I arranged your rescue and you spurned it.'

Stamenka pulled away, dropped the needle, covered her face with her hands. Outside the dog began to bark again. Tears were rolling down Mitar's cheeks. Stamenka clenched her fingers and after a moment said, 'Sit down, child. It will be all right.'

Stefan turned from her, marched to the hearth, shouted into the wall, 'He's to come with me. Now.'

She got up from the loom, moved towards the table, her arms outstretched as though to embrace him and Mitar. He took a step sideways, unaccountably afraid of her touch.

With her arms around Mitar, she said, 'It's warm here, but it will be cold in the mountains. Why don't you take him tomorrow when I've had time to look out jumpers and blankets?'

He ought to have sent Mikaiho; she wouldn't argue with him.

As she released Mitar, he climbed back on the chair, put the knife on the table. He pulled out a miniature bronze sword, jabbed it, as though towards an imaginary adversary. Back and forth, back and forth. Stefan almost succumbed; Mitar was a child. If he remained with his mother, Woislav would take them to their home village.

'The army will provide him with all he needs.' There was no point telling her, he would be part of a unit being led by two English women.

'His hair's too long for the army.'

'We have barbers.'

In his imagination, he saw the Bulgarian girl, Mitar's age, in the gutter after the battle of Bregalnica. She lay screaming, her leg cut off below the knee.

Mitar placed the sword on the table and picked up a book. Probably about his hero, Prince Marko. The child was too romantic to be a soldier. The sooner he was away from the fighting and out of the country, the greater chance he would grow into an educated, cultivated man.

'You're not a good wife.' The words snapped from his mouth. She lowered her head. All he wanted to do, was whip Mitar from the room, down the steps, bundle him into the motor car and speed down the street, leaving Stamenka and her loyalty.

He tried to be jovial. 'Come on, Mitar! Let's get away from this war. Say goodbye to your mother.'

Mitar turned a page with his sword, his eyes on Stamenka.

'Where are you taking him?'

'To the place you refused.'

Mitar sat as rigid as the chair's back.

Stamenka stretched an arm towards Stefan. He'd a memory of her gliding towards him in a cream silk gown, of her smelling of roses and geraniums. Of light streaming through the windows of the sleeping quarters. Of her lying beneath him, sticky with semen and sweat. His throat was dry and he found it hard to swallow.

'Please, Stefan. Tomorrow. He's not dressed for a journey. I will pack jumpers, blankets and bread.'

He touched his holster. 'The Germans will be here tomorrow.' She didn't want to be saved, but she wasn't going to stop him doing right for his son. Let her remain with his mother. Let her live under the rule of another nation if she wanted, but not his son.

'Come on, Mitar!' he said again.

Mitar got up, sidled between the chair and the table, taking tiny steps towards his mother. She bent low, wrapped her arms around his narrow chest. When she straightened, she stroked the top of his head.

'Mamma,' he said.

He hoped she wasn't going to kiss the lad. It would be kinder to drag him away, but he couldn't. He was too soft, he knew he was too soft. He turned his head towards the hearth, wiped away the sweat from his forehead.

'What about me?' Stamenka said.

How dare she! He spat at her. 'When the German soldiers march down the street, remember you turned away Tomislav's motor. You said, "No."' Bile rose like a torrent in his throat, threatened to engulf him, his voice broke. Tears were running down Mitar's face.

'Two minutes. I'll wait in the car.' He ran to the door, the candle flames flattening as he passed. When he looked back, she was cuddling the boy, kissing his hair.

Outside he lit a cigarette. He was trembling. He paced from the side of the house, where the dog was asleep, to the well. He forced his arms by his side, flicked ash from the cigarette. The woman didn't understand. She couldn't imagine the sort of future he wanted for his son. Now and again he took a drag on the cigarette, as though he was sipping through a pipette. In the dark he couldn't read the numbers on his wristlet. How long should he wait? What would he do if Mitar didn't come? Light rain fell. He'd never been so alone.

The door at the top of the house steps opened and Mitar appeared. He paused, before running down fast. Stefan, relieved, hurried across the cobblestones and opened the door to the back seat. Mitar, now wearing a green jumper, carried the bronze sword in his right hand, clutched an object to his chest with his left. His bare legs and feet slid over the leather upholstery.

'What's that?' Stefan said.

Mitar's knuckles whitened as he tightened his grip.

'What is it?'

'Mamma said I could bring one thing.'

This time Stefan could no longer contain his fury. He yelled, 'What it is?'

'Prince Marko.' Mitar sounded defiant. He'd carried the doll everywhere during the summer before the war, when Stefan spent the whole day with them trying to be a family.

He shouted, 'You're not a bloody girl.'

Mitar scowled. 'He's a soldier, and grandmother says he brings good luck.'

Stefan was clouting Mitar across the head as Stamenka appeared from his mother's. He hadn't seen her leave the house. She carried a bundle in both arms. Thank God, she hadn't fetched his mother.

He turned back to Mitar, 'Give it to me.'

Mitar glared, but handed over the doll. Stefan felt the uneven wood, the flimsy black cotton his mother used to make the uniform. It looked nothing like a soldier, nothing like the prince it was supposed to represent. Mitar would have been about five when she gave it to him and by rights it should have disintegrated.

Stefan marched across the cobblestones and confronted Stamenka. She was loaded with two thick knitted blankets. He wanted to drop them on the ground, but they'd be useful. He grabbed the blankets and dropped the doll in the pouch of her apron.

'You spoil him,' he said.

She sidestepped and ran to the motorcar. She smelled of beeswax and wood smoke. He tried to snatch her elbow, she shook him off. She deserved a beating; his father had been right; it was the only way to ensure obedience, but Stefan never hit women. Hadn't it been the very thing he despised in his father?

Stamenka half-ran to the open car door, threw the blankets on the seat before leaning in and embracing the lad.

Stefan jumped into the passenger seat.

'May God keep you safe!' she said to Mitar.

'Shut the door!'

'We'll pray every day.'

'Shut the door, Lieutenant,' Stefan said.

Mikaiho jumped out, ran round the front of the car and saluted Stamenka, who stepped back.

Stefan looked straight ahead. The door banged.

'Goodnight, Madam.'

The car accelerated slowly. Through the tiny rear window Stefan saw Stamenka waving her arms above her head. Mitar was watching him in the mirror. Before he faced forward, he noticed the doll on Mitar's lap. He groaned to himself. Mikaiho sounded the horn and they drove out. As they turned into the road, Stefan glimpsed Stamenka, feet astride, black apron covering her face.

Chapter Thirteen

Leaving Dobro Majka, October 1915

Ellen perched on the edge of her bed, feet resting on her kitbag. Through the floorboards the lights flickered from the kitchen where Gustav thudded across its tiled floor. Most of her belongings, like Audrey's, were packed in suitcases, labelled, ready for transport to England. While she, Audrey and Matron ate breakfast, they'd drawn up a list of what they needed before they set off with the cadets tomorrow morning. While Audrey was enthusiastic, Ellen wanted to warn her they could be raped, the women's corpses piled behind the church door, haunting her. She persuaded herself Audrey wouldn't listen, was too committed, wouldn't allow herself to be intimidated.

She let Edward's letter rest on her lap. Surprised at her reluctance to open it, she didn't pursue the possible reasons. As she traced with a finger, the loop in the **E,** she noted Edward's way of reducing **llen** to an indecipherable flow of black ink. *My dear Ellen.* What if she waited till the end of the day, when she and Audrey were in their hotel room in Jevo? It would be something to look forward to, rather than skimming through it in the minutes before Gustav came to collect their kitbags.

The envelope was thicker than usual. She slit it open and she pulled out the pages, and pressed them against her cheek. She was back in Edward's home, watching him at his desk in the study, pen and inkwell to the right of the blotting pad, a bowl of roses on the corner and, through the window, the terrace leading to the formal gardens. She tried to savour the smell that was Edward: tobacco, musky scent of soap, toothpaste. She felt him by her side; he would laugh at her foolishness. Putting the envelope on the bed, she smoothed the folds of the paper and picked up the candle, held it over the first page.

My darling,

I owe you a heartfelt apology.

Sorry! I will begin at the beginning. Your letters have become illegible because of the censor's black ink and I wondered if mine were equally incomprehensible. I spoke to Lady Alice, who agreed that this letter, because it is so important, be included among those of hers delivered by personal courier. I am thus confident that you will receive it and will be able to read all its contents.

Yesterday I returned from France - a hurriedly arranged visit to see the success of our motor ambulances. I promised myself while I was there that I would write immediately on my return. I will describe as best I can what I saw, though I am all too aware, that such scenes will be familiar to you from your experience on the mule-ambulance.

I was put in the care of Dr. Naseby from the Red Cross (who knows your Dr. Gould from the Women's Yeomanry incidentally and speaks most highly of him). Dr. Naseby was most concerned for my safety and it was evident that he was relieved when my visit was concluded—not only because he was no longer responsible for the life of a civilian, but so he could devote himself full time to his duties.

I did not sleep one wink in France. The first night I was given a bed in a house used by the Red Cross for its staff. Although I was in a village several miles from the fighting, and it should therefore have been peaceful, there was a surprise bombardment, after which most of the staff departed to attend the wounded. They returned at different stages during the evening and early morning. At first I attempted to sleep, but gave up and joined the men and women downstairs drinking tea and coffee. Everyone was kind enough to say that the provision of our ambulances was a major improvement, but when I approached the front (or as close as I was allowed) the following day, I was able to see for myself the dreadful task with which they were involved.

My darling, I cannot describe the extent of my shock. I don't think I could ever get used to the blasts, which shook the ground like a series of earthquakes. Trees, farm buildings, churches, hills, the common place of the countryside were transformed into images of hell. I can put it no other way. And you have witnessed these scenes.

I was told that the area where the fighting was taking place was farmland, such as we see in the shires. Yet there was trench after trench, few trees, and no greenery on the ground or above it. I was not permitted to go to the front line itself because that could have inhibited the fighting. (I think the real reason was that Dr. Naseby didn't want me killed, which was fortunate.)

On the second evening, I got as close as I was allowed. I visited (visited!) a casualty station. Ellen, I confess to you that as I write tears are flowing. Men were piled, stacked. I presumed they were dead, which was bad enough, but they were wounded men who had curled into a single mass for warmth.

My darling! I then paid a visit to a hospital, apparently one of the best. The smell was indescribable. The beds were spotless under crystal chandeliers, but the stench of gangrene, the poor green faces, white bandages reflected in the huge gilt-framed mirrors. The nurse at the desk told me that she does everything for these men; washes, dresses wounds, gives injections, enemas, bed pans. The orderlies (and I thought of you) give drinks, adjust bandages, fill hot water bottles. I asked if they ever did more. Sometimes, she said, if we're busy they might wash the men, give out bedpans. I asked how their lives before the war had prepared them for such duties, and she gave no answer. I spoke to an orderly, several lovely nurses and a woman surgeon. None had a satisfactory answer to my question. You are no ordinary woman; women like you should not witness the horror of war.

My darling Ellen! You have been on the front line. You have been in wards more primitive than those I visited. I had a conversation with a nurse who had served in the Crimea. She admitted that what you have seen would be worse than what I witnessed. My darling... legs blown off...men screaming with pain... crawling through earth works like nocturnal creatures.... I cannot write of some of the things I saw, nor will I ever speak of them.

Civilisation has been abandoned.

However, the journey was worthwhile on two counts. On the one hand, all the medics I encountered assured me that motor ambulances save lives. (Remember how I teased you that the Women's Yeomanry's rescue-the-wounded race was outdated?) Everywhere I went, I was urged to increase production, and in that way, my war effort will equal that of officers and men.

On the other hand, I realised I had been a fool to allow you out of the country.

I remember our engagement ball. The fragrance of the roses, the Japanese lanterns hanging in the trees, you in folds and frills, which are so becoming. And I encouraged you, in my ignorance, to leave the beauty with which you deserve to be surrounded. I should have spoken with your father, asked, demanded the reasons for his refusal to give his blessing on your patriotic support of Serbia. We put it down to his bitter memories of Victor's death in South Africa, but I was wrong.

First, my love, I ask for your forgiveness. Had I the wisdom of your papa, I would have persuaded you to remain at home, where you could have played your part without being sullied by the violence and disorder of war.

Secondly, my darling—you must come home. It is too late for me to prevent you seeing the horrors you have witnessed, but not too late for you to spend time in our lovely countryside, putting aside those memories. It is time we married. I have set the date. I have booked the church. We are to be wed on 1st August, the anniversary of our engagement. You should be in England by Christmas and can distract yourself with arrangements for the wedding. Mother is most excited. Perhaps I'll be able to take a few days off to honeymoon in the Cotswolds. A reward for both of us.

I long to kiss your sweet lips, stroll with you along the banks of the Wye as we did on our last evening. Forgive me for asking you to temper your vivid descriptions of the wards and their patients. I realise now that it was not to protect my mother, but myself. I did not want to face the reality of war.

My darling, I love you so and look forward to holding you once more in my arms.

Your affectionate fiancé,

Edward

Slowly she placed the candle on the locker and clasped her hands. He'd been surprised at the question when she'd asked if he cried after his father's death. She wondered what he meant, if it it had been like the the isolating grief that had shaken her at the death of the boy-soldier.

Rapid footsteps thudded up the wooden stairs and she jabbed the letter into the envelope, shoved it into the top pocket of her tunic.

Gustav appeared in the doorway. 'I have come for your kitbags.'

She ought to ask him to leave hers. Edward expected her to go home. He needed her. German, Serb and English words tangled on her tongue. She could only nod. She must go home, but how she was to tell Audrey, she couldn't imagine.

'They want you to hurry.' Gustav struggled from the room.

When Ellen reached the courtyard, Audrey was installed at the front, Matron in the back. Mikaiho shook her hand, loaded her knapsack to the middle of the back seat. He moved to turn the starting handle. The car juddered. Edward wanted her home for Christmas. She tucked herself behind the driving seat as Mikaiho's head appeared in the light of the headlamps, cap badge gleaming. His nose red, eyes closed, cap peak slipping over his forehead. She ought to return to Edward.

The women were silent till the engine juddered. Mikaiho began to manoeuvre the car between a wagon and a group of waving women. Ellen stared at the cupola of the chapel, the trees grey in the dawn light. If she and Edward had seen the war together in France or Serbia, things might have been different. She thought back to the rescue-the-wounded race, her disappointment in not winning, his remark that motor ambulances would soon replace horses. Not here, they wouldn't.

They turned out of the gates of Dobro Majka and onto the track towards Jevo. As the car lurched through deep ruts, Audrey clutched the door handle. Matron sat straight-backed. Ellen didn't know what to make of her silence. Did she agree with other women in the unit, they were fools to remain in an occupied country? Some of the men warned of harsh, Balkan winters.

Edward wanted her home.

'Ma'am,' Ellen began.

Audrey twisted so Ellen could see her face, pale with circles of red on her cheeks. 'You were calling out in your sleep again last night.' She sounded concerned.

The dream returned fleetingly. Women's corpses behind a church door and among them that of the woman soldier. They'd stirred like an anthill before opening their eyes. She'd been pleased in her dream, but couldn't now understand why.

'What did I say?'

Audrey, once more clinging to the door handle, turned forwards. 'Couldn't make out the words. You sort of whimpered.'

Matron coughed. 'I'm glad you have decided to make this journey, Miss Frankland. It won't be as easy as Colonel Petrovic describes. These things never are, but it will give you a chance to redeem yourself.'

Twisting her hands together, Ellen said, 'My fiancé wants me to go home.'

Audrey shouted, 'I thought you might be worried about this adventure of ours.' The car jolted; as she slid towards the dashboard, she glowered sideways at Mikaiho before falling back into her seat. Raising her voice, she went on, 'If we can get the cadets out of the country to a decent education, they might find an alternative to war.'

Like your brother, Ellen thought. In some ways, Audrey was naïve.

She turned to Matron, 'You see, he was upset by what he saw in France.' She didn't want to give the impression Edward was soft. 'The extent of the injuries at the casualty station was a shock.'

'Can you hear me?' Audrey asked.

'Of course.' Ellen was irritated. 'But I'm talking to Matron.'

Audrey spoke over her, 'We'll register the cadets, while you and Mikaiho sort out the camping equipment and extra provisions.'

'We agreed that over breakfast,' Ellen snapped.

To Matron, she gabbled, 'I don't want to cause upset, but I'd like to go home with the others.'

This morning, Matron wore the Women's Medical Corps' navy blue hat, whose roundness emphasised her angular jaw,

160

sharp profile and Ellen recalled their first meeting at St. Thomas' hall. How young she'd appeared, though Ellen now knew she was thirty-five rather than thirty. Her 'I believe we'll be serving King and country together. I look forward to the privilege,' addressed to Audrey, had made Ellen feel unworthy.

Concentrating on the road ahead, Matron said, 'I am sorry. I thought you had spunk. I am disappointed the other women wanted to return to England. I wonder at their spirit when a few months in a foreign country will suffice.'

Mikaiho began to overtake a procession of sheep, goats and geese. The scrambled egg and toast for breakfast somersaulted in Ellen's stomach. Five in the morning was early to eat.

Audrey said loudly, 'Lieutenant Nis's priority is to find another wagon. Two aren't enough.' She spoke as though they'd not discussed it, as though Mikaiho wasn't next to her. She swivelled. 'Are you all right, Matron?'

'Yes, thank you.'

Ellen rested an arm across her stomach. Edward had fixed their wedding date. 'It's kind of you to say I have spunk,' she murmured.

With a snort Matron said, 'You know, I don't waste words in flattery. This is a once in a lifetime opportunity. You and Dr. Eyres are good friends. She is well organised, capable. The experience will enable you to fulfil the process of maturation you've begun. Your ability on the mule-ambulance surprised us all. In the operating theatre, your devotion was remarked upon. As for your young man...'

Audrey shouted above the engine noise, 'When we met this morning, we thought you could approach local shopkeepers and businesses for donations.'

Ellen retorted, 'I know, I was there.'

'Two wagons, half a dozen tents, a few remnants of tinned food aren't sufficient for thirty or so cadets. The Serbs need to be shown how to organise a journey of this nature.'

Ellen wondered if Audrey had sensed her change of heart.

'You see, Edward has written...' She addressed Matron and Audrey.

Audrey said, 'And about time. We've got rice, sugar and tinned meat, but we could do with more, which is why a couple of extra wagons would be useful. Stefan says it will take us two weeks, but any longer we'll need more provisions and I don't trust his expertise frankly. If Lieutenant Nis goes to the Berry hospital for blankets, tents, first aid materials, you could trawl shops and tradesmen for whatever they're able to donate.'

Over breakfast, they'd both been excited, but Edward had cried while he wrote his letter. Never before had he written so openly of his love.

If only he were with her now as they approached the town where trenches were being built. Witnessed people moving, not just their livestock, as they did when they went to market, but all they possessed. They passed cart after cart loaded with furniture, bundles of cloth, stacks of blankets. Mikaiho accelerated as the road improved.

'Are you sure you're all right?' Audrey glanced back, but reverted to watching the road. 'Your nightmare sounded bad…'

It was difficult; she didn't know what she wanted. She said to Audrey, 'I was wondering about Stefan's wife. It seems odd she'd choose her mother-in-law rather than her son.'

'We know so little about these foreigners.'

'Well…' Ellen could have pointed out it was they who were foreigners, but that wasn't the issue. She glanced at Matron who sat rigid, nervous, perhaps, of Mikaiho's driving.

'I'm not interested in his wife,' Audrey continued, 'though I gather she's not bright. I admit I don't want to go home yet. I want to see Douglas as much as you want to see Edward, but the thought of having to battle to operate in a hospital because my professionalism isn't accepted, depresses me.'

'Well… it's just that Edward wants me to go home straight away.'

'It will be good fun, the two of us working together.'

'Oh, yes,' Ellen replied.

Their attention was taken by hoard of dogs that swarmed towards the front of the motorcar, as they speeded towards the town hall. On the pavement, women dozed round

162

braziers, bags piled next to them. Mikaiho speeded up. The dogs ran alongside, barking. Mikaiho sounded the horn. They scattered. The glass in the car windows rattled as they clattered along the cobbled street.

Edward loved her, he'd fixed the date of their wedding. It felt like a bribe.

As they passed the news and tobacco shop where she used to buy *Politika* for the Serb Medical Officer, she noticed it was boarded up. Audrey didn't sound as if she missed Douglas. How did experiences of love compare? Did Audrey love Douglas, in the same way as she loved Edward? When she thought of him, her body ached.

She allowed herself to be distracted. This was no normal week. Usually men in suits were on their way to work, the sellers of fruit and vegetables set up behind carts under street lights, children ambling to school. This morning, the streets were quieter. Their car flashed past a man, a blue *kepi* on his head, holding a clay bowl, the horizontal fold of his trousers marking the absence of legs. A few men waited for news from the front, outside the district office. At midday the drum would announce the arrival of letters from the front and the list of those killed, wounded or missing. The queue would grow.

Mikaiho swerved to avoid children, who ran from behind a wagon throwing stones at each other. A sign above a barber's shop squeaked.

Matron remarked, 'Edward will not die because he's seen the brutality of war, nor need his realisation that you have witnessed and experienced more than he, necessitate your immediate return.'

Mikaiho braked, and Ellen flung out an arm to steady herself, glimpsed through the windscreen the black coachwork of a fiacre and through the side window, breath steaming from horses' nostrils. The cab slid alongside their now stationary vehicle. Mikaiho jumped out, waved his arms and shouted at the coachman. As she watched a man at the top of the town hall steps being escorted by a policeman, she realised why she'd wanted to do as Edward instructed. It wasn't to please him, but to escape the war. She yearned for what

Edward described as 'the beauty with which she deserved to be surrounded'. She'd had enough of seeing behind the scenes.

Mikaiho jumped back in the car, slammed the door.

'Who was that?' Ellen asked in Serbian.

Mikaiho shook his head.

'He looked important.'

'It was no-one.'

She couldn't volunteer to be a soldier one day and run away the next. She said to Matron, 'Please, will you ring Edward when you reach England? Tell him... tell him, I love him and I've been delayed two, maybe three weeks.'

'Of course.'

Ellen lowered her head to peer through the slit of the back window to watch the coachman whip the horses' flanks. As they galloped away, the rim of the cab's wheels jolted their car. Mikaiho shouted through the window, released the clutch with a jerk and with two wheels running along the pavement, they hurtled on.

Chapter Fourteen

Jevo, October 1915

The sun rose on a downcast morning. Ellen, having left Audrey and Matron with the cadets in the market place, stood with her back to the *kafkana,* watching Mikaiho drive towards the Berry hospital. His motorcar followed a line of bullock-drawn wagons laden with families and belongings. She'd grown fond of him despite his disloyalty at the regimental meeting. He was in charge of the withdrawal of all the cadets and at the end of the afternoon, they were to meet for a farewell drink.

Pavements and road brimmed with soldiers, peasants, women, children, mules, donkeys, carts and wagons. Some people hurried, impelled by fear; others shuffled like the very old. Lowering her hat against driving drizzle, Ellen surveyed the street deciding which tradesman to ask first: tailor, baker, gunsmith, dress shop and general store. Many others were boarded up. Straight ahead, a cobbler's. She would start there, having witnessed the arrival of a few barefoot cadets.

She'd never begged. Her father considered it ill-mannered. Even items for sale at a church fete, arrived at the back door of the church hall. She faltered. How would shopkeepers react?

To her side, two men left the *kafkana* like sleep walkers. They nudged her, whined for dinars. It was the impetus she needed. She darted across the road between an old man pulling a handcart and a laden bullock wagon. She rehearsed Serbian for, 'I am from the Women's Medical Corps. We are taking cadets from the Jevo regiment out of Serbia. Can you please help us?'

About to enter, she noticed a priest hurry out of the church on the corner. They needed another wagon. Mikaiho was to ask the Berry hospital, but Audrey would be pleased if they managed two.

Rushing past soldiers propping up each other, she reached the priest as he was about to enter a half-timbered house. She tugged at his flapping sleeve.

'*Oprostite, gospodine.* Can you help me?'

His reply was too fast for her to understand. She told herself she ought to stick to one task at a time; her Serbian wasn't good enough for unprepared conversation. 'Please, speak more slowly, sir. I am from the Women's Medical Corps. We need a wagon and some oxen.'

Under a fringe of white hair, his cheeks were smallpox scarred. His cloak hung in folds from his broad shoulders, trailed on the pavement.

'I have no wagon.' His hand touched the latch.

'I am with the Jevo regiment taking cadets to safety.'

She wondered how her father would respond if a foreigner accosted him on the doorstep of the vicarage and made such a request. Generous with his time, he was suspicious of strangers and yet, the first person she asked for help, was a priest. She bundled away thoughts of her father.

'You'd do better with mules.' His voice, tinny, didn't match his bulk. 'They're nimble and can carry heavy loads.'

'Do you know…?'

'I do not.' He raised the latch.

In frustration she pleaded, 'But sir, we need transport.'

'The old stonemason has mules, but he'll release nothing without papers and money.'

Before she'd a chance to ask where the stonemason lived, the priest slipped into the house. She considered knocking; jaw tight with anxiety, she returned to the cobbler's.

By early afternoon, Ellen was delighted with the number of shopkeepers who'd donated. She was promised bags of apples, a couple of sacks of rice and sugar, matches, candles, several electric torches, one primus stove, and odds and ends of crockery and cutlery. With the help of Mikaiho and a wagon, she would collect them later. The cobbler had no boots, but gave six pairs of shoes and several pairs of woollen mittens. Though the stonemason owned neither wagons nor mules, he'd heard a rumour freight wagons at the railway

166

station contained quantities of tinned corned beef, condensed milk and coffee beans. Having an hour to spare, Ellen decided to investigate.

Funeral flags hung from every house near the railway station and she thought of Edward weeping over the dead in France. If he were with her, he would be filled with admiration for the Serbs who'd lost much and were so generous.

The stonemason warned she shouldn't go alone. If there were provisions there would be violence, but she only intended to ask. She could return with Mikaiho, who'd deal with any trouble.

Nonetheless, she slowed when she saw grey and yellow smoke billowing above the station roof. She jabbed a hatpin through a thick roll of hair, felt the prick on her scalp. The possibility of success kept her pushing through the crowd of people and animals in the station forecourt, enabled her to elbow aside the rump of a horse as skinny as an ox, to skirt gypsies building a fire in the midst of the bustle. The throng cleared. By the side of a stack of army kitbags, a beggar, stinking of urine, snatched at the hem of her greatcoat. He touched his cap when she glowered. She shook free; felt guilty she donated nothing. Smoke stung her eyes. She was tempted to give up. Admonishing herself, extra food would make a difference, she pressed on. She remembered how hungry she'd been at summer camp.

With her head down, it took only a few minutes to reach the steps leading to the station entrance. More beggars. Propped against a pillar, a man in tweed trousers held out an army cap. Passers-by dropped in potatoes, onions, peppers, an occasional dinar. Along the wall, seven or so soldiers thumped crutches on the pavement; they passed round a bottle.

One cried, 'Were we wounded for nothing?'

Back at their lovely Dobro Majka, she pictured bread cooling on racks in the kitchen, vases of autumn leaves in the wall alcoves and the glow of paraffin heaters in the tent wards at night. Enemy soldiers would soon occupy it. She clenched her fists. Had their work been for nothing? She must write to Edward, tell him how attached she'd become to the Serbs, how she'd grown to love them, that she was as distraught as they were at losing the war. Yet, a letter couldn't be posted. She'd keep a journal, include a sketch or two, describe the journey, explain, justify. She shouldn't need to. Audrey didn't, but Audrey had a job, a profession, whereas Ellen, if she was honest, was replacable.

On the platform, she flattened herself against the outside wall of a packed waiting room, uncertain as to where to go. A train whistled from the direction of the forest. Within minutes steam engulfed her, and as the train braked, passengers jumped off at the same time as soldiers, peasants, townspeople surged from the waiting room. They stepped on each other, dragged travellers off the carriage steps, shoved, poked with bags, sticks. She couldn't see what was happening as the exiting passengers trampled over her feet, jabbed elbows and bags into her chest in their rush. When the crush began to ease, she witnessed one woman, in her attempt to board, bite the hand of another who was clinging to the iron bars on the door. The train let off steam. As the platform became less crowded, she relaxed and moved towards the freight sheds on her left, in the same direction as the black and yellow smoke. The stonemason had warned that soldiers guarded the wagons, but all she wanted were a few tins of beef. Her greatcoat dragged as she nudged through the decreasing numbers, to the end of the platform.

Before springing onto the track, she looked both ways. To the left, a party of men, some in army uniform, and to her right, a ring of women scooping something she couldn't identify into aprons. The men seemed to be larking around so she decided to approach the women, but they screeched, waved their arms, threw stones. She withdrew, shaken.

Keeping close to the platform wall, she edged towards the men, two pushing and shoving in a mock fight. They straightened, as she got close. The others, more predictably, were passing round a bottle, she presumed from the smell, to be *rakija*. A tall youth, wearing a suit, white shirt and tie, observed.

'Miss Frankland.'

She recognised Vukasin with relief. He'd left Dobro Majka nine months ago, though Audrey hadn't been satisfied he was strong enough. He was dressed in army tunic and trousers, she wondered where he'd found them. From beneath his cap, his hair had re-grown thick. She stretched a hand in greeting. He would look after her. When she'd brought him from the casualty station by mule ambulance, he'd promised he'd do anything for her. He swaggered fowards, cigarette dangling. They shook hands.

'Will you carry some things for me?' she said.

'I am a soldier. I am in the Third Ban.'

Was he refusing? Maybe she'd not exchanged the necessary courtesies.

She said, 'That is good. I see you have recovered.' She was pleased her Serbian had improved since his operation. She expected him to compliment her as he used to. When he didn't, she said, 'I am looking for provisions for our cadets. It would help me if you and your friends could carry tins of corned beef.'

She began to walk towards the sheds, noticed he wasn't following. Perhaps he didn't understand. Her Serbian might not be as good as she thought.

She waited a moment. He'd rejoined the group. 'Vukasin!' she called. When she'd first met him, the hole in his head had been open to the sky. He was blind. She'd helped lift him from the seat of the mule, covered him with a blanket on the stretcher. Anger tangled with fear ran through her. She marched back.

One of his mates mimicked her 'Vukasin'.

He dropped the remnant of his cigarette on the track and ground it with the sole of his boot. 'I'm not a servant.'

Her hand flew to her mouth. Uninvited, the picture of him raising the skirt of a peasant woman arose. Arrogant men raped women, murdered children and discarded their bodies on holy ground. She lowered her hand. No. She mustn't allow her imagination to fly free.

In the distance, the departing train whistled. A smell of burning rubber. Needles of pain behind her eyes. Her voice was firm though the words came hesitantly. 'When you were wounded you promised to help me should I need it. I am sorry you're not true to your word.'

Vukasin's glance shifted from her face to the track, over towards the platform, back to his mates.

'I am a soldier, miss.'

She shrugged and walked towards the freight wagon.

She saluted two of the soldiers on duty. '*Dobar dan.* I am looking for tins of corned beef and condensed milk.' She hoped she sounded more confident than she felt.

'Serbia is finished,' said one.

'I'm with the Women's Medical Corps and we're taking cadets out of Serbia. We need tinned food.'

'It is too late.'

He didn't seem to understand. 'Sir, the cadets must eat.'

'Madam, they will never reach their destination.'

In despair she turned to the other man, 'Do you have food in the wagon?'

'We have treacle.'

'Treacle.' She wasn't sure how useful it would be, but it was better than nothing. 'Can we have some?'

'No.'

She'd hoped for corned beef, and condensed milk as a treat. Disheartened, she ambled back towards the platform. What a waste of time. She instructed herself to buck up. They had essentials. She'd go to the *kafkana*, re-read the affectionate parts of Edward's letter. It was reassuring he loved her after her doubts.

As she hoisted herself onto the platform, she was surprised to see the lad in the suit, holding out a hand. They exchanged greetings.

'I'm here to assist,' he said.

She asked his name.

'Branislav.'

'And where are you from, Branislav?'

'Orasac.' His hair, cut above his ears, shone in shades of black, the glints of a dragonfly, the shimmering of sun on the ocean. 'I am a cadet with the Jevo regiment.'

He didn't appear to have started shaving. 'How old are you?'

He didn't reply, but on their way back towards the main street he told her his father was serving in Russia as a medical officer, he was the eldest of five boys and his mother suffered poor health. He was polite and Ellen's enthusiasm returned. She asked him to meet her in an hour's time outside the *kafkana* with a group of cadets to help her and Mikaiho load their promised provisions into a wagon.

Ellen glanced at the sign above the lintel of the *kafkana*, the Cyrillic lettering she didn't understand, the faded paintwork of a swollen bellied pig. On the threshold she glanced round, searching for a seat under a lantern. When she and Audrey drank coffee here on a day off, it was quiet and the barman used to rush across and direct them to a table close to the fire in the middle of the room. While they were taking off their greatcoats, he fetched a woollen cloth to cover the table.

Once inside, she looked for an empty chair. Soldiers crowded around the bar, the long table at the far side of the room crammed with men, women and children. She crossed the room to a group of tables by the fire, her boots sticking to the floor. Only one had a spare seat and excusing herself in Serbian to the three men already seated, she dragged the stool furthest from them, shifted the lamp and sat down. Isolated from the street's bustle, comforted by the fug of wood smoke and tobacco, the flickering lamplight. No one would notice her.

On paper from her pocket, she jotted in pencil the names of shopkeepers who'd promised supplies. Audrey would be pleased. One of the men spoke to her, but not wanting to be interrupted, she finished her list. Two of the men were sharing a carafe of red wine, the other drinking soup with the aid of chunks of black bread. His sucking irritated and she winced.

She would love a coffee. A waitress scooted between tables. She balanced dishes of chicken and paprika stew on one arm, nudged people out of the way with the other. Having finished her list, Ellen unfastened her greatcoat, reached for her letter. She wished she was more useful than an orderly. Any of the Serb orderlies, or Gustav, could do her job.

Audrey pointed out that she should train, but as what? Next year, she was to marry so she'd have no opportunity to work.

One of the men burped; she tried to ignore her distaste. As she re-opened the letter, the door to the *kafkana* opened, bringing in the notes of the *gusle*, the clatter of wheels on cobblestones. The draught fluttered the lamp's light. Wine glugged from carafe to glass. Looking up, a man prepared to sip. Edward loved red wine. The man was staring. She pulled the lamp an inch from her letter.

I urge you to return home as soon as can be arranged.

She heard Edward's voice. *I urge you.* There was no arguing, no room for misunderstanding and yet, she'd given the plea no thought during the day, absorbed with arrangements for the journey. She flicked to the next page, searching for permission to stay. *Ellen, I confess to you that as I write tears are flowing.* Of course, Matron was right, he would adjust, but oughtn't she be there to comfort him? *You have been in wards more primitive than those I visited.* How would he react, when he learned she could have gone home, but opted to stay? Her father had refused his blessing on her joining the WMC. Would Edward stop loving her?

With a jolt she was disturbed by loud glugs as the man lifted the soup bowl, hair jutting over the rim. Straight, thick hair, tinged red. She pressed her knuckles hard on her mouth, surprisingly tense. Her letter slipped and as she gathered up the pages, smoothing them over and over, she tasted blood where her teeth had cut her inner lip. She tried to imagine Edward in his suit at the casualty station, his face splintering as he watched the arrival of broken bodies, smelled blood mingling with earth. He'd been appalled by the war, maybe a little frightened. She pushed the letter back in her pocket, close to tears. The man raised his head from the soup bowl, beamed at her.

When a hand slapped her shoulder, she flinched.

'Miss Frankland.'

'Oh, Lieutenant!'

'I will order coffee.'

While he went to the bar she tried to regain enthusiasm for her mission. The three men at her table were jabbering, the

172

carafe empty. Whatever way she read the letter she ought to go home and yet she wanted adventure.

The man nearest her had teeth as small as milk teeth; his jaw was triangular, his chin unshaven. She wondered if he'd been shot in the face. A drop of wine trickled from the rim of the carafe, slithered down the glass and sank into the wooden table. Edward would expect her home by Christmas. She hoped Matron would reassure him.

Mikaiho returned rubbing his hands. 'I have ordered coffee and cakes.'

'Cakes?'

'English ladies like cakes.'

Mikaiho turned to the man to Ellen's left. 'Sir, may I please sit next to the lady?'

The man looked at his friends. Ellen couldn't understand what Mikaiho said next, but it was evidently good-humoured and the three men laughed. The man with the soup winked, pretended to sit on the knee of his friend. While they moved to share a seat, Mikaiho drew the stool next to Ellen. He lay his cap on the table, unbuttoned his greatcoat, beaming.

'It is a good thing that you're doing, miss.'

She picked up her list, but before she could explain, he continued, 'I, too, have done good things. After our coffee and cake, we will make our collections in the extra wagon I've been able to obtain.' He patted his thigh several times.

On the table, at the far side of the room, voices rose. A soldier sprang, fists raised. A bald man punched him back to his seat. Anticipating trouble, she didn't catch what Mikaiho said. The incident passed.

Not sure if Mikaiho would understand her concerns about Edward, she said tentatively, 'My fiancé wants me to go home.'

'What is home? The enemy is coming. Homes will be violated.'

Again, she remembered the women's bodies piled against the church door and Mikaiho lighting candles in front of the altar.

'My fiancé doesn't know what it's like here.'

Mikaiho laughed, though she couldn't grasp why. 'The coffee, Miss. Here's the coffee.' His world was different from Edward's.

The barman brought a tray with an embroidered cloth, two tiny cups of black coffee, a jug of milk and a slab of cake.

She said, 'I felt sorry for the women in the church.' As she added milk, in her imagination she touched the woollen stockings, knelt on the earth floor, smelled the blood, corpses.

'You're our hero, miss. The men love you because you don't run like many foreigners, but you stay with us even as we leave our country.' He twisted the points of his moustache. 'Miss, I will help you. Every day I will bring you bread.'

She was surprised his duties would permit it, but she was pleased. She assumed they would be self-sufficient; fresh bread was a bonus. It would be a comfort to see Mikaiho.

He pointed to the plate. 'Cake. You will not see cake for a long time.'

She remembered tea with Audrey in Brown's after they'd listened to Lady Alice's speech. There'd been six or seven cakes to choose from and she'd been torn between a butterfly bun, a vanilla slice and an Eccles cake. Audrey dissected a chocolate éclair while Ellen daydreamed of fighting like her uncle.

Here there was no cutlery. She picked up the sticky brown slab and bit off a small piece.

'It is dead,' he said.

'Dead?'

'The cake.' He guffawed and she smiled at his good humour. The cake tasted of fudge, cinnamon and chewy nuts.

Mikaiho raised his cup as though to make a toast. 'I have something important to say.'

She longed for reassurance, to tell someone she didn't want to lose Edward, but Mikaiho couldn't help.

Mikaiho put his cup on the table without having taken a drink. 'Miss Frankland. You will be a soldier.'

She blushed.

'You were dressed in pieces of mud. Your hat was…' he gestured, his hand at an angle against his temple, '… so I laughed, but the men believe you make a good officer.'

Her stomach hardened and she couldn't swallow. She remembered her dream of Victor, of him galloping down the hill to the plain, his men at his heels, her aunt, describing to her as a child, how he'd lain next to his wounded corporal for eight hours before riding for help.

Mikaiho wiped his lips with his handkerchief. 'We need women like you.'

The cake stuck to her teeth, her tongue unable to dislodge it.

'Would you like a Luger?' Opening his greatcoat, he patted a paddle holster on the left of his belt. Logs crackled. Across the room, a stool clattered to the floor.

Mikaiho asked, 'You know how to shoot?'

Recollecting Stefan's teasing, she realised he wasn't waiting for an answer.

'Here.' He removed it, placed it on her lap. It felt heavy, and she didn't look straight away. He went on, 'All seventeen year old cadets have been issued with a weapon.'

'How many?'

'Six. And you.'

Only then did she look down. Black. Shiny. She stroked the barrel, held the polished handle and eyed the trigger. 'Is it loaded?'

His eyes on hers, he took the pistol, opened the cartridge holder. 'Seven rounds.'

'Holster?'

'You have mine.' He unclipped the leather pouch from his belt. A film of sweat formed on her forehead. She'd a role. She would shoot to protect. She could do something Audrey couldn't.

She fastened the holster on the left of her belt. One of the men at the table applauded, she blushed. The others were laughing, sharing a joke. She pictured herself walking at the head of the unit, drawing her gun. No longer an orderly, but a hero.

'It is a good thing you've done,' she said.

She ought not to keep it loaded, Sergeant Sutherland had taught that. Releasing the magazine spring, she removed the bullets. As she was going to put the gun in the holster,

Mikaiho, grinning, took it from her. He pulled the pin, removed the loaded bullet and returned the gun.

Thirty lads, aged between seventeen and fourteen, along with families and luggage, clustered across the square. Kit bags, knapsacks, belongings tied into parcels with twine, string or rope were piled by the wagons. Even though it was dusk, some lads kicked a football, using the water trough under the gas lamp as a goal. Mothers huddled over sons. Animals, refugee bivouacs, carts not belonging to their unit and wounded soldiers fought a passage through the mêlée.

In search of Audrey doing medical examinations, keen to tell her of the Luger, Ellen followed Matron's voice to the back of a wagon. From her tone, clipped consonants, she sounded angry.

She stood between the shafts of the wagon loaded with tents, holding a sheaf of papers and a pencil. A small boy, his face hidden behind shoulder length hair perched on the top of three steps.

'Excuse me, Matron. Have you seen Audrey?' Ellen asked.

Matron jabbed the pencil in the air. 'Miss Frankland! Will you speak to the child? He refuses to move, refuses to utter a single word.'

'I must reassure Audrey about something.'

'According to his father he speaks excellent English, but we have no evidence of it.'

Ellen looked at the child. White shorts, green knitted jumper, bare feet. He peered at her beneath lowered eyelids. 'He's not one of ours, is he?'

'Mitar Petrovic. We've had to load around him,' Matron said. 'It's been most inconvenient.'

She'd expected a mini version of Stefan, but his son barely looked thirteen, slight, arms folded over his chest, knees and shoulders shaking. 'Has Audrey examined him?'

'He refuses to move!'

Where was his mother? Ellen took off her cap, hoping she would appear more friendly. As she edged closer to the wagon steps, Branislav followed. He couldn't do any harm, he might assist.

Distracted, she glanced up at the sound of a motorcar. Three white-bearded officers jumped out. A civilian was pushed into the back seat. She concentrated again on Mitar.

She asked in Serbian, 'Are you cold?'

When she repeated the question, he ducked his head till it touched his chest. She edged nearer, feeling the edge of the shaft against her thigh.

Branislav said, 'Mitar, the lady asked you a question.'

She wondered if her accent was difficult to understand. Sometimes the men laughed at the way she spoke, though she tried to imitate.

Mitar raised his head to Branislav. His top lip trembled.

She sympathised. Cadets shouting, mothers murmuring, a vendor calling out his sale of matches, soldiers arguing, singing. In the distance, the motorcar drove off. She sensed Matron's impatience behind her. Hands on hips, no doubt.

Heavy footsteps approached. Audrey cried out, distressed, 'Matron! An emergency has arisen.'

In singsong English, Mitar said, 'My name is Mitar Petrovic. I am thirteen years old.'

'Have you brought warm clothes?' Ellen said, 'We're going on a long journey and it will be cold.'

Audrey sounded tearful, 'Matron! It is intolerable. The cadets are to be armed.'

Matron said gently, 'We're having a problem with Stefan's son. He refuses to move from the steps of the wagon.'

'We won't go at all if these boys are not disarmed.'

'I don't think it is our business, my dear. They are, after all, cadets,' Matron said crisply.

'We'll attract all kinds of trouble. Ellen and I are women. We don't want to be surrounded by weapons.'

Ellen thought it wise to focus on Mitar. In the excitement of getting the gun she'd forgotten Audrey was a pacifist. How could she? Hadn't Matron accused her of letting her feelings run riot and she'd done it again. Just as well, she'd not found Audrey straight away.

She said to Branislav, 'Can you ask if he's expecting any more clothes?'

Mitar said, 'Serbia is Great!'

Ellen wondered if Stefan exaggerated his son's ability to speak English.

After Branislav repeated the question, Mitar folded his lips. Ellen stared about for inspiration, spotted Gustav carrying a large cardboard box and alongside him Dobrica, loaded with hot water bottles. She greeted them. She'd worked well with Dobrica for several weeks in the admissions' tent; he'd been able to make sense of the men's silences, their strange sounds after the trauma of battle.

'Can you help us, please, Dobrica?'

He inclined his head, but walked on. Gustav, however, pushed his way to her.

'What's the matter, miss?' he asked.

'This is Mitar. Colonel Petrovic's son. He won't talk to us.'

'He is homesick, perhaps.'

A breeze stirred the tarpaulin covering the wagon. Behind her Matron was saying, 'It is up to you, Dr. Eyres, but these lads are soldiers in training. As I understand it, only seventeen year olds will be armed and they'll have been taught how to use guns. Don't get things out of proportion.'

Ellen heard the exchange with some relief.

'Thank you, Gustav. You carry on with your work.'

As Gustav moved away, Mitar was saying to Branislav, 'I've met a school friend. He doesn't have any warm clothes.'

'We'll find you trousers,' she said to Mitar, straightening up. 'We've got shoes as well though I'm surprised your mother didn't make sure you were dressed for a long journey.'

'I want to see mama.'

'Why isn't she here?'

'My grandma is old and cannot fetch the water from the well without her. The jar is too heavy.'

Surprised they didn't have running water, Ellen added, 'You'll need socks.'

'Velimir doesn't have any,' Mitar said.

'Who is Velimir?'

'My friend.'

'Have you another jumper?'

'No.'

'You have no extra clothes?'

'I didn't know I was going on a journey.'

'Your father and mother must have told you.' He must be exaggerating because he was anxious, frightened among strangers.

Audrey pushed between them. She'd exchanged her official cap for a yellow knitted hat, and Ellen was as much taken aback at the change in her appearance, as by her anger. 'Ellen! We're not going. The cadets are armed.'

'They're soldiers in training.'

'I suppose you've got one as well, Ellen Frankland,' she shouted.

'It's what cadets are.'

'If they fire a single shot, we pull out.'

Ellen shrugged. It seemed unlikely they'd be involved in fighting.

'Just one.' Audrey took hold of Ellen's elbow, clenched it resolutely. Ellen sidestepped, aware of the Luger just below her waist.

'I want my mama,' Mitar wailed. He began to sob, his chest heaving.

Ellen rummaged in her pocket, pulled out a handkerchief, gave it to Mitar. 'Very well,' she said quietly to Audrey. To Mitar she said, 'Your father wants you to come with us.'

'I have your word,' Audrey said, 'And I suggest you make sure the child is dressed suitably.'

Ellen was relieved when Audrey walked away. It was a pity their views were very different, but if she or the cadets needed to shoot, there would be no time for debate.

Branislav said, 'I didn't want to leave my mother and brothers, but if my father knew what was happening in Serbia, like your father does, he'd want me to leave. Then, I can return as a soldier.'

Mitar wiped his eyes. Screwing the handkerchief into the palm of his hand he said, 'I don't want to be a soldier.'

'Oh! Now, that's true, but in a few years time you'll be old enough to fight and you'll want to,' Branislav replied.

Ellen let them chat for a moment or so before suggesting Mitar follow her to find trousers and shoes.

The clock was striking the half hour as he climbed down from the wagon. She would keep quiet about the gun. Load it at the beginning of each day once their journey started.

As she lay in the narrow hotel bed, Ellen's mind danced. Thirty cadets registered. Three wagons loaded with tents, food, kit. Branislav, capable with leadership qualities. Mothers: laughing, crying, hugging, waving goodbye. Mitar settled with friend Velimir. So many strange names:Bogdan, Kova, Kostu, Miodrag, Radovan. The drivers silent. The orderlies slow: Timohir, Dobrica, Costic and Gustav, loyal Gustav. She soon fell asleep.

Chapter Fifteen

Belgrade, November 1915

Stefan was sprinting across the Bulevar Foccicia on his way to his compound hoping to find Stamenka, when the searchlight started up again and illuminated the crumbling wall of the Italian legation. He felt a tug on the skirt of his greatcoat, as Rajko yanked him into the shadows. Through empty windows, he glimpsed a chandelier mysteriously hanging, though much of the roof had collapsed. In the distance one of the park's peacocks yowled. Elbow to elbow, they crouched far into the masonry debris, boots grinding shards of glass. Despite the night's drizzle, Stefan's nostrils were filled with dust. He tasted grit. He longed for a drink, but his flask lay miles away.

His hand rested on the butt of his pistol. They shouldn't be here. He'd not slept, thinking of Stamenka. He'd separated her from Mitar. She'd be safe with his brother Woislav, but she'd mourn the loss of their son.

The enemy, having occupied the city, had imposed a curfew. He shouldn't have involved Rajko, but, as Stefan knew he would, he'd responded. They wore unmarked caps, shoulder straps and buttons. Briefly, Stefan spoke of committing suicide if captured. The bodies of their compatriots, which hanged from lampposts, from the cannons of Kalemegdan fortress, signposted retribution was immediate. Nonetheless, with sweat running down his forehead and Rajko panting at his side, Stefan wasn't sure he would have the courage to place the muzzle in his mouth, press the trigger and wait for the sound of his brain exploding.

Rajko's body tensed beside him.

'Two more. Then we'll run,' Stefan ordered.

The last circuit of light lit up the edge of a crater in the middle of the *bulevar*. From the Royal Gardens a peacock screamed. Stefan grabbed Rajko's arm and keeping his face close, he whispered, 'Straight to Ulicia Morava.'

Despite the danger, Stefan was enjoying the escapade. It reminded him of a time when risk was fun, when dreams could come true. Their boots pounded over cobblestones, echoed along the deserted street. The city, foreign already. The Karakjodj obliterated, its pillars, glass roof, beautiful pictures destroyed. Most of the restaurants and shops fronting the *bulevar* were piles of stone, timber, splinters of glass, dissembled furniture.

They planned to follow the road to the Military Academy destroyed in last year's bombardment, past the rubble of the Gornji café and through the streets leading to the Turkish quarter. As they neared, Stefan smelled the stench of the 'death wagon' that had rolled past on the evening of Tomislav's celebration, the evening he'd delayed going home, reluctant to finalise the deal with the journalist. If the American were to appear at this very second, Stefan would take his hand, pay double, to secure Stamenka's safety.

On the corner of the Gornji café, the two men paused. There'd been no attempt to rebuild it after the recovery of bodies. The Austrians had removed the wooden cordon constructed by the army and decorated with rough crosses and prayers written on scraps of paper. But if the enemy thought the destruction of the heartland of student life reduced morale, they were wrong. That Belgrade resisted total occupation for three days was due not only to fierce army defences, but also to the fury of its citizens.

Cautiously, the men advanced. The sound of distant voices, caused them to step into the front garden of a former stylish house. Slabs of stone, window frames, pieces of metal remained. Wrought iron railings were twisted and distorted. In silence, they stood side-by-side, their breath mingling. A cat streaked from the darkness, towards a street where trees had been chopped to build trenches.

Perhaps because he couldn't rid himself of the memory of defeat, Stefan needed this adventure. The fighting had been bloody and cruel. Men and women used pistols, knives, kitchen utensils and manned the artillery guns when their soldiers fell. His eardrums teemed with his order, 'Retreat,' after his men had bolted when their big guns were captured and their brothers lay dead. His men had scrambled over corpses and Stefan feared horror would prevent him giving the leadership they deserved. Nonetheless, the call to the buglers, his words reminding the men they were Serbs, that even as they ran, they should look out for each other.

The Austrians took revenge. They murdered men, women and children without distinction.

From the other side of the Drina, the roar of big guns. Drizzle seeped through the gap between collar and coat. He'd not worn a scarf thinking it could too easily be used as a noose.

They were safe for a few moments, though Stefan feared Rajko's carelessness of life. Rajko boasted that if he died tonight it would be of no consequence, but Stefan didn't want to die. He wanted to see his home. Even though he was defying the curfew, disobeying Tomislav's orders that the curfew was to be respected, he wanted to see if Stamenka had survived, and if she had, to live with her again.

Stefan stepped back onto the pavement, skulking close to the edges of the ruined houses. The route, littered with debris from the bombardment two days ago, reminded him of his father telling of a visit he'd made to a ruined temple in some far off, foreign place. He had described the silence of stones, the arches of doorways and windows, the search for what was missing creating a sense of holiness. Tonight he understood his father's experience. He felt as though he and Rajko weren't simply looking for his family, but they were pilgrims, honouring the city they'd abandoned.

After a mile or so, they left the city centre and continued into the Turkish quarter. More walls, roofs of collapsed houses. Mitar's school was in the area, but though Stefan was accustomed to the darkness, he couldn't see if it was standing. Inside his gloves, his palms were wet. In the distance, a baby cried, beyond comfort, without pause.

Stefan tightened the grip on his pistol. He'd boasted to the women of the Medical Corps that Belgrade was safe, that it was in isolated villages the enemy took its revenge. He'd believed it at the time, hadn't he? He hadn't deliberately left Stamenka behind. She did that by refusing Tomislav's car. He strode on, trying not to listen to the accusing voices in his head, not to admit he'd wanted to punish her, not wanting to implicate himself in his wife's predicament.

With Rajko a step behind, he didn't notice the corpses on the pavement as he turned into the lane, which led home. His toe caught in an arm or a leg. He cried out, sprawling across the uniformed men. He smelled blood and excrement. Rajko collapsed on top, slid to his side.

Before either of them could get up, footsteps pounded down the street from the *kafkana* where he used to buy tobacco for his father. Stefan wriggled closer to the dead. His belly began to heave. He shoved his fist in his mouth.

'Who's there?' a man asked in German. He repeated the question in Serbian and Stefan guessed from his accent he was a Bosnian-Serb serving with the Austrian army. They could silence a single soldier.

From a few meters along the street, another called out, 'Anyone there, Grigoric?' He thundered nearer. Stefan's heart hammered against a skull. He tried not to move, to hang on to the scream, which began in his stomach and rose to the roof of his head.

A lantern flashed. Stefan could rely on his friend not to move. He thought his gut would explode, but after several moments, the light drifted on.

'Can't see nothing.'

'Fucking peacocks.'

'Peacocks don't cough.'

'Let's finish our drink. We'll look again later.'

Once more the light flickered, and then the soldiers strolled back up the street. Every now and again, the lamp shone in their direction. Stefan waited five minutes before inching himself upright. His mouth and throat tasted of bile, but he'd no longer the urge to be sick. He was enjoying the excitement; he guessed Rajko, creeping behind, shared the feeling.

When they reached the compound, the gates were open. Stefan was relieved there were no lights. Rajko crept across the courtyard towards the well, but Stefan didn't follow, keen to check no one lurked in the shadows of the high walls. Drizzle

184

dampened his cheeks and he allowed it to quell his rising fear. He smelled vomit. Touched the front of his greatcoat, felt the stickiness between his gloved fingers. He despised his body's lack of restraint, its independence of will and remembered when he was a boy on the hillside guarding the sheep at night, perhaps seven or so, he'd shit himself without being aware, preoccupied by the eerie sound of wolves. He brushed down his coat as best he could, wishing Dragan were there.

He didn't walk all the way round the compound, but at the foot of the steps to his house, paused. They'd never seemed steep before. Rajko appeared from the side of the house, moved close enough for their coats to touch.

'Dog's dead,' he said without expression.

Sweat ran between Stefan's shoulder blades as he climbed the steps. He clutched at the wall.

By the door, he listened. Not far away, an owl hooted. He swallowed, hand on pistol, he raised the latch, fraction by fraction. Dankness drifted. He pushed the door fully open. Because the shutters were fastened, it was darker inside than out. Stamenka always had a fire; he couldn't remember the room being cold. The air smelled as damp as the caves by the edge of the Danube. He stepped into the room. The wind howled through the chimney hole. He smelled wood ash, and strode to the table. He'd a desire to howl along with the wind, to open his lungs and yell.

He misjudged the distance, banged his thigh on a corner. With his left hand he pulled out his torch, switched it on, circled the beam once round the room. It was, as he'd last seen it. The candelabrum in the centre of the table, candles in the alcoves, the chairs tucked under the table, Stamenka's loom at the far end under the window. It was as though she'd slipped out to his mother's.

'Open the shutters, brother,' he said.

On soft feet, Stefan began to feel his way along the length of the table. The shutters clattered as Rajko raised the wooden bar, which held them. While Rajko unfastened the window behind the loom, Stefan walked slowly towards the sleeping quarters. He remembered Mitar peeping from behind the door.

When he entered the sleeping area, the smell of lavender and rosemary was so strong, he almost called out, 'Stamenka' so certain was he that she was there. Stepping onto Mitar's palister, he opened the shutters and assessed the scene. Nothing had changed. He crouched on his haunches, touched the crocheted blanket on their bed. She loved reds and yellows, though he preferred the gentler colours of the tapestry above their palister. He'd forgotten it. He took off his smelly gloves, leaned across to touch the stitching. He resisted the desire to flash the torch on the rose pink of the apple blossom. After their betrothal, Stamenka had sewn it for their wedding night, though they'd shared his parents' house, and she hadn't been able to hang it. His hands shook as he picked up his gloves.

'No sign of a disturbance,' Rajko announced as he entered the sleeping area.

'No.'

'She can't be far away.'

'The Austrians would leave her body.'

He couldn't think of harm coming to her. 'She's a good woman.'

Crossing to the wardrobe, he felt inside. His suits occupied most of the space. Mitar's clothes were folded on the wardrobe floor. As far as he could make out, Stamenka's dresses and coats were there. He longed to stroke the silk, the lace over the bodice. Stamenka had never been pretty, but she'd been romantic.

'She expects to return,' he murmured. He turned to see Rajko kicking the bedclothes. What the hell was he doing? He burst across, too late to stop Rajko picking up the pillows and tossing them aside.

'Hell.' Stefan grabbed Rajko's arm, dragging him away.

'Are those yours?' Rajko asked.

Stefan's skin felt as though it was on fire. Stamenka's night attire lay next to his. She'd not given up. He was grateful for the darkness. He remembered their first night, her lips hard against his, the oily smell of her skin, her wetness, nails which clawed his back as he entered her, her snake-like movement as she twisted on top of him, hair damp on his chest.

'She might have taken a lover,' Rajko said.

'Never.'

'You stopped coming home.'

Stefan said sadly, 'The army claimed us both in the end.'

'Don't blame the army.'

Stefan began to return to the living quarters. The accusation was unjust. He'd gone home even when exhausted after work. It was hard to leave the barracks sometimes, but Stamenka drew him. And he'd travelled all over the Balkans, to Bulgaria, Roumania before the Turkish and Bulgarian wars, lectured in Paris and Berlin. It was after he'd been wounded, he'd not gone home and Rajko knew it.

He became entangled in the curtain. When he extricated himself, he asked, 'Who else is to blame, brother?'

As he fastened the latch to his house, he imagined Stamenka lying on her side of the bed, his nightclothes under his pillow. Had she lain waiting? Longing? He hurried down the steps, striding across the courtyard to his mother and brother's house, angry with Rajko.

Stefan thought they had become overconfident. The only sinister sign was the dog, but his brother could have shot her before they'd left. His mother's quarters in Woislav's house, were as he'd last seen them. He was struck by the orderliness of the kitchen. Knives in the drawer, pans and enamel bowls hanging on the wall and from ceiling hooks. His mother's apron lay over the back of a chair. His mind was reluctant to contemplate the possibility they'd been captured. Woislav, injured in a farming accident as a child, was no use to the army and none of his children was old enough to be cadets. He tried to convince himself the whole family, like many others, was returning to their birth village. Stamenka's parents lived in Orasac, as did his mother's sister. Relatives would take them in.

By the well, relieved he'd not found Stamenka's violated corpse, Stefan stuck out his chest, flung back his shoulders.

'Thank God, I got Mitar out.'

He was offering Rajko a cigarette when Rajko said, 'You ought to have got them both out as soon as war began.'

Rajko's cap was tipped off his face, his teeth grey in the darkness. He'd never been so critical before.

Stefan's stomach wrenched; he swallowed pieces of vomit. He explained, 'I didn't want to dishearten the men. I waited till Belgrade was lost.'

They walked towards the gates, their boots echoing around the compound.

'He's too young to leave his mother.' Rajko sounded angry.

Stefan spat, 'She spurned the General's car. What else could I do?'

'He's the sort who needs his mother.'

What the hell did Rajko know about children? He'd none. Not seen his wife for years. Ready to swing a punch, he turned on Rajko.

From the street, a voice called in hesitant German, 'Who goes there?'

He laid a pacifying hand on Rajko's shoulder, stilled his breath.

A big boned fellow, tall and lean, stood against one of the gateposts holding a lantern. Stefan strode towards him, noting he wore the field fez of a non-Austrian, probably Bosnian. Their luck might hold.

In German, Stefan replied, 'This place is empty. We can use it to bivouac our men.' As the man moved towards Stefan with his lantern raised, another soldier raced in from the alley. Shit. Rajko was so close, he smelled the tobacco on his breath.

Stefan spoke conversationally, 'Couple of habitable houses. Oven.' Even as he noted both men were armed, that the second had the facial features and bearing of a well-to-do Austrian, he was eyeing the gap between the soldiers and the gateposts. If necessary they'd make a dash for it. Rajko would be making similar calculations, ready for the order. Once out of firing range, they'd escape, more familiar with Belgrade's streets than these men.

'Papers,' said the Austrian. By the shifting light of the lantern, he showed himself to be a gangly character with chestnut coloured eyes. Ten years younger than either himself or Rajko, it was unlikely he knew the Bosnian. For a second, Stefan worried what Tomislav would do, if he heard of their escapade. Too late to think about that. Pretending to fumble for papers with his left hand, he pulled his pistol from under his greatcoat, directing it towards the man in the fez.

'Step aside,' Stefan ordered.

In an instant, the Austrian leapt at him, tried to grab the pistol, but collided with his compatriot who dropped the lantern, extinguished the flame. Stefan squirmed from the tentative grasp on his sleeve, managed to release the safety catch.

'Run, brother, run,' he shouted to Rajko.

He aimed for the chest of Bosnian. The Austrian fell back, struggled to position his rifle, evidently not a regular soldier.

As the Bosnian collapsed, convulsing on the cobblestones, Stefan turned. Rajko had jumped on the Austrian. Stefan slammed the butt of his gun against a skull and prayed it wasn't Rajko's. He edged forward, ready to shoot. He'd two cartridges. Crouching over the wrestling bodies, he tried to distinguish his friend. Grabbing the shoulders of the enemy, he put his arm around his neck, squeezing till the next cartridge slipped into the firing chamber.

There was no sound from the bullet. The smell of carbide filled his nostrils.

Only when Rajko said, 'Brother, my brother,' did he breathe again.

From across the river, an exploding bomb wailed. Two, three soldiers, he couldn't see clearly, ran through the gateway as he stretched his hand out to help Rajko to his feet. How many would follow?

Stefan called out in German, 'They're ours. See what you can do for them.'

He peered beyond them into the street. The newcomers fingered their rifles and edged forward.

'We'll fetch reinforcements,' Stefan declared.

Followed by Rajko, he marched to the gates, turned right, in the opposite direction to the *kafkana*, broke into a run when they reached the end of the compound wall. A siren sounded, as they padded towards the city.

Chapter Sixteen

On leaving Jevo, November 1915

I am writing this journal in the middle of our second day, ten miles outside Jevo. I was too tired last night. I'm sitting on a bench, by the fire in the schoolhouse, where 20 cadets and Audrey slept last night. The shutters are open, so we have light, but because there's no glass in the windows, we're cold to the bone. Some of the cadets are chatting, some playing games with stones and Audrey has gone for a walk. We're all hungry because the provisions' wagon, (laden with 47 loaves, packets of rice, sugar, tinned meat, beans, enough food to last 3 weeks), along with our other two, hasn't kept pace. A party of French and Russian doctors gave us bread, onions and cheese last night. Fresh bread from Mikaiho would have been welcome but Mikaiho didn't come.

At ten o'clock yesterday morning, we waved goodbye to the mothers, in particular Kostu's (lad with yellow scarf) and Radovan's (one less mouth to feed, she told me) who were weeping. I felt sorry for Mitar, still in his green jumper, but wearing the long homespun trousers and leather shoes we'd obtained for him. Clutching Prince Marko, a peg doll made by his grandmother, he was tearful. I felt sad his father hadn't sent him a message.

Audrey led our unit with Gustav. Where the road allowed, cadets walked in fours. The 6 with guns swaggered behind Audrey, jostling each other for a position at the front, providing Audrey with the 'protection' she doesn't want.

I brought up the rear, followed by our wagons.

The whole country is on the move: refugees, caravans of gypsies, troops of Austrian prisoners of war, army officers on horseback, in motorcars and carriages, unsupervised lads, the same age as ours. Occasionally, German planes buzz overhead.

We soon overtook cars, motor ambulances, cavalcades of gun carriages and wagon upon wagon of military equipment. I was surprised at how many ordinary families were leaving with us. Road noisy with animals (pigs, sheep, chickens), people talking, shouting to each other, soldiers singing. All seem in good spirits.

Mitar seems too young for this group. He has long, wavy hair, isn't tall like his father, walks with hand in his trouser pocket where he keeps Prince Marko. Mikaiho told me Marko is a Serb hero who appears when times are tough. Mitar's friend is Velimir (who's a year older) and they've palled up with 2 others, Kostu and Dusan, both with guns. Kostu told Mikaiho he was seventeen, but Branislav says he's only 15 and has 16 siblings! He's weighed down by cartridge belt and an ancient rifle and wears opanki sandals.

In the hotel in Jevo, Audrey and I worked out our respective duties. She is to offer first aid at beginning and end of each day, while I check we've not lost any of our 30 cadets.

Today Audrey decided we should rest because our supply wagons haven't caught up with us. Audrey didn't heed my concerns that the men at Dobro Majka had warned of snow, possibly blizzards when we reach the Albanian mountains. I proposed we buy bread and cheese in villages on our route.

I've used the delay to learn some names: the cadets who carry guns are: Bora, Bogdan (burly Bogdan), Kova, Zivoli, Kostu and Dusan. The latter is broader and taller than the rest, looks slightly more military. All look younger than 17.

Don't think much to Stefan's choice of 3 drivers, they're sullen, uncooperative and I can't understand their dialect.

The orderlies, Cosic, (already complaining of painful feet), Dobrica (lost a hand in the last war) and Timohir, all volunteered. We know and like them but, they behave differently away from hospital. They've to be told repeatedly to do each task. eg. I'd to ask Dobrica twice to fetch water from the well for Gustav. 1st time, he pretended he didn't understand. Audrey had similar problem with Cosic. Perhaps they're homesick.

Gustav is unpopular with other orderlies, possibly because he's Austrian.

The next morning, Audrey was up before dawn. She ordered Ellen to rouse the cadets: they were to leave the village without breakfast. Irritated she hadn't been consulted, didn't understand the reasoning behind the instruction, Ellen busied organising the incredulous drivers to travel ahead of her, Branislav and the group of cadets bringing up the rear.

When Audrey ordered a halt by the roadside mid-morning, Ellen ran across to where Audrey stood on a hummock, a few feet from the unit, stamping her feet to keep warm. Greatcoat collar raised, hands tucked into her pockets, woollen cap pulled over her ears, she appeared to be watching a team of bullocks pulling a gun carriage, overtake their column of cadets and wagons. Mitar scurried after Ellen.

Assuming they were stopping for breakfast, Ellen asked Audrey, 'We'll pull off the road, shall we?'

By now, Velimir had joined his friend so one stood either side of Ellen, Mitar tugging her sleeve.

He pestered, 'When will eat? I'm starving.'

'Please, wait,' Ellen reached for his hand, but he pulled away.

Puzzled that Audrey didn't respond, Ellen went on, 'We can't cook on the side of the road.'

Audrey was rubbing her hands up and down her arms, frowning.

'What's the matter?' Ellen pleaded. If she hadn't known Audrey so well, she'd have thought there were tears in her eyes.

Without glancing at Ellen or the cadets, Audrey strode down the slope, to rejoin Gustav at the front of the unit.

The remaining orderlies were huddled round the provisions' wagon, muttering. Just as Ellen decided Audrey was expecting her to organise the meal where they'd stopped, Gustav approached.

'Dr. Eyres says, no time to eat; we must press on.' He lowered his eyes, not looking at her and hurried back.

Ellen was hungry. Everyone was hungry. She ordered Dobrica and Cosic to distribute two apples each, Timohir, to give out Huntley and Palmer biscuits taken from the wagon.

At half past three, when it was starting to get dark, Ellen pushed her way to Audrey's side.

'Don't you think we should stop?' she asked, 'The lads are exhausted.'

Audrey didn't answer, but said to Gustav. 'See the drivers light the lanterns, will you?'

Ellen returned to the rear. What had got into her? When Gustav brought her a lighted lantern, he confided, 'Dr. Eyres is worried the enemy is closing in.'

'Why doesn't she speak to me?'

'The cadets will hear,' was his reply. Ellen didn't know what difference that made.

By the time Ellen reached the field Audrey had chosen to set up camp for the night, frost was forming along the branches of the hedgerows. Some refugees were settled at the far side of the field, by a stone wall and the smell of their barbecued meat drifted towards her, as she waited for Mitar. Other travellers continued on their journeys. Cursing drivers and orderlies were heaving their wagons through the mud, the oxen having been unhitched, were tethered several feet away. Dobrica was marking the boundary of their pitch with lighted torches, Gustav was building a fire. Mitar, clutching Branislav's hand, wimpered for his mother, Velimir, by his side paused in the gateway as though frozen to the ground. They'd both struggled all day and had fallen behind the main group.

Cosic declared, 'We'd be walking yet if we'd not refused.'

Ellen nodded sympathetically. However, it was the cadets she felt most sorry for. The jauntiness of the first day was gone. The joviality of yesterday's rest day, forgotten. Without having eaten, they'd to erect tents and help in the kitchen.

Audrey marched over. 'So, a third day without Mikaiho's fresh bread.'

Ellen wanted to point out they had loaves in their wagon. They were three days old, but arguing wouldn't help.

She tried to sound apologetic. 'I'm sorry.'

'I hold you responsible.'

Relieved she'd an explanation for Audrey's silence, she said, 'I'll arrange the meal, shall I?'

'It's too late. Dobrica can help put up the tents. You check the register.'

'Don't you think they ought to have something to eat? You said yourself they need three meals a day.'

'I know what I said and you said Mikaiho would ensure we had fresh bread.'

'Gustav could prepare cocoa. Perhaps biscuits?'

'I'm going to bed as soon as the tents are up.'

'You'll speak to Dobrica will you?'

'Yes, yes.'

'What about first aid? Cosic's feet...'

'In the morning.'

Ellen had never seen Audrey like this. Used to being in charge, she could be abrupt, preoccupied, but she was generally courteous. Nor was she known for sulking if she didn't get her own way—too pragmatic for that. Ellen decided to act as if nothing was untoward. When they were alone, she would find out what was on her mind.

Having given Gustav his orders, Ellen began to tick off the cadets on the register as she walked round the field in the dark. On the first day, she'd asked them to line up, but some were waiting for first aid from Audrey, others were eating or playing and it had proved impractical.

Gustav lit a fire, put on the kettle and distributed chunks of cold bully beef. Branislav seemed to be helping Audrey unload tents from the wagon. The drivers and other orderlies were sitting round the fire. Cosic, who wore the *sajkaca* round his head with the rightful pride of one who'd served the army for twenty years, sat smoking, while the others drank from bottles.

Mitar was lying on his back next to Dusan, Velimir and Kostu. The older cadets grouped around Bogdan and Kova, grabbing pieces of bully beef from the tins Gustav handed round. Ellen felt uneasy that those with guns seemed to get the most. They complained they were starving and Ellen asked

Gustav to slice several loaves of bread before he made the cocoa.

The drivers round the fire, were beginning to laugh, not in the drunken, goodhearted way of the men on the mule ambulance, but edgily as though a fight might erupt. Seeing no tents had yet been erected, she glanced over to the wagons. All the orderlies had joined Audrey and Branislav. Too tired to chat, she passed round the biscuits, trying to ensure the bigger lads didn't pinch more than their share. Alert to what was happening with Audrey, she noticed that Dobrica was helping her climb into the wagon.

Five minutes later, having made sure those who wanted seconds of cocoa got one, she realised that none of the tents had been erected. Quite a crowd had gathered round the wagon.

Carrying slices of bread to Audrey and the orderlies, too weary to smile, she was unprepared when Audrey screamed, 'You didn't check the tent poles.'

'What?'

'The tent poles, Ellen Frankland.' Audrey's woollen hat had fallen over an eyebrow.

'Mikaiho…'

'Lieutenant Nis.'

'He got the tents from the Berry unit. I didn't check them because I assumed they wouldn't give us with tents we couldn't use,' she objected.

'You were in charge of supplies.'

The orderlies were smirking. How had she and Audrey ended up bickering after only three days?

'Oh, Audrey!'

'You were too busy flirting!'

Ellen flushed. 'I don't flirt.' She kept her voice low, even. 'I'd no time to do a thing except get extra supplies so the cadets have warm clothes, boots and…'

'So what were you doing in the *kafkana*?'

Ellen shuffled, resisting the urge to touch her gun. 'Not flirting, I assure you. I had a coffee like you and Matron.' She ought to have admitted the truth from the beginning; cowardice, no doubt, but too late now. She added, 'I'm sorry about the bread. Mikaiho must have other duties. I didn't think to question how he'd fit it in.'

Cosic muttered in Serbian, 'The gypsies have stolen our tents.'

Ellen translated.

Audrey remained angry. 'If you'd done your job we'd know for certain whether they've been taken or if we've never had them.'

'I'm sorry,' Ellen said. She'd not considered ensuring Mikaiho had included tent poles. 'There's nothing we can do about it. We're all tired. We'll make up beds as best we can in the wagons for the youngest. The others can sleep either under the wagons or by the fire.' Stefan's comment that cadets were used to sleeping under hedges popped into her mind.

Gustav said, 'I will make a bed up for you, Dr. Eyres. You have led all day from the front. It is exhausting.'

Turning to Cosic, Ellen asked in Serbian, 'Do we have ground sheets?'

'Ground sheets, but no poles.' He shook his head dolefully. 'Thieved.'

She nodded, dismissing the niggle that Mikaiho might have been preoccupied with pleasing her. The Berry hospital had intended to help. Someone must have taken them, whether it was gypsies, or other thieves. All they could do, was get some sleep and in the morning move on.

An hour later, all the cadets were bedded. Orderlies and drivers lay close to the wagons. Gustav placed hot water bottles in sleeping bags for her and Audrey, stacked the folded tents as a windshield. The pine torches were allowed to burn out.

Ellen, the last to settle, made a final check. She was troubled when she couldn't find Bogdan or Kova, but when Mitar and his three friends were also missing she hurried to Audrey.

She flashed her electric torch. Audrey lay still, hair and forehead hidden by the woollen cap, her body covered by sleeping bag, several blankets and a mackintosh.

Crouching, Ellen whispered, 'Audrey, Audrey.'

196

Her friend didn't move. To lose Bogdan and Kova was bad enough, but not Mitar. On their first night outdoors, six cadets were missing. She'd seen enough of the older boys to imagine they might have joined the soldiers or moved out of the camp to smoke, but not Mitar and his pals.

She shook Audrey's feet.

'Damn!' she thought. She didn't want to face Audrey again. Yet, something had to be done. She inched nearer. Why she raised the edge of the sleeping bag with care, she wasn't sure. After all, she wanted to wake Audrey. She tapped Audrey's face with her fingers.

More urgently, 'Audrey! Wake up!'

She pulled back the covering blankets. 'It's important.'

'Go away,' Audrey pulled the blankets around her.

'Mitar's missing,' Ellen yelled.

'Go to sleep.'

Ellen envied her. She'd not even opened her eyes. Had she heard what she'd said? For a moment she was tempted to do as she was told, let Audrey deal with the consequences. Yet, Matron had said they must share the responsibilities. Standing up, she glanced round the field. In the distance, artillery fire shuddered across the horizon. Thousands of stars glistened and she thought of Edward. She should have gone home; she wouldn't be worried there. Instructing herself not to be a wimp, she decided to scour the field. She poked her head inside and under wagons, along the hedge, stumbled over the part of the field they weren't using.

In the end, Gustav told her to go to bed. They would turn up for breakfast. Boys were like that.

She was reassured. She removed her boots, crawled into her sleeping bag fully clothed. Audrey was snoring on her back. Despite thick socks, jumper and greatcoat, Ellen shivered. What a day. She remembered Brown's tearoom and the conversation with Audrey about Lady Alice's speech. Ellen had misunderstood what Lady Alice meant because she'd longed to be part of the action.

Audrey had over-reacted. Waved her cake knife in the air, sniffed in her annoying way and addressed Ellen as someone from the criminal classes. 'Of course, she didn't mean women

197

would become soldiers,' she'd lectured, 'Do you think I'd have volunteered? I'm a pacifist.'

And now she'd suffered the humiliation of Audrey not speaking to her all day. Gustav pitied her. The other orderlies despised her. As she curled up, the gun dug into her hip. Well, she wasn't going to give that up. Yes, she'd felt guilty when Audrey accused of her flirting, but she'd got it wrong and her intention was honourable. No, it served Audrey right. In any case, there were men so she wouldn't need a gun. She felt better; that was all.

The ground shuddered. The doctors had told them yesterday that the area was subject to thunder, but it could be the enemy getting closer. She wondered where Mikaiho was. Maybe he was dead. As they'd left Jevo he'd reported Belgrade had fallen, the rearguard had retreated and hundreds of civilians killed. There was no reason to suppose because she knew Stefan, Rajko and Mikaiho, they would be safe. Thank goodness, Edward had returned home. And England wasn't occupied.

It was no use; she wasn't going to sleep. She'd get up and have another look around. She inched out of the sleeping bag, trying not to disturb Audrey. When she put her boots back on, she touched her gun.

Wasn't Gustav implying that the boys were sleeping outside the camp? She'd questioned Branislav, but he denied any knowledge. Now she reflected, he hadn't been worried, so maybe he knew where they were. Perhaps they'd gone for food. They'd complained of hunger. She tip-toed past the wagons. The frost had frozen spears of mud, which collapsed, landing her in puddles, as she drew nearer the road. Through the hedge, sparks of light from lanterns flared as other travellers continued their journeys.

At the gate, calf-deep in mud, she walked along the bottom rung of the wooden gate, clinging to the top edge, till she was able to clamber onto the grass verge. Two mules, laden with panniers, led by women in black dresses, plodded by. Having forgotten her gloves, she rubbed her hands together, wriggled her fingers. A covered motorcar followed the mules. In the back seat a cigarette glowed. Someone else who couldn't sleep.

As a line of field kitchens approached, she was excited, optimistic they might belong to the Jevo regiment. When they weren't, she was disappointed. A breeze ruffled the hair that escaped her hat and chafed her cheeks.

'The nurses are way back.'

Ellen was startled by the American accent. A tall man, in a long jacket, withdrew from the cavalcade and leapt from his horse. It nuzzled her pocket and slipping off balance, Ellen was glad of the American's steadying arm. The distant hillside fizzed with sparks, an explosion, a flare.

By the time she asked, 'Is it the Austrians?' the hills had fallen once more into darkness.

'No, ma'am.'

She tried to inject some cheer into her, 'Of course not,' though she felt despair.

'Are you on your own?'

A Ford ambulance chugged past, splattering her greatcoat. The American steadied his horse. She couldn't see his expression, but he curved towards her, reminding her of Edward's attentiveness in the rose garden at their engagement ball. 'I want it to be perfect for you,' he'd said.

'I'm with the Jevo regiment. We're taking cadets to Durazzo.'

'Glad to hear you're not on your own. Good luck!' He saluted. 'I bid you goodbye.'

As she watched him remount and edge his way into the line of travellers, she felt tearful. Edward hadn't written because he needed her, but because he'd wanted to protect her.

From behind, a figure scurried towards her. 'Mitar!'

'No, miss.'

Branislav.

'They're not back?'

'You mustn't wander about on your own, miss.'

He was kind, sensible. From time to time during the day, he'd dropped back to chat; moved to Gustav to help set up the kitchen as evening approached; he encouraged those who were tired with stories of Serb heroes.

'Don't worry about them, miss. They know how to look after themselves.'

'Yes...' she said doubtfully.

'They're looking for the thieves in the hills. They won't go far. Bogdan is in charge.'

'I hope they bring back our tent poles.'

'The gypsies will have used them as firewood.'

Back in her sleeping bag, she remained restless. Distant shots could be Bogdan and his pals. It might have been better if the cadets hadn't guns; Audrey had a point.

The next morning the temperature lifted, the frost melted, rain threatened. Oak bushes and hedgerows appeared dipped in a vat of mud-coloured paint. Grass was churned up by vehicles, animals, boots. The stink from latrines on the far side pervaded the field.

Till her arrival in Serbia, Ellen had pictured war as colourful. Red jackets, gold braid, buttons and medals, the flash of weapons, the glisten of men's teeth as they smiled, happy to fight. The painting of her uncle in full dress uniform, over the sideboard in the breakfast room, contributed to this view. Women's Yeomanry camps took place during summer. Yet sepia was the colour of war. Nor had she contemplated defeat. She'd assumed the British would win, though they'd lost against the Boers; her uncle's medal for heroism obliterating that inconvenient fact. Not from the moment she'd volunteered, to the announcement the Women's Medical Corps was to return to England on the arrival of Austrian and German troops, did she reflect on how she might feel about the Serbs losing the war. Loss sapped her energy. The absence of Mitar worried her. A cigarette would have been a distraction, but Matron had persuaded her to pack a jumper and socks instead.

After breakfast, leaving cadets and Gustav washing up, she roused herself to make her peace with Audrey. She found her sitting on the bottom step of one of the wagons bathing Cosic's foot with surgical spirit. He stood, a discarded wellington in the mud, shoulders hunched, looking back to camp. He'd not shaved; his hair, grey and long under his *sajkaca*. He was difficult to fathom. When she'd worked with him in the operating tent, he was silent, somewhat morose, though Audrey spoke highly of him.

Audrey was twisting Cosic's foot to reveal raw, bleeding skin on its sole. 'Pass the lint, will you?' she asked.

Every now and again, Cosic slipped and splayed out his arms to retain his balance.

Ellen moved behind Audrey. Picking up the roll, which lay on a tray on the second step, she said, 'Did you sleep well?'

Audrey had tied a scarf on top of a black sou'wester. 'In the circumstances.' Her tone was cold. 'Pass the scissors.'

Ellen did as she was told. 'We can't continue like this for two or three weeks, you know. We have to be friends.'

Audrey sniffed. 'And the plaster.'

Ellen didn't move. Audrey wasn't looking at her, but holding out her hand. Cosic's foot was blue.

Audrey glanced back at Ellen after a moment. 'This is not a game. Pass the plaster.'

'You've only to twist and you can reach it yourself.'

Audrey tapped the step with her scissors. 'Cadets are missing. We've received neither bread nor the necessary papers to buy it.'

Cosic wobbled. Audrey snapped, 'Keep still.'

'I can't co-operate if you don't talk to me.'

'I am talking to you.'

Cosic gazed at his foot; he'd the look of men in the ward when they feared gangrene. Audrey glared at her so Ellen almost weakened, but she'd to make her point.

'You know what I mean. A proper conversation. Tell me what's troubling you.'

'I told you.'

'In addition to that.' She hesitated, reluctant to betray Gustav's confidence. 'Are you're worried the enemy will catch us up?'

With a sigh, Audrey turned and picked up the scissors before cutting into the roll. The wind whistled through the wagon. In the distance the sky was beginning to lighten. 'Look at Cosic. I never had any trouble in the operating theatre. He did whatever I asked when he got used to the routine; he anticipated, emptied the basket of limbs, brought in patients and made them comfortable. Now, he tells me he doesn't understand English and never does as I ask. And he's not the only one.'

'You mean Mikaiho.'

'It's all of them. Stefan didn't warn us it would be like this, with half the country on the move.'

'The orderlies don't understand English.'

'They're not co-operating.'

'No.'

While Audrey smoothed a piece of plaster over the heel of Cosic's foot, Ellen said, 'Would it help if you told me what you'd like the orderlies to do and I translate?'

Audrey, a hand on Cosic's foot twisted round to say, 'Frankly, I don't think you're on my side.'

'That's unfair. That the lads have shoes or boots and warm clothing is due to me. I've run up and down our line to make sure they can all keep up, helped to distribute food. I'm always the last to bed.'

'You didn't support my demand to have weapons banned.'

Ellen's hand instinctively reached across to the Luger under her tunic. For a split second she considered getting rid of it. 'I don't agree with you, that's all, ' she said keeping her tone conversational.

'You undermined my authority.'

'I agree with Matron. The cadets and the orderlies are armed because it's their job, but in every other way, I'm with you.' She wanted to add that sulking all day created a barrier, not togetherness.

Having stuck down the plaster, Audrey sprang to her feet leaving Cosic, his foot dangling. As he toppled forward, Ellen caught his hand. He was trembling. He raised his eyebrows as much to say, '*What do you expect?*' before planting his foot where Audrey had sat. He stroked his foot before starting to put on his sock.

As she released Cosic's hand, Ellen looked across to see what had prompted Audrey to shift. Mikaiho headed the missing cadets. He'd not shaved; the hem of his greatcoat was thick with mud. He'd never looked dishevelled on the mule ambulance.

In delight, Ellen exclaimed, 'Oh,' and leaving Cosic on the wagon steps, ran towards the group.

Mikaiho saluted.

Mitar flicked his fingers. By his side, Velimir stood, head down. One of his shoes was missing and he rested the bare foot lightly on the ground. Kostu's yellow scarf was smattered with mud, Kova's sleeve ripped. Only Dusan and Bogdan appeared defiant, hands on hips.

'Where've you been, Lieutenant Nis?' Ellen was surprised by the fury in Audrey's voice.

'I've found your charges.'

'You promised bread.'

'You ladies are a grave disappointment.'

Mitar raised his head. One cheek was scratched. In Serbian, he said to Mikaiho, 'You're a bully.'

Wondering what Mikaiho had been doing, that resulted in him coming across the lads, Ellen frowned.

'This one,' Mikaiho pointed with the butt of his gun to Velimir, 'led an attack on gypsies.'

'Velimir?' A skinny youth with no muscle?

Audrey said, 'We didn't give them permission to leave camp, but they went in search of the thieves who stole our tents poles. If they were stolen. Did you check that all parts of the tent were there when you collected them from the Berry hospital?'

Mikaiho seemed uncomprehending and gazed at her. After a moment he said, 'The boys have been punished. I have whipped them and taken their guns. They're not to be trusted.'

Audrey snapped, 'They shouldn't have guns in the first place, Lieutenant.'

Mikaiho clenched his fists.

Ellen said, 'Lads, please go to the kitchen orderly and see if there's any breakfast left.'

Bogdan sneered, 'There'd better be.'

The cadets turned to follow Bogdan. Mitar took Velimir's hand, 'You're a bully!' he shouted at Mikaiho before walking away.

Ellen was about to ask Mikaiho if he'd like something to eat when Audrey, her cheeks red, shouted, 'Where's the bread you promised?'

Mikaiho shouted, 'You've a wagon full of food! We Serbs are starving.' He stepped towards Audrey, his body tensed, an arm raised.

Afraid he was going to hit Audrey, Ellen moved between them. 'Please, Mikaiho.'

Audrey went on coldly, 'We have provisions because Serbs gave us them. They support their country. And as for you, you are a vain, boastful man, showing off to Miss Frankland. Telling her what she wants to hear.'

Mikaiho, his hand on the butt of his pistol, stamped his foot. 'You're lucky you're not a man or I'd kill you. You who speaks no Serbian and do not love us. You're on your own. I will not help you again.' He spun round, walked away.

Ellen began to follow.

Audrey cried, 'Don't you dare.'

Ellen paused. Audrey was in the wrong. Mikaiho must have duties they knew nothing about.

Audrey said, 'Ellen! See to the cadets.'

Mikaiho was striding across mud and ruts, leaping across puddles. Ellen wanted to say goodbye, to thank him, they might never meet again. He'd been glad to see her. Now he hurried away.

She took another step towards him.

Audrey whispered, 'No.'

Audrey didn't understand, but they must get along. She couldn't bear another day of silence.

Not moving, she watched Mikaiho till he left the field, lost behind a gun carriage. Maybe he would relent. He might return. She swallowed.

Without looking at Audrey, she began to walk towards the kitchen. On the edge of her vision, she noticed Cosic hadn't moved from the wagon steps. She wondered how much of the conversation he understood and what he made of it.

Chapter Seventeen

Along the Ibar valley

30th November 1915

We arrived in Kraljevo late last night and luckily were able to camp close to the Scottish Women's Hospital. The journey is more arduous than we expected. Cadets have swollen feet, blisters and, despite my efforts in Jevo, some remain inadequately dressed. We decided they'd benefit from a day's rest. We discarded the tents from the Berry hospital, and SWH gave us 3 large ones and a two-man.

I suggested we divide the cadets into 3 groups (something I learned at Women's Yeomanry) with Dusan, Bogdan and Branislav as leaders. I organised groups, according to their friendships. Kitchen chores are on a rota basis, with orderlies cooking under Gustav's charge. Drivers are spared additional duties.

Gustav provided an excellent chicken dish: red and green peppers, hot spices with rice and couscous.

Already we've been on the road for 1 week. Stefan's 'two—three' was optimistic, I'm afraid.

Cosic didn't return to camp last night. I learned from other orderlies, he's 40, married with son and son-in-law in the army, none of which explain why he's missing.

1st December 1915

Yesterday I wrote to Edward, leaving letter to be posted by SWH. Audrey knows some of the doctors and nurses at the hospital. While we all drank coffee she told us she'd almost returned to Jevo that day she didn't speak to me. She felt threatened by the cadets with guns walking behind her. She's glad she didn't, because we're now 'working as a team'.

We moved on after breakfast of porridge prepared by Scottish nurses, though the cadets prefer their popiri.

Ibar is magnificent valley. Road a thousand feet above river in places. Miles from artillery fire.

Cosic returned just as we were leaving, he told us, 'woman trouble.' I pretended not to notice him loading bottles into the provisions' wagon, hoping I'd imagined it.

The following day, late afternoon, the unit pulled into a field of unharvested maize. Despite the ground being wet from the previous day's rain, the cadets flung themselves down, while the drivers and orderlies manoeuvred the wagons to the shelter of the stone wall. On Audrey's instructions, Ellen asked the orderlies to dig up the maize so the cadets could erect tents.

Cosic complained he was exhausted.

Timohir argued it wasn't his job when there were thirty cadets, fitter than he.

Dobrica shrugged, 'I sleep under the wagon. Why should I help?'

Ellen wasn't surprised by the refusal; Audrey was.

It was Branislav who offered to clear the field with Bogdan and Dusan, describing the orderlies as old. Audrey was angry the orderlies did nothing to help; Ellen was relieved conflict had been avoided.

Some cadets murmured they were hungry and tired, yet as soon as Audrey told Mitar, 'You are too young for this,' the rest of the cadets jeered and he saw Audrey's protectiveness as an insult. He grabbed the plant with both hands, raised his arms, tumbled backwards when it freed. Audrey shrugged. The laughter made him work harder. Bogdan and Dusan challenged the other's team. Branislav boasted his would beat them both. Ellen distributed apples and biscuits thirty minutes later, when the site was ready.

Branislav organised a competition as to which group would erect its tent first. Ellen offered first in the queue for tea as the prize. Half an hour later, Branislav asked the women where they would like their tent. Satisfied Gustav could manage, that the orderlies and drivers weren't going to help, Ellen proposed they might erect their own. She wanted to prove this was something she could do better than her friend, aware that though Audrey had camped, men did the 'physical work'. Having finished first aid, Audrey agreed.

For ten minutes or so they unpacked the bag of equipment, laid the ground sheet, securing it with their own kit bags. Without too much difficulty, they pieced together the poles, accepting Branislav and Bogdan's help to throw the canvas over the ridge-pole.

Ellen considered herself skilled at hammering in pegs. Having stuck one in the soil, she raised the mallet and whacked it. The mallet reverberated against metal, sending ripples up her arm; the peg barely moved.

'It's not going to be easy,' she advised Audrey.

'We can take it in turns.'

Ellen angled the peg and tapped. It needed to nudge into the soil. It took several minutes and sweat trickled under her arms by the time it held firm.

Convinced Audrey would be less successful, she handed her one saying, 'You'll need gloves.'

With a couple of smacks it was in.

In disbelief, Ellen commented, 'I thought you'd not pitched a tent before.'

'I haven't.' Audrey dabbed her forehead with her handkerchief, adding, 'You must be stricter with the orderlies and drivers.' She gave the mallet to Ellen.

Some cadets gathered and Mitar jeered, 'Slow, too slow. We work faster.'

Irritated, Ellen said, 'Get on with it then,' but he called Velimir to watch. Ellen picked another peg. Even though they were sheltered from the worst of the wind, damp rose through the soles of her boots. Her body ached with the day's accumulated anxiety and tiredness. Pine torches flickered, threatening to blow out.

Pausing with the peg in her left hand, mallet in her right, she remarked, 'I don't understand all they say and I'm not sure I use the best words when I give orders.'

'You speak well enough.'

Ellen knew her ability in Serbian relied on the goodwill of the person she was speaking to. If he didn't want to do what she was asking, he didn't understand.

Her fingers slipped. Maybe she should remove her gloves. She slammed the peg but the mallet bounced back.

Ten or so cadets gathered. Audrey said, 'You need to say, "No drinking till duties are completed."'

And how would they stop them drinking? Pouring it away wasn't an option. The men were strong. Drinking was what they did when they finished work; the problem was agreeing as to when duties were over.

The lads offered to take her turn. She ought to have whizzed round like she used to. When the next peg sank in, she handed the mallet back to Audrey with relief.

She belonged on the mule ambulance, but not here. She missed Mikaiho's companionship. On the mule ambulance train he taught her Serbian, encouraged her when she made mistakes, whereas there wasn't a cadet, certainly not an orderly, who'd either the patience or the interest to teach her new words or expressions.

She leaned forward to discover how Audrey angled the peg. Straight in. Whack.

She always felt inadequate next to Audrey. It was her own fault for wanting to impress. She raised the mallet; the muscles at the top of her arm tensed. Imagining Audrey's head she brought it down. The peg sprang out. A burst of applause from the cadets.

'Well done, miss!' giggled Mitar.

'Tomorrow,' she said to Audrey, 'I'll go early to the village and see if I can buy bread.'

When she asked the orderlies to prepare the meal with Gustav, they turned their backs on her. Audrey wanted her to insist, but Ellen refused, certain they'd argue hot food was of no consequence to them; they were content with beef from the tin.

During the early hours of the morning, Ellen was woken by raised voices. She slept in tunic and culottes so Audrey wouldn't see the Luger bulge and she was stiff from the awkwardness. She eased out of bed. She'd been dreaming of her mother throwing a red ball. Wearing a turquoise dress she adored when she was eight, Ellen chased the ball aware of someone else competing from a different direction. Her mother was laughing and the recollection of her mother, happy and strong, saddened her and she sat up. She stretched her neck, first right, then left, wondering who'd been racing against her to catch the ball. Outside, men clapped to the sound of a reed pipe.

Not wanting to get cold, she twisted to unfasten the flap. Through the gap, she spied orderlies and drivers huddled around the fire, Cosic with his back to her. Dobrica who'd refused to fetch wood for Gustav's fire, was throwing on a log. Timohir, the eldest at fifty, had confided at Dobro Majka that one of his sons had been killed, a son-in-law wounded in the war. They used to chat; now he averted his eyes when she passed. In the darkness, the group morphed into a three-headed monster. They began to sing, 'Uncle Petar rides a horse, Old Franz rides a donkey.' She slipped back into her sleeping bag, the gun digging in.

When she woke Gustav was on his own, stoking the fire for breakfast. She dressed, took Audrey a beaker of tea and set off across the field to the village. In the dark, her electric torch shone on tents, wagons and finally the road along the Ibar. Despite gloves and woollen socks, she felt a shiver of apprehension. The traffic was unceasing. She waved a greeting to a man in a turban walking by the side of a caravan, said, '*Dobar dan*,' to a bare foot woman next to their horse. She flashed the beam on the road ahead. Stones of all sizes, ruts and puddles made walking difficult. She pulled her hat closer to her ears, her coat collar up.

Last night some cadets had gone exploring; they told her the village lay off the road by a bridge. When she followed their directions, the path became narrow and it took her a while to adjust to the darkness. She stopped at the bridge, leaning over, her thighs cold against the stone. She shone her light to the water some three feet below. Waves lapped the banks; in comparison to the Ibar it was shallow, but still fast. It reminded her of the Dove, pretty in summer, wild in winter. The thud of approaching footsteps disturbed the thought of needing to write her journal. Had men from the road noticed a woman on her own? Were they following her? She switched off her torch, shoved it in her pocket. In the distance the jangle of oxen bells, wheels rolling on. She tensed, unfastened a button on her greatcoat, prepared for an attack.

'It's all right, Miss.'

Kostu was wrapped in his yellow scarf and a woollen coat she'd not seen before. He and Zivoli were the only cadets with spare clothes. He strode towards her, followed by Mitar and Velimir. She relaxed, stepped away from the wall.

'Oh, oh,' she stuttered as Bogdan, Dusan and Branislav joined them.

'You can't carry all the bread,' Bogdan said. Though he spoke lightly, his height, broad shoulders, alarmed her.

She spoke calmly, 'I won't need six.'

'You might.'

She was being foolish; they were on the same side. If she'd been sensible, she'd have asked for volunteers last night, but she wanted to go on her own, bring back loaves in triumph.

'Come on then.' She swung the torch in an arc, rebuttoned her greatcoat. The track was too narrow, too uneven for her to march ahead as she wanted. Instead, she stumbled, boots slipping. Kostu repeatedly flung his scarf over his shoulder. The wind rose and Mitar crouched close behind. His teeth chattered. Velimir was panting.

Unnerved the others remained by the bridge, Ellen called, 'Come on, lads!'

'They'll catch up,' Kostu said.

As the track rose, Velimir slid on scree, fell. She helped him up, reminding herself he didn't have the advantage of a torch.

'Walk slowly, brother,' Mitar said. His manner of speaking reminded her of Stefan. She wondered if he'd considered how arduous the journey would be for a thirteen year old.

The sky lightened, the path widened, shadows became grey, tree trunks black.

She turned to ask, 'Are you cold?'

'No, miss,' said Kostu.

Velimir skidded and as he steadied himself, Mitar put an arm around his shoulder. It was silly to feel apprehensive. They were struggling too. Kostu and Mitar missed their mothers. Branislav told her Mitar looked for his every day among the crowd of refugees, convinced she would find him. Velimir, undernourished from the start, didn't like the food, existed on biscuits and bread. He'd taken the brunt of Mikaiho's whipping; the wheals on his back were slow to heal.

'It is cold this morning,' Mitar said slowly in English.

In Serbian, she replied, 'Would you like my gloves?'

He shifted a fraction away from her, edging closer to Velimir.

'Damn,' she thought, 'I got it wrong.'

Again the track narrowed, so they reverted to single file, Ellen leading. A mist swirled, hiding and revealing rocks on each side, dulling sound. Wings fluttered, startling her. She began to rehearse, 'We are from the Jevo regiment. We need bread.' She wondered what Bogdan and the others were up to.

She flashed the torch when they reached the first dwelling, a mud daub hut without glass in the window. Behind her, the voices of Bogdan, Dusan, Branislav. She saw again the man with his eyes gouged and began to tremble. She kept moving. Wood smoke mingled with the smell of the earth. She tried to forget the church with corpses. Mitar, Kostu and Velimir stayed close, the other cadets moved off. She thought the village would be bigger from what the cadets described last night. She did her best to ignore the smell of rotting bodies. She must bury the memory. The cadets talked of a bakery. She must keep going. She blew her nose.

In the misty gloom, she made out five houses on either side of a path. Serb villages spread out, sometimes into the hillside. No bakery. The three friends stood inches behind her. One of them prodded her in the back when a woman in long, black dress and sheepskin waistcoat emerged from a house. Dragging part of a tree trunk, as long as she was tall, her breath rose in a mist. When Ellen turned the torch in her direction, illuminating her face, the woman lifted her head, but continued her task.

Switching off the light, Ellen said, '*Dobar dan.*'

'What do you want?'

'Bread.' Mitar sounded threatening.

'We have no bread.'

'Please. Where is the baker?' Ellen's voice shook.

'We have no bread.' The woman stared at them before hauling the trunk with both hands towards an oven by the side of the house.

'She's lying,' Velimir said.

'They have some,' Kostu added.

Ellen shushed them. To the woman she spoke softly. 'We have money.' Annoyed with herself for not using her rehearsed phrases, she paused as a man emerged from the same house as the woman. The shadowy figures of cadets crouched on the other side of the path. In the distance birds squawked. The man shouted to the woman, who replied without pause, at length. He shuffled towards them, a rabbit skin wrapped round his neck, a rifle slung in a holster over his woollen coat.

'I am old.' His accent was educated and he looked into Ellen's face.

Overwhelmed, not only that he spoke, but she understood him, Ellen imitated the voice Audrey used to the orderlies in the operating tent, hoping it would give her authority.

'I am Ellen Frankland from the Jevo regiment. We have thirty cadets and they need bread.'

'All our men have gone to fight.'

'We have dinars.'

A door slammed. Bogdan shrieked, Branislav's voice reassured. They must be inside houses.

Not wanting to be complicit in their behaviour, she shouted, 'Bogdan! Come here.'

'Give me your cadets to plough our land and I will give you bread,' the man said.

'We are leaving Serbia. One day they will return as soldiers.'

Water rushed down the steep-sided rocks behind them; it mingled with the boys' distant voices, Mikaiho's whisper, 'villagers will return and bury their own.'

'Who will be here when the Swabos come? Who will protect us old men and women?'

'Swabos?' she asked, 'I don't know "swabos".'

'Murderers.'

212

'These cadets will come back brave soldiers,' was all she could say. The man grunted to the woman and looked to the dwellings behind her.

The woman spoke rapidly. He raised his rifle and waddled towards their house.

'They've gone for bread, miss. He'll shoot them,' Mitar said.

Her mind was in turmoil. Even Branislav was a thief.

With small steps, she followed the man, flashing her torch in time to see Branislav and Bogdan charge at him from different directions. They reached him simultaneously so he collapsed, dropping his gun.

Branislav grabbed it and Ellen shouted, 'Drop it.' He took no notice. Shoving the torch in her pocket, she raced to seize it.

Dusan emerged from the greyness. Behind her, Mitar, Velimir and Kostu, 'Get him, Miss'.

She skidded, knocking down the old man who was struggling to his feet. She snatched the barrel of the rifle shouting, 'Branislav, let go!'

She dug in her heels, prepared to wrestle it from him, but Branislav released his hold and the gun was hers. By now the man was standing, his face red.

'I am sorry, sir.' She handed him the weapon.

'I am sorry for you, lady.'

There was no point remaining, so she said goodbye to the woman and began to walk away. She heard Branislav's voice close by, cadets' laughter and scuffles. She felt let down, particularly by him. Matron had suggested Ellen redeem herself during this journey, but so far she was proving to herself and to everyone else, she was useless. Summer camps had been no preparation. The orderlies and drivers drank and the cadets, having become a team as a result of her suggestion, had turned against her. Audrey would continue to despise her.

She kicked at stones on the track, slithered down the slopes. By the time she reached the bridge, a watery sun had risen. Branislav, Bogdan and Dusan were sitting on the parapet, holding loaves on their laps. She didn't know how they'd got there, didn't care.

Branislav called, 'Hello, miss.'

Waiting till she was close enough for him to see her face, she burst out, 'You have disgraced the good name of the Jevo regiment.'

He looked surprised; the others clapped his back. As best she could, she strode on but moments later they overtook her, Mitar, Velimir and Kostu close behind.

Mitar called, 'We have bread, miss.'

Velimir struggled to keep up and though he shouted something, she couldn't make out what it was. Theft didn't seem to be a concept they understood. The warmth of the sun did nothing to cheer her. It took all her courage to return to camp with her head high, her shoulders back.

By the time Ellen reached the camp, the cadets had started to take down the tents. She gave Audrey a brief account, apologised, proposing that at the next village she try again, taking a couple of cadets, possibly Mitar and Velimir. Audrey was more concerned about Cosic's feet, even though she suspected his plea to ride in the provisions' wagon related to his desire to dip into the tins of meat and packets of cocoa rather than difficulty walking. The women agreed priority for space in the wagons would be given to the younger cadets, but that everyone should walk initially.

Ellen was supervising the loading of tents and blankets when the woman and man from the village appeared. The man, out of breath; the woman bent over a cooking pot she was carrying.

'For the little Avengers of Serbia,' the man said solemnly.

The woman swung what looked like washing up water and pieces of carrot at Ellen.

'There is no bread,' she said, 'Your brave boys stole it.'

Ashamed, Ellen ordered Gustav to distribute the *popiri* to any who wanted.

The next morning it rained till about eleven thirty, when the sun began to ease its way through the cloud. Most of the cadets were in good spirits. A discussion with Branislav before they'd gone to bed had cleared the ill will between them. Ellen accepted the older cadets had wanted to protect her, understood that they considered the baker and his wife mean spirited, when they'd left their homes and families, in order, one day, to fight the Austrian oppressors.

Before breakfast, Branislav and Mitar accompanied Ellen to a small village where they were given newly baked bread and sweet corn to roast for their evening meal. Ellen persuaded a reluctant Audrey that tired cadets could ride in each of the wagons. Despite the validity of Audrey's reasoning: the cadets stayed up too late, the authors of their own weariness, Ellen wanted to keep morale high. They compromised: no more than two cadets in a wagon, replaced by two others when they stopped for a break.

If Ellen hadn't been worrying about Edward's reaction to her remaining in Serbia, she might have been able to enjoy the journey. For miles the road rose six hundred feet above the roaring Ibar, while it looked up to promontories of castle ruins like those she enjoyed in childhood storybooks. The ground was sticky with mud; the rocks shone in the sunlight, drops glistened like pearls on bare branches. This was the land of Serb heroes. Many cadets were superstitious like Mitar, who swore King Marko walked with them, kept them safe. There'd been no glimpse of his Prince Marko doll and she wondered if he still had it.

Walking between Mitar and Velimir, Ellen listened to them chattering about teachers. Some nasty, some nice. Ahead was a family with belongings and livestock, Audrey and the leading wagons were out of sight. Their provisions' wagon having earlier overtaken the family and its cart, swayed voluptuously a few yards ahead along the uneven track.

Velimir nagged, 'Our legs are tired, when can we have a turn at riding?'

Mitar complained, 'Look, miss! They're passing the old bullock and Zivoli and Kova will have our seats.'

The chance to ride was becoming a source of dispute.

The 'old bullock' was pulling one of the heaviest artillery guns Ellen had seen; it was part of a long, wide army convoy, which would take several minutes to pass.

Ellen was about to reassure the boys, when the provisions' wagon lurched sideways and began to overtake. Amazed at the risk, she clasped her hands as the wagon veered close to the precipice. The rear wheel thumped into an axle deep hole. She stopped walking, waiting for the wagon to steady, but it hung in space over the canyon. As the edge of the path crumbled under the front wheel, roaring rocks distracted her from grasping that the wagon was tipping sidelong into the ravine. She tried to run, but the men pushing the handcart in front of her blocked the way, shouting, 'Thief!' as if she wanted to steal their squawking hens.

By the time she reached the cliff edge, the whole wagon had collapsed into the abyss. She heard herself screaming, 'No! No!' Rocks rattled and clattered. The canvas roof floated, before resting on a juniper bush. The frame had snapped like dry twigs. She'd not realised it was fragile. She'd encouraged cadets to travel in a contraption as flimsy as a moth's wings. Boxes broke, tins of beef, condensed milk, rolled down the gorge. Sacks of cocoa, sugar and curry powder burst. Bottles of wine smashed, discolouring limestone. Her scream bounced round her head, joining the torrent of the Ibar, the cries of Mitar and Velimir, the bellowing of the oxen.

She and an army officer reached the spot where the wagon had skidded off the path at the same time. The sun dissolved the grey cloud and burned her face. There was little evidence from where they stood, of the catastrophe, other than a gouge made by one wheel in its attempt to stay upright. The air was scented with chocolate, tinged with curry, but though Ellen crouched as close to the ledge as she dare, she couldn't see the driver, the cadets or the oxen.

The valley echoed with their names as she called, 'Miodrag, Radovan,' her voice rising as she realised the futility. Hands on her face, she scanned each rock, each bush, but could see nothing. Below them, the gleaming Ibar swirled and dived. The wagon and its cargo might never have existed.

Ellen didn't want to move till she'd seen the bodies, but the army officer assured her no one could survive the fall; he insisted she move on, as more accidents would be caused with traffic building up. Mitar and Velimir's distress persuaded her they must keep going. The army officer sent word to Audrey and their other drivers and they pulled in at the next village.

It was fortunate they were able to secure accommodation at a small inn for half the cadets. The rest slept in a hayloft while orderlies and drivers remained with the wagons. For the first time since they'd left Jevo, Ellen and Audrey slept in a room, each with a bed and straw mattress, each with a separate washbowl and water jug. The landlady in full skirt and embroidered bodice brought them coffee and walnuts.

Ellen doubted she'd sleep, wanted to talk about the accident, but Audrey was reluctant.

When Ellen told her a driver said his brother was drunk, Audrey shrugged. 'How do we know? And if he was, there's nothing we can do.'

'I should have forbidden them.'

'The damage is done.'

'I shouldn't have let the boys ride in the wagon.'

'It's over.'

In bed, Ellen ached with tiredness, hunger and loneliness. She smelled the creepers on the veranda, smoke drifting through the floorboards from the inn below. She kept seeing Mitar's tears, Velimir's white face. Audrey insisted children were resilient, but Ellen didn't agree. Papa had said as much when her mother died and it wasn't true. Over and over, she pictured the wagon tumbling down the gorge, distraught she couldn't remember the faces of the cadets who died, anguished they might not be dead, were dying slowly or being eaten by animals.

For a few hours she slept, though it was still dark when she woke. She dressed without disturbing Audrey, put on her boots and greatcoat and crept down the wooden stairs. At the bottom, she pushed the door, which led into the courtyard. It was raining hard, and she pulled up her collar. Where was Mikaiho? Perhaps he was dead too. In the distance, carriage wheels, men marching, talking. She walked across the courtyard to the well.

'Foreign louse,' Mitar spat at her when she checked they were settled for the night. Surely he didn't blame her for the accident.

She wound the bucket up from the well, splashed her face with icy water. She prayed they'd no inkling of what was happening. She recalled the day the unit left Jevo, how naïve she'd been. She imagined they'd walk in crocodile for an hour before stopping for tea and sandwiches. Not for an instant had she contemplated the physical conditions of the cadets or the journey. Her jaw ached. What about King Marko? She wanted to ask Mitar. Why hadn't he come galloping on his piebald steed?

And then she remembered Miodrag's face, pretty with long lashes, followed by Radovan's, long and earnest and his mother's tears as she'd waved goodbye.

Chapter Eighteen

Orasac, November 1915

Lamps were being lit in Arandjelovic as Stefan stabled his horse. He left the town by the alley, which led across fields and paths. It tracked the stream; the stream not as vigorous as he remembered. Within minutes he and Dragan reached the old bridge and the climb to Orasac. Flakes of sleet stung his eyes. He strode without pause, not caring a breathless Dragan struggled several feet behind. From the top of the crest, he gazed back. He used to love market days: the smells of roast pig, chestnuts, earth on potatoes and root vegetables, the stink of sheep and chickens. He took a cigarette from his inside pocket, a box of matches and turned three hundred and sixty degrees to face home.

Tomislav wouldn't approve. No matter. Tomislav envisaged a hero's welcome such as they'd received in Jevo. Townsfolk lined the streets garlanded for the arrival of the allies; allies who never arrived. On the steps of the town hall, Tomislav thanked the crowds for supporting their army and people cheered rapturously. He described the retreat as a strategic triumph, promised an imminent return, a final, resounding victory. But Tomislav departed before the mood changed, before angry peasants surrounded Stefan's motorcar, before they couldn't be soothed.

The last time he visited Orasac, had been his wedding day, fifteen years ago, but what he remembered now was his boyhood. He used to run between the village and Arandjelovic most days. As a shepherd in the hills below and to the east, he became familiar with the tracks during the night as well as the day. Through a haze of cigarette smoke, he saw a smattering of lights like glow worms. At first, he did his best to explain to Tomislav the village was insignificant and with men of fighting age away, moreso. But as soon as he realised Tomislav wanted him to get used to being treated with honour, to appreciate flag waving, Stefan stopped trying. It was too good an opportunity to miss. He yearned for Stamenka, to hear her say he'd been right to take Mitar, to be reassured she was safe. And if Tomislav believed it was an opportunity for a defeated army to comfort its people, what was the harm?

When Dragan joined him, panting, Stefan said, 'See that light? She will be at Ljubomir's, her father's house. Next to it, is her uncle's.'

'Will Lieutenant Nis have made arrangements for us to sleep there?'

It would be crowded. Though one of the largest houses in the village, it accommodated not only Ljubomir and his wife, but their youngest daughter, her husband and children. A brief letter from Woislav informed him their mother was living there, presumably with Stamenka.

'It's the place we're making for,' he replied.

'Where does the Lieutenant live?'

'The other end.'

He'd have to pay a call on Mikaiho's mother. After all, her husband had provided his education. Stefan fulfilled his obligations by sending money each month, but it would be necessary for her standing within the village, little though it was, for him to visit.

He began the descent, making his way with ease round roots and rocks and after half an hour came upon the main road.

At the stunted clump of acacias, which marked the turn to the lane leading to Stamenka's father's house, he stepped more cautiously. He manoeuvred through troughs of mud to higher clay ridges. A dog barked and didn't stop until they passed its domain; another picked up the signal. It was as well Tomislav wasn't there to witness Stefan's return through darkening, empty lanes.

The moon rose, silvering the falling sleet. Ahead the whitewashed oblong of Ljubomir's house. Stefan's spine tingled as he pictured Stamenka running down the path. The dog in the kennel growled as they neared the house; he pushed open the gate. From the door, Stamenka's mother called, 'Who's there?'

'It is I. Stefan Petrovic.'

'Welcome home, son.'

Stefan found it hard to cope with the disappointment. No Stamenka. He looked over Juliajana's head. His mother leaned on a broom; his sister-in-law squatted next to a cradle, rocked a child of two or three within it.

'Where's Stamenka?'

No one answered.

Juliajana raised a cheek for a kiss and as his lips skirted her skin, he glanced around. Strange how memory obliterated things it didn't want to recall: earth floor, smoke filling the room for want of a chimney, stink of bodies too long in close proximity. The child had shit itself, and though cleaned, the smell lingered. A garland of chrysanthemums on the wall had dried to cracking point.

Half an hour later, having shared the customary *shlatko* and having washed and shaved, Stefan sat in a wicker chair by the fire, Dragan on the footstool next to him. A bowl of stewed apple and maize bread on his lap, Stefan watched his mother who seemed not to have moved since he entered, while Juliajana sat on the mattress, apparently in charge.

Leaning forward, Juliajana was saying, 'I'm sorry I can't provide the food a hero deserves.' Fifteen years ago, Juliajana was round and cheerful, but this evening she looked as shrivelled as the old corncobs on the windowsill above the sink.

'We have no better in the army.'

'It's not what your mother tells us.'

It would be disrespectful to point out his mother hadn't experienced army life, but he raised his head as he chewed waiting for her to comment. She remained arched over a broom, her white hair partly covered by a black scarf.

The logs spat sparks. Stefan unfastened the top button of his tunic. Did his medals intimidate his mother? It was many months since he'd seen her; time at home was spent with his wife and son. Suddenly he felt awkward, unable to ask how she was.

He spoke kindly, 'It's hard for us all.'

His mother's voice quavered. 'We're proud you dined with the King.'

He didn't correct her. As a child, he recalled her being cowed by his father.

'Your hospitality is generous,' he said to Juliajana. He dipped his fingers in the bowl, tore off a piece of bread and raised it to his mouth. Stale. Anywhere else, he'd have asked for the fresh loaf in his knapsack.

The sister-in-law had moved to the other side of the fire and was singing to the child. He recognised the tune; they sang different words in the mess. On his arrival, he'd learned the family was in mourning for her husband killed ten days ago during the defence of Belgrade.

After a moment, he spoke to his mother, as though to the child being rocked, 'Did Stamenka bring you?'

Juliajana answered. 'We do not speak of her.'

'Why?'

'Mucak says she's a lost soul, and for once he's right,' Juliajana added. The old nickname, 'Rotten Egg' and her tone reminded him Mikaiho used to be a figure of ridicule.

'Stamenka is my wife.' He didn't raise his voice. Bile rose into this throat.

'She has brought great shame on you, so also on us,' Juliajana said. Hugging her chest, Juliajana rocked to and fro. 'In the city it may be acceptable to disobey a husband, but not here.'

Dragan's jaw cracked as he chewed.

Juliajana went on, 'We pity you.'

Angrily Stefan retorted, 'I don't need your pity!'

Juliana shook her head. 'You have no wife and we have no daughter called Stamenka.'

He stood up, put his bowl on the earth close to the fire and walked towards the window. He tapped the pane, 'Who paid for this, the new distillery, the cradle for your grandchild? You'd have none of these if Stamenka hadn't told me of your need. Have you forgotten?' Someone whistled a dog and he peered through sleet and darkness to passing shadows.

He held clenched fists to his mouth. These relatives, with whom he was supposedly connected, were strangers. He'd greater understanding of the thought processes of the enemy.

He said to his mother, 'It's different in the city, isn't it? Belgrade has been bombed, many of its buildings destroyed. Mitar's school...' She didn't respond and he began to pace between the mattress and the window. He didn't know how to reach her, to get her to grasp the village hadn't experienced war. He assumed she told Juliajana what happened but, of course, he didn't know what explanation she'd given or what Stamenka had told his mother.

Juliajana struggled to her feet. With one hand on her hip, she said, 'Sir, it is your poor mother who says she has no grandson, no daughter-in-law.'

So, it was his mother who was to blame? Pausing in front of Juliajana, he spoke quietly. 'Mitar is being taken out of the country with a unit of cadets on my orders.'

Juliajana crossed to the fire, poked it so sparks flew, tossed a log into the centre. The room darkened. 'Mucak says war is good for Serbia, that soon we'll have peace, but peace will come too late for us.'

He looked down at his sister-in-law. How would she manage without a man? She'd been a child when he married; he didn't know her husband or his regiment. Though he was sad for her, his priority remained his wife.

After a moment, he went on, 'Mother, Stamenka refused the General's motorcar because there was no room for you. Do you understand? Did she travel here with you?'

Her face showed no expression. She could be obstinate, unable to admit she was in the wrong. 'Listen!' He clasped his hands together. 'The enemy was at the gate and I was afraid for Mitar so... Do you understand, woman?'

Juliajana said, 'The war has brought many deaths and you're wise to protect your son, but your wife disobeyed you. You say yourself she refused the General's motorcar. And you. A colonel. A man with many medals. That is why your mother is right to tell us she has no daughter-in-law.'

'Mother.' He stopped pacing, touched his mother's shoulder, but she shrank from him as she had when his father beat her. He'd forgotten how ignorant she was, how all women were. They based opinion on few facts and much imagination. There was little point in arguing.

Juliajana picked up his bowl and carried it to the sink, saying, 'All I know is, we're proud of you, our defender, but not of our daughter. She's brought shame on the family, which will last the rest of our lives.'

At around mid-night Ljubomir returned home, urging Stefan, already in bed, to see the improvements he'd made. Putting an old pair of trousers over night attire, donning his greatcoat and knitted hat, Stefan joined him at the back of the house. Stamenka resembled her father; she was tall with black hair. But while she was generous, he was sly, looked after himself.

Ljubomir showed him the distillery, the stables, the sheepfolds, corncribs and barns. Despite stars, it was too dark to see the ash trees or the apple orchard. Side by side, they smoked by the boundary fence, listened to the wind through the trees. This was the peace Stefan longed for. The anger which had burned while he lay in bed, slipped away. His gut eased. He and Stamenka held hands here on the evening of their betrothal.

The recollection prompted him to speak. 'Belgrade was badly bombed. Something you're spared. After the curfew, I returned home. Neither my wife, nor my mother were there. You can imagine my distress. Now, my mother is safe. I'll send money. She is not to sweep floors.'

'It's women's work.'

'I am Colonel of the Jevo regiment. She's old. Do you understand?'

'Even when she asks, "what shall I do?"'

'You're to remind her who she is.'

'Very well.'

He was a miserable little man. Stamenka's goodness must have come from her mother.

'Where is Stamenka?'

'She's not our daughter.' He spoke disparagingly.

Rage struck and he seized Ljubomir's shoulders, dropping his cigarette. 'Where is she?' Seconds later, embarrassed by his loss of control, he loosened his grip, let his arms fall. 'Where is she?'

'We set the dogs on her.'

Dogs, Stefan murmured. Bats skimmed among the silhouettes of the trees. He shivered. He'd deceived himself. His childhood was an illusion he'd outgrown the day he arrived in Belgrade. His father deprived him of nothing.

'You set your dogs on my wife?' Ljubomir was a fool if he believed the words of an old woman.

'You're one of Serbia's heroes. One day, you'll be a General and Orasac will be as famous as Struganica.'

They set dogs on her like they did on the insane. He pulled out cigarettes, lit one. Stamenka didn't deserve to wander the country searching for Mitar; he couldn't admit to Ljubomir he'd wanted to punish her for the slight he'd felt. He must find her, ensure she, too, got out of Serbia.

'In any case, she didn't want to remain with us, wanted only her son.'

Stefan didn't believe him; all he could do was try to put the matter right. 'Women are simple creatures. I trust you to make sure the village understands Stamenka wouldn't leave my mother. Stamenka is good. You've done her a grave injustice.'

'We're proud, sir, of what you've done for our country.'

The next morning as Stefan walked down the street towards the *kafkana*, more snow than rain mingled in the sleet. It touched his cheeks, prettying the mud road, the wood fences.

Tomislav had urged, 'Enter Orasac in triumph. Allow the villagers to wave their flags, raise their voices in praise of their most famous son.'

As he thought back to his last conversation with Tomislav, he realised he'd been carried away by Tomislav's words, but here, among the people he grew up with, he was affected not by glory but loss. Not simply of Stamenka. Black flags hanged from nearly every window, just as in Jevo, yet no one spoke of the deaths. Not even of his brother-in-law who had marched from that house to defend his country. By his side, Dragan whistled a one sound tune consisting of long and short notes. Stefan was amused and irritated.

At the door to the *kafkana,* he paused. Dragan began to brush his greatcoat, beginning with flakes of snow on the shoulders, moving down to mud on the hem, caught as Stefan picked up a ball for a child as they left the house. He ran his tongue over his teeth; the *popiri* his mother insisted on preparing for breakfast coated his teeth and tongue with grease. He pulled down the lapels, glanced down at his boots where Dragan was rubbing with a cloth. He caught sight of his boyhood self, running down the street with a hoop he'd whittled from willow. He pushed it with the palm of his hand, preoccupied with running down the street.

Inside, the *kafkana* though it wasn't yet mid-day, lanterns hanged from the ceiling, candles stood on tables, the glass in the windows dark with dirt. The room was packed with some thirty men, mostly older than Stefan. As a child he'd never been allowed in, though occasionally he waited outside with other boys for a meeting to end, when they'd walk home with their fathers.

Each man had his own place. Ljubomir and his relatives sat at the long table by the windows. Mikaiho, who as the son of a widow was lucky to have a seat at all, was perched on a low stool at the opposite end. One of Stefan's uncles sat in a lowly position, near the kitchen door with Woislav. Had that been his father's place or had he, too, occupied the long table, the family losing its seniority with his father's move to Belgrade?

Mikaiho stood up and urged the men to make room for Stefan in the middle of the long table, facing everyone. Stefan removed his cap and gloves. Men around the room, left their seats to shake his hand. Introductions were made, acquaintances renewed, many, contemporaries of his father.

Stefan recognised some. Vojin Kardelj, the blacksmith. Streten Rasic, who lived in the next house. Milenko Trajkovic, known as *Konjska,* Horse-face. Gusts of smoke from the central stove, drifted over the table. Stefan asked each man, 'How is the war going for you, sir?' He expressed sorrow at the death of sons, urged patience for those waiting for news. For a few, he related stories of bravery.

After three quarters of an hour, he rose, glass in hand. Everyone crowded around the long table except a young man sitting on the floor, his back against the kitchen wall, and a begging bowl between his legs. Stefan had noticed him as soon as he walked in, but only now remembered who he was. Danilo, a student officer, son of the mechanic, who'd fought alongside Mikaiho at Chekoj ridge. Stefan had lost track of what happened to him. His right arm amputated from the shoulder, the stump bandaged. It was too late to greet him, but he would have a word before he left.

Stefan raised his glass. 'King Petar.'

Men chanted the toast. Danilo, struggling to stand, didn't have a drink.

Ljubomir announced. 'Serb heroes.' Shuffling of feet, slurping of beer.

Mikaiho sprang from his stool and in a loud voice proclaimed, 'King Marko.'

The hairs down Stefan's back stiffened. It wasn't Mikaiho's place to make a toast; these old men could be insulted and yet, to rebuke his lieutenant in public was unthinkable.

Stefan intercepted with, 'To the brave men of the Serbian army.' Danilo raised an empty hand.

Ljubomir was standing up, 'To our brightest son. To Colonel Stefan Jovan Petrovic.'

'Thank you, gentlemen.'

'You have brought us news?' Ljubomir asked.

Stefan planned to address the men as Tomislav urged but, preoccupied with Danilo and his apparent desire to join in, to belong, he changed his mind. He was not an orator like Tomislav and after Glisic, he was doubtful of the usefulness of speeches, however eloquent.

'Let us talk as brothers,' he said. He waited for everyone to sit down around a table, in front of the stove or against a wall. He wondered what his own father would make of him standing before these men.

'Your army has many victories. Cer. Subovor. Kolubara. Twice we pushed the enemy back from the gates of Belgrade.' Despite his conversational tone, he heard Tomislav's voice in his. 'A few days ago, our depleted, but heroic forces, alongside the brave citizens of Belgrade, held on for longer, much longer, than we or our allies, expected.' He paused to sip his drink, observe expressions.

Someone shouted, 'Miserable allies.'

'Yes, yes, I will talk of them later,' Stefan said, ' In Belgrade, men, women and even boys assisted us, so the occupation was delayed several days beyond what we thought possible. For that action we've won admiration from our allies.

'In spite of numerical superiority and their attacking from three directions, the enemy has been unable to destroy our army.'

Ljubomir was nodding and silently clapping his hands. He'd been his father's best friend, hence Stefan's betrothal to Stamenka, but what had Ljubomir made of his father moving to the capital? Had he been disappointed, resentful? Stamenka never hinted.

Stefan went on, 'That was, of course, their principal objective. However, brothers, we've saved most of the army and we'll retreat to the island of Corfu.'

Shouts of: 'Shame on them. But for our allies we'd be victorious.'

Stefan added, 'Your army is weakened, we're not defeated.'

Ljubomir raised a hand. 'We're proud of our army, our King and our leaders. You grew up among us and know no men can be more loyal than us, but we're disappointed in our allies.' He pulled down the corners of his mouth. 'Austria and Germany are mighty empires. What chance do we stand against them?'

Stefan looked at the men around the table, then beyond, to those leaning on the wall next to Danilo. He said, 'It's unfortunate Greece has betrayed us. It's regrettable Roumania doesn't allow Russia to cross her territory to attack Bulgaria. The Russians are willing to help us, but they need time. Be assured, our Russian brothers will never abandon us.'

'It's true the Russians are a brave and loyal ally. As for the rest?' Ljubomir shook his head. Men around the table muttered, shouted expletives about the British and French.

'The British and the French,' Stefan went on, 'have battles in the Dardanelles and elsewhere, but we must be patient. Brothers, we are a patient people and will be rewarded. The

French and British praise our bravery and tenacity. They'll unite with us in ridding Serbia of the hated Austrian oppressor.'

Men hammered on the table with their fists. 'We're ready!' shouted one.

Before sitting down, Stefan said, 'The Austrians and Germans will do their worst and it is now up to you to hold out against them while we, your faithful army, re-build our strength, wait to be re-armed and then return.'

The blacksmith said, 'We've given our horses and oxen to the army so we and our women pull the wagons.'

Next to him a man said, 'Women are slow.'

'Quick with their tongues.'

'They stir to the sound of the whip.'

The men laughed. Stefan's empty glass was replaced with another. His throat was dry, but he wouldn't drink much because during the afternoon he'd return to his regiment and had yet to visit Mikaiho's mother.

A voice from near the door, came clearly through the general chatter. 'We can't harvest what we used to. Much goes to waste.'

Another said, 'Even though I'm old, I do the work of a young man.'

Ljubomir said, 'We send our sons away to die because we love our country.'

Stefan nodded. 'I'm proud to be born in Orasac, where its people are well-respected and loyal to the King.' The words flowed though he no longer respected these villagers.

'We are wise, too, my son. We will not let the enemy take our wine, for we hide it… underground.'

Another laughed, 'Nor our grain, which is hidden under the stones in the yard.'

'They'll find us stubborn people, who'll not yield to the yokedom of any Empire.'

Stefan could only nod. When he considered the quiet bravery of his men, he resented the ease with which these villagers lived out the war. 'Our country is in safe hands till the army returns.'

He sat down. Foam clung to the side of his glass as he drank. He tasted the barley. He wondered if all those years ago, his father had sought sanctuary here; he doubted his old friend provided it. Candles flickered. The blacksmith leaned between two of those seated, to light a cigarette from the candle flame. When it was lit, he moved to stand by the stove. The smell of pig roasting wafted from the kitchen. As Stefan's thoughts returned to Stamenka, he began to sweat. The sooner he left, the sooner he would find her.

The expression on Mikaiho's face reminded him of Tomislav's celebration in the Karakjodj restaurant.

He said quietly, 'Not now, Lieutenant.'

Mikaiho frowned. 'The men here ask me, "What deeds has the army done?"'

'It's not for you to say.'

'General Stavisto expects us to talk of heroes.'

Stefan couldn't disagree. 'Keep it short.'

Mikaiho raised his arms. 'Gentlemen! We fought hard. Hundreds of brave men slaughtered. I will tell of one battle, though there've been many. I'll show you can rely on us, your army.'

Some heads turned to Mikaiho, many didn't. The old blacksmith was tapping his glass, eyes rheumy. In the distance, church bells rang out mid-day.

Mikaiho gesticulated in Stefan's direction, 'At Chekoj ridge, Colonel Petrovic, our esteemed leader, kept vigil with the priest as we climbed in the darkest of dark nights, up to the heights of the escarpment, where the enemy attacked with the very guns they'd captured from us. I've fought many campaigns, but I swear, this was the worst.'

Stefan squirmed. In the mess, officers would jeer. These men must realise their Mucak exaggerated, but even so there was Danilo, wounded at Chekoj, how would he react to a romanticised account of the battle? Mikaiho waved an arm at Ljubomir.

'We lost two units that night, and three the following. I admit that I survived not as a result of my bravery alone…'

Only a handful of men were heroes. To fight required courage and some men were timid and needed more than others. Some sacrificed their lives because they wanted to save those of their brothers, but not Mikaiho. He remembered the lad being carried between two of his men, his eyes lifeless.

'... nor the valour of the men fighting with me, but through the might of King Marko himself.'

'Lieutenant Nis,' Stefan said.

Mikaiho didn't hear. His gaze remained on Ljubomir as the most senior man, who applauded, nodded. 'Men fire at me from the big guns on the ridge. Three, four, five rounds a time. I shout, "I am ready to die."'

Stefan half-rose. 'That is enough.'

Ljubomir intervened, 'No.' The old fool was enjoying himself.

'The Major is shouting, but his words disappear with his breath.' Mikaiho's cheeks were burning. Stefan wondered if his story, for that was what it was, for there had been no major on Chekoj ridge, was a form of shock. A mask to whatever he'd witnessed. Brief sympathy gave way to irritation. War was terrifying without distortion.

Mikaiho went on, 'I fall into the snow, into the mud and stones. Men call for their mothers. Shots come at me from all directions, but I am loaded with knapsack and rifle and water bottle and can't get to my feet but,' Mikaiho paused, 'King Marko himself galloped down from the ridge, on his white steed and leaned over me.'

There was silence throughout the *kafkana*.

' "Arise, soldier," he said. I am on my feet. I pick up my rifle. I fire. I jab my bayonet in the chest of one who falls.'

Mikaiho picked up his stool and stepping away from the table, jerked its legs as though ramming them through the wall. 'I stab like he's a pumpkin, but he's a heavy brute and it's hard to remove the bayonet from his bones and gristle.'

There was a murmur of laughter. Some-one said, 'That's right!' Some else, 'That's the way!'

'Blood runs over my boots.' Mikaiho dropped the stool to the floor where it rolled over and over. No one stopped it and it clattered against the wall. 'I'm lucky because one of my brothers knocks the enemy to the ground.'

Stefan began, 'Most amusing, but...'

231

Ljubomir interrupted, 'Have you forgotten, son?' He spoke loudly, 'We need stories of brave deeds. Why else would we fight?'

Half an hour later, when Stefan stooped to speak to Danilo on his way to visit Mikaiho's mother, her son was regaling a rapt audience with more of his exploits.

Chapter Nineteen

Mitrovica, December 1915

I've not had an opportunity to write during the past five days.

Today we covered only 6 miles, stopping outside Mitrovica.

After Raska, the road along the Ibar became difficult. Because of heavy rain and snow in the mountains, frequent landslides and mountain torrents flood its narrow, zig-zag route.

Having lost our provisions' wagon and in absence of Mikaiho, we've relied increasingly on gifts of food. We'd no bread for 2 out of 6 days. All of us are tired and hungry. Audrey becomes more and more silent as her anxiety increases after each surgery. Kova (frost bite along with 3 others), Velimir and Branislav are particularly weak. Cosic has a fever. Luckily, SWH gave us medical supplies at Kraljevo. Problem is all travellers need food; therefore prices high.

One evening we camped near a group of Serb officers travelling by motorcar. They were good enough to share their hamper with us, including a bottle of red wine. They left us bread and cheese for the following morning's breakfast. Events like this are restorative.

We're staying in a small holding three miles from the town. Milena, the wife, is very kind. Dobrica and Timohir have gone ahead to military hospital where we're to rest for 2 or 3 nights.

20 of the lads are bedded in schoolhouse under supervision of schoolmaster. The remaining 7 are in Milena's stable and loft, Audrey and I are wrapped in blankets on living room floor. Luxury is relative.

When Ellen woke, it was dark, her feet and legs numb because her blanket had slipped off during the night. At first, she thought she was in a bad dream, a giant in boxing gloves pummelling as she tried to sit up. A glance reassured. She and Audrey lay in front of a now extinguished fire, hams hanging from beams. She stretched before easing out of bed; she envied her friend's ability to sleep even though she too was hungry and anxious. She decided to search for wood to light the fire in the courtyard; she could boil the water for tea. If she was lucky, she would have hot water for a wash.

In the passage she smelled bread baking. It wouldn't be for them. Last night Milena apologised; she'd only a portion of corn and could barely feed herself and her husband. Stone walls, stone floor. Ellen's feet felt tiny inside her boots. Clothes added weight, not warmth.

She couldn't decide which way to go, not recalling the fork in the passage. Understandable, perhaps. Last night she'd felt empty even after eating. Gustav did his best with a scrawny cockerel and a few grains of rice, but it lacked sustenance. The lads had complained. In the darkness, she listened. Heavy stillness. Shivering, she veered off and within a few yards reached a long, narrow chamber.

As she glanced around, she was sure they'd not come this way. No windows. A kerosene lamp on a table by the wall, *putt putted*. Shuffling on, she wondered what it was used for. It smelled damp and fusty. She stopped at a curtain, sensitive she might be encroaching on Milena's private rooms. She understood curtains were used as a door to a kitchen or sleeping quarters. Her stomach gurgled. She wasn't sure if she heard footsteps on a stone floor or if that was what she wanted to hear.

She called out, '*Dobro dan*', her voice feeble.

She returned to the room, reluctant to admit she'd taken the wrong turning. Her fingers were stiff with cold. One by one, she unbent each into the palm of her gloves. Then, the thumb. Pain signalled the return of feeling. If she were at home, the maid would run her hot bath. She gazed at her hands; many of the cadets didn't have gloves. The air stirred. Milena dressed in black and *opanki* sandals, slipped through the divide of the dark curtain, approached like a shadow. Taken by surprise, Ellen mumbled thanks for her bed by the fire.

The woman's eyes and forehead were wrinkled, her lips narrow. She seemed not to notice the cold. She'd not been fazed last night when they arrived unannounced. She was welcoming, practical. Milena chattered, using simple vocabulary, short sentences. Yet, as soon as one word was uttered, Ellen forgot it to listen to the next. It was as though she was still a novice in Serbian. Cold and hunger were affecting her mind. When Milena hurried from the room, Ellen worried she'd missed her explanation. She couldn't quash the thought she wasn't up to the task, she'd taken on too much, should have gone home when Edward asked. She hated being out of her depth. She left the room and began to walk down the passage.

'Miss Frankland.'

Ellen turned around, feeling dizzy. Milena. Gilt-edged combs flashed in grey hair and Ellen was back at her engagement ball. Standing next to Edward, greeting her sister and husband in the reception hall, she'd caught her reflection in the mirror: the elegant gown, hair prettied with combs, make-up which blanched her outdoor skin, emphasised the plumpness of her lips.

Milena approached, touched Ellen's arm. She held out a chunk of black bread. On it, lay two sardines. Ellen's mouth watered. She hadn't tasted fish for over a year.

Milena spoke in simple language. 'For you. We do not have enough for your children. This is for you.'

Ellen snatched the bread, smelled fish as she bit into the crust. Her mouth full, she said, 'Thank you.' She chewed the sea and its bones.

After eating, her voice returned. Even though she talked for no more than ten minutes, it was a relief. To admit she feared some cadets weren't strong enough to cross the Albanian mountains, Mikaiho hadn't provided bread and she missed Edward.

Milena stroked her sleeve and thanked her for enjoying the fish.

When Ellen stepped into the courtyard, cadets were arriving in the wagon, Gustav was roping in water from the well, Branislav lighting the fire. She opened the stable door. She would make sure the younger ones in the hayloft were awake, preparing for the journey.

Palisters and blankets were being stacked in piles. Her relief at the general air of activity was tempered by the sound of voices shrill in argument in the hayloft. Velimir and Mitar. They were being increasingly fractious with each other. Mitar was disappointed his mother hadn't found him; Velimir wished he'd never joined the cadets.

Ellen sprang up the ladder and as her face drew level with the floor, she saw they were tussling over Kostu's woollen coat watched by a pale Zivoli.

'Stop it, at once! It's not yours. It's Kostu's.' She was surprised he wasn't defending his own coat. He was capable of looking after himself.

Mitar wearing Kostu's yellow scarf, shouted, 'He stole it. It wasn't his.'

Squeaky-voiced, Zivoli said, 'Kostu's dead, miss.'

The words didn't register.

She concentrated on settling the quarrel. She'd to establish order so they could move off, reach the military hospital.

'It doesn't belong to either of you.' She leapt off the ladder, into the loft. It wasn't until she marched across the boards and shouted into Mitar's ear, 'Drop it, this instant,' her presence become apparent to either of them.

Velimir let go. His freckles looked like specks imprinted on cream silk.

Ellen said to Mitar, 'You as well or you won't get any breakfast.'

'I'm a Petrovic.'

'That makes no difference.'

Beneath the crocheted hem of the coat, she saw a bare foot. Black as a bruise. She couldn't look further. Zivoli's words became real. Kostu was dead. She was lost. She didn't know whether to give in and let Mitar keep the coat. She didn't care. Her belly ached. She ought not to give in.

'And if I can't, then Velimir must have it because he's my friend,' Mitar said sulkily.

He must have just died. She dreaded seeing his body. She must fetch Audrey. She said sharply, 'It's not for you to decide.'

'Dr. Eyres is the boss,' Mitar said, 'She's the one who'll choose.'

Ellen snatched the coat from him, not looking down. Mitar wiped his cheek with the yellow scarf.

Zivoli said quietly, 'Dr. Eyres is Miss's friend so she'll agree with her.'

Mitar kicked at the straw. 'Well, my father is the proper boss. He's Colonel of the regiment.'

Velimir bent to fasten his shoes. He was wearing Kostu's socks. Her stomach lurched. 'Your poor friend has just died and you bicker about his belongings.'

Zivoli looked as though he wanted to say something. Wanting to weep, Ellen couldn't speak. Audrey would be upset.

Mitar said, 'You don't give us warm clothes and boots. We've no bread. You're...' She couldn't understand the gabbled words, but guessed at insults.

She wanted to grab his skinny shoulders and shake him. It wasn't her fault his parents had dressed him in jumper and shorts. The trousers she'd found were inadequate in the cold and rain. Nor had his father prepared her or Audrey for the chaos and short supplies. If anyone was to blame, it was Colonel Petrovic.

She said, 'You're cold, Zivoli. You take it.'

Zivoli held the coat in his hands for a moment before turning it over, tucking his hands in the sleeves. Over a thick jumper, he'd a jacket. He wore both socks and stout shoes. Everyone had seen the spare clothes his mother packed. Ellen felt ashamed; she'd been unjust. Moreover, she'd a greatcoat and boots; she'd eaten bread and sardines.

Zivoli passed the blanket to Mitar, put his hand on his shoulder.

'It's yours. You're the youngest.'

While the cadets descended, Ellen knelt by Kostu. A fog of breath separated them. He was naked but for a ragged vest. His eyes shut. A sob rose from her belly. The sun slanted through the gaps in the roof. The wind chilled her hands as she touched his flesh. It shrank into his bones, reminding her of a translucent skeleton of a bird she found on the banks of the Wye when she was a girl. One of his arms was twisted

237

back, probably broken as the boys wrenched off his tunic and jumper.

'Kostu,' she whispered. She stroked his icy cheek. 'I'm sorry.' He'd run off with Bogdan and the others at the beginning; it seemed a long time ago. She fingered strands of hair, which straggled to his shoulders. Black tinged with grey. Audrey told her she considered him too frail to walk so far, but his mother said, he was stronger than he looked. And he'd missed her.

Ellen wanted to cover his body. His ribs, his hipbones protruded. His penis lay tiny. She looked round for something to hide his nakedness. Pieces of hay scattered across the floor. The remains of a bird's nest lodged between the roof and a beam. From the courtyard, Gustav's accented voice, the murmur of the cadets.

'Have you seen a dead body, Miss Frankland?' Dr. Gould had asked at her interview to go to France with the Women's Yeomanry. She'd blithely spoken of her mother's death, but hadn't been prepared for the deaths of soldiers, far less of Miodrag, Radovan, Kostu. A mouse scampered across the boards. She stamped her foot. Glancing down at her boot, she felt frozen inside and out.

Walking to the ladder, she decided they'd bury Kostu before they left. Milena would find a place. She wondered how her father would conduct the service, how they could.

At the military hospital, Dr. Dacic, the director, provided clean, warm accommodation in a wooden annexe used in the summer for convalescing patients. It was small for the twenty-seven lads, four orderlies, two drivers, Ellen and Audrey, but despite the food shortage in Mitrovica, they were served three meals a day. Most shared a palister though there were ample blankets. During the two nights, Zivoli sleepwalked and was guided back to bed. Several had nightmares and needed to be comforted. But on the whole, the change lifted spirits. Those who needed medical attention were given it and Audrey, as soon as they arrived, began to help with surgical operations.

Ellen wrote to Edward.

We've reached Mitrovica where we're staying in the military hospital. We're being treated like kings. We move on in two days time.

My resolution to keep a journal is intermittent. The journey is taking longer than expected though it's proving most interesting.

I read and re-read your letter. You're in my thoughts so many times a day and I'm looking forward to seeing you. Sadly, it will not be till after Christmas.

The weather is bitterly cold. It's hard to remember the warmth of our engagement ball, the heat of my last summer camp.

I am looking forward to being with you soon, feeling safe in your arms,
Your ever-loving fiancée
Ellen

The letter took an hour to write. She struggled over each sentence, not wanting to admit this wasn't the journey she'd delayed her return for. The recollection of their engagement ball hurt. She didn't want to think about how they'd both changed. What he wouldn't want to hear, what she wanted to talk about.

She tore up the letter and instead suggested the cadets explore the town with her. No one took up the offer, preferring to play cards or a game, which involved dice and sticks and she took her walk with the loyal Gustav. She considered telling Mitar that according to Dr. Dacic, his father was in town. Audrey, working in the operating theatre, wasn't aware of it, but they could hardly make a social call.

That evening, Dr. Dacic joined them again. This time he brought cakes and biscuits from a Red Cross parcel. The room was lit by lamps hanging from beams and heated by a kerosene stove in the centre of the room. The lads sat on palisters chatting or playing cards, the adults around the table. Ellen and Audrey shared a bottle of red wine donated by a local Italian count, the orderlies *rakija*. Zivoli was given the task of distributing biscuits from a tin, while Dr. Dacic sliced the Dundee cake.

He asked, 'When will the unit be ready to leave?'

Ellen said to Audrey, 'I think two more nights, don't you?'

Audrey sniffed. 'I've decided we stay.'

Ellen was surprised, wasn't sure if she agreed. 'You didn't mention it.'

Audrey, appearing not to have heard, addressed the doctor. 'If you'll have us.'

His knife poised, he queried, 'May I enquire the reason for this change of plan?'

Audrey folded her hands on the table in front of her. 'Our unit is not medically fit. You can see for yourself.'

Next to the doctor, Branislav fidgeted. Ellen wondered what he wanted; if he still intended to be a soldier.

'I've offered to keep the frost bites,' Dr. Dacic said.

Mitar sprang to his feet. He had been lying on his bed playing cards with two others, but now he waved his arms, stamped his foot. In Serbian he said to Ellen, 'It's not what my father ordered. He's paid you to take us to safety. You will be shot if you disobey.'

Ellen wanted to giggle. Yet, she took his point.

Audrey, glass raised, said, 'We can't continue to what, for some, will be certain death.'

Mitar glared at Ellen.

'That is because *she* didn't get us bread.' Mitar stood, hands on hips, glowering at Ellen. Supposing he imitated his father, she was irritated even as she pitied him. Yesterday, he'd chatted about his mother and grandmother. How they trusted in God to bring them safely through Austrian attacks. How their father intended to get them out of the country at the beginning of the war, but the man due to take them, was killed by a bomb.

Dr. Dacic removed his pipe with one hand, and waved the cake knife with the other, 'That is not the way to speak to ladies. Both Dr. Eyres and Miss Frankland are on this mission because they love the Serb people. If they'd wished they could have returned with their friends to their own country.' With a flourish of the pipe, he said, 'Please apologise to them.' He picked up the cake knife. He didn't have an obvious air of authority like Edward or Dr. Gould, but Ellen thought him determined.

One of the card players said, 'Sir, it's true we'd no bread.'

'We'd no food at all one day,' another added.

'That was because we lost a wagon down a ravine. There was no food to be had. It wasn't the fault of the ladies,' Gustav said.

'Please, apologise,' Dr. Dacic repeated.

Mitar muttered, 'Sorry.'

Neither she, nor the cadets had been prepared for the journey; if they were to continue, they would need to be realistic. The doctor resumed his cutting.

Audrey snapped, 'The point is the unit isn't robust enough to last the journey.'

'What's robust?' Mitar asked Ellen.

Branislav said, 'It means that our brother, Kostu died because he wasn't strong enough.'

Mitar began, 'But…'. Velimir nudged him and he said no more.

Branislav picked up a plate and held it under the wedge of cake as Dr. Dacic dug it out of the tin. Crumbs fell to the table.

Audrey asked, 'Can you accommodate us, Doctor?'

He let the knife fall and began to light his pipe. Smoke drifted, masking the raisins and sultanas that made Ellen's mouth water. Treats made a difference. Branislav dabbed the crumbs on his fingertips.

Sucking on his pipe, the director continued, 'I have to remind you, food is severely rationed here. We've given you our portions because you need to be built up for the journey.'

He cut another slice. The afternoon with Audrey in Brown's teashop belonged to another world. They'd laugh if they could see themselves now, in woollen hats, without make-up, pretty dresses and jewellery.

Dr. Dacic said, 'When the enemy arrives, many will starve. Mitrovica is full of refugees because they haven't the strength to continue. The more who stay, the more who'll die.' He paused, prodded the pipe bowl with a match before resuming, 'I urge you to keep going. I can take the frostbites and the chest. The Colonel's lad, if you like.'

'No! My father ordered it,' Mitar said.

'It's a matter for Dr. Eyres and Miss Frankland.'

Audrey was shaking her head.

Ellen recognised that if they moved on, they'd need total commitment from the drivers and orderlies. They appeared more co-operative but they would have to rely on them if they faced another disaster.

Ellen asked them, 'What do you think?'

Timohir swore, ran his tongue between his teeth and gums. 'Do you think sticking with this rabble will save our poor country?'

Having topped up his glass, he pushed the bottle to Dobrica and went on, 'He's got two little ones and his father is old. He's needed in his village. One of my sons is dead. Two are on the eastern front.'

'Lieutenant Nis said every Serb wants to die for his country,' Ellen said. Even as she spoke, she wasn't sure; two years ago, it was one of life's certainties.

'Then Lieutenant, whoever he is, is an idiot,' Cosic said. 'I don't want to die miles away from my family.'

'So why did you volunteer to come with us?'

Cosic said, 'What choice did we have?'

'Aren't you afraid the enemy will imprison you if you stay?'

Dobrica shook his head. 'We won't be hanging about, miss.'

'We'll be on our way home,' Cosic agreed.

'They won't catch us.' Timohir was reaching for the bottle.

Ellen glanced at the director. Stefan argued the enemy would kill the cadets. Having witnessed the corpses in the village church, she'd been persuaded. Dr. Dacic didn't talk of murder, but starvation.

Timohir wiped his mouth on his hand. 'You mean well, miss, but you're wasting your time. We've lost. The best we can do, is get on with our lives under enemy rule.'

The director tapped the table with the tip of the knife. 'Enough! That is not patriotic talk. When or if these ladies leave, you go with them.'

Ellen said to Audrey, 'Don't you think it's as much a risk to stay as to travel on? You heard Dr. Dacic.'

Audrey, her cheeks burning, turned on Ellen, 'When we left Jevo I knew they weren't fit to travel. I was wrong to take

242

the risk. Colonel Petrovic said two to three weeks and we're nearing the end of our third week. We've done the easy bit. How do you suppose we'll manage through the mountains?'

'If we've another day of recuperation?'

Audrey shook her head. 'You just don't appreciate how weak they are. Kostu seemed resilient...he starved to death.'

'A day to get through the highest peaks and we'll be in Albania.' She didn't mention the military escort, doubted it would materialise.

'You're talking like a Serb. A day! Two or three weeks. And the Albanians hate the Serbs. They won't give us food.'

In desperation Ellen asked Gustav, 'What about you?' While they'd explored, he said he was keen to see the cadets deposited in Durazzo, so he could return home through Italy.

'I'll do whatever you ladies decide.'

With a sigh, Ellen let the discussion drift into chatter. Her mood shifted. One moment, she'd be glad to stop struggling. At others she felt as committed as Mitar. Without the weaker cadets, they'd get on quicker. They'd promised Stefan. There was risk whatever they did.

That night, Ellen woke up screaming. She smelled burning wood, saw smoke and tried to run. As soon as she realised she was tucked in a sleeping bag under the table, she fell back to the floor.

Audrey's face hovered over hers. 'What's the matter?'

'A nightmare.'

'Tell me.'

'It's all right.'

Audrey settled back under her blankets. Ellen was trembling. She tasted blood, the tallow from the candles Mikaiho lit in front of the altar screen.

She ought to warn her friend. She touched her hunched body. Calmly, she said, 'Audrey, the Austrians will rape the cadets if we stay. Colonel Petrovic said.'

'Don't be silly.' Audrey patted her shoulder. 'You've had a nightmare. Lie down, think of going home to Edward. This country's getting to us.'

She'd not meant 'rape'. She'd decided a long time ago not to tell Audrey about the village. She closed her eyes.

'I'm all right now,' she whispered.

As Audrey turned on her side, Ellen felt her heart thudding faster and faster. She placed her hand over it, tried to calm it, ease the panic. She was afraid, frightened because the world wasn't as she imagined when she waved goodbye to Edward. She'd never thought that soldiers might rape women. And a whole village. Murdered. War was about protecting women and children. Another of life's rules shattered.

Nonetheless she wanted to move on. She didn't want to watch the cadets die. Cadets she was getting to know, brave Branislav, loyal Zivoli and little Mitar. She'd rather face the unknown than wait.

Leaning up on an elbow she whispered in Audrey's ear, 'Dr. Dacic says the colonel's in town.'

'He didn't mention it to me.'

'He told me before I went out with Gustav. He's part of the rearguard.'

Audrey sat up.

'Shall I look for him tomorrow? I can ask if we can stay.'

A cadet whimpered.

'I forbid you.'

'He's in charge.'

'You don't know where to find him.'

'I can find out.'

Audrey fell back onto her bed. Ellen's stomach felt tight, her scalp ached. 'Will you come with me?'

'It's not safe.'

'Are you frightened?'

'We're staying.'

Ellen stretched out in her sleeping bag. Stefan would forbid their journey if he thought it too dangerous for his son.

Chapter Twenty

Outside Mitrovica, December 1915

As soon as he heard Rajko had been killed, Stefan drove to the scene; all that remained were smouldering ruins. Six men had been exploding a small arsenal so the enemy couldn't use the bombs. There'd been no need for Rajko. The men were experienced. They sheltered as soon as the fuse caught; when they looked for Rajko, he couldn't be found. Stefan half-expected him to walk through the rubble, waving his stick.

As Stefan slipped into the back seat, sleet lightened the night sky. Huddled in greatcoat, black scarf and gloves, he was insignificant. The journey could never be long enough. He needed time to reflect on and accept Rajko's death. With Mikaiho driving, Dragan by his side, he imagined Rajko's last moments. Over and over. Bones, skull, flesh dissembling in the morning air.

It was eleven in the evening when they reached the General's temporary headquarters. Stefan marched across the courtyard, Dragan followed in silence, Mikaiho remained with the car. Through the open door, men's chatter, cigarette smoke billowing into the entrance. The door closed as Stefan bounded up the steps, pretending all was well, acting as if he wanted to talk to Tomislav.

Despite the open fire where Tomislav was positioning a log, the room was chilly. A whiff of thyme lingered. Stefan was reminded of the vigil in the Hotel des Balkans: the table by the window, cap on the white linen cloth, greatcoat folded across the back of a chair, wine bucket and two glasses.

'Your orderly can wait downstairs.' Tomislav's eyes were bloodshot, strands of hair curled over his tunic collar. He put an arm around Stefan and accompanied him to his seat. Even Tomislav was affected, Stefan noted with satisfaction.

'Sit down, my friend.' Tomislav pointed to the turquoise cushion on the chair.

Stefan gazed through the pane. The flakes were getting larger. He'd a desire to open the casement window, let them lie in his palm. The rising wind whistled through the trees, which bounded the courtyard. In the light of the street lamp, Dragan and Mikaiho, appeared as silhouettes in the motorcar.

When he turned around, Tomislav was at the far side of the room. While Stefan removed his cap and gloves, Tomislav carried a lighted candle from the desk littered with papers and placed it between them. Shadows slipped along the white walls.

The smell of tallow tightening his throat, he asked, 'Sir, I'd like permission to search Mitrovica for my wife.' He longed for Stamenka's arms around him; the look of concern between her brows; her body holding his grief.

Tomislav, his hands, white-knuckled on the folds of his coat, leaned forward over the back of the chair, appraising.

Yesterday when Stefan learned of the death, he'd cursed his father because he'd taken the family from Orasac so Stefan could take advantage of his uncle's money, to be educated as an army officer. He remembered pleading, 'I don't want to fight. I want to be a man of letters. I want to study, to become a diplomat.' He'd been unfair to blame his father, as if he'd caused Rajko's death.

After a moment, Tomislav walked to the hearth, picked up a dish, and brought it to Stefan. 'Help yourself.'

There were hundreds starving in the town and Tomislav was serving olives.

'The finest Greek, though, of course, we're no longer allies.' He picked out a couple, left the dish on the table and meandered to the fire into which he spat the stones.

Nonetheless, there was something reassuring in the actions and Stefan took one, held it between finger and thumb and raised it towards his mouth. Oil dripped from his fingers, his throat contracted. Following his silent prayer for the soul's repose at the arsenal, a sob had swelled from his belly. Aware of the men, he'd suppressed it. He'd not eaten since the news. He was still holding the olive when Tomislav placed a loaf on the table, three slices already cut.

Stefan put the olive into his mouth. He chewed, spat the stone into his hand. The effort of walking to the fire was out of proportion to the action. He ought to buck up, but Tomislav's kindness allowed him to wallow. Stefan recalled Rajko was a child when his mother was raped and hanged herself. At the start of their friendship, Stefan understood Rajko's military life was unusual. Each time Rajko killed a soldier, it was for his mother, for his boyhood self.

Tomislav raised the dripping bottle from the bucket. 'Pour, my friend.'

He thought Tomislav was playing a game. Observing, judging. All he wanted was permission to look for Stamenka.

With a steady hand he filled both glasses.

Tomislav sat down. Snow splattered the pane. A wagon and oxen clattered into the courtyard. Stefan was sure, Stamenka was close by; he sensed her presence.

'To victory!' Tomislav said.

Stefan found it hard to move; he'd to force his arm to raise the glass, inch by inch.

Tomislav sipped; he wiped his mouth with a napkin. He'd always been particular. His moustache waxed, his buttons polished. They were alike in that respect.

'I'd like permission to look for my wife,' he repeated.

Tomislav said, 'I haven't had your report. Three times, I ordered you. Give me a reason, I shouldn't discipline you.' He picked up a slice of bread and broke it into pieces, placing them in front of him like markers in a game of chance. 'Have your men mutinied?'

'No, sir.'

'Deserted?'

'No, sir.'

'Why no report?'

Running his finger around the rim of his glass, Stefan murmured, 'I've been sick, sir.'

Wearily Tomislav replied, 'Freedom requires sacrifice, as Major Kostic understood. We'll avenge his death.'

He reached to touch Stefan's arm, but Stefan drew his glass to his chest, nursing his wine.

'You were friends, I know. Were you more than that?'

'We go back…'

'I've the records. I want to know if there was an emotional attachment than can exist between men?'

Stefan was puzzled.

'You've not filed a report since the Major's death. Every day men lose their friends in action. Was there a sexual relationship between you?'

'You think we were queers?' Such things happened though Stefan couldn't understand why. 'When I ask permission to find my wife?'

'Every day men worry about the safety of their women. Do you think at a time like this I can allow an officer to chase a silly woman?'

Stefan's thigh itched. He was as exhausted as after a day's fighting. He reflected Tomislav had been too long away from the battlefield and become a political animal. He shrugged, 'We should never have invaded Bosnia.'

'You're talking treason.'

'We fought to bolster your reputation.'

'Your second and third assaults regained Chekoj ridge. Your men are loyal. They volunteer for the most difficult assignments.'

'His death was needless.'

'Nonsense.' Tomislav picked up a piece of bread, dipped it in his wine, popped it in his mouth, 'I, too, grieve for Stamenka. She's a good wife. When you chose the army rather than the civilian life, she backed you to the full.'

'I wanted to be a diplomat…'

'Till I offered you a position and a future.'

'My father…'

'You're like a son to me.'

Stefan thought, He's got his own sons. Let them fulfil his dreams.

Tomislav continued, 'I want that report. When it's completed, an officer can organise a short service to remember those who died in action. The people will attend, the priest reassure.'

He heard Tomislav's kindness, wanted to respond but felt too remote. He began to shake, put down his glass and watched spilt wine bleed onto the cloth. In Jevo, when despair threatened, he would jump on his horse, gallop across the fields, canter through the woodlands till restored. Drink wouldn't help.

'I'll have your reports within an hour of your return to your rooms.'

'Yes, sir.'

'Finish destroying guns that can't be moved. You, and your regiment will continue to bring up the rear.'

The next morning Stefan was on his own in their living quarters when he heard a knock on the kitchen door. He'd crawled into his sleeping bag at four, awoken by Dragan at five thirty. The strip wash, taken in privacy, away from Dragan and Jovan, not because it was his right as senior officer, but because company, any company irritated him.

He heard Dragan invite in visitors. Stefan was annoyed. He'd given instructions not to be disturbed. Jovan laughed. He was taking Rajko's death better than Stefan expected.

While he was tucking his shirt into his trousers, there was a tap on the door and Dragan slid through the narrow opening.

'Whoever it is, the answer's "No".'

'Miss Frankland accompanied by the Austrian.'

She wants to become a soldier, he thought. We're in the deepest shit and she's come to rescue us.

'What does she want?'

'A private matter.'

'And Lieutenant Nis has arrived,' Dragan added. Stefan would tell Mikaiho he no longer needed him. Last night, having completed his paperwork, defying Tomislav he'd decided Mikaiho would search the town for Stamenka. This morning, it seemed wiser to ask his orderly, who would be more discreet.

'Tell the lieutenant to wait. I'll speak to Miss Frankland, but her chaperone can wait in the kitchen.'

Dragan beamed. 'It's fortunate she found us.'

'And bring us tea. Miss Frankland likes tea.'

It was difficult to be tidy in a small space. He'd no desk, his papers stacked on the floor by the telephone, secured by a block of masonry. They'd slept with their heads against the wall, Stefan near the stove because he couldn't get warm. The card table by the window overflowed with maps and engineers' drawings. He grabbed his sheepskin gilet from the back of the chair, shoved one arm through a sleeve, sprang to the sleeping area. He should have asked Dragan to adjust the bedding rather than make tea. The gilet flapped loose as he crouched to fling his palister across the others. Throwing the blanket over it all, it occurred to him he was protecting Miss Frankland from the fact that she was in a bedchamber. Straightening, he looked to see what else was out of place.

'Colonel.'

'Oh.' He stumbled, pushed the other arm through the gilet, stepped to greet her.

'I did knock, sir.' She shook his hand, but he was shocked by her appearance. Her face had grown long, accentuating the bones of her nose. Her cap was tipped away from her face. Lines he didn't remember scoured her forehead. Her ears were small, their lobes pink, her cheeks as red as those of peasant women. He marvelled he'd ever felt attracted.

'Please.' He waved her to the table. 'Sit down. Dragan will bring us tea.' He swept the maps into his arms, lay them across the bedding.

She watched, her face grave. 'It is a little different from the last time we met,' she said.

'You've lost weight.'

'You too.'

He held the chair as she lowered herself down. Still a lady.

'The journey's been bad,' she said.

'We've never had a winter like it.'

As she removed her gloves, she asked, 'Are you well?'

Conversations with Matron taught him the nastiest of situations could by masked by pleasantries. It took several months to realise the lack of a cover over the cesspool wasn't an aesthetic failure, but contributed to the deaths of his men.

'I think so,' he replied.

He walked over to the stove and picked up the towel he'd left on the floor expecting Dragan to remove it, dropped it on the maps.

'If we win, I suppose it will be worth it.'

She sounded despondent. 'It will, Miss Frankland.'

He was aware of her watching as he removed socks drying on a log in the hearth and flung them towards the towel. Jovan's grey, knitted vest hung over the log basket; he ignored it as he threw logs in the stove, embarrassed she might think it his. She was examining her boots and he glanced out of the window as he went to sit opposite her. Horses clattered down the street. Men shouted. The gas lamp was still lit.

'The weather has been atrocious and we've not yet reached the Albanian mountains,' she said rubbing her hands together.

'It's winter.'

'We don't have such winters in England.'

'That's the place to live. My son will be happy in England. My wife also.'

'She didn't join us. Didn't you know?'

'Yes.'

'So, how will she get to England?'

'Like Mitar. Like the cadets.'

'Mitar thinks his mother will find him.' Stefan was surprised. She went on, 'When we have snow, we dress in warm clothes.' There seemed reproof in her words. 'Mitar, and many of the cadets were poorly clad. If we'd known how cold and wet it was going to be, we wouldn't have taken them.'

He didn't know how to respond. 'England is wealthy. Our General tells us that we're a peasant army.'

She licked her lips and he saw her as she'd been. Red lips, full cheeks lightly rouged. She was young and strong; she would survive.

He leaned back, stretched his legs, careful not to touch her. He said, 'You've come to see me, for what reason, Miss Frankland?'

'Many of the cadets struggle.'

'That's all?'

'Dr. Eyres thinks it best we remain in Mitrovica.'

'That's out of the question.'

'Many are tired.'

'We're all tired.'

'I know.' When she rested her hands on the table edge, they trembled. Quickly she lowered them.

In an even tone she continued, 'Dr. Eyres is concerned because some cadets have bad chests or frost bite and aren't fit for the journey. Also, she wants to remain in the town to help in the hospital.'

'Then that is what she must do.' On impulse he added, 'Lieutenant Nis will find you an Albanian to escort you through the mountains.' He was pleased with himself. It would be a simple task for Mikaiho, one that did not involve any danger.

She glared at him.

'You don't want an escort?'

'Such a person doesn't exist.'

She was probably right. 'I'm sorry,' he said.

She tucked strands of hair under her cap. 'I'm afraid for Mitar.'

'It's not what I want for my son, but in truth, hardship has made our people resilient and it will be the same for Mitar.'

'Sir, he was dressed in short trousers. He'd no shoes, coat, gloves, carried only a blanket and Prince Marko.'

Rajko was right. He should have got his family out when the Archduke was assassinated. He cleared his throat.

'You made promises you couldn't keep so we'd do as you wanted.'

'You've survived.'

She leaned forward, her hands clasped the edge of the table. With surprise, he realised this protected young woman was furious and blamed him.

He looked away, towards the door.

'Please don't ignore me.'

She didn't understand how resilient the Serbs had to be. He remembered Mitar sliding across the leather seat clutching Prince Marko.

He sighed. After a moment, he returned her gaze. 'I didn't expect the journey to be as difficult.'

'Lieutenant Nis promised bread. He brought none. The drivers got drunk; one of them drove a wagon over the edge of the road killing himself and two cadets. The orderlies have been unco-operative.'

'Are you willing to take the unit on your own?'

'If you think we'll reach Durazzo.'

He wouldn't send his son to his death. Surely she'd grasped that? 'You will succeed, I'm convinced.'

She said, 'Dr. Eyres will remain here.'

He wondered if the women had quarrelled. 'I'm confident you'll care for Mitar. Does he have warm clothing now?'

'Yes, Dr. Dacic provided boots, but he's frail, sir.'

She was mistaken. 'My son is strong.'

'He may not live.'

He folded his arms. He wanted his son to enjoy the peace he'd denied himself. Looking up, her eyes were wet. What had he given away?

The knock on the door saved him from explaining he loved his son, recognised the risk. Dragan and Jovan bustled in, carrying beakers, the coffee pot and a chopping board, bread, cheese and a knife.

Dragan was still smiling. 'We've no tea, only coffee.'

'Bread and a little cheese.' Jovan spoke as though he was offering top cuisine.

'Are you hungry, Miss Frankland?' Stefan asked. His men did, after all, know how to treat a lady, but seeing Jovan reminded him of Rajko.

After they left the room, he asked, 'You remember Major Kostic?'

'Of course. I nursed him in hospital and he drove me home after my silliness ... He's a delightful man.'

'He, my best friend, is dead.'

At first, he thought her melodramatic. Both hands rose in slow motion to rest on her head. Her face crumpled, she covered it, tried to hide her tears, folded over her chest. She sobbed.

Embarrassed, he murmured 'We trained together. He was my hero. He won the gold *Oblilich* medal.'

After he'd sent his report to Tomislav, in the early hours he'd walked through the graveyard on the edge of the town. Rajko could have no burial. Snow gleamed blue in the moonlight. The gold and black of the skeletal trees. Listening to the earth, smelling the nearness of wolves, he heard Rajko, 'Your wife can look after herself.'

His friend. He remembered him dancing, his stick, held between both hands, raised above his head. His own impatience as he ran ahead to the destruction of the Gorniji café. While Stefan was coughing, choking on masonry dust, Rajko commented, 'You're wasting your time, brother.'

'They're lads like you and I.' Stefan continued to pull at the rubble, shift pieces of stone. 'We can't leave them.'

'They've done what they lived for.'

Ellen wiped her eyes and blew her nose. Her voice broken, she spoke tentatively. 'I never thought he'd be killed.'

'He died as all Serbs wish to die, on the battlefield.'

A cart rumbled along the road and in his head he heard the words of the song, '*Ruza, Ruza.*'

From his pocket he fished out a packet of cigarettes, feeling there in its depths the whistle he'd found among Rajko's possessions. He offered Ellen a cigarette.

When she declined, he took one, saying, 'I smoke too much.'

He drew on his cigarette. Last night, they slept as close as children. He loved his men, not as Tomislav implied, but through the companionship of battle, breath mingling, pain shared.

'I'm sorry he's dead. He was kind,' she said.

'He wasn't a woman's man.'

'He was kind to me.'

'I tried to persuade him to go back to his wife, but he said, "We are married to the army." He included me in that.'

'He could have laughed like you, or ignored me like Mikaiho, but he took me seriously, though he said it was hard to be a soldier.'

'Yes, I remember…'

There was silence between them.

In Belgrade art gallery, he'd long admired a portrait of a Western woman, a lady, like Miss Frankland. Until now, she'd been as distant as the elegant line of her brows, the lace on her cap, the polished lips. He'd done his volunteer soldier a disservice.

The logs in the stove stirred.

Ellen cleared her throat. 'I'd better go, sir, but I ask if there's any little thing, something of a personal nature I could give Mitar. To encourage him.'

'His mother is better at that sort of thing.' He put his cigarette on the edge of the table. 'You haven't eaten,' and picking up a piece of cheese placed it on the bread. 'Eat it.'

She flushed. He thought she was discomforted, but perhaps the room was too hot and he recalled her carrying the tray in the kitchen at Dobro Majka. She took the cheese, bit into it. She'd known hunger. Not wanting to embarrass her, he moved to the stove. Warming his hands he crouched in front of it, turning back to look at her after several moments. Cheese gone, she was tearing the bread. Maybe she would remember him as kind.

He thought of Rajko playing the whistle in his hospital bed. She, too, had been close.

Putting his hand in his pocket he held the rough instrument between finger and thumb. To hang on to it was mere sentiment; it would change nothing.

'Give Mitar this. Tell him to play '*Ruza, Ruza*' to encourage the cadets when they're struggling.'

After she'd left, he realised he'd not asked for details of Mitar. He missed his mother, that was apparent. He looked at his hands. The nails were almost gone. He couldn't remember biting them; it must have been during the night. He pulled the file from his pocket; only the little finger needed trimming.

There was a disturbance in the kitchen, but he ignored it and added more logs. He'd carry out Tomislav's orders to destroy their cannon, move on and do it again and again until they were out of Serbia. If there were time, he'd arrange a service for the dead on the border. He was sure Stamenka was close by; he sensed her presence. With Dragan's help, he would continue to search for her.

Chapter Twenty-one

Military hospital, Mitrovica. December 1915

Ellen thought the provision of pen and paper were Dr. Dacic's way of saying thank you, his way of showing relief the unit would leave. While he worked in the main block, he let her use his writing room, a windowless space under a staircase between two wards, lit by an oil lamp hanging from a beam and a candle on the oak table.

Her last letter to Edward had been business-like rather than romantic. Now feeling optimistic, was a good time to write. She picked up the pen, dabbed the drips on the rim of the inkwell. She glanced at books crammed on narrow shelves, piled high on the floor, distracted despite being of little interest. Written in Russian with a few illustrations, she guessed they were medical textbooks.

My darling Edward,
We have reached Mitrovica. Tomorrow we move on. The few days'
rest has revitalised the cadets. Two will remain in hospital with severe
frostbite.

Would that pass the censors? Perhaps she ought not to say she'd given the orderlies the option of staying or moving on. Cosic wanted to go home. Then, there was Audrey. She didn't want to admit their disagreement.

Her hands and knees shook in the cold. At home, she had no difficulty in talking to Edward, but they were apart and she didn't want to worry him.

We're loading the wagons with…

'Miss Frankland! A telephone call for you.' Dr. Dacic's secretary was excited.

Ellen ran after him as he belted along the corridor, not answering her, 'Who is it?' She wondered if it was Matron, but why her and not Audrey and how did she know their whereabouts? As she sprinted out of the building across paths covered with snow, she realised where they were heading.

'Quick!' he shouted.

At the door to Dr. Dacic's office, she asked, 'Who is it?'

Dr. Dacic pushed the receiver at her. The two men withdrew.

'Hello,' she said cautiously. She'd not spoken on the telephone for fourteen months.

'Ellen Frankland. I must speak to Miss Frankland as a matter of urgency.'

'Darling Edward!' Only Edward could manage to get through. She couldn't stop smiling, but how did he know she was in Mitrovica?

'Where have you been? I've been stuck for ten minutes on the end of the line not knowing if I'd be disconnected.'

'Oh, how wonderful to hear you…'

'It doesn't matter now.' He sounded cross. In the corridor Dr. Dacic was dictating. His back to her, she couldn't signal a request to lower his voice.

'The point is I'm coming to fetch you.'

She was a girl again. Sitting in the rose garden at Oaklands, Edward producing the ring, insisting she wore it from that moment. She'd not worn it at Dobro Majka, afraid she'd lose or damage it. Now it was wrapped in tissue paper in the folds of the bodice of her day dress, locked in the suitcase awaiting the journey back to England.

'That would be lovely except we're separated by the English Channel and several hundreds miles…' she teased.

'Didn't he tell you I'm in Belgrade? The idiot.'

'But, we move tomorrow. I was writing…'

'Stay where you are. I've told Dr. Dacic you're…' His voice changed. Loud. Intrusive.

The line rustled. She held the receiver from her ear. What would she do if they were cut off?

'Damn.'

He was back. She spoke apologetically, 'I was saying we're leaving for Albania. The weather's been atrocious and we've to get across the mountains before it deteriorates. Snow…'

'I'm in the hands of a journalist who has agreed to drive me to Mitrovica. It will take a full day...'

'It's not that easy...'

'For God's sake! Dr. Dacic has told me all I need. You must not proceed.'

'We can't wait. The snow's early this year.'

'Woman, you're in the middle of a war zone. Don't you realise the Austrians have occupied Belgrade with the Germans not far away?' He was emphatic. 'I'm risking my life.'

If only she could explain the implications. 'I suppose if Dr. Dacic agrees we could delay one day and you could travel with us or better still could catch us up.'

'Us! It's you I want. I want you home.'

She didn't want reminders of a comfortable life. 'We leave tomorrow. The cadets are Serbia's future. Victory...'

'You're my fiancée. I can't allow you to continue with this undertaking. You must wait and I will bring you home.'

With the best motorcar in the world they wouldn't pass the traffic of refugees. The weather was deteriorating even in the north and the whole country would soon be occupied. Stefan and his unit would be the last to leave.

She tried to distract him. 'I often think of our last evening together. Do you remember? We'd a lovely dinner at...'

'I've spoken to Sir Edward Grey, the Foreign Secretary, and he advises all Britons evacuate Serbia. I'll be with you in twenty four hours. Otherwise, I cannot vouch for your safety.'

She picked up the anxiety in his voice. The desk was littered with papers. She pushed them to and fro, wondered at the conversation between Edward and Dr. Dacic. Tempted to reassure she would wait, till she remembered Mitar's delighted face when she'd given him Rajko's whistle.

She pleaded, 'Please don't make it difficult. I've been commissioned by Colonel Petrovic to accompany the unit out of Serbia to Durazzo.'

'One of his officers can take your place for God's sake. He can't rely on women.'

'Please, my darling, go home and wait for me.'

The receiver was slammed down.

'Edward!' she cried out, 'Edward! Don't go.' Through the roar of static she whispered, *Please Edward.* Go home and wait for me. She didn't mean she didn't want him. She was trying to say it was too late to turn back. What if, like her father, he stopped talking to her? What if, he broke off their engagement? And he'd reached Belgrade. What would he do?

She put down the telephone, picked up papers she'd knocked on the floor. She'd been feeling optimistic. Fears returned. The orderlies might not be true to their word; they might get drunk. The cadets might be ill and if she couldn't persuade Audrey, she would be on her own without medical knowledge. And Edward was in Belgrade… If only she'd known what Edward was going to say, she'd have responded more elegantly, more lovingly.

When Dr. Dacic returned, she described the situation. He listened, assured her Edward ought to return home. If she waited and he'd to turn back, what would happen to the cadets? She was wise to move on.

When she sat once more with her letter, her hand was shaking too much to pick up her pen. Mixed feelings competed to take hold. She marvelled at the hurdles he'd overcome to try and rescue her. She felt tearful. She didn't know if Matron had telephoned him. He wasn't angry with her, but worried. Desperately worried.

Yet even now, she wanted to travel on. She didn't know why.

Eventually she settled into the letter. She wouldn't mention his call or describe the journey.

Major Kostic was killed in action.

She wasn't sure if she'd written about Rajko. She could never admit to Edward she'd volunteered as a soldier. Looking at the wet ink, she recollected Rajko's patience while they waited for the car, his attempt to keep her dry and the touch of the clothes brush on her back. How naïve she must have seemed, how sensibly he answered her questions.

The Major was in Colonel Petrovic's regiment. He and the Colonel used to leave the barracks at Jevo for weeks. As one of Audrey's patients he'd a knee operation. Audrey warned him relief was temporary; ultimately the damage would spread. His death was a shock, though during a war, it shouldn't be.

She'd never thanked Rajko. Holding the pen, finger on the nib, she felt the brush on her back, the steadiness calming her.

She saw Rajko's curls under the tip of his cap, his weathered skin, his eyes. She mustn't dwell on him. How had her aunt accepted Victor's death? Mikaiho said after a battle there was no time for funerals. Though she admired Victor, not once had she asked if there'd been a funeral, if he'd been buried.

Despite winning the highest military honour in Serbia, he was easy to talk to.

Her mind drifted to her meeting with Stefan. It was the first time she'd seen him out of uniform and she'd been struck by how ordinary he was. Where'd she got the idea soldiers looked heroic? She couldn't remember Victor; she was ten when he died. She recalled him in dress uniform because of the painting. He would fight in khaki, not white. And her father could never have opened a parcel containing his white jacket stained with blood; yet the memory was as vivid as if she'd been in the room.

Tomorrow the unit leaves. I hope, my darling, you do not attempt the journey from Belgrade, or if you do, turn back as soon as you realise how impossible the roads are. Even military motorcars have problems because of the amount of traffic.

I was surprised you weren't more interested in the cadets. It's flattering, of course, that your priority is me, but, Edward, I am doing this because of our country's involvement in the war. Britain declared war on Germany in defence of 'poor little Serbia' and the fact the Serbs are losing, must surely be of concern to you. I am beginning to think that unless you experience an event, it is of no significance. Your belated letter, which reached me as I was leaving Dobro Majka suggested you'd not tried to imagine what I'd be doing, despite my giving as honest an account as I could. As you pointed out, your request I temper my letters was to ease your sensibilities, not to help me.

When we spoke on the telephone I was upset. I didn't want to disappoint you by refusing your request. Now I'm angry. How dare you presume from your limited knowledge of the situation in Serbia, to advise me? Had you considered my request to join me as I take the cadets to Albania, I might have waited, but you didn't listen. I think you knew what you wanted, to get me home so you needn't worry about me. I've seen more than you'll ever know. Will you be receptive when I get home to my telling you about the deaths of two of our cadets over a ravine, one beautiful boy who dreamed of becoming a soldier and fighting for his country, or the raped, murdered corpses in a country church? Not if today's conversation is anything to go by. We promised each other we'd be as honest as we could, but ordering me to do something when you know nothing of my situation, doesn't aid truth telling. There are times I can't admit the truth to myself.

Her palms were sticky with sweat. The pen slipped, splattering the page with ink. Quickly she blotted it. She was tempted to sketch through the splodges so they resembled roses or hearts as she did at school. She stared and stared at the page. She remembered Edward's embrace as they stood on the banks of the Wye on their last evening together. Felt his heart beat against her breast. His fingers stroking her hair, his pulling away, 'May I?' How long would it be before she felt his lips on hers? During that evening, he'd spoken in support of Lady Alice's belief that women should play a part in the war, but it wasn't a simple matter. Being a witness was more complex than either of them expected.

She picked up the first page, ripped it. Edward had been anxious, afraid she would be killed. He meant to be loving, not controlling. As the shreds gathered on the table, she wondered how many soldiers began by promising to write faithful accounts of their adventures, but ended wanting to protect the innocence of those they loved.

*

Ellen spent the afternoon finalising the next stage of the journey. Every cadet was provided with boots and socks. Each one was given either a jumper or a jacket. All received scarves and woollen hats. Their two wagons were filled with whatever provisions the town could spare: - a few tins of meat, sacks of rice and beans, tins of dried milk, a dozen bags of sugar, half a sack of cocoa and biscuits from Red Cross parcels. They were found extra blankets, their tents repaired.

Having delayed asking Audrey to continue the journey with her, when she didn't appear for tea at six o'clock, Ellen decided they must talk. The operating theatre was closed because of lack of medical supplies, and Dr. Dacic thought Audrey might be in one of the ward offices.

Rather than use up the batteries of her electric torch, Ellen borrowed the lantern Dr. Dacic used on his night rounds. The bitter wind cut through her greatcoat as she hurried from their quarters into the main building. Having searched the wards, on impulse Ellen veered towards the operating theatre.

The doors were shut. If there was one place she hated, it was this. The stench of ether mingled with disinfectant. Nurses, orderlies, surgeons shrouded in gowns, masks, Wellington boots. At Dobro Majka she'd held cigarettes to the mouths of patients before their operations, nursed their bowls of sick, endured the sound of the relentless sawing. She recalled the basket of limbs that stood outside the tent door and Gladys's refrain, 'It wasn't like this at St. Barts'. Her fingers on the door handle, she was loath to hang around.

To her surprise, the door opened with a slight push. It was the first time she'd been in this operating theatre. It was cold, dark, a single lantern on one of the tables. There were no curtains or blinds at the window. She shivered. An old woman was bent over a walking stick. The figure turned. Ellen was amazed to see Audrey holding a mop. The damp floorboards smelled of Jeyes Fluid.

For a moment neither of them spoke. Ellen cleared her throat.

'What are you doing?'

'What does it look like?'

262

'I came to look for you.' She prayed for right words. 'Are you coming?' she asked.

'Where?'

Anxious, Ellen decided not to say outright what was on her mind. 'Tea.'

Audrey hurried across the boards towards Ellen. The sound of her heel tips echoing around the theatre felt threatening, and for a second, Ellen thought her friend was going to strike her and backed till she touched the coats hanging on the door.

Audrey switched on the electric wall light. Two narrow beds, bare bulbs hanging, palisters covered with white sheets, occupied the vast space. Ellen imagined men crying out.

'Dr. Dacic said you might be here.' Not strictly true, but it gave her authority. 'He doesn't need you.' She modified her words. 'He's happy for you to leave with us tomorrow.'

'You mustn't go,' Audrey pleaded.

'We have to.'

'I don't care what Colonel Petrovic says, or what Dr. Dacic thinks. It's dangerous.'

Afraid Audrey would notice her shaking, she stepped into the room, strode towards the nearest table. She placed her lantern next to Audrey's.

Audrey accused, 'You've not been affected by our experiences.'

'I *have*.' Ellen clasped her hands across her stomach. Audrey's face looked pale under the bulb. Her eyes dark hollows, her nose sharp mountain edges.

'Three cadets died. One driver. You witnessed the fall of that wagon, heard the screams of the children as they fell thousands of feet. We've been near starvation, exhausted. Colonel Petrovic promised his support and we've had none.'

'It wasn't his fault Mikaiho…'

'What has he offered this time?'

'Nothing.'

'You're simple minded, believe what people promise even when they've been shown to be dishonourable. I'm not prepared to risk my life, or the lives of others, for a lost cause.'

It wasn't 'a lost cause.' Ellen was sure. The deaths of the cadets had been shocking, but there were the rest of the cadets to consider. And she'd turned down Stefan's offer of Albanian guides because she didn't trust him.

'We agreed to take them to the Albanian coast,' she said feebly. It was an argument that wouldn't convince.

'Colonel Petrovic said it would take two to three weeks,' Audrey snapped.

'I've got a map from Dr. Dacic, which shows the shortest route.' She didn't add it was strenuous; they would need to exchange the wagons for mules when they reached Pec.

'The orderlies don't do what we tell them.'

'They're more committed now.'

'Cosic has frost bite and will lose his feet.'

'We can manage without him.'

'That's all right then.'

Ellen glanced at the white painted instrument trolley and above it the windowpane and their reflections. Elongated faces superimposed. Endlessly shifting. An overhanging branch scratched at the outside glass. She turned towards the hard angles of the lamp stands remembering how she learned to adjust them.

'I didn't mean it like that.'

'Like what?'

'That I don't care. Matron said we shouldn't get emotionally involved.'

'She didn't say we should ignore facts. Fact One: If Branislav continues on this mad escapade he'll die. He'll probably die here, but it will be with a degree of comfort.'

'He insists.'

'He's sixteen. He does as we instruct.'

'Colonel Petrovic wants Mitar to have the chance of freedom.'

'Freedom for what? I don't know how many will die, but it'll be more than three I'll warrant. And Branislav will be the first.'

She supposed Audrey knew about hearts, but he did seem less breathless. He could travel in one of the wagons if he'd agree. 'If he's going to die, isn't better to give him hope?' She could provide extra blankets, a hot water bottle, even during the day.

'I'm needed here.'

'No, you're not.' The words were out; she must learn to keep quiet. She went on with greater kindness, 'On the road, it's different. We don't know the cadets, we thought we knew the orderlies, but we didn't and we've no control over the weather.' Audrey had turned away and thinking that she was beginning to persuade her friend Ellen pleaded, ' Please! We can work together like you said. The lads are on our side now. We've learned...'

'Don't tell me what I've bloody learned.'

Ellen gasped. Audrey's cheeks were blotched pink and white. She fluttered her arms like a butterfly caught in a jar.

Audrey went on, 'I've learned you don't give a damn about anyone but yourself.'

'Don't be rotten.'

'It's true.'

'Like you showing off what a great surgeon you are.'

'You don't give a damn what happens to Branislav, Mitar, to any of them, just as long as you get the chance to play the hero. And don't think I don't know about the gun Mikaiho gave you.'

'What?'

'Without the trappings of a man, you're nothing.'

She was played out again. She retorted, 'We had them in the Women's Yeomanry to protect the wounded.'

'You imagine the great Ellen Frankland will save twenty-five cadets with how many shots- five, six?'

Two of the orderlies were armed, but she'd tried not to imagine the unit being attacked by Austrian or German soldiers. She would be helpless against a group. The Luger would make no difference.

'You can't be a soldier so you pretend to be a twentieth century Joan of Arc.'

She marched past Ellen, slammed her hand against the handle. It didn't move. 'Damn,' she said. She tried again, breezed through the door.

Audrey had kept quiet about the gun. Ellen leaned against the table, her arms and shoulders aching. She clenched her fist, banged it down hard. Pain shot through her wrist up the arm, jolting her shoulder. She remembered poor, delirious Sibin, how she'd jumped on his foot and how his pain struck through her body. If she thought about being attacked, she would give in. Audrey had never understood her. It was Audrey's mother who explained that Ellen's aloofness was a twelve year old's way of coping, packed off as a weekly boarder only days after her mother died.

She picked up her lantern, not sure whether to take Audrey's. She blew it out, left it. Audrey presumed to find a role for her, was angry when she couldn't. She was right in one respect. That Ellen saw herself as Joan of Arc was too fanciful, but a woman with a gun protecting cadets? The Luger was vanity. She'd leave it with Dr. Dacic. But she would lead them to freedom; there was nothing wrong with that. Switching off the light, she stepped towards the door, closed it silently.

Chapter Twenty-two

Pristina, December 1915

The fire in the schoolmaster's office was heavy with logs, flames roaring. Frozen all day, Stefan had requested a warm room when he came to write his report, but within a few moments of sitting at the desk, he was sweating, his skin itching. In a burst of irritation he cursed Dragan, well meaning, but over-solicitous since Rajko's death. He unbuttoned his jacket, hung it on the back of his chair, smoothed the shoulder straps. He was tempted to forget work and drink a glass or two of *rakija* as he used to with Rajko.

Through the unshuttered window, darkness. Church bells had been ringing since he arrived with a small unit at six. They weren't sombre like those of Belgrade's St. Petka's, but peeled celebration in contradiction to the town's edginess. Not all houses were shuttered; lights flickered at other windows. Pristina was used to war. Young children, sly as rats, ignored the curfew, scurried through the streets. Though the air was tinged with smells of roast pig, chestnuts, food wasn't shared with new arrivals. He didn't blame them; they'd to live.

His reflection, broad shoulders, face of shadows, revealed nothing of his anguish. Rajko was everywhere. He smelled him, heard him breathing. If he were superstitious like Stamenka, he'd believe his ghost occupied the room, though Rajko had no interest in haunting. 'Once we're dead, we're gone, brother' was his creed.

He must start. He tucked his chin in his hands, elbows on the table as he stared through the window.

His relationship with Rajko had changed after Bregalnica. They'd escaped injury till then, presumed they were special. A bullet skimmed Rajko's skull in 1912 and Stefan twisted his shoulder during a training exercise earlier that year. Of course, promotion created a wedge, but Rajko had his medal. Rajko being unable to fight did it. Not that they referred to it.

He picked up his pen and began, 5 *decembar Pristina*.

Tomislav should have telephoned hours ago. Without turning, Stefan fumbled in his jacket pocket for cigarettes. He thought of Ellen's worries for Mitar. Her anxiety would ensure the lad's survival, but what about Stamenka? What if she was dead? He'd seen hundreds of starving refugees on the roads between Belgrade and Pristina. On her own; who would look out for her?

He searched wherever they halted. He walked the streets where families slept in doorways. He flashed his lantern over dozing bodies, proclaimed her name hundreds of times, hammered on doors, intruded homes, insisted on inspecting cellars. No one had heard of Stamenka Petrovic.

Running the cigarette between thumb and index finger, he remembered their last evening together. He'd been wrong not to return immediately after Tomislav's celebration, but on reflection admitted he'd not wanted to finalise arrangements with the journalist. That night, that night of the bomb he felt he wasn't helping them escape, but abandoning them. And briefly, as they lay in bed, his body remembered their closeness. He could have told her—he'd have struggled because words, intimate, soul-words, didn't come easily- how much he yearned for peace. She might have understood, but he missed the chance. His humiliation at not managing an erection, her whispered, 'You're tired,' added to the blanket of despair.

He rubbed the scar on his thigh; it always itched in the heat. Damn Dragan. To think Stamenka, who admired his patriotism, proud he was a soldier, had suggested, perhaps because she sensed his disappointment, suggested he desert. She wasn't as docile as he presumed. He couldn't face letting Tomislav down. He put his pen down, lit a cigarette. Smoked.

He was inspecting the schoolmaster's choice of books when the telephone startled him. He leapt to grab it. Inevitably, the line crackled.

'Petrovic.'

'Yes, sir.'

'What have you got to tell me?'

'We've withdrawn from Hill 247.'

'Your report?'

'Writing it.'

'You're to attack at dawn.'

He wondered how Tomislav retained his self-belief. In Mitrovica Stefan, trudging down the main street after searching for Stamenka through queues at the military hospital, encountered the General's cavalcade. The pavements were overcrowded, the road impassable with carts, overladen packs of mules.

Tomislav's motorcar was bombarded with snowballs. The vehicle slowed. Stefan willed it to press on, but Tomislav—defiant? optimistic?—opened his door, stepped into a stream of slush. He made the speech he'd used in Jevo, promising a revitalised army to bring victory. No one listened. They chanted, 'Coward!' They threw lumps of wood, snow balls packed with pebbles, till the adjutant bundled Tomislav into the car, shooting into the air to ensure safe passage for the 'people's General.'

The incident confirmed he could never desert.

Tomislav was saying, 'I want to know what you don't want me to know.'

Rubbish, Stefan thought.

'Now, Petrovic. Now.'

Tomislav had been wrong about the war. To please the people wasn't strategy. The more Stefan reflected, the more convinced he was they'd wasted resources in Bosnia. Tomislav had taught at Military Academy a General looked beyond the immediate.

'We've dismantled the guns, sir.' He spoke with an authority Tomislav wanted to hear.

From the moment Austria delivered its ultimatum, Stefan had despaired. He'd done his best. Yesterday, outside Pristina, he'd joined his men on a howitzer positioned on the far side of a tower. Vojin, who boasted of seeing old Milan Obrevonic driving through his village in a horse drawn cart when he was a boy. Milorad, nursed back to fitness at Dobro Majka, sang in a haunting tenor as he worked. Bozdan, who couldn't read or write, had fought at Bregalnica.

A German plane hovered in the area all day. It passed over where they were working and dropped nothing.

Later, Stefan left to go to the other side of town, preparing two units to move on to action in Pec. Mikaiho brought news the tower was hit and during a blizzard Stefan drove to it. The car stuck in drifts several times. Eventually, he got out, struggled through blinding snow for twenty minutes.

There was nothing he could do; he'd known it from the start. At the time, he thought it a decent instinct; he loved his men. In retrospect, he recognised regret. Regret he'd not remained with them.

The tower was burning. The plane overhead. He wasn't sure how the tower was destroyed. It might have been enemy action; it might have been their own explosives. Field glasses showed rubble. He witnessed too many similar scenes to feel optimistic there would be survivors.

Tomislav was saying, 'Well done.'

'Thank you, sir.'

He chose not to mention the losses. They would be in his report. Twenty volunteers. Elsewhere men were deserting so perhaps his presence made a difference to morale. He and Tomislav had that in common.

During the night, having completed his report, he ordered food. Liver. Red wine. Bread and cheese.

Later, he wandered narrow streets looking for Stamenka. The place was prettier than Mitrovica, reminding him of the town he was taken to after Bregalnica. On the stretcher, he'd wanted to die. Because of the pain. Because he was afraid.

What if he died before he found Stamenka? He was running out of luck. He wanted to tell her he loved her even though he'd not gone home as he ought. It mattered she knew. It wasn't enough she might sail with Mitar to England where they would be provided for. She must understand he loved her; the trench-ridden tapestries weren't her fault.

The church clock struck three. Rajko condemned him for not getting them out before the war. Rajko was right; he'd been self-centred. How could he live with himself?

He contemplated writing to her. He'd seal a letter in his kitbag so it could be returned with his possessions if he was killed. During campaigns or long training schedules he used to describe the scenery, the colour of the sky, the snow, conversations he overheard so she knew what was happening to him. But not after Bregalnica.

He composed in his head,

My Dear Stamenka,

I have not been the husband I intended to be... No. ... the husband you deserved.

He must explain how he changed.

You remember I was wounded at Bregalnica. I fought bravely and was promoted for my actions that day.

She knew that. Something happened inside him. Loss. 'Of innocence'? 'Illusion' was more accurate.

I was wounded in the thigh and was carried off the battlefield on a stretcher.

It was difficult to put more than facts into words. Could he admit his first thoughts, through the pain, had been the appearance of his leg—not whether he'd lose it, or be disabled, but how the scar would affect the texture of his skin? As though he was an artiste for whom a blemish was disfiguring. How could he expect Stamenka to understand, if he didn't? Nevertheless, he experienced something like shame. At being bayoneted? No. That was agony he thought would never stop, but no...

He was carried through streets, helpless, unable to stop clutching the edge of his canvas bed, aware that if his porters slipped, he would be on the ground, too weak to defend himself. He dozed in and out of consciousness. They reached a street where men were running, shouting, 'We've avenged Kossovo!'

Their triumph chilled him.

He remembered returning home after his convalescence. There was something about that visit... He struggled to remember... He hadn't announced his intention by sending Dragan ahead so Stamenka could dress appropriately, prepare a celebratory meal. At lunchtime, he drank a bottle of red wine, then a glass or two of *rakija*, perhaps more, to give him courage. He didn't know why he needed courage.

September 1913. His favourite time of year. It was six on a beautiful evening when Dragan drove him into the courtyard where the dog was barking. Usually he spent a couple of weeks at home, his mother or Woislav's wife looking after Mitar for the first night so he and Stamenka could be alone. But this time as he watched Dragan reverse ready to return to barracks, Stefan anticipated he wouldn't be at home for more than a day. He ought to have heeded his foreboding.

The sky over their house burned the colours of autumn. He wore his dress uniform. Another departure. Off-duty he preferred a suit; it helped set their mood, but that evening he was regaled in cap, campaign medals, riding boots, pistol in a leather holster. What must she have thought?

Just to prove he could, he took the steps two at a time. The wound wasn't as bad as he feared. Certainly not as serious as Rajko's. On the top step, he stumbled. He didn't fall, but collapsed on one knee. Though unhurt, he felt foolish.

As he straightened, Stamenka's face appeared at the window to the outside door. He remembered thinking they were like actors in a drama over which they'd no control, as though his return was happening to another couple.

The skin across the wound burned. He'd donned long johns to protect where the stitches had been, but even so, the rough wool of his trousers was an irritant. He pictured the jagged marks enflamed. He flung open the door so Stamenka had to jump out of the way.

Disappointment with her appearance tasted of bile. His reaction was unreasonable. Nonetheless, he was angry she wasn't wearing Serb costume. White suited her olive skin and the colours of the embroidery across her bodice were pretty. She adorned her hair with tortoiseshell combs, not dissimilar to those worn by Ellen on the day he asked her to take Mitar to freedom. But, he hadn't forewarned Stamenka, so understandably she wore her working clothes. He shouldn't blame her, yet he did. A rod tore through his gut. He experienced a slight erection.

She rushed to kiss him, but she stank of garlic and onions and he recoiled. He was reminded of the women going to the well in the village of Kadavsic. Rough, enemy women.

He pushed her so she knocked her hip against the edge of the long dining table. He wanted to hurt her. When she cried out, he didn't care.

He demanded food.

He marched over to the fire, rubbing his hands as he pulled off his gloves. He crouched in front of the logs, placed his gloves in the hearth, thinking they'd be warm when he came to leave. She was talking, but he wasn't paying attention. The logs were fresh and he thought of the forests around the barracks where he'd started to run again without Rajko. He'd not enjoyed exercising alone. She went on and on in the way women did. He wanted food and a good fuck.

She began to walk towards the kitchen. Normally they ate as a family at Woislav's where there was a stove and a fire. But for occasions when they were intimate, they used the little eating area, separated from the rest of the room by a wooden screen. They could have improved on it, but it had the merit of being simple and it held their memories. Usually on his first night, Stamenka prepared little delicacies: stuffed olives, cold meats, sausages, breads and he expected something of that sort. When she brought out the serving board with a shrunken piece of goat's cheese, a crabby crust of bread and olives the size of peas, he was furious, knocked it from her hands. It crashed to the floor. The knife glinted as it fell. Mitar called out in his sleep.

Stamenka bent down to pick up the food from the floor. 'It's all right, sweet heart.'

Sweet heart, the lad was eleven. Her back was turned against him. He told her to leave it, but she scrambled about the floorboards, collecting not only the part loaf, but also the crumbs. Licking her fingers, sticking a single crumb on it, scraping it off against the side of the board. She was behaving like a pauper.

He stamped on her hand. Or intended to, but misjudged and caught only her fingertips; she squealed as though he'd broken bones. He yelled at her. Red sparks dotted in front of his eyes. He bellowed for the child to quit bawling or he'd give him something to bawl about. He snatched the knife from the board she placed with exaggerated care on the table.

He instructed her to come to him. To take off her dress. She refused.

'I'm your husband. You do as you're told.' He heard his father's voice inside his own.

She laughed. He'd been surprised at her laughter. He held the knife to her throat. The blade was shining in the candlelight. He again instructed her to undress.

'No, Stefan. Please. It is not the time. Our son is too close.'

Women argued. He'd been away a year. Some men went with gypsies, prostitutes; found lonely women, the wives of officers. He waited till he was with his wife. He kept clean.

He grabbed the hem of her skirt, dug in the knife. As it tore, the material whimpered. He dug deeper. He remembered the bayonet in his thigh. Some Bulgarian bastard, waking them during the night so he'd no time to wash, say his prayers, piss properly before he rallied his men for battle. Later, he learned traitors let the Bulgars into their encampment so the enemy slept in tents next to their own, roused them from their beds.

He relished the rip of the cotton as he held the knife steady till it reached the waistband. He instructed her to unfasten her belt. Her face fast with tears, her skin blue.

Her hands could not, would not undo her belt.

'Let me help you,' he said, 'If you keep crying I will hurt.'

He snipped the front buttons of her dress with the knife. By now he was fully erect. He gave her the knife as he fiddled with his own buttons. His hands were sticky. He heard the knife drop to the floor, skim across the boards. His cock was hard, he could smell his juice. Through the skirts he saw white long johns thick and ugly. Where were the frills and lace she wore when they bedded? She was set against him. She despised him because he provided for her, was wounded for her, nearly died for her and she chose not to be ready. He snatched at her underskirts, pushed her against the chimney-breast. The heat from the logs burned through the trouser leg. He couldn't wait. He forced his lips against hers, pressed her head against the stone.

'Bitch. Be ready next time.'

He tried to pull down her long johns, leaning against her body. He'd to hang on, not come too soon. He must drive inside her, so she knew she was his. He was in charge. Not her with her wily ways. His hands reached up to her waist. Into the elastic. More knickers beneath. He put his hands over both sets of elastic, yanked them over her thighs. She tussled. He slapped her face. Dragged the pants down to her knees.

He was overwhelmed. He couldn't stand against the wall to fuck so he pushed her to the ground, where she pulled her knees to one side, then the other, closed her legs. Pushing her thighs apart, he ignored her pleas. He was glad she struggled; it made it easier to ram into her. Even so, she resisted. She wasn't wet, but held her body stiff, arched her back not with pleasure, but to force him away. He wouldn't go away. He came quickly, lay on top, panting.

His eyes closed, he waited. She was lying still. Her heart heavy against his breast. The logs burned. Sobs wrenched her body. He was pleased. He hoped she understood how much it hurt to be a soldier. He rolled off her, overcome with tiredness.

When he opened his eyes, Stamenka was standing, examining his face. Streaks of grey glinted among her black hair. Her thick eyebrows were damp. He touched her forehead with his fingers and she flinched. As he raised himself on his elbows, he noticed Mitar at the door to their sleeping quarters.

Stefan said, 'Go back to bed.'

Mitar didn't move. Stefan opened his mouth to repeat his command. The child had gone.

Chapter Twenty-three

Pristina, December 1915

Journey to Pristina
Hard, steep climb out of Mitrovica which gradually fell to a plain.
We're on the same route as the Army. Enormous gun carriages pulled
by huge oxen: 10 or 12 in a team. Have passed many burned
skeletons of motorcars and lorries by the roadside.

Took 4 days to travel 25 miles. Mitar, Velimir and others are
weak but determined. Orderlies, Timohir and Dobrica, can be sullen
at times.

Pristina, December 1915
Turkish town at head of broad valley. Quite poorest we've seen. Bitter
wind. Sleet, snow. Hundreds of minarets covered with ice and snow.
Very pretty.

Found a dying man in the street. Wrapped him in blanket.
Dobrica gave him sip of rakija and carried him to hospital.

Camped outside town in woods by river along with others. Mile
upon mile lit by our fires. Ate mutton and sweet biscuits. Atmosphere
better among cadets, but Serb orderlies unpredictable. Good to talk to
Gustav who gets on better with other orderlies since Mitrovica.

Worry about Edward.

On leaving Pristina, their unit re-joined the exodus. For several
miles, Ellen and Zivoli accompanied the second wagon with
Timohir who shared the driving. The cadets, in twos and
threes, marched behind soldiers in black and brown
homespun trousers, tight in the leg, billowing in the seat.
Although Mitar was apt to be moody, Ellen was sorry he and
Velimir weren't with her, but with Dobrica at the front. They
liked chatting to the soldiers, feeling part of the army.

From time to time she witnessed the destruction of
vehicles. Two soldiers wearing gauntlets and sheepskin gilets
doused a French limousine and several army vehicles with

petrol. A gun-wielding private dashed up and down the road shouting, 'Danger! Danger!' It was amusing until the flames whooshed as they took hold. Yellow, green, orange and purple devoured what were once recognisable vehicles. The smell of petrol was followed by that of rubber and leather. While Ellen daydreamed she'd a motorcar in which to drive downhearted cadets, two soldiers with long poles, prodded the whirlwind of fire. It trembled on the brink of the hill, before somersaulting down to the stream. She saw the exercise repeated. Each time, Ellen grieved for Radovan and Miodrag, their wagon shuddering on the precipice, tumbling a few feet before disintegrating.

Because it was important the unit stay together, Ellen ordered Gustav to move between wagons so Dobrica didn't get too far ahead. Using Dr. Dacic's map, she decided they would stop for the night at a monastery a day's journey out of Pristina. Other travellers had the same idea. There was no room in the dormitories or outbuildings and rather than erect tents because they were exhausted, they were given permission to sleep in and around their wagons in the courtyard in front of the marble church.

Ellen asked Timohir to check the register while she held a surgery. She missed Audrey. It would be a long time before she could make her peace.

Her first patient, Velimir, squirmed as she rolled up his trouser leg to examine the graze on his shin. Moving the torch close to his skin, she glimpsed Dobrica on the other side of the courtyard, kitbag between his knees. He and Timohir remained a source of anxiety. Gustav admired Dobrica because, having lost his hand, he still longed to be a soldier.

'Velimir, I have to remove the dirt,' she said, 'See!'

She held the piece of lint in front of him, flashing the light. 'Grit. I have to remove each piece or it will poison you.' The boy shuddered.

She glanced again at Dobrica, but it was too dark to make out what he was pushing into the depths of his bag.

'How did you do it?' she asked. It would have been hard for Audrey to make conversation. She ought to have treated her with more sympathy.

While Velimir described running to catch up, having stopped for a pee behind a bush, slipping on black ice and unable to steady himself because he was carrying Mitar's mascot, Ellen pondered whether to question Dobrica. She feared he planned to abandon them.

An hour later, surgery finished, she followed Dobrica who'd gone to tether their oxen in the field outside the monastery. She exchanged pleasantries with the guard on the gate and turned down the lane where refugees were sleeping in the hedge. The lighted fires reminded her of Women's Yeomanry camps. The conditions during that summer before the war were idyllic, luxurious. The smell of wood smoke. The warmth of Prince's breath as she stroked his head after the 'rescue-the-wounded' race. Her friend Maud's laughter as they drove home. The experience that had given her a yearning for adventure.

The muddy track was beginning to freeze. She allowed herself the childish pleasure of digging a heel into an untrodden patch of snow, cracking its crust. Giggling at her silliness, she pressed on through the mud, ice and snow towards the orderly, pulling up her collar against the cold. As she pushed open the gate into the field, she imagined the unit's arrival in Durazzo, the cadets in twos, the orderlies and drivers at the rear and Stefan's arms reaching for his son.

Dobrica had cleared an area as large as a football pitch so each animal could wander the three-foot extent of their rope. He covered the ground with straw, filled improvised troughs with hay. As he held out a bucket of water for the smaller animal to drink, he sang what sounded like a lullaby. Gustav told her Dobrica had two young sons. Her eyelids prickled with tears as he stroked the animal's large forehead, still murmuring his tune. For several moments she didn't move.

When he saw her, he raised his eyebrows, averted his face. They'd not spoken since early morning. The urgency to sort out the problem waylaid the part of her that recognised patience was more productive.

'Are you planning to leave us?'

'Good evening, Miss Frankland.'

'I saw you packing your kitbag.'

278

'Unpack.'

'Do you intend to abandon your army?'

'I am a patriotic man.'

A grey, knitted sock, which he raised to push his cap away from his forehead, covered the stump of his wrist. The ox nudged the bucket, shuffled its feet.

'Dr. Dacic said those who don't stick with us are deserters, but I don't want to be accompanied by reluctant men.'

'No one is reluctant.' He seemed amused rather than angry.

'It's true you behave better than you used to, but compared to cadets like Branislav, I don't find you enthusiastic or co-operative.' She almost praised Gustav. Gustav who chatted to everyone, encouraged the cadets to help each other, even the sulky Mitar. She trailed off. 'I know it can't be easy. You were badly wounded.'

Dobrica let the bucket clatter to the ground. Water splashed his *opanki* sandals and trousers. With one foot, he shoved the trough towards the ox whose blue bead of fortune in the centre of the yoke, glistened in the moonlight.

His manner was serious, courteous. 'You do not understand Serbs. You think you do, but you are mistaken. Dr. Dacic flatters, Colonel Petrovic also. You cannot see our souls.'

Ellen was taken aback at this reference to religion.

'You think only the English have souls,' he added.

The soul wasn't something she gave attention to; it related to the dead, her mother, her uncle. The part that lived on. But oddly, not Rajko. She'd not thought he might have a soul. He'd disappeared. There was nothing beyond.

Her, 'I'm sorry' was as much for Rajko as Dobrica.

In the distance, the laden waters of the narrow stream, running by the side of the wood, gushed and raced. Who would have thought she'd have a religious discussion in Serbia at this momentous time? Neither Lady Alice, nor Audrey. She felt a flicker of self-satisfaction.

'Do your souls live on like ours?' she asked.

'I don't know. I love my country. This Lieutenant Nis you talk of can tell you, but he is not right that we want to die. I am too young. I choose to help my country instead of staying at home, which I could have done because, as you say, of my wound.'

He was staring so intently she thought he might read her mind.

The ox kicked over its trough and feeling she ought to do something to show she was sorry for her ignorance, she walked to the far side of the animal, bent down and righted the trough. The animal's breath smelled warm, reminding her of steaming porridge on the breakfast sideboard at home.

She said, 'What has that to do with souls? You said I cannot see into your soul.'

'The Serb soul.'

He was talking of a living thing. 'So it's different from the English soul?'

'The English have money. Money buys special treatment. For the cadets and for you. You get wagons, plenty of food while others starve. You choose plump animals while our poor are left with beasts that collapse.'

She remembered Rajko saying the British let the Serbs down by not sending troops; nurses wouldn't have been needed if the British army had turned up.

'I'm here! I could have gone home to my fiancé.' Her cheeks burned.

'We fight for our land. We have no money, so no weapons. We fight with our wits to keep out the oppressors.'

'I'm taking the cadets so they can come back with the army.'

'In the meantime, what happens to our people? How will they endure the enemy's rod?'

'I can't tell the British army to send troops...'

'You can remember we have soul.'

She still wasn't sure what he meant. She took his point about the Serbs being poor. With a twinge of shame it struck her she'd viewed Rajko, despite his kindness, as not quite as significant as herself. Even though she compared him to Victor, she hadn't regarded him as quite Christian.

The oxen munched hay loudly. This was an adventure for her, but not for the Serbs.

She asked, 'You are leaving, aren't you?'

'I want to join the rebels. We'll hide in the hills and attack. I'll ask the older cadets to join me and of course, my brother orderly.'

'That's for Colonel Petrovic to decide.'

'He's not here.'

'The cadets are too young.'

'At sixteen and seventeen?'

'They're not strong enough.'

'We're used to weakness.'

Stefan had said something similar, but Branislav was breathless and even Zivoli, the strongest, found the climbs arduous.

She turned to walk back. There was nothing she could do to stop anyone going with Dobrica if they chose; guns, immediate fighting, would tempt the cadets. Matron would have handled the situation better. She wouldn't have lost two orderlies.

She paused. Dobrica's damaged arm rested on the ox's rump; she saw a brave man.

She pleaded, 'We can't reach Pec without you. At least accompany us that far. Help us get a good price for the oxen and the wagons so we can buy mules for the journey through the mountains.'

'Give me half the money.'

'I forbid you to take cadets.'

'You can't stop them.'

'Will you stay till Pec?'

He nodded.

She went on, 'And Timohir?'

'It's his choice.'

A gust of wind blew surface straw across the snow. She shivered. She would leave Pec with one orderly, probably without the older, capable cadets. Her dream of reaching Durazzo leading the unit of twenty-five cadets was receding.

'Thank you.' She prepared to return to the monastery. 'I see you truly love your country.' She thought he was a hero, but hesitated to say so.

'I'm not the one you need to watch.' Dobrica pulled down his cap so his face was hidden.

'Who?'

'The one who doesn't like being told what to do by a woman.'

As she plodded back through the snow, she reflected. Gustav was loyal. He showed no resentment. It had to be Timohir. As she waited outside the gates to be re-admitted, she wished they were all on the same side.

The next day's travelling was enjoyable. Following discussion with Gustav, they experimented with a late start, after breakfast of tinned meatballs, bread and cheese. The plan was to stop for a rest at midday rather than a meal and cook dinner in the evening.

It worked well. Most of the cadets walked, lessening the weight of the wagons on the oxen. Ellen was mindful of Dobrica's comment about getting a good price. Nonetheless, Velimir remained weary and despite Mitar's protests, she insisted he rode in the afternoon.

Although the unit was positioned behind a slow-moving platoon of Serb artillery, their wagons kept together. In an effort to humour Mitar, she pointed out they were marching close to soldiers in his father's regiment. Mitar sneered their trousers were scruffy, their boots unpolished. As if his appearance was superior. When she praised the kindness of the men who lifted two children carried by their weary mother, covering them with a blanket and sitting them inside the big guns, Mitar pulled a face.

That night they camped in a hillside adjoining a farmhouse. The cadets, despite the cold, quickly erected tents and the orderlies provided a meal of chicken stew, rice, apricots dipped in *rakija* and gallons of tea.

Timohir, having persuaded the older lads to collect branches and twigs from the hedgerows and nearby woods, built a fire. Ellen saw he'd the marks of a leader and wondered at the truth of Dobrica's accusation.

By eight o'clock, tempted by the heat, biscuits and the unusual good humour of the orderlies, fifteen cadets remained crouched round the fire. Worried they wouldn't get enough sleep, Ellen announced, 'We need to breakfast before dawn tomorrow. Please get yourselves to bed.'

Several stood up and moved towards their tents. Gustav followed with the biscuit tin.

About to repeat her order, Ellen was surprised when Timohir said, 'If you please, miss, I think they're old enough to decide for themselves.'

Ellen glanced down at Dobrica. Was this the sort of thing he meant? Dobrica wasn't looking her way, but began a recitation. Sparks blew, popped. With a sigh, she plonked herself down between Zivoli and Timohir. Tomorrow they would reach Pec. Timohir passed her a blanket; she pulled it round her shoulders.

She was reminded of summer camp. Maud had narrated the whole of *Sir Patrick Spens* to Ellen's amusement. Dobrica's Serb poem was unfamiliar to her, though she picked up the gist: King Marko was given a choice of either victory on earth, or death and eternal life. That he chose the latter resulted in the Serbs losing the battle of Blackbirds on the plain. She remembered Rajko saying soldiers needed stories to persuade them to fight and she wondered if that lay behind the church's teaching about heaven. As a twelve year old, it had been comforting her mother was safe in heaven. It was an uneasy thought.

When Dobrica finished, Zivoli slid a whistle similar to Mitar's from his pocket. Timohir leaned close to tell her it was a *frula*. He didn't seem to dislike her, but maybe he objected to her giving orders. She folded her legs, rested her chin on her knees.

Last night she'd been unable to sleep, obsessed by the women's corpses. As she lay, her back cold on stone, it struck her again the rapists, the killers, were soldiers. The soldiers who raped would be known to those who didn't. Heroes and villains side by side. Two kinds of violence co-existing.

As she looked at the stars, those her beloved Edward could be gazing at, she reflected there could have been rapists in Victor's unit. Was there good violence? Victor and Rajko fought for a just cause; among their men were some who hated women. Victor might not have realised the possibility, but Rajko had. Maybe rapists hadn't wanted to be soldiers. She found, in the darkness, in the midst of Zivoli's playing of the *frula*, tears for the women whose lives she'd touched. Tears she'd been too shocked, too frightened to shed when she'd discovered them.

Zivoli nudged her. She thought he'd seen her crying. She brushed her face with the back of her glove and looked where he was pointing. Beyond the sparks and flames, a shape, dark as a shadow, emerged from a tent. Mitar's gangly figure. Velimir's squat. She'd been relieved when they went to bed, but now they were inching down the slope, Velimir leaning on his friend's arm so they shifted from side to side like a man with one leg shorter than the other. They were lurching towards Branislav and Kova. Branislav must have heard their approach for he turned.

As Ellen flung off her blanket, Timohir said, 'Let them sort it out.'

Even as she hesitated, she remembered Dobrica's warning. Nonetheless, she pulled the blanket back.

Branislav was on his feet, running towards his friends. He put an arm around Velimir, frail as an old man. In the flickering light, he swayed; unable to contain her anxiety, Ellen was up, the blanket tumbling in folds.

On reaching them, Velimir's face reminded her of Kostu's corpse. She longed to put her arms round him, wished he'd eat more. 'Did you have a nightmare?' she asked.

Velimir shook his head.

Zivoli was playing a tune containing the sadnesses of the past and present.

Mitar shouted, 'He's not ill. He wants to join the fun. Why should he miss out?'

Timohir appeared at her side. 'Miss Frankland, may I have a word?'

Mitar spat, 'Foreign witch.'

Having no idea how to persuade Velimir to return to bed, Ellen followed Timohir up the slope to his tent. He took her hand, slipped a flask into it.

'What is it?' It looked like the ones the orderlies passed to one another. She knew where that led.

'Taste.' His voice was as gentle as her mother's.

She wiped the rim with her gloves, looking at him. She saw someone wiser than she was. Holding the leather bottle in both hands she raised it to her lips. At home, a sherry, champagne, a glass of wine added to an enjoyable occasion, but she was responsible, there was no Audrey, and tomorrow they'd to reach Pec. She tipped it on her tongue. It was sweet, too sweet, but her hand, stiff with caution, slipped and she swallowed more than intended. The taste reminded her of cough mixture and she returned the flask with a smile. As she did, her throat burned. She jolted in surprise and Timohir laughed.

'Forgive me, miss, but that boy is spoiled. He doesn't take well to being told what to do.'

She opened her mouth to speak, but the cold air made her cough. When she recovered, her voice trembling, 'Velimir is frail. I fear for his life.' Audrey had warned against him travelling. She dreaded finding him dead in his sleeping bag.

'He will die.' Timohir was matter of fact.

'No, no.'

'And the other one, he'll never take orders from you.'

'Only from a man. Is that what you mean?'

'From no one. His father spoils him.'

'If Velimir rode in the wagon, he'd stand a better chance, but Mitar sees it as weakness.'

'You could ask Branislav or Zivoli to persuade him.'

When she returned to her place, Zivoli was saying to the cadets, 'I will teach you a song. First the words. I will sing the words.'

His voice was beautiful.

She recalled riding Prince through the hills on the evening war was declared; the canter had calmed her.

Zivoli sang the words through twice. When he played, they joined in, *A jag ga kelti necu. Jer sam ga ljubila.* A love song. And I love her still.

The wind was bitter and Ellen shrank into her blanket. Velimir and Mitar were wrapped in the same blanket. Perhaps it was better Velimir wasn't on his own in the tent; here he was warmed by his friend. As she looked around, there wasn't one she wasn't attached to. Branislav with whom she'd wrestled for the baker's gun. Bogdan one of the original leaders whose father died the day he was born. Dusan who loved the way Gustav made cocoa. She wanted to get through to Durazzo and yet she missed Audrey, dreading the consequences of defying Edward.

And beneath that, she feared rape.

As the fire began to die down and smoke drifted, Zivoli played another tune she'd not heard. The cadets knew it and began to sing. Picking up the two four beat, she clapped her hands. Though the voices merged she distinguished each. On the other side of the fire came the whistle of another *frula*. Mitar was playing the whistle given by his father, the one she'd bought for Rajko. When the tune finished on a surprising high note, she applauded; Timohir and the rest joined in.

'You have beautiful voices,' she said.

Dobrica said, 'You, also, Miss Frankland. Many of the men at Dobro Majka heard it as they lay in pain. They will say it gave them the fight to live.'

She was taken aback. In the hospital, she and the other women received compliments, but since then, no praise. Quite the opposite, she felt to be under constant attack.

Timohir said, 'And now, miss, I think it is time these young men bedded down.'

Chapter Twenty-four

Pec, December 1915

Last night as we followed our wagons through Pec I was filled with sadness at the prospect of losing Dobrica.

The smell of wood fires and barbecued food couldn't mask the stink of sewage, which ran raw in the gutters.

I was relieved to find space for us in grounds of monastery. I write on my own in the little tent I used to share with Audrey.

Tomorrow we move on.

Dusan, Kova (despite frost bite) and two other cadets have chosen to join Dobrica. I'm delighted Bora, Bogdan and Branislav are staying with the unit. Bora will replace Dusan as team leader. Zivoli is distressed he'll lose his friend, Kova, but from my point of view all are committed to the journey. With the possible exception of Timohir who's angry Dobrica considers him too old to fight. Our drivers were reluctant travellers, their absence less troubling.

Dobrica sold our wagons and oxen in exchange for 9 mules. He'll help us load in the morning. He advises we take the shorter route through Cakor Pass to Androvica, allowing 3 days supplies: tea, sugar, sack of rice, can of oxo, tins of condensed milk, bully beef and 2 loaves of bread apiece, loaded on 6 mules. The other 3 carry hay. Each of us will carry on our backs personal items wrapped in 3 blankets and protected by a rubber sheet.

Bitter winds cut the valley as Ellen's unit set off the next day. Timohir overslept; some of the cadets took a long time to pack their bundles in a manner they could balance. It was noon when the mules were roped in a train and they clattered on the frozen track out of Pec.

Ellen was delighted when Timohir volunteered to lead with the older, fitter cadets. The younger ones liked the mules and when the path narrowed, they patted their laden rumps, whispered encouragement. Gustav scurried up and down the line checking the baggage remained secure, rallying the lads.

Blue sky and sun brought optimism and the cadets laughed and chatted in groups of three or four as they walked between the animals. Ellen was surprised how the mood could shift and with it, hers.

Towards sunset, they reached a farmhouse, the only habitable building they'd seen for an hour. Timohir persuaded the farmer to accommodate them, rather than other refugees, in the stone sheep pens. Ellen bought goats' cheese and fresh bread from the farmer's wife. Under Gustav's guidance, Branislav's team prepared a substantial supper.

Wedged in a corner between Velimir and Gustav, Ellen couldn't sleep. The wall prodded her back and the distant murmur of the river didn't sooth, but stirred fears. The mountains were unattainable, their pace fatefully slow. She heard Edward's voice, harsh as barren slopes, cold as sunless peaks. She imagined he tried to reach Mitrovica, his motorcar tipping into the ravine, his cries filling her head with accusations. She rehearsed a more pleasing telephone conversation, her concern expressed with love.

The next day Velimir was one of the first up. Because he appeared stronger than yesterday, Ellen's spirits rose. They breakfasted on bread and goats' cheese and were on their way as dawn broke.

After a mile, they reached the Rugovo gorge where they were to separate from the army and the rest of the refugees and follow Dobrica's route through the Cakor Pass. The path became steep sooner than Ellen expected, shrubs and saplings, sprinkled with snow, sprouted from rock crevices. At the foot of woods where the ground levelled, a bitter wind battered their faces. The occasional splashes of sun coincided with shifting stones underfoot, so they could never relax. Their pace slowed.

Ellen wasn't sure if it was a particular Serbian trait, but like Stefan, Dobrica anticipated it would take half a day, not a day and a half to reach the turning to the Cakor Pass. He estimated they would cross the Bistrica River twenty-four hours later. Ellen alternated between anger at the miscalculation and frustration at being unable to move faster.

At three thirty in heavy sleet, Ellen suggested they stop for the night in what she presumed was a shepherd's hut some yards from their route.

Timohir corrected, 'It's a summer dwelling for many families.'

The roof leaked. There was no glass in the windows and Gustav contended with fierce winds and wet to build a fire; the cooking team did well to provide a meal of stew, bread and tea.

Once again Ellen didn't sleep. Cold after feeding the mules, a draught on her feet increased her discomfort. She worried how the cadets, Mitar and Velimir in particular, would cope when they got to the heights of the Pass.

The next morning, she and Gustav, up before dawn, prepared breakfast of bread and tea. Despite squalls of sleet, the unit set off cheerfully as the track descended and curved round a low ridge. Then began a sharp climb. Sheer cliffs rose thousands of feet from the swirling river below. In addition to sleet, gusts of snow blew from the hillsides into their faces. The path proved icy, sometimes deceptively coated with snow. The mules walked steadily, but the younger lads found it hard not to slip. From time to time, water, ankle-deep, cascaded across their path so Gustav and Timohir carried the bundles of the weaker cadets. Ellen fought thoughts of the comfort of the hospital in Mitrovica, Audrey's wagging finger.

From time to time, Ellen reminded the lads they were soldiers, suggested they sing. She hoped Mitar would get out his *frula*, but it was Zivoli who began to play. Some, encouraged by Timohir, sang words to popular tunes. The wind grew more powerful; they stopped mid-tune, needing to concentrate on keeping upright. Branislav tried to lighten the mood, pretended he was a kite and would fly over the mountains. Mitar smiled for an instant, as if to laugh outright, would further enrage the wind.

Snow layered their caps, the shoulders and fronts of jackets and when Velimir fell on his knees, he let out such an anguished cry Ellen thought he was dying. Mitar helped him up, pressed Prince Marko into his hands. Velimir protested. The mascot was pushed between them till Velimir relented and tucked it in his jacket pocket. For the next mile Branislav and Mitar walked on either side of him, holding his hands, promising it wasn't far. When the track became too narrow, Ellen suggested they walk in pairs and Gustav walked with Velimir.

That night they slept in a shepherd's hut. Sleet had turned to snow and after discussion with the orderlies, Ellen decided it was too difficult to build a fire. Supper consisted of the last of the bread, remnants of goats' cheese and spoonfuls of condensed milk.

No one disagreed with Timohir the next morning, that having fed the mules, they discard two bundles of hay allowing two cadets to ride. Despite the snow, they settled into a steady march, heads down against the wind, their feet taking tiny steps to avoid slipping. Velimir spurned the offer of a lift, made a walking stick; Mitar imitated. Ellen dismissed any thoughts of Durazzo, their unit being greeted by Stefan, or even more tempting, the taste of champagne bubbles as she sat with Edward in the rose arbour at Oaklands.

It was one o'clock by Ellen reached the river. She saw the mules waiting in line, the cadets in groups on either side of them and presumed Timohir and Gustav wanted lunch. They ought to push on though hungry after the simple breakfast. She prepared to negotiate. They would cross the river, walk an hour, but stop before sunset.

'The bridge is down, miss.' Timohir crossed the shingle to her.

'Can we mend it?' At her first summer camp, Sergeant Sutherland and a few of his men showed how to build a pontoon from trees fallen in the nearby woods, but here, they'd no axe, ropes or crucially time.

Timohir shook his head. 'See, it's crashed on the other side.'

'Overloaded,' Branislav suggested. 'They must have set off…'

'If it can't be repaired…' Ellen was impatient. 'How do we cross?'

Some of the cadets crowded round while others skimmed pebbles across the water.

Gustav said, 'The best thing is to turn back. We'll be in Pec in a day.'

To Ellen's annoyance, Timohir agreed with him.

'We must push forward,' she urged.

'I'm starved,' Mitar said. He sat on his bundle next to Velimir. Others did the same.

Ellen walked over to the rickety remains of the bridge. The river was flowing fast, shallow at the edges, about three feet in the middle. She despaired of reaching the Cakor Pass. But for the swirling pools in the centre, they could wade across. Except the water would be freezing and the pebble bed, shifting.

'Can the mules cross without being unfastened?'

'No, miss.' Timohir reverted to sulky mode. 'If one slips, we lose the lot.'

'It's quite deep in the middle,' Branislav observed. 'It's too deep for the cadets.'

'Can they sit on a mule?' Ellen asked.

'They're already heavy laden,' Timohir said.

'What do you suggest?'

'We go back.'

'That's not an option,' Ellen insisted.

Timohir and Gustav glanced at each other.

Branislav said, 'If we remove the hay, those mules can carry the cadets. Put the hay on the strongest ones.'

'It'll take too long,' Timohir snapped. Gustav nodded.

Ellen said, 'Gustav, can you see to lunch and we'll do as Branislav suggests.'

It took over twenty minutes to separate the animals. Bogdan volunteered to take the first loaded mule across and tie up the others as they arrived. Timohir decided he should go first, test the waters and Bogdan could follow with the other loaded mules. The cadets lined the bank and watched Timohir lead the animal into the water. Occasionally in the heat of summer, Ellen paddled bare-foot across the Dove and the sensation of the first chill on her feet always sent a frisson up her spine. Timohir plunged in as though the waters were warm. The animal trotted alongside with ease and aplomb. Even in the middle of the river where they stepped more cautiously, there didn't seem any danger of them falling. The water swished against the base of the panniers, Timohir's thighs. When they reached the far side, Mitar led the cheers.

While Bogdan took the other mules, the rest of the unit sat in a circle eating rice and beef out of a common dish, sharing a spoon, their own packed in their bundles. There was a general discussion as to how best to manage the crossing of the cadets. Branislav proposed building a raft from the remains of the bridge; Gustav agreed, but Ellen said it would take too long. It was finally decided each rider would be accompanied by Ellen, Branislav or Zivoli; Gustav would remain a constant on the bank. Some cadets were nervous, couldn't swim. Some were frightened of mules. Ellen strove to reassure and hearten.

Branislav said he would take the first mule with a cadet. Mitar volunteered in order to show a reluctant Velimir how easy it was. Soon he was sitting like a king, his bundle on his back, Velimir's in front. Zivoli and Ellen followed with their cadets. All reached the other side successfully. The feeble sun dappled the water and Ellen relaxed, accepting the delay, optimistic they would have half an hour of daylight in which to continue.

It was three in the afternoon by they were ready to make the last crossing. Zivoli remained on the far bank, the plan being Branislav would accompany Velimir; Ellen, would take Bora who was frightened of water and mules, despite his age and size; Gustav would ride on his own.

The problem arose when Velimir refused to mount his mule. Branislav promised to stay close, to hold his leg while Velimir put his arms round the mule's neck, but Velimir said no. Branislav offered to hold his hand. Velimir shook his head. Only when Ellen suggested Gustav walk with him, did he agree.

Gustav backed from the group gathered round the mules at the water's edge. His bundle at his feet, his face twisted in a frown.

Glancing at her watch, Ellen hurried over. 'If we don't move now, we'll get no further today.'

Gustav examined his feet. 'I am not a brave man.'

'Nonsense.' She couldn't waste time humouring an orderly; the cadets were her main responsibility. 'If you prefer I'll take him.' She checked her watch again, 'But he likes you. You make him feel safe.' Gustav had been walking next to Velimir all morning, chatting encouragement.

'The river god will devour me,' Gustav blurted.

Ellen tapped her foot. He was an educated Austrian, a librarian. How could he believe such rubbish?

'Well....' she began.

She turned round distracted by Branislav's, 'Miss!'

Branislav said, ' I need a pee.'

She snapped, 'Not now.' To Gustav she said, 'Please, Gustav. Velimir will be fine with you.'

Gustav clenched his hands into fists. 'I can't swim.' Gustav spoke as though confessing he'd assassinated Archduke Ferdinand.

Ellen resisted the urge to laugh. 'No one need swim. Branislav and I will be right behind you and it's only three feet in the middle.'

When they rejoined Branislav and the other cadets, Ellen asked Branislav to bring up the rear, he said, 'Sorry, miss. I can't.'

She didn't need him behaving like a prima donna.

She hoisted a trembling Velimir onto Gustav's mule, which had become reluctant. The sun had disappeared. Sleet smudged the grey sky.

'You're a brave lad,' she said to Velimir. He was sitting upright, his hands clutching Mitar's Prince Marko. Ellen hugged him. 'You'll be fine.'

From the far bank, the cadets whoopeed encouragement. Maybe it was a mistake to leave Velimir until last. She couldn't blame him for wanting Gustav. If Gustav went first, she would go next. It would be easy to shout instructions if necessary.

'Put your hands around his neck,' she said to Velimir. 'Tuck Prince Marko away.'

Velimir leaned forward. He was making it hard. Sleet driving downstream, cut their cheeks. While she was thinking how she might persuade him to release the mascot, Branislav pushed her aside.

To Velimir he said, 'Let me,' and shoved the Prince in the top pocket of Velimir's tunic. 'See. Arms round his neck like this.'

Velimir lay as rigid as a broom handle across the mule's back.

'Off you go!' Branislav smacked the animal's haunches; it began to step across the stones. Gustav, taken by surprise, ran to grab the reins and stumbled alongside his rider. As the hooves splashed through the shallows, Gustav soothed Velimir. Ellen felt reassured.

She anticipated she would need to give Bora, a robust lad, no more than a hand up. His trembling, she attributed to his standing around for two hours and the drop in temperature. Like Gustav, he couldn't swim, like Velimir he was nervous of animals. Earlier in the day he told her, he'd been tempted to join Dobrica, but had been persuaded by Branislav a more exciting future lay with the army proper.

Sensing his anxiety, she said, 'The mule knows its way. All you have to do is hold on.' He pulled his knitted hat over his ears, closed his eyes. As they entered the water, she advised, 'Try to keep in rhythm with his movement. You're just a load to him.'

This last crossing proved the most difficult. Quite apart from the sleet, the wind rose and Velimir's mule remained lively and splashed water into their faces. Bora was sobbing to himself.

Ellen murmured, 'That's it. Very good. You're doing fine.'

Behind, she couldn't hear Branislav's mule enter the water. Why was he so slow? She debated with herself whether they ought to camp by the river. She'd like to find some habitation or shelter so they could build a decent fire and dry off. Tonight of all nights, they would benefit from hot food and protection from the elements.

'I don't want to be a soldier, Miss.'

She was surprised both at his comment and that he wanted to speak. 'That's a long time off.'

'I never wanted to be a soldier.'

His face was waxy against the mule's neck and she remembered his pleasure at being part of the group on the bridge when the cadets had stolen bread. She wasn't sure, but thought every man in Serbia had to do military service.

'You're brave enough,' she said.

'My father wants me to be an officer. I want to be a doctor."

The water was three or four inches up the mule's leg, but ahead she noted Gustav and Velimir were approaching the deepest part.

'Serbia won't always be at war,' she said. Through the sleet she observed the heights of the mountains they'd to climb. She must concentrate, not worry about the struggle ahead. A bird let out a piercing cry. She glanced up, but could only see whirling snow. It sounded like Mitar. No. Velimir. He was falling towards the river. Slowly. Imperceptibly.

'Don't leave me, miss,' Bora shouted.

'Hold tight,' she urged him, 'I have to help...'

She splashed through water a foot deep towards Velimir. It reached her thighs. It was passable; she'd done it several times without feeling unduly anxious. Gustav would push Velimir back on the saddle, but she couldn't see Gustav. The mule plodded on. Without Velimir. Without Gustav. For a moment, she lost sight of all of three.

She was scared there was no sign of the orderly. She glimpsed Velimir's head, his shoulders in the river and she strode forward, a sudden tempest hitting her chest in waves. She couldn't work out how he came to fall, why Gustav wasn't there. When she instructed, 'Whoa!' the mule stopped.

She shouted, 'It's all right, Velimir.'

To her relief, he was struggling to his feet. Sleet stung her eyelids, blinded her and she reached out till she touched his shoulder.

Turning back to Bora, she shouted, 'Hold on! The mule will take you.'

No sign of Gustav. Bile rose in her mouth. Where was he? Where was he? She'd heard nothing.

'Well done,' she said on reaching Velimir and she put her hands under his armpits, helped him wade towards the mule.

They were both shaking. Her teeth chattered though she tried to control them. Her ice-cold arms were heavy. Water poured off Velimir.

'Gustav!' she called.

'The river god took him,' Velimir said, 'I saw.'

She froze, trapping her breath. She forced her legs to move and as she neared the mule's reins, raised Velimir onto the saddle.

'Well done, brother,' she said.

She ordered the mule, 'Walk. Walk on.'

Stones stirred under her boots and she peered into the dark waters in the middle where the river eddied and swirled. If she moved inch-by-inch, careful not to disturb the riverbed, she would be able to watch Bora behind her. Branislav had just left the shore. What a fool she'd been. Was it too late; was it even possible to put both lads on the same animal? So much for Branislav. He'd probably gone into the bushes for a pee when he should be helping. And where the hell was Gustav?

'Miss! Miss!' Velimir was pointing left.

Snow floated like petals on the surface of the river. No Gustav. All she saw was the movement among the depths. All she heard was roaring in her head. She glanced behind. Bora was crouched over the mule, his head raised, one hand over his eyes.

'Steady does it, Bora,' she shouted back.

As they reached the bank, the sleet slackened though her eyes and cheeks were stinging. She put a grateful hand on Velimir's thigh as Bora approached the shore. In an instant Velimir flung himself from the mule, attached himself to her. Arms round her neck, legs round her waist. Relief at Branislav's approach mingled with dismay at Gustav's disappearance.

'Mamma, mamma,' Velimir said.

'It's all right.' She kissed him on the cheek, rocking him as she kissed the top of his head. She noticed Mitar, standing on his own on a bank of gravel, too far away for her to read his expression.

Minutes later Branislav reached them. 'Sorry, Miss. I was taken short.'

*

Ellen didn't expect to sleep, lay apart from the rest, longing for the numbness to pass, to feel pain. But something had woken her. At first she thought a dream had disturbed her though she couldn't recall it. Her body was stiff, consumed with unease and she remembered Gustav. His arm bandaged, lying on a palister, one of her first patients. Gustav handing her a beaker of sweet tea after the incident with Sibin, walking with her through the streets of Mitrovica listening to her talk of Edward. And finally, her ridicule of his fear.

Snow fell lightly but steadily. She smelled cigarette smoke. She sat up and gazed at the circle of cadets sleeping round the fire, which Timohir had banked up ready to heat water in the morning. Behind, she heard the mules tethered among the bushes that edged the river.

As she became more awake, she became aware of a figure smoking on the beach. Timohir. He'd spoken little last night, after they'd agree to camp where they were, dry off by a fire. She guessed he was worried. He'd been shocked by Gustav's death; it would be sensible to discuss how best to manage the day's journey.

She shook snow from her rubber sheet and wrapped in a blanket, tip-toed around the sleeping cadets. Timohir wore his greatcoat and a woollen cap with earflaps he'd bought in Pec.

There was a mist over the river. She recalled the Wye and how she loved to ride along its banks on Prince. She flushed with longing to be held by Edward. Though the stones crunched as she approached, Timohir didn't stir, not even when she asked, 'Can't you sleep?'

She wondered if he was thinking of Gustav. Perhaps he witnessed what happened, but couldn't speak of it. Uncertain as to how to break into his thoughts, she waited. He took another drag on his cigarette before throwing it towards the water.

She cleared her throat, began, 'It's not easy, is it?' when he spun round, grabbed her shoulders, shook her so hard her cap fell off. He was six or so inches taller than her and as he released her, he put his hands round her neck. She remembered her dream. She'd been pressed against a tree

297

trunk, a man in a dark cloak forcing his lips on hers. Breathing heavily through her nostrils, she shuddered. Timohir stepped back.

She was shaking and out of nowhere came the picture of Gustav flaying in the river, frightened and cold. She pulled the blanket tight.

'And what would you do, Miss Frankland, if you or any of these kids were attacked?'

Before she'd fallen asleep the same thought occurred to her. She banished it, not wanting to frighten herself, but the answer was obvious. Timohir would protect them. Uncertain of his reaction if she said so, she remained silent.

'You've taken them from their homeland with no chance of reaching Durazzo. Dobrica directed you this way because he was desperate for wagons and provisions. Gustav drowned because he couldn't disappoint you, even though he was shit-scared of water and now you expect these half-starved kids to walk unprotected into bandit country.'

'Shut up!' she screeched, 'It's up to us to keep them safe.'

'It's up to you!' He stepped so close she thought he was going to knock her over. The tighter she drew the blanket, the less she shook. He went on, 'When they wake, I'm asking these kids to come back with me. I'll warn them of the dangers ahead. Of a severe Balkan winter, climbing mountains in blizzards, starving, hunting animals, bandits. Tell them they'll be safer to return to Pec.'

Hugging her quivering body, she thought fast. Some might go. And what of those who didn't? What was the point of alarming them with an onslaught of possible dangers? He wasn't to be persuaded to stay. She saw that. Her teeth chattered. She must challenge him. She let the blanket fall.

In a shakey voice, she said, 'If you want to go, go now.' She pointed in the direction of the river.

He edged closer, hands on hips. 'Answer me this, who will protect the kids when I've gone? You?'

Her legs ached with holding firm.

The snow stopped. Her vision cleared and she saw an ashen face, eyes dark with fear. The tension began to dissipate.

'Just go, Timohir.'

'I'll take a mule.' She recognised the old sulkiness, but hesitated. She didn't want to comply.

'Very well.'

She watched him untether the last of the animals in the train. She supervised emptying the panniers; he took a tin of bully beef, biscuits and his bedding. She longed to deny him everything, but she couldn't risk his death on her conscience. Only when the hooves splashed in the shallows did she recognise what she'd done. She was a virgin, scared of a man's rough hands. She chided herself. Her job was to cajole twenty-four tired cadets through the Cakor Pass. As she lost sight of him in the mist, she wondered how she could ever defend the cadets.

Chapter Twenty-five

Pec, December 1915

Stefan awoke to a familiar prod on his arm. His back ached and his limbs were stiff with cold. He must have dozed. Mikaiho had driven from Prizren to the frontier town of Pec. A blanket covered his legs, his cap lay on the leather-upholstered seat and Dragan was opening the car door.

He was moving further and further away from Stamenka. Dr. Dacic promised to send word if she turned up, but she might be on her way through the Albanian mountains. Or dead.

He picked up his cap, shoved the blanket to one side and stepped onto the narrow pavement. A pale sun was rising from behind a minaret. He stopped to admire the softened edges of the buildings. Pan tiled roofs lay thick with snow, windows shuttered.

'Mind your feet, sir.'

Stefan glanced down. Reddish water overflowed from the gutter. The place stank of urine.

He was reminded of Kadavsic, the town he'd been taken to after Bregalnica where blood flowed through the alleys as Serbs fought resisting civilians. Why blood here? Had Albanians and Bulgars united to attack the fleeing Serbs? God help them if their escape was cut off.

He brushed his cap, reshaped the crown with his fist before putting it on.

Dragan, buried in sheepskin gilet, looked morose. 'Our poor people are killing oxen and horses in the street. They tear whatever meat they can from the carcases.'

There were increasing signs Tomislav's 'people' were becoming disillusioned, angry with the army. Adjusting the peak of his cap in line with the tip of his nose, he worried Stamenka didn't know how to look after herself where food and a place to sleep, were fought over. The poverty she experienced as a child was not on this scale. He prayed, *God keep her safe.*

Dragan stamped his feet, bounced his arms against his chest as Stefan opened the passenger door and shouted across to Mikaiho, 'Wait here, Lieutenant. I'll be no more than an hour.'

At the door to the stone built Turkish house, a sentry he recognised from Tomislav's entourage, greeted them. The candles in the holders at the foot of the steps wafted sickly smoke and he wondered why his suspicion of the Turks persisted. As a boy from the country he'd been taught mistrust. When they moved to Belgrade he carried ignorance with him, but the Turkish craftsmen liked his father and proved respectful, helpful neighbours. Yet, his first reaction to anything Turkish was dislike. He wasn't sure what was cooking, but that made him angry. Perhaps, he was tired. Or lonely in this alien part of Serbia.

As he reached the top of the steps, he heard a woman's laugh. The sort that rose from the heart and he remembered sitting with his wife in front of their fire and her giggle at something he said. He preferred the humour of the mess. Jokes about the enemy, sex, women. Nevertheless, he missed the simple laughter of the hearth.

Recognising Tomislav's voice, he turned back to Dragan who was concentrating on not losing his foothold in the gloom. Stefan couldn't catch what was being said, but there was a teasing, flirtatious quality to the exchange. It seemed unlikely Tomislav had a mistress; he was a family man.

The door was opened by an orderly. For a moment, Stefan felt he was intruding on a domestic scene. Tomislav in uniform, with the top few buttons of his tunic unfastened, was standing by Louise's side at the far end of a long table. Louise was mixing yellow dough with a spoon in a stone bowl and she greeted Stefan with a smile. Her flushed cheeks were smudged with flour.

Behind her, along the length of the wall, were a stove oven, a hearth and an open fire where a girl was turning a pig on a spit. In the corner close to the stove, was a dresser, the kind Stamenka loved, shelves for displaying pots at the top, a couple of drawers and a cupboard beneath. Dawn light was struggling through the large windows; candles, on the table and in the alcoves, illuminated the room.

'Come in! Come in!' Tomislav was cheerful, 'Your orderly can wait downstairs.'

Having kissed Louise on both cheeks, Stefan said, 'I hadn't realised you were still in Serbia.' He was fond of her. On the occasions he and Tomislav dined with their wives, she offered to lend Stamenka Serb translations of European novels.

Tomislav, with a wink at Stefan, tapped his wife on the bottom. 'Louise is as reluctant as I to leave our country.'

With a gesture, which combined sweeping over his shoulder his white silk scarf, he said 'Join the party, lad.'

Stefan hid his irritation; it was a long time since he'd been a 'lad'.

'Louise will brew tea when she's finished the bread. You've not had breakfast?' He strode to the opposite end of the table to his wife. Stefan began to remove his gloves.

Louise was spooning yoghurt into the dough. 'How's Stamenka?'

Stefan began to explain he didn't know when Tomislav interrupted. 'Headstrong. She put us to some trouble.'

With a smile at Stefan, Louise said, 'You know he doesn't like a woman to refuse him.' She dipped her hands into the mixture and began to swirl it around the bowl, her hands and hips maintaining a rhythm.

'Add more oil,' Tomislav said, 'It's not moist enough.'

In Stefan's view, the woman was in charge of the kitchen. He would no more think of instructing Stamenka on how to make bread as she would military strategy. Louise appeared to agree with him; holding a goat's cheese between thumb and fingers, she chopped it into the bowl. Stefan's mouth watered.

Stefan placed his gloves on the chair next to him.

'Where is she?' Louise asked.

'Get along with your duties, my dear. I wish to talk to Stefan.'

Feeling it discourteous to ignore Louise's question, Stefan said, 'Stamenka left Belgrade, and took my mother …'

Tomislav slammed the table with his fist so hard the bowl jumped. 'Colonel! I've not invited you here to discuss the whereabouts of your errant wife.'

'I didn't expect you had.' Anger impelled his words, fuelled both by Louise's physical presence and the memory of the earlier laughter. He took a deep breath, began to remove his greatcoat. 'What's on your mind, sir?'

Leaning back in his chair, Tomislav's good humour returned. The aroma of the roasting pig, which the girl turned every minute or so, filled the room.

Tomislav swung forward as though to tell a secret. 'I'm the only General left in the country.'

Stefan wasn't surprised. In Prizren he'd seen old King Petar travelling in a horse-driven cart; he would be out of Serbia by now.

Thinking of Louise's safety, he said, 'The sooner you leave, the better.'

Louise interrupted, thumping the bread from the bowl onto the table. 'You know Stefan, our eldest has been taken prisoner in Austria.'

'Personal is not the point,' Tomislav flipped an arm, 'We have to consider our people.'

Stefan sank into the chair opposite him. Here was Tomislav with his wife in the most domestic of situations, while outside in the street 'our people' ate the flesh of their animals.

'My view is this, Petrovic. We make one last attack on Mitrovica. Nothing to gain by abandoning the country. If we fail, we surrender. That's when we make peace.'

Stefan checked to see if Tomislav was serious. His hands folded, he faced Stefan square on. Stefan was tempted to tease, ask what they would do if they won.

Louise was scooping the dough into tins. Outside a wagon rattled along the cobblestones. Stefan tried to distract himself by working out if horses or oxen were pulling. Horses were faster even when they were starving.

He asked, 'Are those Putnik's orders, sir?'

'We're out of touch with High Command.' Tomislav, his eyes sparkling, spoke as a child who'd just dipped his fingers in a sugar sack.

'What do you consider are the chances of success?'

'You've become too cautious since your promotion. You regretted our incursion into Bosnia, doubtful we could push the Austrians out of Belgrade. You should be honoured I'm talking strategy with you, my friend.'

'Cautious? What about the lives of our men and how does an attack on Mitrovica help our people?'

'Impertinent, Petrovic,' Tomislav commented.

'Think about it this way. We can't afford to lose men. Hundreds died in Bosnia because we overstretched ourselves in order to 'please the people' as you say, but at some point, enough is enough.' Stefan's fists were clenched, his heart thundered against his ribs.

Tomislav pushed his chair away, one hand flicking his scarf against the edge of the table. His tone was equable as though the matter of academic interest. 'Still, you haven't grasped the purpose of leadership. The men's deaths, regrettable of course, spur survivors to continue the fight. Hence, our success at Kolubara. Yours, on the second and third assaults of Chekoj ridge.'

Both men turned, as an empty bread tin crashed to the floor.

Louise asked, 'I'm about to take the first batch out. Would you gentlemen like cornbread with a little cheese?'

'Thank you,' Stefan said.

Tomislav nodded, but said to Stefan, 'Other than the prospect of defeat, what's your objection?'

'That's the most significant consideration. In addition, on your instructions we've destroyed our weapons.'

'Faith. Leadership. They make a difference.'

Stefan wondered what had got into his old friend. Perhaps he was more worried than he was letting on about his son. Or maybe it was a kind of grief, a reluctance to abandon their homeland.

There was a sharp knock to the door and the orderly who'd admitted him appeared.

'Telegrams, sir.'

While Tomislav began to read, Stefan got up and strolled to the window. Faith. What the hell did he mean by 'faith'? In God, in the army, in the people? The sky above the rooftops was a cloudless blue. He pictured a tired Stamenka stumbling along blood stained pavements. He remembered Tomislav's defence of Glisic and wondered if war affected men's minds or if romantics like Glisic, Tomislav, even himself were attracted to the utopian dream war offered. He flattened his face against the pane trying to peer into his car below, but could only see its white-crusted top.

The orderly departed and Tomislav continued to read. Stefan shifted closer to Louise. He said, 'Your bread reminds me of home.'

If Tomislav ordered an attack on Mitrovica he would desert. He felt lighter at the possibility. Louise had her back to him and was rummaging through the crockery in the dresser cupboard; he wanted to ask if she was worried at the delay. Was Tomislav intending to hang around till the army was annihilated? What was Louise supposed to do in the meantime? Keep baking?

'We must attack.' Tomislav sounded less certain, as though he was trying to convince himself. Maybe he was pretending, acting as if he'd an option.

'What do the telegrams say?'

'The Germans are on the run. They've capitulated. Also the Austrians.'

The maid at the spit raised her head, glanced at Louise who was frowning as she held wooden plates mid-air. If Tomislav wanted to fight on, why hadn't he let her leave?

Tomislav flashed the telegrams in triumph. 'They've their tails between their legs and we've the element of surprise.'

Rumours were rife during a war, particularly when defeat was in sight. Stefan asked, 'Are you sure?'

Tomislav insisted, 'They've suspended operations in Serbia.'

'What specifically will we attack?'

Tomislav pronounced, 'Intelligence reports that Austria is to withdraw troops from Serbia in order to concentrate on attacks from Russia.' He dropped the papers and said to Louise, 'Breakfast, my dear. We'll have breakfast.'

He picked up the telegrams again as though to read them out, but scanned them before putting them down. 'Pity you can't dine with us this evening. I spent the last of my dinars on that pig.'

Louise gave a little cough. She tapped the bread tin hot out of the oven on the edge of the table. Stefan noticed liver spots on the backs of her hands. Looking at Stefan, she said, 'It's difficult. Putnik has given orders without consulting all his Generals.'

Tomislav shouted at her, 'It is a dereliction of our oath to the king to abandon the people.'

'What orders has he given?' Stefan addressed Tomislav.

Sitting upright in his chair Tomislav glared not at Stefan as he expected, but at Louise. Stefan wondered if there'd been a disagreement. What happened before the laughter?

'Since your promotion I've had to drag you like a child having a tantrum…'

Stefan's stomach heaved. He strode to the window, peered down to the stricken street. This wasn't the victory Tomislav pretended. With his hand on the sill he admitted, 'I want peace.' He felt honest. 'That's all. For myself, for my wife and son and my country.'

Tomislav jumped to his feet. 'Are you refusing to attack Mitrovica?'

Stefan wanted to shake the old man by the shoulders. 'What orders has Putnik given?'

Tomislav flung his scarf round his neck, 'I am a true patriot. I love the people and I am willing to die as did our heroes on the Field of Blackbirds.'

'It was pointless then and it's pointless now.' Stefan snapped. His palms were sticky with sweat. Some streets distant, the muzzerin called the faithful to prayer; he understood the need. He wished Louise hadn't heard him. He hadn't meant to sound unpatriotic. He'd been trying to say there was a point at which the fighting had to stop and this according to the politicians and the King was the time. He gave her a sidelong look. She was easing bread from the tin.

He went back to sit opposite Tomislav, watched his fingers flick the fringe of his scarf.

Having served Stefan, Louise walked across to her husband. Putting an arm round his shoulder she lowered his plate. Kissing the top of his head, she rested her hands on his shoulders, massaging deep into the flesh. Tomislav sank into his chair.

Straightening, she addressed Stefan, 'There are many who would agree with you, but are too cowardly to say.'

'Nonetheless, I spoke out of turn.'

She said to her husband, 'Tell him what your friend Putnik has done.'

He pushed her to one side, but leaned over his shoulder and began to unwind his scarf.

'We fight for freedom for our people.' Tomislav was no longer convincing.

Louise said, 'Tell him, Tomislav.'

From the street a woman screamed. Stefan tried to hide the trembling, which started in his chest and spread to his hands and knees.

He saw Mikaiho in the lights of the motorcar, head down, running crouched. Soldiers' boots clattered on cobblestones. Flurries of snow beat his eyelids. A blanket lifted in his head. He remembered the struggle in and out of consciousness, being jolted on the stretcher, a girl child, eyes gouged, lying in the gutter, a woman accusing him, her head thrust against a wall, desire firing through his body, the ejaculation.

He tried to regain control, but the plate shook under the flat of his hand and his fingers refused to tear the bread.

Louise was stroking Tomislav's cheek, removing his scarf, and letting it fall over the back of his chair. She bustled to the stove. Tomislav loved his scarf. Louise knew that.

Tomislav blew his nose. He said, 'My services as General have been terminated.'

His men had charged alleys, down to the well where women gathered to raise buckets of evening water.

He must pull himself together. 'I'm sorry sir.' He must concentrate on success: the celebration at the Karakjodj—

glistening glasses, food fit for the King, Tomislav's gesture of concern when the bomb exploded. 'I'm sorry, sir,' he repeated.

Stefan kept his eyes on his bread. The smell was no longer enticing, his appetite faded. A ball formed in his stomach. When he looked up, Tomislav was tweaking his moustache; searching for words. The sharp knock on the door, the entrance of the orderly, provided respite.

Stefan focussed on the restaurant, the candelabra, the gusle and the gleam of medals.

The orderly handed Tomislav a letter.

Stefan called down the table to Louise, 'Your cornbread is delicious. As good as Stamenka's.' His effort at lightness failed; he dabbed at the bread, put a drop of soft cheese in his mouth; he couldn't swallow. The fragrance of lime wafted along the table as she poured boiling water into the teapot.

Kadavsic. He'd seen the women huddled round the well as he and Rajko were stretchered to hospital. Fighting had stopped. His men turned to carousing, celebrating victory. The women shouldn't have been allowed out. Fetching water together was no protection. They should have had more sense.

Without raising her head, she said, 'Stamenka is welcome to travel with us, should you find her. The lad, as well.'

Louise was an innocent. He wanted to tell her to forget the bread, the pig and leave before the enemy arrived, before war spoiled her. Tomislav sighed and groaned and Stefan didn't want to know the contents of the letter.

Stefan spoke in a low voice to Louise. 'I've not told her, foolishly, but if I'm killed, her fare is paid to England. She'll have money there. If you could reassure her she'll be provided for. The British Matron knows what to do. '

Louise picked up the teapot and carrying it to the table, commented, 'I admire your wife. She understood what Tomislav refuses to accept, that you didn't wish to replace him.'

He was surprised.

Tomislav shouted, 'Bugger.'

'What's wrong?' Stefan asked.

Louise said, 'What does it say?'

Tomislav jumped up and began to pace the length of the table, his arms wrapped around his head. 'The Austrians have killed our people in Djakovica.'

What must I do brother? he'd asked Rakjo, *How can I stop this?*

Stefan shivered. He was glad to be sitting so he could hide his shaking knees and hands. Sweat broke across his forehead. He wondered if this was battle trauma; if it had afflicted Glisic. He pulled out a handkerchief, mopped his face and the back of his neck.

A howl leapt from his stomach and whined through his head. Again he heard the laughter of the women at the well, the men's boots on the cobblestones. He gabbled to Tomislav, 'The sooner you depart the better.'

Louise was gazing, mesmerized at the teapot. They'd guards. No harm would come to them.

Tomislav said, 'I'm out of favour. I'm old and should have known better. I saw at the Karakjodj, you feared it.'

Rajko's silence came back to him. The little boy watching his mother's skirts being raised.

'Sir. I have to report an incident. Wrong word. Wrong word, sir. I have no excuse other than I chose to protect a brother officer.' He ought to be on his feet, but his legs might not support him.

Tomislav seemed relieved at the change of subject; he walked across to Stefan, placed a hand on his shoulder, said, 'I knew there was something. Tell me.'

As a child Stefan made confessions to the priest. He'd not made them up like some boys, but admitted, 'I stole a bottle of my uncle's best plum brandy. Drank it all myself. Drop by drop every night when I kept watch.' It kept him warm, gave him courage till he got used to the barking of the wolves.

When Tomislav sat down, Stefan did his best to describe Kadavsic. While he was speaking, Louise joined the maid by the roasted pig. Their murmurs were comforting.

Sweat rolled down his back and chest. He longed to unbutton his tunic, strip to his shirt. The uneaten bread accused him. Louise and the maid were attentive over the spit, Tomislav shaking his head.

'What did Major Kostic say? What were his exact words?'

'Nothing. He was in pain, but I expected him to curse our men… in view of…'

'If he said nothing… You didn't witness anything. Silence isn't guilt. Screams aren't women under attack. Men running…'

Tomislav covered his head with his arms. Stefan glanced over at Louise, but she'd her back to them as the maid fastened the strings of a black overall round her waist.

After a moment Tomislav said, 'We had such hopes, my friend.'

'I'm sorry, sir.'

With lowered head, Tomislav continued, 'You were my future. All the things I believed in, we believed together. We deplored the acts of oppressors who stole our young men, put them in foreign armies and turned them against us, their fathers. We fought for our women, children, our old men to live gracious lives…'

It seemed a long time ago, a time of innocence when they lauded such ideals. They'd been young and optimistic.

'…And you, above all, taught our soldiers to honour all women.'

Stefan thought, *I was afraid Rajko would be court martialed and shot.*

'Is that why you stopped going home?'

'I tried to forget.' He could never admit to anyone, not even a priest, of his attack on Stamenka. Only she could give absolution.

Unable to bear Tomislav weeping into his hands, Stefan turned to watch Louise and the maid, armed in leather gauntlets, hoist the pig from the spit to a tray at the end of the table.

He struggled to work out why he'd forgotten the incident, how he was certain Rajko gave the orders.

'I cannot carry on, sir.'

'You must.'

'I must face a court martial.'

'There's no evidence.'

Stefan was overwhelmed with tiredness; he wanted to sleep. He repeated, 'I'm sorry, sir.'

'If you'd reported your suspicions, who knows, but it's too late. It's a mistake you'll have to live with.'

'Court martial.'

'Self indulgence, my friend.' Tomislav looked up, his eyes rimmed red. After a moment, they turned to watch Louise who raised a hatchet and in one blow removed the pig's head. Stefan shivered.

With a sigh Tomislav said, 'We'll do as the King requires. Dismantle the guns in the presence of the people. They must be shown that its army doesn't abandon them.'

There was a limit to how often he could apologise. Tomislav was right to order they carry on.

He jumped up, called goodbye to Louise and extended his hand, across the table, to Tomislav. Tomislav held it, patted it before walking to the door. He told Louise to pack; they'd be away by mid-day.

The men embraced for several moments. Tomislav said, 'Victory will be ours.'

Stefan replied, 'May God keep you safe.'

Stefan spent the rest of the morning organising the dismantling of the field howitzers. Units transported the barrels for burial in the forests behind the monastery. The wooden mounts and gun carriages were set alight, or tipped into the river. The breech and aiming devices were loaded onto animals and began the journey through the mountains.

As he stood with Mikaiho, to watch the first batch of mules leave for the mountains, he reflected on the foolishness of trying to protect Rajko. Why hadn't he voiced his suspicions to his superior officer? There'd been no need to mention Rajko. Why hadn't he thought of that? And Tomislav was too generous; he ought to be punished.

Mid-morning a group of priests asked to speak to him. They wanted the military band, which had played the army out of Mitrovica and Prizren, to do the same in Pec, preceded by a service in the cathedral. Stefan envisaged prayers of thanksgiving for those who died for their country, prayers for protection during the army's retreat. But, the priests and the town council, had developed the idea sown by Tomislav. The populace would celebrate resistance, hold mass followed by burial rites for one symbolic gun. There'd been discussion about numbers and size, but the military insisted on a single gun in the interests of safety. In being persuaded to hold the ceremony, Stefan recognised Tomislav's confidence in the people was well founded and his admiration returned.

Smoke darkened the afternoon sky. Anything of use to the enemy was being burned, wheels, axles, documents, even telephone and telegraph wires. Outside the cathedral's west door, at the top of the steps in the centre of the open space, they positioned a French 75mm gun covered in holly, rosemary and ivy wreaths. Town councillors in traditional costume stood on one side of the gun and army personnel on the other. Public turnout was impressive. These were not the flag-waving optimists of Jevo, but a solemn, defiant people determined to unite in adversity. Dragan stood on Stefan's left and around them officers and orderlies, all those engaged in the final acts of military withdrawal.

During the mass, Stefan's anger towards Tomislav shrank. He imagined Tomislav and Louise striding up mountain slopes. If only he'd warned Tomislav, told him what he suspected when they'd promoted him. The priest's petition of forgiveness reminded Stefan of his own faults.

As he glanced down at the crowds at the foot of the stone steps he thought again of Tomislav. He'd treated Stefan as a son. He'd wept. Yet, he was not a friend like Rajko. The difference in age and rank created a gap, whatever Tomislav said to the contrary. Stefan considered him a wise father despite his faults. A priest gave him a lighted candle. Stefan gazed into its trembling flame. He prayed for Stamenka and Mitar. That they reach the coast. Another priest was chanting, others were swaying incense over the gun. He prayed for the women of Kadavsic, that they were alive. That they could forgive.

'Holy God, Holy Strong, Holy Immortal, have mercy on us.'

Stefan turned his head from the priests as the bells began to toll. Anguish roared through his veins, leaving him close to tears. He was glad Rajko was spared this. His attention was drawn to movement in the crowd where a woman dressed in traditional costume grabbed a child of no more than three years. Would the child remember anything of the occasion in years to come? He started at the profile of a young woman behind that of the boy. Stamenka. No. Too young. He tried to concentrate on the ritual. He held the candle in front of his face as the priest chanted,

'Holy God, Holy Strong, Holy Immortal, have mercy on us.'

Through the flickering candle he sensed rather than saw movement, a familiar gesture. A hand pushed back a scarf, tucked in stray strands of hair. He adjusted his candle so he could see better. He was too far to be sure. He eased towards the platform edge. She looked directly at him. His heart stirred.

He whispered across to Dragan, 'Stamenka.'

He hesitated. He didn't want to be disrespectful to those who gathered to pray for these symbols of retreat. To Tomislav. He took one step. Dragan was by his side. He stopped. He needed God's blessing. Yet, he couldn't risk losing her. There were hundreds at the foot of the cathedral. That he'd glimpsed her was, perhaps, a sign from God.

'Hold this,' he handed his candle to Dragan and ran down the steps.

The crowd parted as he barged towards her. She smiled. Sixteen again. Her clothes hung lose; he didn't recognise the jacket buttoned to her chin, nor the blue scarf. But the smile was Stamenka's. He couldn't believe she was pleased to see him.

'I'm sorry.' He clasped her arm, 'I'm truly sorry.'

The women around her began to mutter and he gabbled, 'Come with me.' He grabbed her hand and pulled her along. At first, she followed, but at the foot of the steps she resisted. He couldn't force her.

'Will you wait here?'

Only after she nodded, did he resume his place, checking now and again she was there. As soon as the gun was carried down the steps, he would be free to find somewhere private to talk. Tomislav would have left. He'd send Mikaiho to the

Turkish house. With luck, there would be roasted pig Dragan could use for their meal.

'Holy God, Holy Strong, Holy Immortal, have mercy on us.'

'Amen,' Stefan responded.

Chapter Twenty-six

Pec, December 1915

Stefan should have been enjoying himself. He sat with Stamenka on the sofa in what had been Tomislav's sitting room. She was prim, hands on her lap; his fingers crept towards her. The log fire roared; sparks blew into the hearth in front of them. The smell of lavender oil on her wrists reminded him of the closeness they once shared. Bending across he kissed a clutch of scratches on the back of her hand. She didn't withdraw. Her nails were as neatly clipped as his. He marvelled she was as well scrubbed as at home in Belgrade, evidence of her journey limited to cuts and the worn hem of her skirt. Her breath came evenly, relaxed. It was he who was on edge.

This was no ordinary reconciliation. The shutters were closed. Candles filled the room with fragrant light. Though their hostess placed carafes of wine and of water, along with a dish of raisins, on the low wooden table to the side of the sofa, they were untouched. He'd removed his jacket, unfastened the buttons at the top of his shirt; he straightened against the back of the sofa. He folded his arms. They must talk.

'Where's Mitar?' Stamenka asked.

'I told you. He's safe with Miss Frankland and because I want you safe also I'll arrange for Mikaiho to get you to Louise and Tomislav while I finish my duties.'

'The child will expect me.'

So she must have reassured Mitar during the few moments he'd allowed.

'Louise will take you to him.'

Stamenka pulled her hand from his. 'Mrs. Stavisto doesn't approve of me.'

'She's promised to look after you.'

With a grimace she queried, 'Did *she* reach Pec unaided?'

'You've done well.'

Shouts, wagons rattling rose from the street. He was tempted to open the shutters, scrape frost off the pane, but it would delay what needed to be said. Downstairs there was hammering on the outside door. The house reverberated. If someone came in, told him they'd to depart, he needn't say sorry. He'd have no peace of mind either, yet how to start?

Stamenka clasped her hands as in prayer, her lips parted.

The words were easy enough, but how to describe, explain his actions. To admit he'd threatened her with a knife, slit her skirt, was out of place.

After a moment she said, 'It might seem to you that I'm obstinate, but I couldn't leave your mother. When you and I married, we became one family. Do you understand? I confess also I don't like the way Mrs. Stavisto speaks to me as if…'

'She likes you. I assure you.'

She raised her hand. '…as if I were a child.'

He patted her lap. He didn't want to get embroiled in a discussion about Louise. 'You've found your own way and…'

'It's true that Louise Stavisto has travelled in comfort, but I disobeyed you and that displeases you.'

He'd forgotten how spirited she was. It used to be a joke between them. The seventeen-year-old Stamenka persuaded her parents to shun convention and spend the night before the wedding in Belgrade rather than Orasac.

He half-smiled. 'It's like old times.'

'My mother warned not leaving from home would bring bad luck,' she said.

He guessed it brought estrangement between them. Her mother didn't attend the births of their three children.

'Did she think it "bad luck" when you remained in Belgrade because you loved my mother?'

'When we were young, we did not care what others thought.' She held out a hand and he took it, stroked her fingers. He might not need to ask forgiveness. She put a hand on his knee.

'You would have made a fine diplomat.' She spoke gently.

So she'd not forgotten, any more than Tomislav had. It was he who'd buried the dream. When she showed him her walnut tree, he'd confessed he wanted to leave the army.

Wearily, he stood up and walked to the window. Below men spoke Turkish; yet he was certain the disturbance had something to do with their house. About to unfasten the blind, he changed his mind. An apology wasn't necessary. Stamenka was happy. It was a pity they couldn't stay for the duration of the war. They'd a kitchen, a bedroom and this little sitting room. They would be warm, well fed.

Turning to her he pleaded, 'Let Mikaiho take you to Louise and Tomislav.'

'You idolise them.'

Surprised at her astuteness he explained, 'I want you out of this war.'

'Then I will go.'

He rejoined her on the seat, fidgeted, uncertain. There was a report to write. She could leave as soon as Mikaiho arrived. No. It would be best to wait till dawn. They could sleep in the bed with silk cushions, the coverlet drawn back on cotton sheets.

What if Mikaiho had been knocking? It was unlikely as they'd been Turkish voices. He twisted to face her, longing to touch her ankle where the summer skirt peeped beneath that of black wool. The curve of her breasts showed through the knitted jumper and as his eyes moved up her body, she raised her face for a kiss.

He kept thinking of the afternoon she showed him the walnut tree. Her hair as dark as night, her complexion, as now, full of sunshine. He'd been prepared to defy the marriage their fathers arranged till he saw her and when she looked into his eyes and asked if he wanted to be a soldier, he admitted the truth.

He placed his hands flat on his lap, blurted, 'I'm sorry. I failed you as a husband.'

'You are a brave soldier who will revenge Kossovo.'

He lowered his head, looked down at his hands. He folded them to hide their shaking. 'After Bregalnica I didn't come home for a long time. When I did, I came to hurt.'

Stamenka shifted away. He remembered her with her apron over her face as the car pulled out of the courtyard. That too had been an act of revenge.

317

'A man has desires.'

'I tore the clothes from your body,' he whispered. Her skirts were still. Her boots firm on the polished boards.

'It's not important, husband.'

When he managed to raise his head and face her, her eyes brimmed.

'You deserve better.' He remembered arriving home after their daughter was born. Stamenka wearing the smock she made when pregnant with Mitar, was cutting dough into strips of noodles while Mitar played under the table. The gold embroidered thread reflected in her eyes. He'd left for the campaign against the Bulgars before typhus took the child; he'd been unable to attend the funeral.

'When I became old you chose other women.'

Her words didn't register and he continued with his own line of thought. 'I attacked you. That was wrong.'

Without malice she said, 'A husband who saves his country has his choice of women and if his wife is no longer pleasing…'

'No,' he wailed. She didn't understand. He stood up. Sat down. He sighed. Wept into his hands.

In an instant she knelt at his feet, enclosed his knees with her arms. 'When you no longer came to me, I went to our home village and *baba* Mira told me. I did as she ordered, but you did not return, so I knew.'

He blew his nose loudly. He wasn't interested in *baba* Mira. Superstitious nonsense like taking a lock of his hair and walking through the house with it at midnight.

'You told that old crone I took a knife to your dress and forced myself on you?'

'I said you came to me no more.'

'Do not crouch before me like a servant.' He jumped from his seat and knelt in front of her, took her hands in his. They clung together till their trembling stopped.

'There are no other women,' he said. 'There never have been.' He sat back on his haunches rubbing the scar on his thigh. She was biting her lower lip. He stuttered, 'I saw… things…they happen in war… things… women are attacked

318

by soldiers... girls are as well... I didn't, of course....' He couldn't use the word *rape*, '... I lost my tenderness.'

The fire crackled. A log began to roll towards the hearth and he bounced to his feet. With his boot he prodded the log back, feeling its heat. It hadn't occurred to him she'd do other than despise him. He turned to her. She was sitting on the sofa, hands on her knees. 'I don't blame you, husband. I haven't witnessed the wicked things you have.'

'We can start again,' he said when he joined her. 'We can be lovers...' He put a hand on hers, not sure if she grasped the enormity of his violence towards her. He'd dreamed of forgiveness; yet, she didn't blame him. He wished he could express the feelings deep within him.

After a moment, he said, 'You walked all the way from Belgrade to Pec.'

'Not all the way. I had rides in cow carts, ox wagons, even an army limousine that would have driven me here, but I was sick. Do you think I might be as capable as the General's wife?'

'There's no comparison.' He put his arm round her waist, kissed her lips. She cupped his head in hands. Tears threatened again. He smelled rosemary and lavender.

'Lie with me,' she said.

Patterns flitted across the kitchen walls, over the scrubbed table and floorboards. The roasted pig lying across the top of the stove caused him to think of squealing pigs behind the woods in Orasac, their bodies twitching till enough shots had killed them.

The ghosts of Tomislav and Louise pervaded the room. The perfect couple. He, the people's soldier, she, educated, wanting more than Serbia for her children. Stefan had watched her hands knead the dough, cut the cheese, remove the scarf. They sat in the back of a French limousine, hand-in-hand.

He saw his father's hands raising the belt, his mother's covering her face.

He put down his pen, rubbed his hands, shivered inside his greatcoat as he recalled Tomislav's, 'It is a mistake you will have to live with… Perhaps you will have an opportunity to make amends…'

Stamenka had forgiven him, but what about the women at Kadavsic? He couldn't apologise to them. As a young man he'd abhorred rape as a weapon of war. Boasted he couldn't do it because the enemy's women were like Stamenka, like Rajko's mother.

He picked up his pen, somewhat comforted by Dragan snoring in front of the stove fire his head lolling, jolting upright from time to time. He'd left Stamenka in bed. The woman he loved. Earthy, rooted in her country, not a dreamer like himself.

The streets were quieter now. The occasional wagon, footsteps along the cobbled street. The clock above the entrance to the guest house chimed the quarter hour. Past midnight. Where was Mikaiho? No curfew had yet been imposed, but it was accepted everyone be indoors by ten. Gypsy girl, no doubt.

He poured ink into the well watching shadows darken the report. With a sigh, he read through what he'd written. He hoped he was doing right in entrusting Stamenka to Mikaiho. She'd never disguised the fact she despised his cousin, considered him irresponsible, but that didn't mean he wouldn't get her to Tomislav and Louise. He would ensure she'd mules and provisions. She would catch them up in a day, a day-and-a-half. It surprised him how much store he put on getting her to Louise. Yet, when they talked after lovemaking, Stamenka explained she resented the emphasis on reading foreign novels, when her lack of schooling resulted in her missing out on Serb poetry and literature. Learning about Serb heroes was what she wanted.

Well into the second page, he was startled by a rat-tat-tat on the doorknocker downstairs. As he held the pen a blob of ink scurried along the nib and plopped onto his report.

Reaching for the blotting paper, he shouted to Dragan, 'See who it is, will you, brother?'

Dragan unravelled from the chair, put on his cap and hurried to the door.

The bolt was pulled back, and even as Dragan put his hand on the latch, rapid steps clomped upstairs. Mikaiho, he presumed. He'd make sure he gave an explanation for staying out late.

Voices drifted in from officers chatting in the opposite room.

At first, Stefan thought Mikaiho shot into the kitchen because he wasn't expecting the door open, but his cheeks were flushed and he was out of breath. Something other than women was affecting him.

With a sigh, Stefan smoothed the blotting paper. Mikaiho could sleep for a few hours before he began his journey with Stamenka.

Dragan closed the door and stood to attention. Mikaiho marched to the side of the table where Tomislav had sat several hours earlier. He saluted. His bearing was triumphant and whatever criticism there was of him, none could be made about his appearance. His trousers retained creases, his tunic well brushed, his moustache waxed. Only after Chekoj ridge had Stefan ever seen his cousin dishevelled. For an instant Stefan wondered if the Germans truly had withdrawn, the Austrians actually shifted their forces to the eastern front.

'You bring news, Lieutenant?' Stefan continued to rub his hand over the page.

Mikaiho sort of leered, as though he wanted to smile but dare not. 'Sir! I bring bad news, sir. Your son along with...'

The hairs along Stefan's fingers rose like hackles on a dog's back.

Mikaiho's voice built up steam. '... our cadets. The infidels have killed them all. Not one is left. May Serbia live forever.'

Even as he breathed the smell of Mikaiho's cigarettes, caught in anger and disbelief, Stefan was on his feet, fists knotted.

Turning to Dragan he shouted, 'What the hell is he saying?' In his head he repeated, *your son, your son*. He couldn't be dead. Stamenka was going to join him. He'd promised. They were to sail to England.

He planted himself in front of Mikaiho who was grinning. The conflict between Mikaiho's expression and his words confused him.

'Speak plainly!'

'He is dead.'

Stefan steadied his knees with his hands. 'Are you sure?'

'They have been murdered by Albanian guerrillas. Not one is left alive.'

Dragan put a hand on his arm as Stefan slumped into his chair. He asked, 'How do you know? Have you seen the body?'

He longed to be outside. In the woods around Jevo or taking the western path above the Sava River, climbing the heights of the Kalemegdan Fortress, not imprisoned with his damnable cousin. He twisted from his seat; his boots skimmed the floor as he paced towards the roasted pig. Walking away from Mikaiho, thinking of Stamenka asleep after they made love. How would he tell her? Every nerve throbbed. Mitar was dead. Their son. His head raged with the sounds of a thousand rivers. It wasn't true. Mikaiho was lying.

He returned to stand in front of his cousin, who saluted.

Ready to collapse again, Stefan said to Dragan, 'What do you think?'

'Who told you?' Dragan asked Mikaiho.

'Major Zariya.'

He was a reliable man, not given to exaggeration. He would question him; find out one way or another. Stefan fumbled for his cigarette case, taking deep breaths, trying to marshal his thoughts. Stamenka mustn't be told. He tried to concentrate, decide what to do. His mind refused to obey his wishes. Just when he didn't want to remember the physicality of his boy, he saw Mitar skinny in those hours after his birth. Stefan had been relieved when the midwife wrapped him in swaddling strips. The same coloured strips for the son who lived for a few days. He'd go on his own, find his son's body and see he was given a decent burial. No, no. He must talk to Major Zariya. A sensible man.

'I swear on King Marko's heart that I will avenge these slaughters,' Mikaiho pronounced.

Stefan's fingers, sticky with sweat, let his cigarette case slip with a clatter. After Chekoj ridge he'd done his best to protect his cousin, but Rajko had been right, his cousin was a lost cause.

'Lieutenant Nis, you'll do no such thing.' He was tired of doing his best for him.

'Sir! Revenge will be mine. Just as at Bregalnica, so now. No Albanian woman will be safe.'

Stefan was being crushed. Unable to believe what Mikaiho said, his cousin went on, ' Sir! You have been a better father to me than my own and King Marko demands vengeance. I am a true hero of Serbia.'

Tears sprang from Stefan's eyes. He'd protected a villain. Steadying himself with his hands on the table, he said, 'Dragan. Please call the arresting officers.'

His orderly was out of the kitchen so fast he might have anticipated the instruction.

The oven fire crackled. He wondered if Mikaiho might make a run for it. He half-hoped he would. Candles shimmered. Retribution for what happened at Bregalnica. Mikaiho still as stone.

'I'm sorry, cousin,' Stefan said.

'Sorry I avenge the murder of your son?'

'Revenge serves no one.'

'After Bregalnica we got our own back on those foreign whores for desecrating…'

'Women had nothing to do with the fighting.'

'You knew what we did!'

'I was unconscious.'

'You were not unconscious when you were taken by stretcher and the streets ran with the blood of infidels. Major Kostic wasn't unconscious when he gave orders!'

'No!' The word bounced in his head.

Stefan reached for his pistol. He remembered one evening emerging with Stamenka from the cathedral after a candlelit service, seeing Rajko. The men had exchanged glances, but they never spoke of the encounter. For Stefan it cemented their relationship, his fighter friend had another side. They shared a love of the mystery of their religion.

As his grip tightened on the butt of the pistol, he wanted to obliterate Mikaiho, destroy him so he need never see him again. Rajko was wounded too. Rajko had been in no position to give orders and yet Mikaiho described what Stefan feared; his friend had, might just have, given authority for the women at the well, to be raped.

Even as his arm moved to his holster, ready to smash his cousin's head, he remembered Mitar whittling wood with his knife just as his own father had. What good had turning his father out of the house done? What good had violence ever done? Exhaustion once more engulfed him. His jaw ached; he let his hand drop to his side.

'Major Kostic! Your hero!' Mikaiho taunted.

'Enough, Lieutenant. You will be arrested and court martialled and…' he paused, appalled, '… and face the consequences.'

He was relieved to hear footsteps. Moments later, a handcuffed Mikaiho was taken from the room.

Stefan walked back to the stove fire and, with shaking hands, lit his cigarette. He shivered. Were he a superstitious man he would believe he was cursed at Bregalnica. Rajko had given the orders. They'd fought, slept and ate together. They were brothers. And now, Mitar was dead. No. He must first check with Zariya. He tried to convince himself Mitar's death wasn't linked with his failure to question, to investigate. He must find out if Mitar was dead. There may yet be hope. He'd been too cowardly to voice his suspicions, afraid for his friend, but the gods hadn't been silenced.

His palms were sweating. His skull felt ready to shatter. He tried to concentrate. Stamenka mustn't be told until he was certain. A couple of officers would take her to Tomislav as soon as possible. He would give instructions she mustn't know, not till she was with Louise. After he'd spoken to Zariya, if he gave any hint the attack was true, he would travel with Dragan to find his son's body and bury him. Should Stamenka be summoned then? No, no. It would distress her. He couldn't face that. Over and over, as he smoked the cigarette, then another, he rehearsed his plans.

He didn't hear his wife come into the kitchen. 'What was the noise?' she asked.

He flung the stub into the fire. She was smiling; his sunshine. When she saw his face, she strode towards him, 'What's the matter?'

'Mikaiho has been arrested.'

There was a knock on the door, but before he'd time to answer, Dragan rushed in. With tears running down his cheeks, he approached Stamenka.

'I am so very sorry, ma'am.'

Turning to Stefan, she frowned. He rested a hand on her sleeve. To Dragan he said, 'Bring me Major Zariya, please.'

Dragan sniffed, blew his nose. 'The men offer their sympathy, sir.'

Stamenka gave a little cry like a creature caught in an owl's clasp. 'Stefan!'

He tried to hold her hand, but she snatched it away and he was left clutching the tip of her sleeve.

'We don't know,' he gabbled. 'It's no more than a rumour. There are always rumours in war.'

'Tell me.'

'It's a rumour. No more. I am making enquiries.'

'About what?'

'Some cadets have been killed by brigands.'

He grabbed her hands, which she flapped. 'We don't know.' He tried to touch the possibility that all wasn't lost. 'He might not have been with them.'

Stamenka's scream tore through him. He released her and turned away. Dragan had moved to the head of the table, his shoulders were hunched; he mopped his face with a handkerchief. Stefan glanced down to where he'd been writing his report, the blotting paper, the ink well. He remembered sitting on the banks of the Sava watching Mitar throw a line into the river.

'I am sorry,' he said.

'My son.'

'I wasn't going to tell you till I was sure.'

'If he'd been with me…'

'Please, Stamenka.'

'He should have been with his mother. He should have been with me.'

Her cheeks were awash with tears. She grabbed strands of hair, yanked them from her scalp, doubled up. He flicked the sheets of paper, wished Louise was there. Women knew how to comfort, how to ease pain; he was at a loss.

'You have ruined my life.'

'Please…Please…'

'You were meant to protect him…' She arched her back, '… because of you, my son is dead.' She straightened, strode towards him waving her arms. 'How could you do this to me?'

'We don't know.' He stepped back felt his legs against the wall.

'You thought you knew best, but you didn't. I shouldn't have let you take him away, but I am a good Serb who obeys her husband even when he is wrong,' she shouted between sobs.

'It's not my fault.' He took a tentative step towards her, wanting to hold her, but as soon as he touched her arm, she shoved him.

'Stamenka please,' he said.

He placed both his hands at the top of her arms, pressed them. She shook him off with a strength that shocked him.

'Don't do this to me,' he cried out. He ran at her, locked his arms round her shoulders, clutching her to his chest.

'You bully! I hate you!' she sobbed as she wrestled against him.

He released her and as he did she leaned against him, weeping. He would speak with Major Zariya himself. If the rumours were true, he'd abandon his men, accompany Stamenka and travel through the mountains on mules till they found their son. Together they would bury him.

Chapter Twenty-seven

Cakor Pass, December 1915

Sheltering during a heavy snowstorm in mountain hut. Walls covered with raw ox-hides. Wild looking men made us smoky coffee, drank from the same bowl! Very kind. They pointed out several murder stones. Traders, not travellers like us, killed by Albanians.

We're all tired. Cadets try to work out why Timohir left us. Fear after Gustav's drowning is consensus. They're more distressed by Gustav's death than Timohir's desertion. Velimir cries a lot. Can't eat.

Yesterday when the sun came out and warmed us, the lads laughed and chatted.

Ellen roused the cadets two hours before dawn on the day they were to begin the ascent through the Cakor Mountains.

Only Mitar argued. 'It will be best to wait till light.'

'No.'

'We'll fall.'

'It will be light when we leave.'

Mitar was in the habit of disagreeing with everything she said and though she tried to take no notice, Ellen was edgy. Timohir had warned the track was steep, twisting, treacherous even in summer. The previous evening she discussed with the group leaders and Zivoli how to organise the journey. The snow was two and three feet deep in places; none of them had experienced conditions like these.

After breakfast it took Ellen and Bogdan an hour to re-load the mules and secure the panniers. Most of the cadets carried their bundles. They debated whether to dump sacks of rice to enable cadets to ride, but decided against. Though rice was slow to cook in these conditions, they might be able to exchange one bag for bread in Androvica.

The distance between the mules was increased to enable two cadets to tuck behind each animal when the track narrowed. Ellen and Bora led Tola, the lead mule. When she suggested Velimir ride between the rolled up blankets on Tola, no one objected and Mitar offered to walk by his side. Zivoli followed the last animal, Bogdan brought up the rear, while Branislav took on Gustav's role of ensuring neither mules nor cadets had problems.

Before they moved, Ellen checked and re-checked each rope was secure. She flashed her electric torch over the snow-crusted rocks, indicated the steep drop on their left to each pair.

If anyone fell, it would be exhaustion, not ignorance.

Ellen ordered Tola, 'Walk,' and she and Bora set off. Velimir, perched on the saddle, leaned into the blankets, Mitar by his side. The easterly wind pierced her greatcoat. Now and again a flurry of snow.

For the first few steps, Ellen skidded till she remembered to shorten her stride; she shouted back instructions for the cadets to do the same. Her throat dry, she'd to remind herself not to lick already chapped lips. Physically she felt strong, more confident than when she first left Audrey. As they plodded through dawn becoming light, she missed Audrey, Timohir and Gustav. During the night she heard Gustav calling; she tried not to reflect on her anguish, her involvement in his death. She tried not to think about any deaths. Listening to the steady mules behind, she concentrated on positives. The leaders, the mules. Tola was sure-footed, agile and used to the conditions. Not usually superstitious, Ellen was glad each wore their blue stones. For a few miles, the path remained level and Ellen believed they would reach Durazzo. Instead of her initial picture of Stefan greeting them, she now imagined standing alone on the quayside, waving to the cadets on the boat for Corfu. Mitar was no longer more important than the others. Certainly, she'd a soft spot for Branislav because she met him first, but she'd grown fond of Bogdan who'd led the rebellion on the first day, timid Velimir, Bora who overcame his fears to ride across the river, brave and just Zivoli. She loved them all.

After ten minutes, Zivoli pulled out his *frula* and began to play *Ruza, Ruza*. He was proving an exceptional leader. A second *frula* picked up the accompaniment and Ellen turned to see Mitar's fingers poised on his whistle. He, too, was growing up.

The tune changed. Recognising its haunting sadness, she wished she could remember the words Zivoli taught around the campfire on the road to Pec. They reminded her of Edward picking and presenting her with a rose from the arbour at Oaklands, her father in his study, in the armchair in front of the fire, bible open on his lap, fingers nudging the words. From the middle of the train, Branislav begin to lead the singing. Others joined in, but the words still eluded her.

As the path curved into a long ascent, the wind drummed her cheeks. Snow whizzed in front of her eyes so she could barely discern the track. A movement from high above drew her attention; she noticed a boulder, its nearside bare. A slow running rivulet crossing their route, obliged her to look down.

'Watch for ice under the water,' she shouted behind. The warning passed down the line.

Her satisfaction faded as Tola, nudged her from behind, and broke into a trot. It startled Velimir, his body bouncing out of kilter. Ellen dropped back quickly, pushing Mitar to one side. A pannier veered towards the edge of the track, alarmingly close to the precipice. Zivoli and Mitar stopped playing.

The mule flicked her ears, wobbled and refused to move. Ellen reached forward, grabbed the reins. Cries of alarm sounded from the cadets.

Zivoli shouted, 'Halt! Halt!'

Ellen coaxed the mule a step forward.

She tucked the blanket round Velimir. 'I've got you.' A wave of anger engulfed her. Why had their pleasure been spoiled? She looked around for the cause of the animal's distress. The mountains were dark with snow, clouds drawing in and when she turned to reassure, Bora was waving and pointing. She followed the direction of his hand; high in the purple sky, eagles hovered.

Zivoli began to play his *frula* again.

'Walk,' she instructed the trembling Tola. Trying to sooth the mule with, 'It's okay,' a whistle split the air and too late she spotted the movement, rubbed the side of her head and felt stickiness on her glove, the trickle of blood. She remembered the mock battlefield at summer camp and Captain Bagshaw. His, 'You damned near killed me,' when all that had mattered to her was that she won the race.

Stones careered on their path. Torn between looking to discover who'd shot at her and helping Velimir, she chose the latter. From behind, she grasped his waist with both hands and pushed him upright. He leaned forward on the blankets again as the mule trotted on. Striding on too fast, she slipped and weighed down by her backpack, crashed to the ground. The edge of her little pistol dug into her leg.

Velimir cried out, 'Miss! Miss!'

One of the cadets held out a hand and helped her regain her balance.

Bora reassured, 'Miss is fine now.'

The track broadened unexpectedly into an area suitable for camping. Sheltered from the snow, its rocks were bare, but for a desolate, skinny tree and a few shrubs. As she hurried to catch up, Ellen looked around for her attacker. Powerful mountains ranged on all sides. Beech, fir and silicate spruce, sharp, barren edges, glacial ridges. She observed the lower slopes and spotted a flash of metal. From a boulder no more than three hundred yards ahead, a man pointed a gun.

Bora tightened the reins as Tola stepped out.

Ellen said, 'Stand still.' There might only be one. What a fool she'd been. Scared of such an attack, she'd no strategy on how to respond.

Mitar was sobbing, 'He's going to kill us!'

As the rest of the mules reached the clearing, Zivoli pointed further up the path. Struggling to contain a hysterical Mitar against his chest, he shouted, 'There, miss.'

Two men were in conversation until the nearest began to edge towards them. He didn't look like a soldier, in trousers fastened at the ankle with string. Nor did he wear a jacket, but a garment more like a knitted cardigan and under it, a shirt buttoned at the neck. She noticed his weather-beaten hands, an infected wound on one of his fingers. She hoped they hadn't been mistaken for merchants.

With hands raised, she began to walk towards the men, who were both motionless. The second man in a fez and a black coat was watchful. If she'd seen him in Jevo, she'd have presumed him poor, old and decent. If their intention was to murder, she would soon know.

She announced, 'Sir, we are unarmed, innocent travellers.'

Her words were lost as Mitar screeched, 'May Serbia live forever.'

She wheeled round. Mitar, having escaped Zivoli's grasp, stood by the mule, waving Prince Marko above Velimir's head.

'Don't…' she shouted to Mitar, but the man in the cardigan darted past her. She shuddered at the sound of the shot.

Mitar screamed. Tola howled, her cries echoing across the valley. Some lads whimpered.

She thought, he's murdered a child in cold blood. When she looked back, Mitar and the mule lay on the ground, Zivoli crouched by them. Bora leaned across the mule's head to hold Velimir. They *were* all going to be killed. Murder stones would mark their absence. Their bodies would be left on the path for the next travellers to discover. They would be gossiped over at the end of someone else's journey.

As she raced to Mitar's side, more cadets arrived and she tried to decide what to do. What did these men want? The man who'd shot Mitar was immobile, watching, but the man wearing the fez, ran towards them with a crab-like gait.

She crouched next to Zivoli who said, 'He's got him in the gut.'

'Stem the bleeding if you can,' she said. Their attacker's gun remained directed at them.

Mitar's eyes were full of tears. 'I only…'

'It's all right.'

Hands raised, she stood up, joined the cadets who'd grouped round the last the mules.

Bogdan indicated with his head. 'Another.'

Orders were shouted from a man perched on the top of a rocky outcrop who ranged his rifle along the line of mules and cadets. So far away, she couldn't make out his features.

The man who'd shot Mitar was slashing the rope that separated Tola from the rest of the mules. Now and again, he glanced up to the man on the ledge. The man in the fez remained pointing his gun, but didn't approach further. She must do something.

'Don't move and don't speak,' she advised the cadets.

Guessing the man above them was in charge, she began to stride towards him. In her haste, she stumbled on stones, her cap dropping over her eyes. From below, shots were fired into the air. She daren't look back. She kept moving. The leader shouted and the firing stopped.

Her eyes fixed on the ledge; she plodded on, her chest tight. She looked for kindness, generosity of spirit. She first saw a faded army cap. As she drew nearer, homespun trousers tucked in boots and over a shirt, a sheepskin jerkin worn by artillery soldiers. They could be stolen, but she remembered Rajko's account of his mother's rape and she was afraid.

When she was within hearing distance she called up, 'Sir! Have mercy on us.'

To her relief, he replied though she couldn't understand him. They must be Albanians. Montenegrins were allies.

As she began to scramble up the ledge, she could no longer see the one she dubbed leader. An avalanche of scree fell from under her feet as she clung to an outcrop. She smelled sweet pipe tobacco, a sweet pipe tobacco like her father's. Her feet became entangled in the hem of her greatcoat and she paused, panting. He was probably a soldier, maybe a rebel like Dobrica, though not a Serb. She heaved herself onto the ledge, her knees scraping the frozen ground. Not much older than her, she noticed his hazel eyes.

She fumbled for the pistol Edward had given her. The firearm Stefan had ridiculed. The mother of pearl handle she loved.

'Sir.' She flung it at his feet.

She removed her cap and a hairpin loosened. 'Take me,' she said, 'Not these boys.'

The young man was looking beyond her to his men. What if he killed the cadets and still raped her.

She said, 'These boys have done no harm. Let them go on in peace.'

He fired into the air and she followed his gaze. The cadets had huddled into two groups—one around Mitar and the bleeding mule, the rest around Bogdan and Branislav. The brigands had cut the rope, which separated the mules and the one who'd shot Mitar was leading them up the slope.

The young man ignored her and barked further instructions. The man in the fez was grabbing Bora, poking his gun in his chest. Mikaiho had told her Serbs used to be kidnapped by the Turks and made to serve in the Turkish army. They didn't have the air of a press gang. Or rapists.

The leader wasn't interested in her, had no intention of negotiating. Her place was with the cadets.

As she hurtled down the slope, it occurred to her she was as insignificant as an ant under her boot. The thought gave her strength.

The bitter wind brought flurries of snow. Within minutes, she was back with the cadets. No one spoke. Mitar was leaning against Zivoli, some colour in his face. Bora had removed his coat and boots and the man with the fez was feeling the pockets, the lining of his cap, his boots. If these men were mere robbers, they might yet live.

When the brigand tossed the clothes to one side and began to take apart his bundle, Ellen said conversationally, 'Put your boots on.'

Bora was fixated on his attacker.

'He'd have shot you by now if he was going to. Put them on.'

She drew close to the brigand and pleaded, 'Please, leave some food for the children. We mean no harm.'

She'd no idea if he understood. Like his leader, he acted as though she didn't exist. Despite her words to Bora, she worried they would all be shot when the men had taken what they wanted. She assessed the unit. Bogdan and Zivoli composed, Bora fastening his laces. Branislav looked shaken and many cadets were sobbing. Snow was beginning to fall; cold freezing the fibres on their hats, coat shoulders, surface of their shoes.

Rajko had told her to act like a soldier when she'd least felt like it.

'Hold hands,' she instructed the cadets. It was how she imagined their unit leaving Jevo.

She remembered Victor. Victor on a hill in South Africa where his unit was attacked, where he jumped from his horse, defied the Boers, galloped for help. How had he done that? How had he silenced fears for himself and his men, the chattering doubts?

'Stand together and hold hands.'

The words of the song Zivoli had been playing came back to her.

A jag a kleti necu
Jer sam ga ljubila

A love song. They'd been singing a song of lost love.

She walked along the line. Spoke to each cadet by name. Zivoli was sitting next to Mitar who'd stopped crying.

She crouched beside him and said, 'Remember who you are, brother.'

He said, 'I'm all right now, miss.'

Satisfied, she announced, 'Zivoli! Your *frula*. We'll sing of love.'

He didn't hesitate. With fingers bloodied from Mitar's wound, he pulled out his whistle. The first few notes were shaky, but Bogdan remembered the words. His voice had broken. Gradually everyone joined in.

She thought of the gun she'd left with Audrey. The possibility of using it. Wasn't that what Stefan expected of a woman who volunteered to be a soldier? Wouldn't he assume he'd entrusted his son to someone prepared to use whatever weapon she had? She imagined taking aim as Sergeant Sutherland taught. 'Keep your eye on the target.' Yet her encounter with Audrey had shown, she didn't have it in her to kill.

The man in the fez was searching the bundles on the ground, stealing blankets, coins, medals.

They sang the song through three, four times. The cadets started to whisper about Timohir. Whether he'd been involved in a plot. Encouraged by Zivoli they moved on to remember the evening by the campfire.

Above a black eagle screeched. Ellen's knees knocked together. She'd lost her cap at some point though she couldn't recall how. The side of her head burned.

Zivoli said, 'They're leaving us, miss,' but the man who'd shot Mitar, darted back to Velimir.

Scared he was going to kill him, Ellen ran and flung herself between them. She felt the slow beat of the mule's heart; this was no time to weep. The smell of blood filled her nostrils. The butt of a rifle drove through her greatcoat. Digging her heels into the mud she said, 'Let him be.'

The man shoved her to one side, bent down and knocked Velimir forward and grabbed the blanket. Ellen snatched a corner. He let go and jabbed the rifle into her elbow so she staggered, struggling to keep her footing.

From the top of the hill, the young man shouted. Velimir had curled into a ball, over Tola's head. The brigand swore; moved away.

'Get up,' she said to Velimir, handing him the blanket. 'Go and stand with the others. Hold their hands.' She didn't want him to be sitting on poor Tola when she died.

The young man in sheepskin jerkin skipped down the slope, stones crashing in front of him. When he landed no more than a foot away, his eyes met hers. He winked, handed her her pistol. She blushed, confused and lowered her face. Edward had bought the pistol especially for her trip to Serbia. 'Personal protection.' They'd laughed.

The air was still. She ought to shoot. He was close enough. Tola stirred. She looked down at the mule, mesmerised by the pulse beating in her neck. The robber jabbed at Tola's belly with his boot. Ellen suppressed a sob. He prodded the mule away from the track, pushed her towards the precipice. The faintest of breaths from her nostrils mingled with the falling snow, and Ellen prayed the creature was dead. The mule lodged on a piece of rock for a moment. Ellen swallowed. With a final prod he kicked her down the slope, blood trailing.

The words they'd been singing reverberated in her head...
and I love her still.

The man followed his friends up the slope. The mule train had disappeared from sight. Ellen waited until the path was empty. So much for Joan of Arc.

Velimir was sobbing, slumped where the mule had lay, his blanket trailing in the blood. Bora put his arms round him, rocking him.

Wiping her eyes on the back of her gloves, Ellen walked to the cadets clustered around Mitar. She crouched next to him. Though there was a lot of blood, she thought most of it was the mule's.

'Let me see.'

The bullet had lodged in the surface flesh close to his stomach. Quickly she removed her bundle from her back and took out the first aid kit. There was no time to remove the bullet, but she dressed the wound.

'I don't want you to walk. You'll lose too much blood.' He might work the bullet deeper into the flesh.

'Leave him with me,' Zivoli said. 'You take the others to the next village. You can send us help.'

She didn't want to. Stefan had entrusted his son to her care; she ought not to abandon him.

'I'll be all right, miss,' Mitar said.

'I know.' She handed him her electric torch.

Snow was settling when they left. At first Ellen didn't know whether to lead, or bring up the rear, wanting both to reassure the cadets they weren't being attacked again and to urge them to walk fast. Velimir was distressed at leaving his friend, so she decided to go first with him. Branislav and Bora, not many yards behind, brought up the rear, were instructed to shout if there was further trouble.

Ellen saw a brigand behind every bush, every boulder. She heard a shot in every shifting stone. When anyone slipped she forced herself to turn slowly, not wanting to cause unnecessary alarm. At twenty-two she felt old. Her joints were tight, her muscles ached. When anyone spoke, her hand went to her mouth.

She relived the scene. If only, she'd not slipped. If only, she'd threatened the men. She pictured herself, pistol in hand, the men at her feet sobbing for mercy. She longed to be back with Mitar and Zivoli. As the snow continued to fall, Bogdan began to sing. Her stride lengthened, as did Velimir's.

When they reached the edge of the pine forests, the crumbling stone houses, she was tempted to race ahead, to call out for help, but she kept pace with Velimir, reminding him, repeating, his friend would soon be rescued.

Instinctively, she led the unit towards the church and the houses surrounding it. A man in a homespun suit hurried down the street towards them.

'*Dobro jutro.*' In Serbian she explained the situation.

Branislav and the other cadets joined them. 'Today, we have been saved from bandits by our lady soldier.'

'They killed our mule and took our blankets,' said Bogdan.

'They shot my best friend,' Velimir added.

'And stole our biscuits,' Bora said.

'You will be hungry,' said the man.

'Will you help us fetch our wounded brother?' Ellen asked.

It was dark when she and the rescue party returned with Mitar and Zivoli. The man she'd first met provided them with soup and venison stew. A doctor removed the bullet. Flesh wound. Nothing, he pronounced.

Their rescuer urged Ellen to take his bed while he watched over sleeping Mitar.

The room was sparse, the narrow cot facing a full moon and a sky flashing with stars. Ellen fell asleep within a few minutes, but awoke an hour later.

She was alone in her bed at home, the counterpane silver in the light of the moon. She listened. An owl. Her parents murmured downstairs. Into her mind came a childhood scene she'd not thought of for years. Her mother was playing the piano and her father, his hand resting on her shoulder, sang tenor accompaniment. She, seated in a little chair.

Edward's voice came back to her as he spoke on the telephone at Mitrovica. Suddenly she knew where he was. He'd wait at Durazzo. Overjoyed to see him, she would tell him she loved him.

The Albanian villagers promised help. They would reach the port, not in triumph, but they'd get there.

Chapter Twenty-eight

On the borders, December 1915

When Stefan and Dragan left the house an hour later for the trenches, the wind had dropped. Their boots cracked the crust formed over fresh snow as, single file, they waded down the pavement.

At the gas light on the corner Stefan paused, tempted to admit to Dragan he would rather remain with his men than journey with Stamenka. A vixen padded along the centre of the road, bedraggled, ears back, bush down. As Stefan stepped into the road, avoiding the snow accumulated in the gutter, the fox veered along an alley. Behind shutters, a slither of light, laughter. He felt hollow; his feelings scraped, scoured out of him.

There'd been no reason to leave his quarters. But Stefan, restless, impatient for the report, decided to speak directly to Major Zariya, a quiet hero who'd volunteered to command the final action; his task to delay the enemy long enough for Serb stragglers to escape along the Bistrica valley. He wouldn't expect a visit and would be asleep at one in the morning. Dragan had insisted on accompanying him and Stefan was glad.

As they turned down the lane out of Pec, the ground became rutted where military wheels gouged the earth. Their feet cautious on the uncertain ground; their steps slowed. Stefan's trousers trailed in the mud. He pressed on, facing the mountain peaks, which he and Stamenka must travel. He wondered what she was doing. How would she bear the waiting? In silence, no doubt. After his mistake, Dragan had made lime tea, his laced with *rakija*, Stamenka's with honey. She refused a sleeping draught and sat motionless on the kitchen chair while he paced. Action, however pointless, was preferable.

If Mikaiho was right and the unit attacked by Albanians, the cadets must have been well on their way, perhaps would have covered the worst of the heights between Serbia and

Albania. How would he get Stamenka up there? His mind couldn't settle. There would be bodies. He wanted his son whole, intact. He longed to stroke his hair, hold his hand and watch him whittle wood. For Stamenka, he must hang on till his child-son was lowered into the ground.

The sentry, tall, arms like paddles, showed no surprise at their approach, but flashed his torch in their direction as they climbed the steep slope. While he fetched the officer-in-charge, Stefan tried to work out the position of the trenches from the information he'd been given. 'Trenches' was a misnomer. The engineers would have dug less than two or three feet. They'd no artillery. Ammunition was in short supply; retreating soldiers transported all they could. Zariya's men weren't conscripts, but criminals released from prison. With luck this unit need do nothing but give themselves up.

Minutes later, he followed an orderly through a gap between stone walls into what used to be a sheep fold, common enough on the edge of town. He was reminded, as he tried to make out the shapes around him, of last year's inspection of Glisic's front line. Here, the smell was of wood smoke, damp grass, acidic marshes rather than rotting corpses and the madness of neglect.

'Tea, sir?' It was Major Zariya.

Rage erupted. Sweat broke across his forehead. 'Tea,' he shouted, 'when…' His voice shook. He paused to stop his body trembling, his teeth chattering. '… according to your information… my son and his unit have been murdered… I gave orders…'

Dragan moved towards the fire, filled a kettle with water from a canister.

Zariya was matter of fact. 'It's not my information, sir. There've been rumours the Austrians ambushed a unit of cadets in Puka. On receiving your request, I sent a scout to ascertain the facts.'

Stefan's heart fluttered as he took a deep breath. Puka. How long would it take? Stamenka couldn't wait in Pec; it was too dangerous. Without definitive news could he let her travel without him?

The major handed him a cigarette, offered a light. Their cap peaks touched. Stefan heard the burn as one cigarette lit the other.

The major observed, 'Rumours are rife in war. You know that, sir.'

'My cousin was certain you said Miss Frankland's.'

'Your cousin misheard, sir.'

'Is my son dead?'

'I don't know if a unit was attacked in Puka, never mind if it was your son's. No one mentioned Miss Frankland. And I'll be honest about your cousin. In his world, rumours of disaster become facts.'

'For my wife's sake, I have to know whether my son is dead, or not.' His cousin was in the wrong again. The family tainted. Yet Dragan had believed Mikaiho. Stamenka also. Dragan was crouched by the fire watching the kettle. The major spoke as though offering a distraction, 'We've a personal letter from General Stavisto for you.'

Envious of his friend and his wife, already on the road, he snapped, 'I'll read it later,' and stuffed it into his inside pocket.

Officers bedded round the fire, curled close for comfort. He'd often been in places like this, cold seeping into his boots, the smell of tea brewing. Each time was different; he couldn't imagine other men's fears or their dreams.

Major Zariya said, 'When the scout returns I'll provide a full report.'

Stefan nodded thinking of Stamenka. He wondered if she needed him, whether she was as self-sufficient as she now appeared. Flicking ash from his cigarette, he said, 'You've written to your wife?'

'I've said my goodbyes.'

The major lived in a village outside Jevo though Stefan couldn't remember if he'd sons. A dependable soldier, it was typical he volunteered for this final encounter.

'You're ready to surrender?'

'I prefer to die in action.'

Dragan was striding across from the fire, a mug of tea in each hand. Though Stefan didn't want one, he threw his cigarette on the ground and took it. He could take Zariya's place. He could be killed in action. No need to bury his son, live with the rape of the women of Kadavsic, or his cruelty to Stamenka. Yet each has his destiny; he'd learned that.

He said, 'I'd like you to survive and join the army when it returns. Nothing would suit me better.'

Awkwardly he put his free arm across Zariya's shoulders. Tea splashed from his beaker, burning his fingers. He remembered the night of the bomb exploding next to the Gorniji café. Devotion like the major's often went unrecognised. Embarrassed, his throat blocked, he returned his hand to his side.

Zariya said, 'We came across an orderly from Miss Frankland's unit in the town a week ago. A Dobrica Kuca.'

'Medical orderly at Dobro Majka,' Stefan said, 'Lost a hand at Bregalnica.'

'He's joined a unit planning to cause trouble to the Austrians till we return, you know.'

'Send him to me.'

'He won't come.'

'Deserter?'

'Well...'

'Where can I find him?'

'You can have his address by all means, sir, but...'

'He'll have seen my son.'

There was no point in him staying here. He handed his beaker to Zariya. 'May God keep you safe.'

'And you, sir.'

Though Dobrica was on his own in the shuttered room at the top of the stairs, it reeked of stale sweat, bodies cooped up for hours. A lantern hanging from the ceiling, a candle on the windowsill and several stuck on the floorboards provided dim light. Despite a small fire in the grate, it was chilly and Stefan wasn't surprised the orderly had pulled a blanket over his shoulders. As far as he could make out, there was no furniture, not even a chair. For some students at Military Academy, this was an independent, romantic life. He and Rajko preferred cheap dormitories, saving money for books, wine and the occasional restaurant meal.

Stefan stepped between the candles before squatting next to Dobrica. They shook hands.

'Well, brother…' Stefan began, 'The others are…'

'You've come to turn us in?'

'Why?' He'd gained access by agreeing to come alone. He clarified, 'You were with Miss Frankland's unit, weren't you?'

'I deserted the unit.'

'I'm here as a father. There are rumours…' It was no easier to voice the possibility of his son's death this time. He wondered if he'd be sick; his throat tasted of acid, which he'd to swallow repeatedly.

'It was too much for her.'

'I spoke to Miss Frankland at Mitrovica.'

Dobrica sounded angry, or bitter. 'Did she tell you we lost a wagon along the Ibar? Three dead and no food.'

Stefan struggled to remember; he'd been preoccupied with Rajko's death. 'She wanted to finish the journey.'

'Or the frostbite? We left four at Mitrovica. One orderly lost his foot. Did she tell you one cadet starved to death? Not much to you and I who're used to these things, but for a foreign lady…'

Was Dobrica blaming him for the deaths? His intention had been honourable, to get his son out of Serbia as well as the cadets. About to defend himself, he remembered she'd lost weight. Hadn't she implied Mitar wasn't dressed adequately?

'She could have stayed with Dr. Eyres,' he said, aware he'd encouraged her to carry on.

'It was no task for an English lady. Whoever thought of the crazy idea of cadets leaving the country in atrocious conditions, without food, suitable clothing, must hate us Serbs.'

Stefan felt weary. He wasn't responsible for the war, the government's actions. All he wanted was peace. And now, to discover if his son was dead.

'I haven't come to argue, brother,' he said.

A flea nipped his ankle and rubbing the bite, his admiration for Ellen returned. The journey had been worse than government or army anticipated. The worst Balkan winter in memory and civilians unexpectedly fleeing Austrian occupation. Stamenka could have travelled with Mitar, but not accompanied by thirty untested cadets.

Stefan said, 'Don't think I'm ungrateful. Miss Frankland didn't complain either about you or the cadets.'

Dobrica was scratching his head. He produced a piece of soap and smeared it along his hairline. 'They're everywhere! In the plaster, the palisters. It's like being eaten alive.'

'I couldn't live like this.'

Dobrica put the soap on the floor between them. 'I thought you'd have me shot.'

'Why?' His back was itching. When he got back to the digs he'd need a complete change of clothes. 'You're not a traitor.'

'I pulled out of the unit. The cadets behaved like schoolboys. Especially at first, Mitar played the hero, that's what we reckoned he was up to.'

'Did he misbehave?'

'Well, he is a child. And you know the conditions. When we lost the wagon we lost the best of our food. These days, you know, they're not like we were.'

'I hope to God they're not dead.'

'Who told you they were?'

'My cousin, Lieutenant Nis, brought news. Major Zariya is investigating.'

'Take no notice of your cousin. He's unreliable, sir. I understand he's part of your family, he never tired of telling us, but he was scared witless by the war. I tell you, you saved many lives by your bravery, but your cousin would run sooner than look out for anyone but himself.'

'I have to check his story.'

'Well, after Mitrovica we pulled together. Miss Frankland asked our advice. She was upset when I told her I'd pack in. She tried to persuade me to stay on. Excuse me, sir.' He snatched his cap and scoured his scalp with his fingers. 'They're driving me mad.'

'So there was Miss Frankland, two orderlies and the cadets, were there?'

'Well... Not in the end. You see the Austrian drowned and the other Serb came back here.'

Stefan nodded. Cadets behaving like the school kids they were and an inexperienced woman in charge. 'Do you know why he left?'

'Didn't want to leave Serbia, is my guess but he blabbered about women and the English. The bridge was down, not her fault. I suggested that route and she took my advice.'

'Which was?'

'I misjudged the speed of the cadets, but the Cakor Pass should have been quicker. More arduous, of course.'

'They didn't travel through Puka?'

'Ah! In my view…'

'Tell me, brother! Did they travel through Puka?'

'No,' Dobrica shouted. 'If I gave dud advice, I can only…'

Stefan sprang up. 'The unit was ambushed near a village outside Puka.'

Dobrica grinned. As they shook hands, Stefan felt the stub that remained of the orderly's hand through his woollen mitten. 'We need men like you.' As they moved apart he added, 'I could speak to my landlady. If she's willing, the army can pay for decent rooms for you and your men, at least till the spring. If the enemy allow it.'

'Thank you, sir.'

Stefan lowered his voice, 'You were at Bregalnica. You know what happened in some places…' His voice trembled, '…civilians murdered, houses burned… women raped by our men…' He continued more slowly, 'I ask you to remember our regiment does not rape nor murder civilians…'

Dobrica put his hand on Stefan's sleeve. 'Our intention is to disrupt the enemy and protect our people. Like you, I'm a decent man.'

Snow buntings whirled ahead, black under-wings stark against a grey sky. Sheltered by a stone wall from the north-easterly wind, Stefan gazed towards Pec. He and Dragan hadn't needed to climb high to reach the top of the mound, which looked back into Serbia, forward to Montenegro and beyond to the Albanian mountains. The mud, though frozen in part, suggested they weren't the first to climb the ruins of the tower.

He surveyed the spires of church and mosque, the pan tiled roofs of Pec. He'd been weak. No one else to blame.

Turning to look along the valley floor, the travellers were stragglers. He thought of Stamenka who had left a few hours ago with trusted officers. He wished he was with her. He could smell the lavender oil on her skin, feel the strength of her fingers as she held his hand. He reasoned she was well able to reach Durazzo without him.

When he returned with the good news, she'd wept, leaning on his chest. He wiped her face with his handkerchief and held her steady, apologised she'd been put through unnecessary grief.

Only then had he opened Tomislav's letter. Having scanned its contents, he handed it to her.

'Read it to me,' she said.

Brother! The Montenegrins are holding the front against the Austrians. For as long as they put up their glorious fight we can get through Albania.

This morning we came upon a priest who had spoken to Miss Frankland and her unit in Androvica, despite his emotion Stefan kept his voice firm, *who are in good spirits.*

After visiting Dobrica, he was confident his son was alive. This was confirmation.

'I must leave immediately,' Stamenka had said.

He kissed her, clung to her thinking if they were together, they'd all survive. They didn't speak of England, of the long journey into the unknown. Nor did he tell her Tomislav urged him to leave before it was too late.

'I love you,' he whispered. She was strong, a rock on which to lay his dreams. 'May God keep you safe.' His voice was firm as he released her.

Dragan handed him a flask. As the *rakija* scorched his throat, he watched the last of the troops, in twos and threes, carrying backpacks, march along the valley. They were armed for self-protection. Many, like him, wore knitted caps. He thought of Major Zariya and Dobrica's comments about Mikaiho. He'd not seen him since his arrest, probably wouldn't, until the court martial in Corfu. He regretted overreacting to his cousin's demise at Chekoj ridge, caused by guilt that he'd received Mikaiho's entitlement, overlaid with grief at the loss of his men's lives.

Wiping his mouth on the back of his glove, he thought of Rajko. He would never know whether Rajko gave orders for the rapes. If not him, who? If he'd reported his suspicions, he might have found out. He might have the peace he yearned for.

Within the hour, they would join the last of the departing Serbs.

'We'll be back,' he murmured.

'To avenge the deaths of our brothers,' Dragan responded.

'No. The time for revenge is over.' They must defend their freedom; that was unavoidable, but not a shot more. Looking towards Serbia he said, 'All I want is to walk through the Kalemegdan Park when the trees are in blossom; hold my wife's hand and listen once again to the voice of my son.'